Eileen Townsend

Eileen Townsend is the author of the bestselling novels *Of Woman Born*, *In Love and War*, *The Love Child*, *The Other Woman*, and the forthcoming *Dreamtime*. With her husband Professor Colin Townsend she compiled *War Wives*, the highly acclaimed story of women in the Second World War.

Of Scottish birth, she is an MA graduate in Modern History and Political Science, and now lives in the Midlands.

EILEEN TOWNSEND

CHILD OF FIRE

This edition published by Diamond Books, 1999

Diamond Books is an Imprint of HarperCollins*Publishers*
77-85 Fulham Palace Road,
Hammersmith, London W6 8JB

First published in Great Britain by
HarperCollins*Publishers* 1992

ISBN 0-261-67093-X

Set in Meridien

Printed in Great Britain by
Caledonian International Book Manufacturing Ltd, Glasgow

For Patricia

Contents

Prologue

The place where the story that follows is set, the limestone highlands of north-west Yorkshire, is a dramatic and remote landscape very different in character from any other part of England. It is a tract of white and open land, the original bedrock of warm seas, thrust up to the open skies by gigantic primeval forces, and left to be weathered and fretted by two million northern winters. Lying exposed and bleached beneath the winds, it is the bare vertebrae of the Pennine mountain range – the very backbone of England.

To the south and east the Great Scar limestone falls away in the bluffs of the Craven Fault, to the north and west it ends in high mountain-top pavements, where the soil has been stripped bare to reveal a wide landscape of white stone, cleft and rutted into grotesque shapes, but never levelled by the elements.

But if the work of time and the elements is dramatic enough on the surface, it is as nothing compared to the damage that has been wrought beneath. This land has been eaten from within, gouged and tunnelled by water which, finding weaknesses, has worked at them persistently over millennia. Seeping and percolating for mile after mile, its irresistible, corrosive effect has turned small cracks and fissures into wide passages and gigantic galleries, tiny holes into enormous caverns, and vertical splits into yawning chasms, which around the great mountain of Ingleborough gape open on the surface of the landscape. Nowhere is the scale of these elemental predations more awesome than at Gaping Ghyll, where the waters of Fell Beck, tumbling off the shoulder of Ingleborough, plunge 340 feet in a mighty cataract down into an underground cavern large enough to swallow St Paul's Cathedral.

The Viking shepherds and goatherds of old knew these pot-holes well; they believed they contained the spirits of lost souls, condemned forever to roam their fearful depths till the end of time itself. They gave them resounding names that have echoed their beliefs down the ages: Hell Ghyll, Hurtle Pot and Trow Ghyll, named after the legendary Troll of Ingleborough who is said to lurk there yet.

Still daunting centuries later, these pot-holes continued to provide a challenge for generations of cavers in modern times, their explorations being interrupted this century only by the advent of the two world wars.

It was shortly after the end of the Second World War, in the early autumn of 1947, that Trow Ghyll, a ravine only a short distance below Gaping Ghyll on the flank of Ingleborough, yielded its macabre secret – a secret which has remained for two generations.

Convinced that the two cave systems were interlinked and that a passage could be found which would lead them through to the floor of the main chamber, thus avoiding the long and dangerous winched descent down the main shaft, two young men were removing rocks which barred the entrance to Trow Ghyll when they were halted in their tracks. What confronted them there brought their bodies out in a cold sweat as the full horror of their find began to reveal itself. Their discovery became the talk of the surrounding area and immediately speculation about their find was rife. All sorts of theories were put forward as to the explanation, but it remains unresolved to the present day.

The story that follows could be one explanation. And for

a certain old lady who has lived all her life in that remote and ancient land, and was still a young woman with the bloom of youth on her cheeks that fateful day in autumn 1947 when she first heard the news, it is the only one possible.

'Child of the clouds! Remote from every taint
of sordid industry thy lot is cast;
Thine are the honours of the lofty waste . . .'

William Wordsworth

Book One

CHILD OF
THE CLOUDS

Bethany

Chapter One

'Beneath the shade the Northmen came,
Fixed on each vale a Runic name,
Reared high their altar's rugged stone,
And gave their gods the land they won.'

31 October 1932,
UTHERDALE, NORTH RIDING OF YORKSHIRE,
England

The child's eyes grew wider as the flames grew higher. They had been chanting now for almost two hours and, as the voices grew louder and the dancing more frenzied, it seemed as if the whole village population of Utherby was possessed by some strange power, some ungodly spirit that had claimed their very souls.

Where familiar neighbours had once been, red- and black-clad demons now cavorted with witches in pointed hats, who cackled and screamed ancient curses as they pranced around the flames. Gawky youths with unwashed sheepskins around their shoulders cavorted with others draped in skins from slaughtered foxes, while young girls bedecked in the virgin white of their Druid forebears made eyes behind their gaudily painted masks at the scrawny young bloods in their Viking furs and helmets.

Could these alien creatures really be the same people who attended the Reverend Barden's sermons in Chapel twice every Sabbath? And what would become of these elaborate costumes come the morrow? It was as if they and tonight itself belonged to some other world far removed from the God-fearing Methodist lifestyle carried on in the everyday life of the Yorkshire dales.

A feeling akin to fear crept into the excitement in the child's heart as she watched silently from the sidelines. These costumes could be hidden away when the night was done, but surely not the feelings that went with them. They must always be there, lurking beneath the surface, waiting for an opportunity such as this to burst forth and turn a sober small community into a raving, ranting mob who at heart still worshipped the old gods with as much – no, with far more enthusiasm than they ever worshipped the Christian one. It was a thought that chilled the blood and the bone.

As the child watched, she realized that for all of her twelve years she had never really known the community into which she had been born, had never recognized those other emotions that simmered just beneath the surface of these dour Yorkshire faces. She had grown up in a world within a world, for her strict Methodist father headed a household sober in word and deed as well as in its prohibition of alcohol. Yes, perhaps it was only in her own home that such feelings were frowned upon. Perhaps it did not need the great Fire of Beltane to rekindle these passions in the breasts of the other people of this valley. Perhaps they were there all the time.

'They're a queer lot, Yorkshire folk,' her Cumbrian father, Cheevers Baine, had declared on more than one occasion. 'They don't take kindly to offcomers, that's for sure.' And he had spoken from the heart, as one of that despised breed himself. The 'offcomer', or stranger to the uninitiated in North Country talk, was someone to be tolerated at best, and more often resented for not having had the good fortune to be Yorkshire born and bred.

'But at least thou'll not have that held against thee, lass,' he had told his young daughter. 'Thou art as much a part of this land as that crag out yonder.' And he had held his eldest child in his arms and pointed out of the window to the great limestone bulk that was Uther Crag, and his small daughter Bethany had gazed up at its cloud-shrouded summit and felt, even then as a mere four-year-old, a strange affinity with that enormous mound of rock that overshadowed their village and gave work to most of its menfolk. She was part of it; her father had told her so. It was funny how those first childhood memories often left the deepest impressions.

She shivered now beneath the brown worsted coat that hid her nightdress, and pondered on the many questions that had flooded through her mind since she had climbed out of her bedroom window to make her way up that very limestone crag, which rose to over a thousand feet behind their terraced cottage, to witness the happenings that were taking place on this most special of nights.

She had planned this sin for so long. And sin it was, for there was no doubt that was how her father would regard it, and she had felt shame mingled with the fever of anticipation within her as she bade him goodnight after supper and climbed the steep stairs to her bed.

She had lain where she always lay, on the side next to the window, alongside her younger sister Libby and her little brother Sammy, beneath the patchwork quilt of the big iron bedstead, while the two oldest boys, ten-year-old Tom and eight-year-old Teddy, slept top to toe in a single one against the opposite wall. She felt fiercely protective towards her younger siblings: tow-haired, stocky Tom, with his shirt always hanging out and his bootlaces undone, who was never to be found outside school without a ball at his feet, was a stark contrast to the younger but taller, thinner Teddy who was a quieter, more studious character all round. Libby, their little sister, was more like Teddy by nature and tended to cling to whoever in the family was willing to give her attention. With her straggly, mousy hair, she was not as pretty a

17

child as Bethany, and 'backward in coming forward' was the phrase most often used. Not for her the wild rambles on the hills that so beckoned her elder sister; she much preferred to stay indoors and help her mother tend their cherub-faced toddler Sammy. Sammy was everyone's favourite, for his good nature as a baby had helped cushion the despair his mother had felt at having to cope with yet one more mouth to feed.

The room where they all slept, with its two beds separated by a chipped, marble-topped washstand, was small; claustrophobic in the hot summer months, but chill in the long, dark evenings of autumn. The walls were whitewashed and bare of decoration, apart from a faded cardboard picture from an old calendar entitled 'Suffer Little Children', from which a smiling Christ figure, with arms outstretched, beckoned a host of running, happy children.

A large, mahogany double wardrobe that had once belonged to Grandma Hetherington stood against the far wall at the foot of the beds, its bottom drawer containing what remaining linen their mother had brought into the marriage with her, and its spacious interior holding the one set of Sunday-best clothes the children possessed.

There was no curtain to the skylight bedroom window which slanted into the eaves and for this Bethany was truly grateful for it meant that once the younger ones were asleep, she could gaze out into the night sky and dream of things to come. And it had been a magnificent sky this evening; a special sky for a very special night.

Her feet had dragged slowly on the way home for supper, as her eyes gazed heavenwards at the massing dark-grey clouds with rain wisps dangling from them as they scudded over the hills. Now and again the north wind would tear rifts in them, revealing glimpses of pale-blue infinity. Dead leaves of gold and brown swirled around her feet and crackled beneath the wooden soles of her boots. Winter would soon be here and the boughs of the trees on the hillside behind her home were being stripped bare. Last night had seen the first frost and its chill bite had remained in the air. She had shivered as she looked up towards the top of the crag that glowered over the mean houses beneath, and she thought she felt the spit of rain on her face. Everyone had been praying it would not rain, not tonight of all nights.

They had been gathering on the hilltop since late afternoon – children mainly, and she could see their small antlike figures scurrying around the giant stack of unlit wood as behind them in a wild splendour of crimson and gold the sun began to set. Every cottage window facing west had had panes of fire as she had gathered pace and hopscotched along the unmade-up road of The Row. She could hear her mother calling. Supper would be on the table. It would be like any other night, except that her family would be the only one not to venture beyond their own front door after darkness fell.

The celebrations would go on till daybreak, when each master of a family present would be obliged to carry a flaming cinder home to kindle the fire in his own hearth, to ensure good fortune and good health for his own household throughout the year to come. And this was the part that worried the child most, for of all her friends' fathers, hers was the only one who never attended these ceremonies, whose hands never bore the sacred burning ashes home to protect them all from evil for the next twelve months.

'Doesn't your Dad care about what happens to you, then?' Ellen Capstick, who sat next to her in class, had asked this very morning. And there had been quiet smiles and ill-concealed giggles from the other girls on the bench, for they all knew that Bethany's father was a Bible-thumper and had no truck with such goings-on.

'Happen, my Dad thinks Jesus is better than any of your

old fire gods,' Bethany had replied. But her defensive words held little conviction, for surely the whole village couldn't be wrong?

And it was not just in their dale that such fires were lit. In the Mallerstang valley to the west and on the felltops of Swaledale to the east they would be lighting them this night. In fact all over the North Riding of Yorkshire and on the fells of Northumbria, Cumberland and Westmorland beyond they would be kindling the flames in honour of their ancient god, Beltane. But none, they said, would be a match to that of Utherdale, the red glow from which could be seen as far off as Kirkby Stephen to the north west and on the banks of the River Swale to the east. The great Fire of Beltane. It had been lit on the highest hill above the village of Utherby on this night of Hallowe'en since time immemorial; yes, ever since the great county of Yorkshire itself was part of the ancient kingdom of Deira, and its people still heathen.

The men and women of these parts were a proud race; the ancient Druid blood that had mingled over the centuries with the Viking had produced a people as fierce in their loyalties and strong in their passions as any in these islands, and they clung tenaciously to their traditions. Even the teachings of Jesus Christ himself could pale in comparison to the homage that was still paid to the elements that ruled their daily lives: earth, wind and fire.

And now, in the dark and chill of the autumn night, as the child stood on that hilltop and her eyes continued to survey the scene before her she realized how little she really knew of these her people. These strange beings in their robes and fancy costumes who now pranced and cavorted before her hid their faces well, and not just behind the hand-made masks. The stolid, respectable faces they displayed to the world throughout the rest of the year bore no resemblance to what was going on here

20

tonight. Until now they had simply been 'the folk of the dale' who had been part of her young life for all of her twelve years. But no more. After tonight they would be something else entirely. It was as if at long last she had been allowed to glimpse their other face – to stand on the sidelines and witness this other dimension to their lives that the rest of the world beyond these Northern Pennine hills knew nothing of.

There were more than five million people in Yorkshire; five million people scattered over four million acres – as many as there were letters in the Bible, so her father said. And of the three distinct parts into which the great county was divided – the North, West and East Ridings – it was her own land of the North that was the least known, even to its own.

Yes, the North Riding was a far cry from the industrial towns of the South. It was a hard land that bred even harder people than were to be found in those smoke-blackened cities of Leeds, Bradford and Sheffield. Its inhabitants were mainly sheep farmers scratching a precarious living from the bleak foothills of the Pennine mountains. But it was also a vast and historic land where, long before the ancestors of these her people ever trod its hills, its peaks had stood proud above the great ice sheets that had cut their way southwards as the glacial sea swept over the land, and then melted to reveal the massive beds of limestone beneath; a stone as cold and grey as those far distant seas; a stone composed of millions of sea creatures whose bones could still be seen today if only you knew the secret of where to look. And the child's slim fingers clutched protectively at the small piece of rock in the depths of her coat pocket. In her hand she held her own piece of history, for hadn't her father shown her how to crack open a piece of the rock to reveal the skeletal remains within? Her very first fossil was now her own personal talisman.

21

On such things was the childish imagination fed. And her father knew so much. He had told her of how beneath the land lay an even older world, for in the Pennines' western hills were the entrances to caves and caverns by the hundred that had been created by the slow action of the waters of the millennia; it seemed to her since the beginning of time itself. Strange unearthly places with names like Gaping Ghyll, Jingle Hole, Alum Pot, and the cave of the Giant Yordas, named after the fearsome creature said to inhabit its darkest depths.

And just beyond their own Utherdale loomed the dark, mysterious shape of Wolf Fell, so called in memory of the ferocious beasts that had roamed its slopes for centuries. So common were they that one of the Roman legions, who had built the Emperor Hadrian's Wall to keep out the marauding Scots, had actually used a wolf as its emblem.

Yes, every stony crag, river or small village seemed to link its inhabitants to that past the stranger might think long dead, but which was in many ways still very much alive in its people. There was a darkness here, at the heart of things – a darkness into which no Christian sermons could shed their light. It was a darkness born of another time – another time in this very place, where homage was paid to other gods, gods even more potent than the one brought to this most northern part of England by St Columba and his followers; gods more potent than Jesus Christ himself.

'Aye, Uther Pendragon himself would be proud of this one!'

The voice was that of John Greville – 'Black Jack' they called him in the village, for the local Squire's son had hair the colour of Whitby jet, like his grandfather before him after whom he was named.

Uther Pendragon . . . The child's face turned to the young man who had uttered the name. Uther Pendragon. The very sound of it brought fear to the soul, for she had listened so often to her father speak of that most awesome of rulers, the father of the legendary King Arthur himself who had given his name to their own village. Uther Pendragon, who had founded his kingdom within a day's walk of this very place, in the Mallerstang valley; the man who had tried to divert the rushing waters of the Eden river to create a moat for his own Pendragon castle.

> Let Uther Pendragon do what he can,
> But Eden shall run as the Eden has ran . . .

There was not a child in the whole of the North of England who had not learned those lines before any nursery rhyme. Cannibalistic and ruthless, he had left a legacy of fear and awe that had survived the centuries.

The young man beside the child let out a whoop and threw another branch on to the flames as he accepted a swig from a proffered jug of ale. He kept the jug, waving the owner away with a dismissive gesture as his eyes moved back to the blazing pile of wood. 'By God, this is a sight and no mistake!' His dark eyes gleamed as he turned to the much smaller figure by his side. 'There's none that does it better in the whole of Yorkshire, is there, lass?'

The child shrugged. 'Happen not, mister. But you'll all go to hell, all the same!'

Jack Greville looked down at her, the smugness of his expression giving way to surprise. 'And who says so, may I ask?'

'Me Dad does.'

'And who might your Dad be?'

'Cheevers Baine.'

'Hmm.' The name rang a bell. A quarryman, if he remembered rightly; an obstinate bugger whose sanctimonious tongue would be long enough to strangle him one of these days. 'And you would be?'

'Bethany Baine.' She looked him straight in the eye as

23

she flicked a long fringe of reddish hair back from her brow.

His eyes took in the scrawny little figure in the outgrown worsted coat, the sleeves of which finished halfway to the elbows. From the frayed cuffs two pathetically bony wrists poked as thin little fingers pushed windswept strands of long, unruly hair back behind her ears. A frill of nightgown hung down from beneath the coat, below which two thin white legs stood their ground in a pair of boy's wooden-soled boots at least two sizes too big. The overall effect was a gawky, scarecrow appearance of which the child seemed blissfully unaware. She was undersized and underfed, and no different from any one of the other fifty or so children in the village – except perhaps this one was more forward than most.

'Well now, Miss Bethany Baine, you'd do well to keep your impertinent remarks to yourself, tonight of all nights. If anybody's to be going to hell around here it'll be you, you little squirt, for your bare-faced cheek. Do you know who I am?'

'Oh aye, I do. You're Black Jack Greville and my Dad says if the good die young they'll have to shoot you and your kind!'

She surprised herself by her outburst. Maybe it was that drink she had had from Billy Sedgwick's ale jug earlier on – who was to know? All she was really sure of was that she felt curiously elated and free to think or say whatever came into her head.

'Why you little tyke!' Never in his twenty-one years had he heard the like – and from a chit of girl at that. 'You watch that tongue of yours, my lass, and mind how you speak to your elders and betters!'

He was rattled. She could see that and drew a curious comfort from the fact. Far too many folk hereabouts were afeared of the likes of him. Elders and betters indeed! She kept her eyes on him, staring him out till he was forced to look away. She saw him toss the empty ale jug into the bushes before turning to talk to a young woman alongside him.

Yes, Uther Pendragon must have looked a good deal like Jack Greville, she decided. Tall and broad, with eyes as dark as the curling mass of hair on his head, and a laugh that sent shivers down the spine, for more often than not, if a Greville laughed, the joke was at someone else's expense. He was even dressed like the devil tonight, with his long black cloak and hood, his black eye-mask pushed up into the shock of dark hair. There was a saying in Yorkshire that her father claimed could have been specially written for the family from Wolf Hall:

> Hear all, see all, say nowt,
> Sup all, eat all, pay nowt.
> And if thou ever does owt for nowt,
> Allus do it for thyself!

Yes, that was the Grevilles all right. The family that had inhabited that ancient abode up there on the moors had never been known for their charity. 'Long pockets and short arms' they had when it came to doing any repairs to the much smaller, meaner houses of the village. Almost each and every one of them owned by the Grevilles and never a penny spent on them for generations past. And as for the present Squire, Colonel Philip Greville: 'Talk about hard-faced,' her Dad said. 'You could straighten nails on his!'

Yes, Philip Greville and his three sons were far from being the most respected family in the dale, but like so many of their neighbours, they too had known better times. The retired Colonel's Boer War veteran's pension didn't go far in keeping up a house as old and rambling as the Hall, with three growing lads to educate and clothe into the bargain. Wolf Farm itself didn't bring in much in the way of income, and as for the quarry – well, the least said about that the better, as far as the Colonel was concerned. 'Too little income and too much aggravation' just about summed that up. If he could have found a buyer for it, he would have got rid of it years ago, but who in their right minds would want to saddle themselves with a place like that? The crag was almost worked out, and the same could be said for the men who spent their lives hewing the unforgiving rock – although that was not something that the Colonel would ever agree with. He was firmly of the conviction that, for the most part, his workers were lazy beggars who should be grateful for the fact he supplied them with roofs over their heads and money in their pockets every Friday, for there were many in this dale – yes, and far beyond – who did not have that security. The Depression, as they were calling it down in London, was hitting the country hard and Utherby, like everywhere else, was suffering.

There was no doubt that the Grevilles might still be one of the most powerful families in the area, but even they were feeling the pinch. There was even talk of the Colonel selling up and retiring somewhere down south, but that hardly seemed possible, since their family had been here as far back as the Domesday Book and were as much a part of the local landscape as Uther Crag itself. By all accounts they had been the biggest landowners in the area for most of the past millennium. It was easy to see who had been first in the queue when, after the Battle of Hastings, England's new Norman King, William the Conqueror, came to divide up his newly-won spoils. His old comrade in arms, Jean-Éduard de Greville, made sure he got more than his fair share. But if it was to a Norman Frenchman that they owed their name and lands, legend had it that the Greville family tree went a great deal further back than that and the family's dark colouring and swarthy complexions came not from Normandy, but from a soldier of

26

the Roman Legion itself. But that could be just another of the tall tales that folk loved to tell hereabouts, for this was a place where fact and fantasy were often so bound up it was impossible to tell the difference.

The child squinted back up at the face of Jack Greville, now half-turned from her and illuminated by the full glow of the fire. It would have been a handsome face if it hadn't been for that sardonic smile that seemed to play perpetually about his lips. And of his two younger brothers, Amos had it too – that same superior way of looking at the world. Only the youngest, Edward, better known to the villagers as Daft Ned, did not possess it.

Daft Ned was everyone's friend. 'Ned, Ned . . . Daft in the head!' the village children had shouted for most of the sixteen years of the youth's existence. 'Not right in the garret' he was, or 'two loaves short of the dozen', as Isaac Youdell the baker put it. But Ned didn't care; he was at peace with the world, which was more than could be said for the rest of them.

The Squire himself would be here with the others tonight, no doubt, but it was almost impossible to pick out any individual from the crazily dressed, cavorting crowd. Money and position meant little on a night like this. 'Bow-legged wi' brass' the Grevilles were, so her father said, and too much money gave men a power to use or abuse as they thought fit. The fact that they owned the quarry that bit into the side of this very crag didn't help either, for not only her own father worked there, but it gave employment to almost every able-bodied man in the village; yes, and even them that were not so able. Hewing limestone by the ton from the rocky hillside at the foot of which their village stood made young men old before their time and fit only to meet their Maker long before they had reached middle age.

But the thought of her father brought a pang of fear and young Bethany Baine's brow furrowed. What if he or her

27

Mam were to check upstairs in the two-up, two-down cottage they lived in at the foot of the hill? What if they were to investigate and see that she was no longer abed alongside her younger sister and brother? That she was in fact right up here on the windy summit of this outcrop they called Uther Crag paying homage to the god Beltane with the rest of the village? What then?

Despite the sniggers and scoffs of her schoolfriends, Bethany knew that her father Cheevers Baine hated these pagan ceremonies with a passion. 'Trysts wi' the devil' he called them. 'I'll have no truck wi' the likes of that, nor those who need to call upon dark forces to light our way in this world, for how can darkness shed light? Tell me that, our Beth? Will not the Good Lord take vengeance on those who take part in such foul deeds? Have they not read the Good Book? Know they not of the Commandment: "Thou shalt have no other gods before me"?'

And he would stare down at her with those faded blue eyes of his, as if searching for some trace of those devilish practices in his own child.

He had been a good-looking man in his day, but twenty years of hauling rock had taken its toll, and it was a seamed, weary face that looked down into her own. And his daughter would shake her head and wish that sometimes he would unbend and smile a little, and not make even their own God seem such a fearsome creature.

'Will you take a look at that!'

A woman's voice brought her out of her reverie and she gazed up at the subject of the exclamation. Someone had thrown the remnants of a scarecrow on to the very top of the bonfire and for a moment it seemed to stand there, arms stiffly outstretched, staring down at them all: a black-coated Christ crucified for all their sins and now offered as a sacrifice to that other ancient god they had all gathered here this night to pay homage to: Beltane, the god of fire and fertility, who must be placated and pandered to by all if their small community was to survive yet one more year on these barren hillsides.

'Is it not a sight for sore eyes!' the female voice continued, and the revellers seemed to chant their agreement as they whirled past in their frenzied dance. And all around them the flames leapt and crackled, sending sparks into the darkness of the night sky.

Many of them had their faces totally obscured by their garishly painted masks and they carried lighted torches as they pranced their rhythmic steps around the flames. If there had ever been a set pattern to their footwork and gestures it was only half-remembered, but enough remained to give an eerie ritualistic element to the proceedings that totally mesmerized the watching child. And strange words were being chanted; words as funny and foreign to her ears as the 'Yan, tan, tethera, methera . . .' that the hill farmers still used to count their flocks.

At one point a tall, stout woman, dressed in the flowing white gown of an ancient Druid, the upper part of her face totally obscured by a bird mask, positioned herself just in front of Bethany, between the flames and the dancers and, throwing her arms wide, began to chant:

'Thrill with lissom lust of the light,
O man! My man!
Come careering out of the night
Of Pan! Io Pan . . .

I am thy mate, thou art my man,
Goat of thy flock, I am gold, I am God,
Flesh to thy bone, flower to thy rod.
With hooves of steel I race on the rocks
Through solstice stubborn to equinox.
And I rave; and I rape and I rip and I rend
Everlasting, world without end.
Mannikin, maiden, maenad, man,

In the might of Pan.
Io Pan! Io Pan Pan! Pan! Io Pan!'

And when she had done a lusty shout went up and the watching child was thrust aside as the woman was hoisted aloft on the shoulders of two of the brawnier of the fur-clad young men and she was carried off into the night.

Others took her place at various intervals, chanting strange incantations or declaiming words that made no sense, just like those shouted out by the woman in white. Bethany was both intrigued and perplexed. Who was this Pan that so many of them seemed to call to? The only one she knew of that name was Peter, the little boy who refused to grow up. But the Peter Pan of her story books she knew had little in common with this Pan, whose name sent such a feeling of unease through her that eventually she moved back from the vicinity of the flames to watch from a safer distance. There was a strange atmosphere in that inner circle, where bodies perspired in the heat of the flames and, as the night wore on, the dancing and chanting were becoming ever more frenzied.

On the outer rim it seemed less threatening, more like a wild Hallowe'en party, and many of the revellers there carried lanterns cut out from turnips to represent glowing faces. Each one seemed to leer at her as it swung past. Some of the owners she could recognize, but most were too well disguised to put a name to. It was a disconcerting experience for a child who had grown to her twelve years knowing the name and face of every man, woman and child in their valley.

With the passing of time the heat from the fire seemed to grow more intense, as limbs of trees long dead that had been gathered for the occasion were pulled forth to add fuel to the flames. And as the sparks flew heavenwards and the faces of the onlookers not behind masks grew scorched and red, and bodies perspired even more beneath the elaborate costumes, so the bottles of spirit and jugs of ale began to be passed around more freely. Oaths and curses spilled from the lips of men and women alike as, arms around each other, their steps became more lurching, their footing less sure. Drink, her father never ceased to remind her, was both a loosener of tongues and of morals, and who could argue with that tonight? Never had she seen so many people in its grip.

It was proving quite an education and she watched both in fascination and in fear as women she knew as respectable wives and mothers, as well as young girls, some little older than herself, reacted to the attentions of the opposite sex. Some were quite open with their courting displays, while others made for less conspicuous places out of the fire's glare. High-pitched giggles could be heard from the direction of the scrubby undergrowth just behind them, and the sound of the occasional slap and muffled cry. But the cries of protest held little conviction as the giggling grew louder and other less familiar sounds began to emanate from that area.

In the shadow of a gnarled, wind-stunted tree to her left she could make out the figure of a man dressed in the same costume as Black Jack Greville, his long cloak half-covering the buxom shape of Sarah-Jane Youdell, who was all but pinned to the trunk of the tree. The young woman's face was upturned to the bare branches above her and as Bethany continued to stare, she could hear strange gasping sounds coming from the loose lips of the baker's daughter. The man was making odd pushing movements against her which grew more violent by the second. And the harder he seemed to press against her beneath the enfolding cloak, the more tortured the sounds that were emitted from the young woman's throat. And one of his hands was there, his long fingers encircling the pink flesh beneath her lower jaw, with its faint double chin.

My God, she sounded desperate! She was in trouble. He was strangling her! He must be!

Bethany ran over and began to pull frantically at the black cloak. 'Get off her! Get off her, will you!'

A sound like a roaring animal met her ears as the face that was buried in the fair hair of the Youdell girl twisted round. A pair of dark eyes met hers with a look such as she had never seen before. 'What the deuce!'

It was not Jack Greville at all, but his younger brother Amos. Her own face flushed with alarm, Bethany sought the backing of the object of her rescue. But Sarah-Jane Youdell had other ideas. 'Just clear off, Bethany Baine, will you! Just bugger off out of here!'

Bethany's fingers loosened their grip on the fine worsted of the cloak and she backed slowly away. The dark head of Amos Greville turned from her once more. She could hear him cursing beneath his breath as Sarah-Jane squirmed back into position and the strange contortions resumed beneath the voluminous garment.

'That bitch is always in season!' she heard a woman remark. 'There's not a lad in t'dale that she hasn't favoured. Yon Amos Greville's not the first and he'll not be the last tonight, I can promise you that!'

It was Nancy Turver's mother from Number Nine, The Row — just three houses down from their own. The older woman looked down at her young neighbour. 'Eh, Bethany lass. Dost thy father know, thou'st here this night?'

Bethany shook her head. 'No,' she said quietly. Then her eyes returned to the couple on her left.

'Is it the first time thou's seen a pair at it, then, lass?' There was amusement in Emily Turver's eyes. 'By Jove, it'll not be the last if you hang around here much longer, mark my words! There'll be more than burning wood sacrificed to old Beltane up here this night. If you ask me, half the lasses in t'dale lose their most prized possessions

32

this time each year. And if the likes of yon hussy Sarah-Jane's not careful, there'll be more buns in t'ovens come morning than her old man Youdell could ever cater for in his bakehouse!'

Bethany's hazel eyes narrowed and her brow furrowed beneath the fringe of auburn hair. What was she on about? 'What do you mean, Mrs Turver?' she asked. 'What do you mean there'll be more buns in t'ovens?'

Emily Turver's round face creased with amusement. 'Eh, lass, dost thou not know? Art thou telling me a big lass like thee doesn't know where babbies come from?'

Bethany's brow cleared. 'Oh aye, I do.' She could well remember the procedure for the arrival of all her younger brothers and sister. 'It's right simple.' After all, she had seen her own Mam do it so often. 'All you do is, have a bath, put the kettle on to boil, put on a clean nightie, and send for t'nurse. Or if she's not in, then Granny Hutchins'll do!'

The hoot of laughter that met the child's perplexed gaze was followed by a playful clip around the ear. 'Away wi' you, you young rascal, it's time you were abed. You'd better not let your Dad be catching you up here, or there'll be the devil to pay at Number Twelve, if I'm not mistaken!'

The reminder of her father pricked Bethany's conscience once more. What if . . . ? Yes, just supposing little Sammy, her youngest brother, had one of his coughing fits again? As sure as there was a God in Heaven her Mam or Dad would be up those stairs in a flash. And what then? She shivered in the heat of the fire. Nancy Turver's Mam was right: there would be the devil to pay all right when they found her side of the bed empty. In fact payment to all the devils conjured up here tonight would not calm her father's wrath.

She turned slowly from the fire and gazed back down the hill in the direction of the village. Maybe she should be getting back before she was missed — back to reality. For surely this had not been the real world up here tonight? She glanced back at the scene taking place behind her. For years now she had been the only child in the school not to have attended the Fire of Beltane on top of Uther Crag on Halloween, and to have endured the scoffs of her friends once more in her very last year at school would have been too much to bear. But had the courage it had taken to defy her father and mother been rewarded? She could not answer that, for she felt deeply troubled by what she had witnessed. This was not the Utherby she knew. These were not her people. Or were they? Could it be that she had gone through childhood never really knowing the reality behind the bland and often dour everyday faces of the dalesfolk who were her friends and neighbours?

She pulled up the collar of her coat around her ears. Come next summer she would be thirteen and would have to say goodbye to her schoolbooks for ever. She would be sent into service like the rest of the young girls from the village, and how could she possibly be fit to enter the adult world knowing only half the truth? What she had seen here tonight might have troubled her – shocked her, even – but there was no denying it existed. She had chosen to defy her parents and had opened a door to a part of life that they refused to recognize, but could that really be right? Could you really go through life believing things to be only as you wished them to be? There was no doubt that this was a part of her world that was as real as the people themselves who had kept this ancient tradition alive. She had been brought up for the past twelve years in the sight of God, but now, with her own eyes, she had seen the devil at work among her own people and in so doing she knew she had left childhood behind for ever. Life would never be quite the same again.

It was almost an hour later that her footsteps dragged slowly in the direction of the scrubby wood and tangle of undergrowth that skirted the quarry face at the side of the hill. The path to the village below led through the thick copse of wind-blasted elms and Scots pines before winding its way down to the long straggle of quarry workers' cottages known as The Row that was home.

It was dark in the wood and a shiver ran through her as the sounds of revelry died away in the distance, to be overtaken by the strange, whispering sounds of the night. Somewhere above her an owl hooted and she could hear the flap of its wings as it took off in the direction of Hunter's Farm on the other side of the wood. There was a rustling in the undergrowth just ahead of her. A fox, maybe? The skin of her arms became gooseflesh beneath the thick worsted of her coat sleeves. In the shaft of moonlight beneath the tall trees a figure was looming towards her.

Her breath caught in her throat. She half-turned to run back in the direction of the fire, but the shout stopped her in her tracks. 'Bethany, in the name of God!'

The blood drained from her heat-scorched cheeks as her lips formed the word, 'Father . . .'

'Come here, you young devil!'

But Cheevers Baine's exhortation to his eldest child went unheeded as his daughter made a dash for the undergrowth to her right.

'Come back here, you young whippersnapper! I'll tan the hide off you when I get hold of you!'

And he would too! Bethany had no doubt about that. He had done it before and he would do it again, for there had been no transgression in her past that could hold a candle to this one tonight.

Her breath came in gasps as she stumbled over the tangled undergrowth of the wood in search of another path that would lead her down to The Row and the sanctuary of her mother's arms before her father got hold of her.

'Ow!' Her cry rang out in the darkness as her foot caught on something soft and she went sprawling all her length.

Panicking now, for her father was almost upon her, she attempted to pull herself up, but found her foot caught in something that felt like a piece of cloth.

'Get up out of there, you little devil!'

'I can't, Dad. My shoe's stuck. Honest it is!' She tugged with all her might, only to have her bare foot pull clear of the obstruction, leaving the clog firmly embedded in its snare. Panting now from the exertion, she leaned forward to retrieve it from whatever was holding it.

'Aaaaaah!' Her shriek echoed through the trees and made the blood run cold in her father's veins.

'What is it, child? For pity's sake . . .'

But for a moment she could neither move nor speak. Her searching fingers had probed at the piece of material holding fast her right clog, only to find her hand touching what felt for all the world like human flesh.

Her father was kneeling by her side now, all thought of chastisement forgotten. Together they gazed down at the object protruding out of the undergrowth at the side of the path. Tentatively Cheevers Baine put out a hand and gingerly touched what might easily have been the limb of a tree.

'God have mercy!' This limb had no bark; it was soft and cold to the touch. It belonged to no elm or pine. 'Dear God in Heaven, Bethany child, I do believe it's human!'

The girl let out a strangled sob and clung to her father as above them, beyond the tall trees, the moon shone clear of the scudding clouds and slanted a beam of light on to the body that lay on the ground beside them. It belonged to a young woman and Bethany watched in mounting horror as her father bent down to remove his daughter's shoe from where it had lodged in the torn fabric of the young woman's skirt.

The garment was bunched up over a pair of splayed white thighs, and the lower half of her was naked, save for a pair of lisle stockings, one of which was down around the ankles, its garter still cutting into the pale flesh at the top of her leg; the other stocking was still held fast by its own piece of elastic above the left knee. Her shoes, with their fashionable single-button strap, were still on her feet, but were covered in mud, as if there had been some sort of scuffling fight on the damp ground. As Bethany watched, her father pulled the rucked skirt down past the woman's knees to give some semblance of decency to a being long past caring about such things.

'Who – who is it, Da . . . ?' The whisper almost stuck in the throat.

The young woman's head was turned to the side, obscured behind an upraised arm and a swatch of long fair hair.

Gingerly Cheevers Baine leaned across and removed the arm, which was still pliable, and brushed the hair back from the face.

'Sarah-Jane!' Bethany gasped. The daughter of Isaac Youdell, the baker, had a trickle of drying blood coming from the same loose lips that had cursed her only an hour or so ago. 'Dad, it's Sarah-Jane!' A pair of blue eyes were gazing sightless into the night sky. 'It's Sarah-Jane Youdell.'

'Aye, it's her all right.'

'But what shall we do?'

'We'll get the police, lass. That's what we'll do.'

Chapter Two

Bethany sat in the stone-flagged kitchen sipping slowly from the mug of hot tea as Constable Sutcliffe licked the end of his pencil and balanced the folded notebook carefully on his knee. His was a frame bloated from a lifetime of tea drinking in just such back kitchens and his burly presence seemed to fill the room that was no more than ten by ten, excluding the brick protrusion at the back which held the copper and stone sink. Tonight it seemed even smaller than usual, for today had been Monday — washday — and above their heads four rows of drying clothes and bedding hung from the wooden slats of the pulley. More washing, mainly Sammy's baby clothes, hung on the folding drying rack by the side of the range. A whole day given over to washing, mangling, drying and ironing had lent a dank feel to the atmosphere that did nothing to relieve the overriding impression of gloom that pervaded the place. No one spoke as the officer made himself comfortable and his ruddy face was grave as he eased himself in the chair and unfastened his belt a notch.

He was a dour but decent man of almost sixty who, as the dale's only policeman, could have done without this type of thing happening on his patch. Although he had enjoyed many a brew from the Baines' teapot in the past, this was the first time he had ever had cause to call in any sort of official capacity on the household and he felt as ill at ease as the house's occupants as they sat waiting for his questions and pondering on the awful discovery of less than an hour ago. The mere finding of the body had leant an air akin to guilt to the proceedings, as if that in itself had been a wicked act that had somehow implicated them in the crime.

The visitor cleared his throat noisily, then looked round them all in turn, first at her father, then at Bethany, then at her mother who stood anxiously at the back of her father's chair, her hands, still red and raw from the washtub, resting protectively on her husband's shoulders. Bethany, who was sitting on a stool by the range, had her eyes fixed firmly on her father, whose face was as drawn and as colourless as his lips as he said, 'Well then, let's be having you.'

The officer took a deep breath. It was the first time he had ever dealt with a murder in all his thirty years in the dale. How to begin was the question. 'Well now, Cheevers lad, you'll have to think carefully before you say owt, but how far were you from the deceased when the body was discovered by young Bethany here?'

'Ten yards, two feet and half an inch.'

Constable Sutcliffe looked startled. 'Surely you're not telling me you know the exact distance?'

For the first time that evening Cheevers Baine gave the semblance of a smile. 'Well, let's just say if my answer strikes you half as daft as your question strikes me, Henry Sutcliffe, we'll be well matched.'

The atmosphere lightened somewhat and the constable gave a wry smile and sighed. 'Aye, well that's as may be, but I have to write summat down here. The law demands it.' He tried another tack. 'Tell me then, did you see the deceased, Sarah-Jane Youdell, wi' anybody before her death tonight? It needn't have been a local neither; for all we know it could be an offcomer we're after here.' That thought really appealed, for the idea that one of Utherby's own could be responsible for the young woman's death was not a happy one.

Cheevers Baine shook his head, but before he could answer his daughter broke in.

'I did, Mr Sutcliffe – and it weren't an offcomer neither!'

All eyes turned to the child and interest flickered in the officer's eyes. 'Is that so, Bethany lass? And who might it be that you saw with the victim?'

'It were Amos Greville.'

There was a sharp intake of breath from the other three people in the room. If she had said King George himself there couldn't have been more consternation.

'Eh now, are you sure o' that? I've no doubt young Sarah there spoke to a lot o' folk in the course o' the evening.'

'Aye, but when I last saw her she were wi' him and he were near throttling her. I tried to pull him off!'

The room fell silent as all eyes stared at the child.

'Now there, Bethany lass, tak' heed to what thou's saying.' It was her father who spoke. He looked nervously at the figure in police uniform across from him. It was the first he had heard of such a thing. His own daughter was pointing the finger, and at his boss's son at that! Sweat broke out beneath the hairs of his armpits and a thin film bathed his upper lip beneath the greying hair of his moustache. 'Tak' no notice! She's nowt but a lass, Henry. We know what sort of imagination young folk have these days.'

Bethany shook her head. 'But I did, Dad, I swear it! I saw her wi' Amos Greville. He had her against a tree and had his hand round her throat. I swear to God he had! Like this!' With a theatrical gesture she grabbed her own throat and began to gag in a quite dramatic fashion.

Cheevers Baine shifted uneasily in his chair. He looked at the man opposite him who was staring at the child, not quite knowing what to make of it all, then he looked back at his daughter. Despite the dramatics – and young Bethany had always been prone to exaggeration – he knew she would never make up something like this. He rubbed the palms of his hands backwards and forwards slowly on the rough serge cloth of his trouser-knees and a small knot in the vein at his left temple pulsed as he wrestled with his thoughts. It was not comfortable, what they had just heard, there was no doubt about that, but the truth was the truth, and he had brought his children up to value it as much as he himself did. He sighed and it seemed to come from the depths of his being as he drew himself up in his chair, clasping the wooden arms as he said, 'Aye, well that's it then, Henry lad. No child o' mine would swear to anything in t'Lord's name if it weren't true.'

Henry Sutcliffe's pencil was still poised above the blank page of his notebook. Surely it was more than his job was worth to write down such a thing in black and white? The Colonel owned just about everything – aye, and everyone hereabouts – how could he possibly accuse his son of murder on the word of a chit of girl? And that's what it would amount to if no one else came forward with another name to go on.

He looked imploringly at the child. 'Come now, Bethany love, wi' all them fancy costumes and things on tonight, you could have been mistaken. It could have been any one of a dozen lads you saw wi' poor Sarah up there.'

'Oh no, Mr Sutcliffe. I weren't mistook. I swear I weren't. You can ask Nancy's Mam.'

'Nancy's Mam?' He looked puzzled for a moment. 'You mean Emily Turver?'

'Aye, she were with me at t'time. She saw it were Amos as clearly as I did.'

Henry Sutcliffe let out a low whistle and sank back in his chair, as he pushed the pencil and notebook back into the breast pocket of his jacket. There was no way out of it now, but at least he had more than a bit of a lass's say-so to go on. 'Well now, that's a different matter entirely.'

'Why, Mr Sutcliffe? Why should it be different just 'cause Mrs Turver saw him?'

The constable heaved his great bulk to his feet and, taking his helmet from the scrubbed tabletop, he placed it back on his head with a weary sigh as he made for the door and said, ' 'Cause she's a grown woman, lass, that's why. And you're still nowt but a babby – as far's the law's concerned at any rate.'

He turned to her mother and father. 'Now if you good folk'll excuse me, it looks like I have some questions to ask a couple of doors down before I go any further. But as likely as not I'll be back, mind. Though not tonight.' He glanced at the clock that sat between the two Staffordshire dogs on the mantelpiece of the range. It had gone midnight; his feet were aching and it was hours since he had last had a bite to eat. He tightened the belt of his tunic over the wide girth of his empty stomach. 'Aye, it looks like it'll not be tonight.'

Betty Baine accompanied him to the door and she watched anxiously for a moment or two as he walked the few steps along the road to Number Nine. She could just imagine the shock its occupants would get when they found him at the door and she wished with all her heart that young Bethany had held her tongue. Folks had enough on their plates these days without being implicated in something like this. And with Emily's husband being as beholden as her own to the Grevilles for work, to say it was an awkward situation young Bethany had landed them in was putting it mildly.

For the few seconds the tall figure of the policeman was silhouetted in the moonlight as he waited for a reply to his knock, then, as the door was opened, Betty Baine watched him remove his helmet and bend his head as he stepped down into the narrow passage that led into the Turvers' front room. Her heart went with him, for she knew just how excitable Emily, her neighbour, could get; it took very little to get her worked up.

Once he had disappeared inside, she closed the door and

snibbed it behind her, before walking slowly back through to the kitchen where her husband and eldest child still sat. Her thin face was pinched and pale in the lamplight as she pulled the knitted shawl tighter around her narrow shoulders. The kitchen was cold, for the fire in the grate was little more than a pile of ashes. Coal was too precious to waste at this time of night when they should all be in bed.

She had been a fine-looking woman in her day; she might even have been called pretty if it hadn't been for the large brown mole with its sprouting hairs that blighted the skin to the right of her mouth and some said had caused her still to be on the shelf at twenty-five when the sturdy, sandy-haired figure of young Cheevers Baine had come into her life.

But Cheevers Baine had barely given the mole a second glance that first time those gentle brown eyes had smiled into his from along the hard oak pew of the Chapel. And they had smiled a lot in those days, for the only child of the late Harrison Hetherington, Methodist preacher extra-ordinary, was almost as well loved in the district as her late father had been, and was never short of a kind word or ready smile for anyone, stranger or friend alike.

He had not had the courage to make her acquaintance that first day, but he had made sure he was at the morning service the following Sunday, with his black boots polished as never before, and a fresh white collar about his well-scrubbed neck. In the lodgings he shared with two other of the quarrymen above the village reading rooms there had been plenty of comments as he slicked back his hair and carefully snipped the loose threads from the worn cuffs of his best shirt. They couldn't believe he was taking so much trouble just to go and sing a few hymns and say a few prayers, but he had not had the courage to confess the true reason for his attention to such personal detail. It had taken three weeks of sharing the same pew and polite smiles and nods before he had plucked up the courage to walk with the object of his admiration the few hundred yards to the small, whitewashed cottage on the edge of the village that she shared with her mother.

He had been made more than welcome by Edith Hetherington, the minister's widow, but it had been the still living presence of her dead husband that had made the strongest impression on the young man as he sat sipping tea from a dainty porcelain cup in the tiny living room. Framed beneath a photograph of the kindly-looking, white-haired man in the dog-collar that hung on the wall above the piano, was a cutting from the local newspaper, and Betty had taken it down and handed it to him with pride to read:

> The village wept, the people round
> Crowded the consecrated ground,
> And waited there to see the end
> Of Minister, Teacher, Father, Friend.

'Over five hundred there were at his funeral,' she said quietly. Pride burned in her eyes as she nodded her head and continued, 'Almost the whole of dale were crowded into the churchyard yonder. They said they had seen nothing like it in living memory.'

He had handed her back the picture to be rehung in its place of honour. 'He must have been a fine man.'

'Oh he was that all right. Happen they broke the mould when they made him, for I've yet to meet his match.' And she had looked at him, with those clear, light-brown eyes of hers, and he had known that she was judging him against that man up there on the wall, and he made up his mind there and then never to be found wanting. Whatever virtues she had known and admired in her father, he would endeavour that she would also find in him: faith, temperance, charity towards others . . . In fact, the only ways he could never compare were in book-learning and occupation, and the two went hand in hand.

Coming as he did in the middle of a family of seven children born to an itinerant farm labourer and his illiterate young Irish wife, he had attended very little in the way of school as his family moved around the bleak farmsteads of northern Cumberland in search of work. To have been taken on at Shap quarry at all as a twelve-year-old had been a rare stroke of luck for the young Cheevers Baine, and to have learned a skill by the time he was called to take the King's shilling and enlist in the Great War of 1914 was more than most young men from similar backgrounds could have hoped for.

As he had sat that day on the high-backed wooden chair in Betty's mother's parlour and listened to them talk of the days before the war when Harrison Hetherington himself had still been alive and things had been so much better, he resolved to do his very best to make sure the great man's only daughter could look forward to as good a life as someone in his own lowly position could give her.

They had been married from that same Chapel in which they had first met, and in which her father had preached for over quarter of a century, and their honeymoon had been one night spent in the White Hart in Hawes.

It had been a stroke of luck that the end cottage of The Row had been empty for their return as man and wife. The family that had rented it had moved to Darlington, where the father had been promised a better-paid job on the railways. But neither Cheevers nor his new wife had been prepared for what awaited them. The seam he had been working ran into trouble and, despite the government's need for stone for the 'homes fit for heroes' they had promised, the orders just didn't materialize. Half the workforce was laid off for almost eighteen months, with the rest put on short time.

It was into this situation that young Bethany was born

almost nine months to the day from the day they were wed. Too ill to care, with a bad bout of childbed fever, Betty had left the choice of name to her husband and Cheevers had taken the task seriously, borrowing a book of Christian names from the local lending library. He had chosen well. 'Bethany, it will be,' he told his wife, cradling the infant who looked up at him from wide, knowing eyes. 'It means "born of the house of poverty" in Aramaic, the language of Christ. We couldn't have anything more appropriate than that, could we now, lass?' And his wife had smiled at him from the pillow as she tried the name out on her tongue, 'Bethany . . .' It had a nice ring to it. And wasn't Beth short for her own full name of Elizabeth, anyway? 'I like it,' she said. 'A special name for a special child . . .'

And now, all these years later, that same child looked up at her mother from the stool where she still sat. She had finished her cup of tea and her arms were clasped tightly around her bony knees. She had that faintly defiant look to her face that Betty Baine knew so well, and her eyes took everything in – too much, sometimes. She was a bright child of whom her grandfather, Harrison Hetherington, would have been proud. But he would not have been so proud of the poverty that was now their lot. He had seen too much of it in his long years of ministering to the folk of the dale, and it was no secret that he had hoped his only child would marry into a household that offered at least the minimum of comfort and security. 'The rich man may never get to heaven,' he would say, shaking his head, after a day spent visiting the unemployed of the parish. 'But the poor man is already serving his term in hell.'

No, their lot was not an easy one, and now this had been visited upon them. Betty Baine shook her head as she closed the kitchen door and said wearily, 'Well, he's gone. He's in at the Turvers'. This is a fine do and no mistake. We'll not have heard the last of this by a long chalk.'

'Aye, you're right there.' Cheevers Baine rose to his feet, leaning heavily on the wooden arms of the windsor chair. 'But I've got a job to do in t'morning and if we sit here much longer it'll be daybreak afore we know it.'

He turned to his daughter still sitting silently by the pile of dead ashes in the grate. He felt tired, dog tired. And the energy he had already expended before Henry Sutcliffe's arrival, pointing out to Bethany the wickedness of her ways, he could ill afford. They had problems enough to contend with without this. He shook his head at the sight of those hazel eyes gazing up at him from the stool. 'As for you, young lady, you see where your wickedness has got us all? You see what happens when you play with fire and worship false gods?'

Bethany chewed her bottom lip and said nothing. Because of the chill of the house, she had not yet removed her coat, beneath which the white flannelette of her nightdress protruded, and she pulled it even tighter around her thin body and shivered. Despite the painful thinness of her limbs, she was a pretty child, with pale skin inherited from her sandy-haired father and long reddish-brown hair that hung in a single thick braid down her back. Her hazel eyes were dark in the lamplight and had a worried look as she glanced from one to the other of her parents. Why were they looking at her like that? She had done no more than tell the truth, after all. A strange atmosphere pervaded the kitchen. Her father was upset, she could sense that, but for once he wasn't shouting at her or even attempting to raise his hand. He was looking down at her as if she were the one responsible for Sarah-Jane's awful death tonight. And although he hadn't actually said so, it was as if he was blaming her – as if this trouble was all her doing. As if what had happened up there on the crag was somehow her fault. Gooseflesh covered her skin. She was almost beginning to believe it herself. Maybe it *was* God punishing her. Maybe he was right. It was an awesome thought.

She knew sleep would not come easily this night, and she was right. Beneath her closed lids loomed the white face of Sarah-Jane and she would shudder under the patchwork of the quilt and thrash out in the confined space of the bed as reality and nightmare became inextricably mixed and she wished with all her heart that she had never ventured out from the safety and warmth of this bed to join in the goings-on up there on top of the crag.

This could be a queer place – a frightening place at times – and folk did and said things that could hurt both mentally and physically. Even their favourite pastimes seemed bound up with death and suffering: fox hunting, badger baiting, yes and even cock fighting, if one was in the know and knew exactly where to go for the bouts that still took place regularly in the area. Young and old, rich and poor, seemed to gain some sort of inner satisfaction from seeing other creatures being hounded to death, then torn apart, and none more so than the Grevilles with their Utherdale hunt. The sound of those baying beagles had haunted her dreams ever since as a very young child she had first seen a fox torn to pieces in front of her in the field behind her grandfather's old church.

Colonel Greville had been Master of the local hunt for as far back as anyone could remember, and it was said that the only person to rival his horsemanship in the area was his second son, Amos. Amos Greville, they said, rode like the wind and had the killer instinct so necessary to hound a fox to the bitter end. And it was not just foxes Amos had been good at killing, for with her very eyes she had seen him take a rabbit from a snare on the edge of the moor and, holding it upside down by its feet, she had seen him gently stroke its neck as he killed it. She had watched mesmerized as his long fingers gently caressed the soft fur. 'What are you doing?' she had asked. She could see the look in his dark eyes to this day, and the satisfaction in his voice, as he replied, 'I'm dislocating its neck.' The small, terrified creature had been looking at her as it hung there between his fingers then, under her horrified gaze, it had given a sort of strangled shriek.

'That's the beggar gone!' its murderer had declared with satisfaction, before throwing its lifeless carcase over his shoulder, and making off in the direction of the Hall.

Bethany shivered beneath the bedcovers as the rabbit's petrified gaze merged with the look on the dead face of Sarah-Jane in her mind's eye. Had *she* given that same sort of strangled cry when his fingers found her throat? Suddenly the rabbit and the murdered girl became one, and transposed themselved in some sort of crazy dance of death behind her closed lids. She could feel herself break out in a cold sweat as she struggled to remain awake and escape from the awful nightmare she knew awaited her should she allow herself to fall asleep. This had been a terrible evening, a culmination of all the horror and evil she felt to be at the heart of things in this place that she both loved and hated with equal passion.

Eventually she was aware of a familiar warm, cloying smell from beneath the bedclothes. Little Sam had wet himself once again, but the four-year-old slept on, bliss-fully unaware, as did the six-year-old Libby beside him. Their older sister edged even nearer the wall, away from the damp patch that seeped ever closer to her own precious eighteen inches of mattress, and decided to ignore the accident. There had been enough upset tonight already without adding to it by revealing poor Sam's misfortune.

'Please, Jesus . . .' she began in a hoarse whisper. Then she fell silent. She stared through the darkness at the wall only a few inches from her nose. What could Jesus do to help? What could anyone do now? Sarah-Jane was dead, just like that rabbit. A shudder ran through her and she pulled the edge of the cotton sheet closer around her neck. It would soon be morning, and tomorrow before school she would have to go back up there, up on the crag where that terrible thing had happened tonight. 'Please, Jesus . . . Please . . .' But what was she trying to pray for, she wondered? For protection for herself up there on her beloved crag, perhaps?

Her eyes closed as her thoughts left poor Sarah-Jane and the rabbit and began to roam once more on those lonely windswept heights that she liked to think of as hers and hers alone. Her breathing became more even, until eventually, as the first grey streaks of a reluctant dawn lightened the skies over Utherby, all five children in the small attic bedroom were deep in a dreamless slumber.

As the eldest child of the family, it was Bethany's task each morning before school to carry her father's tin bottle of tea and wedge of home-made haverbread up to him in the dressing shed to have later with his mid-morning break. Her mother would have at least four of the delicious oatmeal loaves sizzling on the bakstone of the grate before the children came down to breakfast.

Betty Baine would have risen just before daybreak along with her husband and while he washed in the stone sink next door, she would be pouring a pint and a half of blue milk, for the want of best buttermilk, into an enamel pail, before adding about three quarts of hot water to bring it to blood heat. Then, while the first morning pot of tea was brewing, she would stir in the sieved oatmeal and yeast, before leaving it for an hour to rise by the side of the fire. It would then be poured on to the hot stone, where it would be steaming and rising with its familiar mouth-watering smell as the children came downstairs.

One of the still-warm loaves would be divided between the two eldest boys to have with butter and milk, and another between the two girls, Bethany and Libby, and their little brother Sam. The bread had a nutty, whole-some flavour and eaten hot from the range it tasted wonderful and helped fill young stomachs that were forever hungry and thankful for whatever food was on offer. 'Hunger is the best sauce,' their father would say as he watched them tuck in to the bread with perhaps a piece of cheese at suppertime, and Bethany would wonder at the strange saying, for she had never tasted such a thing as a sauce to compare the two.

The trek up to the quarry was a task that the young girl had seldom minded, especially at this time of year when the air was fresh and keen, with just the hint of the coming winter on the wind. Once she had completed her delivery, she would often climb even higher, for up there on the felltops she was alone with the elements and at peace with the world.

'A child of the clouds', her mother had once called her, for it was no secret that their eldest child was more at home up there on her beloved fells than anywhere else.

High above the drabness of the village streets and the relentless pounding and grinding of the quarry there was a strange almost ethereal peace to be had. It was a wild, lonely landscape, too high even for the sheep which clung to the more fertile lower pastures. A few lonely, stunted trees still protruded from the thin soil, but they had long since given up, their stiff, dead limbs pointing skywards, and hung with the smoke-coloured lichen they called old man's beard. Lichen covered the rocky outcrops too, but there was very little other sign of vegetation. Only the hardiest survived up there among the clouds, where only the wild purple heather and the occasional blaeberry bush could succeed in drawing sustenance from the barren soil.

On the highest ground no birds flew overhead as she walked, nor rose from the ground at her approach. It was only when she reached the lower slopes and came in sight of the quarry once more that she could see any signs of life, and Bethany got endless pleasure out of watching the birds as they soared and dipped on the eddying currents that played around the nooks and crannies of the crag that she had come to know as well as her own home, and her thoughts and dreams soared with them, far, far beyond this barren land, to a softer, greener place where life was not so hard, and fathers did not die young hacking a living from the very rock on which she trod. But in her heart she knew she was part of this barren land, and bleak and hard though it was, it was *her* land and she would not change it – not for all the green, fertile meadows in England.

It was her mother who had first walked with her up to the very top of the crag and told her of the birds and animals who inhabited these lonely places. And on their return Betty Baine would take from the dresser in the front room her most treasured possession: a clothbound volume of watercolour drawings of these same birds that soared and swooped above them up there on the highest hilltops. Throughout his long years as preacher and friend to the people of the area, the Reverend Harrison Hetherington had captured the essence of the dale's other inhabitants in a way that captivated the childish imagination like almost nothing else. Looking at that precious book brought nature alive almost as much as climbing to the tops of the fells themselves, for her grandfather had depicted the tiny creatures in all seasons, and in all their rich and varied finery.

And this time of year was a special favourite, for the swallows and other less hardy types had already gone in search of warmer climes, and it was now that the great skeins of wild geese traversed the skies over Utherdale. Even the curlews had gone now, forsaking the high fells to sing their peculiar bubbling song and utter their plaintive mournful cries in the wide river estuaries of the Solway.

Thanks to her grandfather's precious book, she knew them all, and she was sorry to see old friends such as them go. And friends they were. But she knew she could not be too sad, for one day they would return – drawn back to this place she too loved more than any other, where the air was surely as fresh and pure as that of heaven itself.

But now even the heather was fading and the vibrant colours of summer and early autumn were giving way to the golds and darker browns that told of the approaching winter. By the banks of the tumbling beck where she had dangled her feet on a summer's day the green rushes had turned to copper and bronze, and the clumps of yellow bent grass now swayed silver in the wind. And the water in the standing pools she would splash through in pursuit of her brothers had turned the colour of old pewter, reflecting a sky more often grey than blue. They would catch newts there in the summer, lying on their stomachs, arms outstretched to grab the slithering little creatures, before they disappeared beneath the water, their golden under-belly uppermost. She would feel sorry for them sometimes, for all they really wanted was to be left alone to enjoy their lives in the little pools and boggy places of the fell. Who could blame them for resisting being cooped up in a jam jar and taken to school to be poked and prodded by a motley assortment of children?

But on the morning after that terrible night Bethany gave little thought to the glories of nature as she set off on her trek up the hillside. There were other things afoot, such things as Utherby and its inhabitants had never known the like of before.

She could sense the tension in the very air she breathed as she picked her way along the rutted track, past the untidy squalor of the spoil heaps and the deep trough of an old working that now served as the local midden. As she turned her nose from the odour another assailed her nostrils when she reached the smithy with its pungent singeing smell and sizzling, spitting forge. It was in there that the horses and ponies were shod for their never-ending treks to the station and back, and the picks and masons' tools were sharpened daily by Ellen Capstick's father, Joe.

She caught sight of her friend's flaxen head just inside the smithy door and shouted, 'Hey, Ellen!' before skipping over to join her.

Both girls stood for a moment or two, mesmerized by the spitting, hissing forge, where the sparks flew from the anvil like windblown chaff as Ellen's father Joe manipulated the white-hot lengths of metal with pliers and a seven-pound hammer that his daughter and her friend could barely even lift.

When yet one more horseshoe was flicked into the hot dust to the side of the forge, Joe Capstick stood back a moment and removed the pipe from his mouth to spit noisily into the glowing fire. He was not a tall man, but what little flesh there was on his spare frame was all muscle and his biceps matched a horse's thigh inch for inch. His wrists and hands too had grown huge from years of toil and the insides of his sinewy arms were covered with permanent raw, red blisters, the pain from which liberal applications of zinc and castor oil ointment each night did little to relieve. The leather apron he wore was held in place with a wide leather belt and was frayed at the bottom, from years of brushing the debris from his anvil with its bottom edge.

'Lean on t'bellows there, our Ellen,' he said wearily, stretching, with one hand in the small of his back. Bending over a hot anvil all day was no joke.

His daughter did as bidden, and the two girls watched as the fine-grained coke took on a lighter, more radiant glow as the pumped air breathed more life into the flames. The warmth caused a rosy flush to come to the faces of the two schoolgirls; inside the smithy was a pleasant place to be at this time of year and, caught in the right mood, Joe Capstick was a dab hand at story-telling. But this morning was not to be one of those days.

'I reckon it's time thou wast heading back, my lass,' the blacksmith said, addressing his daughter, before reaching for another bar of unworked metal. 'The school bell'll be going afore long and I've enough to be getting on wi' this morning without having to keep an eye on the likes o' you two lasses.'

Ellen shrugged and sighed, then turned to Bethany who still had her father's meal to deliver. 'I'll see you in the playground,' she said confidentially. 'Eee, it's terrible, in't it? A real-live murder here in Utherby!'

Bethany was just on the point of saying you couldn't have a 'real-live' murder when her friend turned on her heel and ran off back down the hill in the direction of the village. She watched as the pinafored figure disappeared into the distance and was already imagining the horror and excitement with which the news of poor Sarah's death would be received by the rest of their classmates.

'Aye, lass. It's a sad state of affairs when summat like this befalls the place,' her friend's father said, with a shake of his head. 'We could've done without this, all right. But it's a sign of the times, if you ask me. Things weren't never the same after t'bloody war. Life were cheap then, wi' millions killed for nowt, and things have never got back to what they were. Respect has gone. Respect for life.'

He puffed slowly on his pipe, then glanced down at the young girl to whom he had been addressing his thoughts. Then he gave an embarrassed cough. 'Aye well, you're a bit on the young side to know about that. Just you tek care, that's all I can say. No young lass'll be safe around here till they get the wicked beggar who was responsible.'

Bethany nodded gravely. She had never thought of it like that before, but maybe Ellen's Dad didn't know who did it. Maybe nobody had told him it was Amos Greville. And it *was* Amos Greville, wasn't it?

'I'll tek care, Mr Capstick. Honest I will.' And her face was as solemn as her thoughts as she set off to walk the remaining hundred yards or so to her father's place of work. And it seemed they weren't the only ones to be absorbed by poor Sarah's death, for normally when she passed by the men would be concentrating on their individual tasks, but this morning they seemed to be huddled everywhere in small groups.

Around the gaping, black mouth of the drift she could see what looked like a meeting going on. There was a distinct whispering in the air – an undercurrent of excitement tinged with fear that made the small hairs at the back of her neck stand out as she made her way up to the sheds where her father and the other masons dressed the stone into finely gauged building blocks, or the two-inch-thick flags for house floors or pavements.

They worked outside in the summer months and then the din never seemed half as bad as it did now when they were all inside and the shouts of the men and the sound of their implements vied with the whinnying of the horses as the empty carts were backed into the bedlam till they were hard up against the dressed-stone banker where the finished work was stacked and ready to go.

A shaft of autumn sunlight blazed in from one of the tall windows, causing the dust particles to dance in the air as Bethany made her way through between the long benches in search of her father.

She eventually found him bent over a bench at the far end of the shed. He looked up as she approached and wiped a rivulet of sweat from his brow. The gesture left a dirty streak in the film of grey powder that clung to his face. 'Lay it there, lass,' he said, not looking at her, but nodding his head in the direction of a stone bench opposite, where his jacket lay next to a pile of others. His voice had an edge to it that she immediately recognized.

'Is owt wrong, Dad?' He looked even more tense than she had anticipated and had not greeted her appearance with his usual smile. 'Are you still mad at me?'

He shook his head, still avoiding her eyes. 'Nay, our lass, I'm not mad at thee.'

'What's wrong then?' Something else was up, there was no doubt about it.

Cheevers Baine wiped his hands on the thick apron he wore, but was given no chance to answer as a man's agitated voice rent the air.

'We were right! They've tekken him, Cheevers! They've tekken Tom up to t'Hall!'

Both the child and her father looked round as the owner of the voice came hurrying towards them from the direction of the door. It was Will Dearden, who had worked at the next bench for ten years or more. His square face was even more set than usual beneath the battered tweed bonnet and his eyes had a worried look to them as he cast a glance at the child and attempted a smile.

'What's that you say?' Cheevers Baine's pale eyes stood out in the caked grey of his face.

'Not five minutes since. Old Carnforth's put him in the back o' t'trap and they've set off ower the moor for t'Hall. They say there's blue murder being threatened up there this morning for young Amos has been tekken away for questioning about that lass's death, and his father is blaming the Turvers for pointing the finger.'

Bethany looked at her father, who had gone quite pale beneath the coating of grey dust. His body seemed to slump against the stone bench as he wiped his brow with the back of his hand. 'This land will never be free, nor the folk in it free men and women as long as there are those such as the Grevilles to play God over us,' he said softly. ' "Vengeance is mine saith the Lord". . .'

'But not only the good Lord's while there is a bloody Greville about!' Will Dearden cut in.

All three looked at one another. 'Kick one and they all limp', they said about the Grevilles, and this had never been more true. There was vengeance being sought out there at Wolf Hall this morning. A sick feeling came to the pit of the child's stomach. 'What will happen, Dad? What's going to happen to Mr Turver?' She really couldn't care less about Amos Greville, but Nancy Turver's dad was her favourite among all her friends' fathers. Short and squat, with a ready smile for all, he was one of the few folk who could make a joke out of just about any situation. But she knew he would not be smiling now.

Cheevers Baine looked down at his eldest child and shook his head. 'Only the good Lord knows that, lass. But we should all pray for Tom Turver this day. Yes, we should pray to God that He sends His only Son to help him – and us!'

'Nay, nay, Cheevers man!' Will Dearden cut in. 'If thy lass is going to pray for such a thing, tell her to ask God to come Himsel'. This is no job for His lad!'

They all managed a weak smile as they looked at one another in the dusty light of the dressing shed, and although Bethany was not quite sure exactly what was going on, she had a curious feeling of foreboding, as if things were never going to be quite the same again. Sarah-Jane Youdell's death last night had started a train of events that would not stop with her funeral, she was sure of that. And what was worse, she herself might even be the cause of it.

Chapter Three

'Calm down, father! You'll get more out of the man if you keep your temper.' Jack Greville caught hold of the sleeve of his father's riding jacket and urged caution.

The older man had been beside himself with rage for the past half-hour, ever since Amos, his second son, had been taken off by the police for questioning. The very idea that any son of his could be implicated in such a thing as an unexplained death – he steadfastly refused to use the word murder – was not only unthinkable, it was downright slanderous. The good name of the family was one of the few things they still had intact from the old days and he was damned if some tittle-tattling woman – and the wife of an employee at that – was going to take it away from him.

Aye, so much had already gone . . . He shrugged himself free from his son's restraining hand and his brown eyes beneath the beetling brows clouded as he thought of the difference between the world of Wolf Hall that he had known as a child and the situation that existed now. Just a glance around the walls of the hall where they were now standing would have broken his mother's and father's hearts. Almost half the paintings had gone – the Turner watercolour of the Lune near Kirkby Lonsdale, the Pre-Raphaelite oil by Rossetti that his father had given his mother on the occasion of their Silver Wedding anniversary, the Dürer collection of drawings that had been in their family for over two hundred years . . . All gone, the lot of them – sold to pay death duties and other debts that were mounting still. 'Thank God, your grandparents didn't live to see it,' he said bitterly.

'Don't worry, Father. Amos will be back by nightfall – have no fear of that.' Jack presumed it was purely his brother's predicament to which his father was referring as he pulled back the heavy brocade of the curtain for a better view of the drive.

They were standing by one of the windows in the great hall of the old manor house, alongside the youngest of the Greville sons, sixteen-year-old Ned. The eyes of all three were riveted on the drive outside as the family's pony and trap clattered up to the front door with the object of the Colonel's wrath, Tom Turver, perched aloft, alongside the driver.

They watched in silence as, at an order from Old Carnforth, the Grevilles' general factotum, the quarryman jumped down from the cart and removed the battered tweed bonnet from his thinning hair. He glanced anxiously up at the door of the large house in front of him. It was much bigger close to than it appeared from a distance, he thought as he passed a smoothing hand over the greying strands that covered his scalp, then rubbed first the toe of one boot and then the other on the back of his trousers. It would be the first time he had been inside the Hall itself and he was very conscious of the dusty and threadbare state of his working clothes.

'Well, mek haste there!'

Within seconds he had been prodded up the front steps by the end of a riding whip in the small of his back. The metal segs in the soles of his boots caused his feet to slip on the well-worn stone treads and he had to catch hold of the wooden side of the porch to steady himself as the old man next to him took a firm hold of the wrought-iron handle of the door in both hands and twisted with all his might. The heavy oak panels creaked on their hinges as the door swung open and they passed through, to be met by the stares of three pairs of eyes waiting in the hall beyond.

Tom Turver's insides quaked at his first sight of the huge entrance hall, with its blackened beams and high vaulted ceiling. His whole house could fit into just one corner of it. Out of the corner of his eye he could see the Colonel and two of his sons standing by one of the windows. They made a forbidding trio, and he felt acutely exposed and vulnerable as he stood uncertainly in the vicinity of the front door and waited for instructions.

'That first room to your left,' Old Carnforth said, and Tom headed for it, after first nodding respectfully to the small group on his right.

Within seconds he found himself in a room that he took to be the library, by the rows of floor-to-ceiling bookshelves that lined the walls. It reeked of fresh tobacco smoke and an upturned pipe lay inside an ashtray, next to a paper folded open at the sports page. He caught sight of a photograph of England cricketer Harold Larwood, the Nottinghamshire pitman now hailed as the world's fastest bowler. There was a controversy raging about what the Australians were calling the 'body-line' bowling delivered by Larwood and at any other time he would have been keen to take a closer look and even make an attempt at reading the article. But not today.

Carnforth did not stay, but held open the door for his employer to enter. Tom Turver swallowed nervously as Colonel Greville, resplendent in grey riding jacket and black jodhpurs, strode into the room, closely followed by his eldest son. The youngest, Ned, had been left standing by the window in the hall outside.

For a moment or two no one spoke and the workman's face was pale in the sunlight from the window as, his bonnet clasped tightly in his hands in front of him, he stood looking anxiously at the two men who confronted him.

61

'I don't suppose you need to be told why you're here,' Philip Greville said at last. His was an imposing presence: over six feet and built in proportion, his military bearing seemed to dwarf the stunted growth of the man opposite and the expression on the patrician features underlined the divide that existed between the two, both in class and character. This was a man as used to giving orders as the other was to taking them, and it was more of a statement than a question he threw at his employee as he glared across at the clearly worried man.

Tom Turver flicked a tongue over lips still caked with powdered limestone. His mouth was as dry from nerves as the dusty floor of the dressing shed from which he had just been plucked. His eyes darted apprehensively from father to son. Young Jack, now every bit as tall and well-built as his father, avoided his gaze, as if the whole business embarrassed him.

Tom looked down at the carpet in front of him. Should he brazen it out and pretend he knew nothing of the goings-on of the previous night and this morning? One look at the set faces before him told him otherwise. There was nothing to be gained by antagonizing them any further. 'Happen you're referring to that lass's death,' he said at last, barely recognizing his own voice. Usually abnormally deep for such a small man, it had risen in tone and cracked to an embarrassing croak in mid-sentence.

'I'm referring to the fact my son Amos is now sitting in some police cell somewhere answering a load of damn-fool questions on your say-so!'

'Nay!' Tom Turver drew in his breath sharply. Surely they didn't imagine this was what he wanted? Couldn't they see he was almost as upset as they were over the whole sorry business? 'Nay, Colonel . . . I . . .'

'Don't "Nay, Colonel" me, Turver! I have it on the best authority that it was your wife who pointed the finger at my lad and that makes you responsible. What have you got to say to that, that's what I want to know?' Philip Greville, who was standing legs apart, hands clasped behind his back, was clenching and unclenching his fists as he spoke and his son, Jack, standing just behind him, knew his father was having a hard job controlling himself.

The accused man made a hopeless gesture with his hands. 'There's nowt much I can tell you and that's the God's truth, sir. From what I can gather the young lass next door told the bobby that she and my missus had seen your lad Amos wi' the Youdell lass just afore she were killed, and that's as much as I know of the affair.'

'Young lass next door?'

Tom Turver's face flushed beneath the caking of dust and grime. It sounded as if he was pinning the blame on a bit of a girl. 'The Baines' lass, Bethany. She were wi' t'wife . . .'

'You mean that skinny little thing? Why, she's still in short skirts!' It was young Jack who broke in. He was surely not referring to that forward young brat in the undersize coat and outsize boots who had cheeked him earlier on in the evening?

'How old is this Baine girl?' the Colonel asked in irritation, reluctant to be sidetracked.

'She's not more than eleven or twelve, Father,' his son answered. 'Just a bit of a kid.'

The Colonel gave a derisory snort and looked contemptuously at the unfortunate man before him. 'Don't tell me you're attempting to shift the blame for Amos's abduction by the police on to a mere child, Turver! Shame on you, man!'

Tom Turver shifted uncomfortably from one foot to the other. He felt no higher than the expensive Persian carpet on which he was standing. 'No, I'd not do that, Colonel,' he said quietly. 'If my wife is the cause of your son being arrested, then happen you're right and as head of t'household then I must tek responsibility . . .'

'Arrested!' The word exploded in a shower of spit from Philip Greville's lips as he stared at the man in front of him. Flecks of saliva clung to the grey hair of his moustache as he contemplated the dreaded prospect. He pulled a linen handkerchief from his breast pocket and wiped his mouth, adjusting his top denture back into position before dabbing his brow. 'By God, Turver, you had better pray it never comes to that, for if it does then I'll have you and that wife of yours out of this village – nay, out of this dale – before you can draw breath!'

The ex-military man's dark eyes bulged and his already ruddy complexion became even more florid as he leant over and gripped the edge of the desk beside him. His son came forward, anxiety etched on his features as he took his father's elbow and helped him into the nearest chair. He had been told he must not excite himself; his blood pressure was already dangerously high for a man of his age. 'Take it easy, Father. You'll only make it worse by getting in a state.'

His father drew in a deep breath and nodded as he stuffed the handkerchief back into his pocket. 'I'll make it worse all right!' he promised. 'I'll make it a damned sight worse for those who are responsible for this travesty! They'll find no sanctuary in Utherdale after this! You'll be out on your ear, my man, if this doesn't blow over good and sharpish!'

Tom Turver's heart pounded. He had been born and bred in this village and his father before him. He worked for this man, who owned the very roof over his family's heads and was now threatening to ruin him. Sweat broke out on the skin beneath the striped flannel of his shirt as he shook his head at the hopelessness of the situation. He felt dog tired. He had been up all night consoling Emily after the bobby had gone, and what little courage and energy he had managed to muster on entering the Greville household seemed to evaporate in the glare of his employer's eyes.

He took a deep breath in an effort to gain control of himself, then his whole being began to shake and he was standing there quivering like a small child about to be struck for some misdemeanour. All he could see was his few sticks of furniture being thrown out on to the road. He had seen it happen before in the village. And it had even happened to his own grandfather, Septimus Turver, when old Henry Greville, the Colonel's grandfather, had been told of his employee's attendance at a local Chartist march. Even today Tom could feel the smart of tears in his eyes when he remembered his own father tell of witnessing the event as a child. And local Chartist sympathizers had composed a poem about it; he could still remember part:

> He's spent his life in breaking stones,
> With saddened heart and aching bones;
> So why did he grumble? he got good pay,
> A house of his own and a sixpence a day . . .

'No, please, Colonel . . . Please, don't do that . . .' His grandfather's experiences had been etched on his soul by his father, whose childhood the affair had blighted, and never could he let his own family go through such a thing.

And suddenly he was begging, begging for forgiveness for a supposed crime he knew he had not committed, begging for himself, for his wife, Emily, for his whole family. In fact, he was grovelling — prostrating himself before this man who held his whole future in his hands. 'Please. Colonel, I beg of you. Don't let my family suffer . . .'

Jack Greville turned and walked from the room, unable to bear the sight before him. Humiliation, in any form, was not an edifying spectacle. He was glad it was his father's problem to deal with and not his.

Tom Turver did not return to the quarry, but was

ordered to keep away from his place of work until Amos Greville had been safely returned to The Hall, with the assurance from the police that no further action would be taken.

Shocked to the core at being banned from his work, and gaining no crumb of comfort from his employer as to the future of his family home, in a state of shock, he was left to walk the two miles back to his home in The Row to contemplate the future that might await himself and his family. He dreaded telling Emily, for she never was one for coping with bad news at the best of times, and things couldn't get much worse than this.

Betty Baine was scrubbing her front step when the sound of his booted feet coming up the road made her turn. But gone was the familiar sprightly stride of her usually chirpy, good-natured neighbour; this time the metal-studded soles of Tom Turver's boots made a weary, dragging sound as they approached their destination. As always he tipped his cap, but for once he did not manage his usual smile or joke before disappearing over his own doorstep.

Betty Baine stood up and wiped her hands on her apron. Never had she seen such a picture of dejection and the vision was still with her when her three eldest children returned from school at twelve-thirty.

'I don't know what was said to poor Tom before they sent him packing, but I can guess,' she confided to the four young faces gathered round the kitchen table as she lifted the heavy pot on to the wrought-iron stand and dished a boiled potato into each waiting plate. 'It'll be the Poor House for the lot of them if young Amos is not released, for the Colonel'll not keep him on at t'quarry, that's for sure. Not if he holds the family responsible for his son's arrest.'

Bethany was horrified. Did the Poor House still actually exist? And could Nancy and her family really be bound for it? Solemnly she dug her spoon into the hot potato and placed part of it in her mouth but, strangely, she wasn't hungry any more. She sucked thoughtfully on the white, floury substance and swallowed with difficulty. It was all wrong, somehow. She had walked home from school with Nancy this dinnertime and she had never known her friend so worried. Her mother Emily had been up all night in tears after Henry Sutcliffe, the bobby, had left, and had kept crying out that they would be the ones to face the consequences if anything happened to young Amos Greville.

'What does she mean, "face the consequences"?' she had asked Nancy, but her friend had only shrugged as she sucked on a chewed-out piece of liquorice root.

'I don't rightly know,' Nancy had said eventually. 'Happen it means summat bad though, otherwise she wouldn't have been crying, would she?'

Bethany could only agree with the logic. And now her own mother was talking of the Poor House and the Turvers in the same breath. It wasn't right somehow. The Turvers were being punished for something that wasn't their fault at all. In fact, if it was anybody's fault that Amos Greville had been arrested, it was really hers. She was the one who first mentioned his name to Constable Sutcliffe. And she was the one who would have to do something about it.

She told no one of her decision to skip school that afternoon, and merely told Nancy and her brothers and sister that she had an errand to run when she left them at the school gate at just before one-thirty.

It took her all of three-quarters of an hour to reach Wolf Hall, running all the way.

The half-timbered old house, with its tall twisted chimneys, stood three storeys high at the end of a long drive bordered by ancient spreading oaks said to have been there long before the original Wolf Hall was partially destroyed by fire at the time of Cromwell. With its wisteria-clad walls and mullioned windows, and with much of its original Tudor exterior still intact, it remained a fine-looking building despite its peeling paintwork and general air of neglect. On the whole it had withstood the ravages of a Civil War and centuries of wild Yorkshire winters remarkably well. It was certainly the grandest house Bethany had ever seen, totally unlike any of the other manor houses in the dale. While most of them were built in the usual solid limestone style, Wolf Hall had been designed in the fashion of the grand houses of the South, and this was something that had always lent it a certain air of mystique as far as the child was concerned. The only others she had seen like it had been in the pages of some of the old history books inherited from her Grandfather Hetherington.

Even the two ornamental statues of running wolves at the foot of the stone steps leading up to the front door had been specially commissioned in Italy and the original gardens laid out in an Italianate style during a period when most other such houses in England had made do with open parkland. Style had been important to the Grevilles then, for they had always considered themselves a cut above their neighbours. But a love of drink and gambling had been inherited by enough Greville men to make a difference to the family coffers, and this, combined with punitive death duties, had meant that succeeding generations had found it increasingly difficult to keep the old place from crumbling at the edges.

Little was left now to remind the eye of the ornately laid-out lawns that had once graced the front of the house, and the urns on the shoulders of the marble cherubs which had once stood proudly in the middle of them had long since given up spouting water. With toes and fingers missing and faces ravaged almost featureless by severe North Riding winters, they, like the house and the family which owned it, had seen better days.

While nature had been given leave to claim back what was rightly hers outside the house, inside little had been done to either add to or restore an interior originally designed by its first inhabitant, a certain Right Honourable Archibald Greville, who had led his young wife and family over the threshold in the reign of Elizabeth I.

It had been an expensive business, pulling down the original house and replacing it with one of the finest and most expensive family homes in the county, but he had considered it was well worth the money; after all, the Grevilles were one of the oldest and proudest families in Yorkshire and they deserved the best.

But, despite its present air of genteel decay and neglect, even he would have been surprised to see how his creation had lasted. It had already been standing proudly overlooking the village of Utherby for almost three centuries when, during Victoria's reign, the street of cottages known as The Row was built to house the workers from the newly-opened quarry.

Its tall, twisted chimneys could be seen from Bethany's bedroom window on a fine day and the child had often gazed across at them. They had seemed a whole world away from the mean streets of her village. Throughout all her young life, The Hall had stood there, aloof and above it all, so near and yet so far from her own small world of The Row. And now, as she ran the two miles that brought her to the front steps of Wolf Hall, it had seemed a very long way indeed. Now she was actually in front of it, it seemed even bigger and more imposing than she had ever thought it from afar.

Her face glowed with the exertion, and her breath still came in gasps as she gazed up at the life-size stone carving of a running wolf inside its elaborately carved shield that had pride of place above the great oak door. Cut into the stone above the shield were the Latin words: *Homo homini lupus*. 'Man is a wolf to man,' she murmured under her breath: the age-old motto of the Grevilles. Miss Meldrum, her teacher, had translated it for the class, and there was not a child in the dale who did not know it off by heart, for the Greville shield embellished the front cover of almost every school jotter in the district. Ever since slates had been replaced for special tests in the classroom by paper and pencil, the Colonel, as chairman of the school governors, had presented the cluster of local schools with which he was personally involved with special jotters for the children.

And now as she looked up and beheld the creature face to face, it was every bit as fearsome as she had always imagined it to be – a bit like the inhabitants within, she thought to herself, as she stood uncertainly on the front step and regarded with some apprehension the heavy, wrought-iron bell pull in front of her.

For a moment she panicked and wanted to turn and run, but the thought of poor Tom Turver and his family hardened her resolve. She had come this far; there could be no turning back now. She had just pulled her socks up above the laced tops of her boots, and was contemplating what to say if she gave the bell a tug and the Colonel himself appeared, when, from round the edge of the porch, another face grinned.

'Why, Neddy, you didn't half give me a start!' she gasped. She smiled nervously back at the gawky youth who now stood beside her as she pushed windswept strands of hair back behind her ears, then pulled her fringe back down into place.

Philip Greville's youngest son snatched the cap from off his head and his dark eyes shone at the sight of the visitor. Bethany felt an immediate sense of relief at the sight of the young man who was not above joining in their childish village games. He might not be all there, as they all claimed, but Ned Greville was the nicest of the lot as far as she was concerned.

He had a bag of boiled sweets in his pocket and she watched as he pulled it out and extricated a black-and-white bull's-eye from the sticky mass and handed it to her.

She took it with a smile of thanks and stuck it in the corner of her cheek. 'Ta, Neddy,' she said, with a now bulging cheek as she licked her fingers and nodded in the direction of the closed door. 'I've come to see your Dad. Will you take me to him?'

Ned's permanent smile remained intact as he shook his head and screwed up the paper bag and pushed it back into his trouser pocket.

'But I must see him. It's important. Honest it is. Please take me to him, Ned, please!' Her voice rose as she pleaded.

But again Ned shook his head and gestured with his right arm back down the drive. 'Ay-y-mos . . .' He at last succeeded in getting out his brother's name. 'Fffaaa . . .'

Bethany squinted up at him in the early-afternoon sunshine. If it wasn't for the slackness of his mouth and that silly permanent grin, he wouldn't be a bad-looking lad, really. He had the Grevilles' dark colouring and, like his eldest brother Jack's, his hair was curlier than Amos's, and he had the dark, walnut-brown eyes common to all three sons. They said his half-wittedness was due to his difficult birth and that might have been true, for it was common knowledge in the village that his mother, Margaret, had had a hard time of it and had never fully recovered. She had died before he was three weeks old, leaving the Colonel to be both mother and father to all three boys. The only female attention they received was from Tabby – Miss Tabitha Fleetwood –who had been housekeeper to the Grevilles for the past two generations.

'What's that you're saying, Ned? Has your Dad gone out?' Bethany's heart began to sink. Had she run all this way for nothing?

The youth nodded his head vigorously. 'Ay-ym . . .'

'He's gone to see your Amos?' she interrupted. 'Is that it?' She might have known – all this effort for nothing.

Again he nodded and grinned, as Bethany sighed deeply and gave a disconsolate shrug and kicked at the stone step in frustration, before beginning her descent. But Ned grabbed her hand. She began to snatch it back but he was quite insistent as he pulled her, half-stumbling, up the steps behind him.

He was surprisingly strong for all his slight build and she could do little to stop him as, still holding tightly on to her right hand, he pushed open the heavy wooden front door and almost hauled her over the threshold behind him.

The door closed behind them with a sonorous clang and she gave a gasp as she looked around her. It was the first time she had been in so grand a place and she gazed in awe at the huge vaulted ceiling of the great hall, with its centuries-old beams. The oak-panelled walls with their tall, mullioned windows, were hung with what looked like family portraits, although some pictures were obviously missing; you could tell from the much lighter colour of the wood in places. But what oil paintings remained were interspersed with framed game trophies, varying from glass-cased salmon to a huge stag's head which had pride of place over the enormous stone Minster fireplace that dominated the far wall. An open-mouthed tiger rug – a souvenir from one of the Colonel's earlier Indian trips – lay in front of the open grate, in which a fire of oak logs crackled. She stared in a mixture of fascination and apprehension at the bared teeth of the animal, then made a face in its direction, as if to say, 'You can't scare me!'

Ned beckoned for her to follow him and, still gazing about her, she did so, her booted feet slipping on the polished floorboards as they made their way to a door at the far end of the hall, to the left of the fireplace.

Ned opened it and almost pushed her into the room

within. He motioned for her to take a seat on the leather chesterfield in front of the fire, before he, himself, began to back out of the door. She made to follow him, but he held up his hand and indicated for her to stay. The door closed behind him, and ignoring his invitation to sit down, she stood looking around her, marvelling at the sumptuousness of the surroundings. Her eyes shone in her still flushed face as she drank it all in. It was obviously some kind of an office or study she was in, for a huge mahogany, leather-topped desk stood in front of the window, covered in papers.

After several minutes' waiting she became bored and picked up a copy of the *Daily Mail* lying on the desk among the other papers. There was an article about the Reverend Harold Davidson, Rector of Stiffkey in Norfolk, whom it was said had recently been defrocked for having had carnal relations with women. Carnal relations . . . the words had a wonderful ring to them as she devoured the lurid details. Having been brought up in awe of her Grandfather Hetherington's memory, vicars held a real fascination for her and this one seemed to have got himself into a real bit of bother. What exactly were they, these carnal relations? she wondered, as she turned from the newspaper to take in the other wonders of the room. She would endeavour to find out as soon as she got the chance.

The walls were hung with a heavy, red flock wallpaper that looked as if it had been up as long as the house had been standing, and on it hung several pictures in gilt frames, with their titles inscribed underneath on small brass plates. They were all of various Lake District scenes. She had never actually been there, but had heard tell it was a beautiful part of the world, and at school Miss Meldrum, the schoolmistress, made them recite poems like 'The Daffodils' by a man called Wordsworth who had once lived there.

73

Apart from the desk and chesterfield, the other furniture consisted of a tall mahogany bookcase, filled with bound volumes, and two matching green leather armchairs, one on either side of the fire. Two small, round tables stood on either side of the fender, covered in a plush red chenille, the fringes of which reached to the floor. Their tops were covered in a collection of sepia-coloured photographs, mainly in silver and polished wooden frames.

Fascinated, she walked over and picked one up. It stood out because it was smaller than the rest, being no more than three inches in height, and was in an exquisitely carved ivory frame. It was a head-and-shoulders portrait of a very beautiful young woman in a high-necked Victorian blouse, her dark hair piled high on her head, with a frizzed fringe in the style made popular by the King's mother, Queen Alexandra. How wonderful, she thought, to have all these family pictures – to have a personal record of all the people you have known and loved, and many you never even had the chance to know, for they died years before you were born. The only photograph their family possessed was one of her grandfather Harrison Hetherington, inherited from her grandmother, and proud though she was of it, it paled into nothing in comparison with all these.

The noise of the door opening made her jump back guiltily and sit down with a bounce on the sofa as originally instructed. She gazed up curiously at the tall figure who now entered the room. It was the eldest of the three sons, Jack Greville himself. His dark brows furrowed as he stared curiously at the young girl in the white school smock and brown worsted coat perched on the edge of the chesterfield. She had a disconcertingly pert way of looking at you, with her head to one side. 'What in heaven's name do *you* want?'

Bethany edged back to the very furthest corner of the

cushion and swallowed the remaining piece of boiled sweet. She opened her mouth, but no words would come as she suddenly became aware of the small ivory frame in her hand. Dear Lord, what if he thought she was stealing it? Her face flamed at the very thought as she guiltily slipped the article down the side of a cushion, meaning to replace it later. 'If you please, Jack Greville, I've come to talk to your Dad.'

'And if I don't please?' One dark brow rose in sardonic fashion as he looked down at her. With the sunlight from the window playing on her auburn hair and those wide hazel eyes of hers, she might even have been quite a pretty child if it hadn't been for those awful clothes and those skinny wrists and legs.

Bethany rose to her feet. He was for playing funny beggars – she might have known. She bent down and pulled up her socks once more, then straightened her coat. 'It's your Dad I've come to see, Jack Greville, not you, but if I can't see him, then happen you'll have to do.'

'Is that a fact, then?' He grinned at her. She was a funny-looking kid and no mistake, but spunky. He liked that. 'Well, fire away.'

Bethany moved behind the arm of the sofa, as if to distance herself even more from the tall figure on the other side of the room. 'Your Dad's blaming the Turvers for your Amos being taken by the bobbies – and that's not fair.' The last part of the sentence came out in a rush.

The smile faded from Jack Greville's face. 'So what's not fair about it, may I ask?'

Bethany took a deep breath. Her father always said you couldn't suffer half as much for telling the truth as for staying silent and have someone else be punished for your sin. ' 'Cause I saw him too!' she declared. 'I saw your Amos wi' Sarah-Jane as well as Nancy's Mam. We both saw him, so it's not fair that your Dad's just blaming her.' There, it was out.

75

Jack Greville looked at her curiously. She was a funny kid and no mistake – coming up here and confessing like this. That must have taken some doing. Amusement flickered in his eyes as he said, 'Tell me, squirt, does your mother or father know you've come here this afternoon?'

A look of horror passed over Bethany's face. 'Oh, please don't tell them, Jack Greville – please don't tell them!'

The other occupant of the room gave a knowing nod of the head. So she had come here of her own accord. He dug his hands deep into the pockets of his trousers and walked to the window, where he looked out over the green lawns leading to the tall beech hedge that marked the start of the moor. 'I won't tell on you, little Miss Baine, but neither can I do anything about your friends the Turvers. You're just a child and must understand that when one grows up one becomes responsible for one's own actions.' He didn't talk like other people of the dale, but had a faint South of England drawl indicative of his class, although he had gone to the relatively nearby public school of Sedbergh. She particularly noticed his accent, because as the child of a preacher herself, her mother Betty was very insistent that all the Baine children learn to 'talk proper'.

Jack Greville perched with one hip on the edge of the desk, pushing the copy of the *Daily Mail* out of the way as he did so. Noticing the newspaper once more, Bethany's curiosity got the better of her. 'Can I ask you a question?'

He looked amused. 'Fire away.'

'What's carnal relations?'

He looked startled for a moment, then burst out laughing. 'What in heaven's name do you want to know that for?'

She looked hurt and didn't take kindly to being laughed at. ''Cause my grandad was a Reverend,' she said proudly, 'and so is that man in the paper who has had carnal relations. Happen I'd like to know if Grandad Hetherington had them too.'

Oblivious as to the misdemeanours of the Rector of Stiffkey, Jack Greville looked puzzled as he glanced down at the paper, and his dark eyes shone with amusement as he nodded his head most emphatically. 'Well, I can't speak for the Reverend What's-his-name, but your grandad most certainly had them, young lady. You wouldn't be here asking me such daft questions, otherwise!'

He looked almost human when he laughed, even although she had the distinct impression he was laughing *at* her and not *with* her. She shifted her weight from one foot to the other. This visit didn't seem to be doing an awful lot of good as far as the Turvers were concerned. She plucked disconsolately at the silk fringe of a cushion on the sofa next to her as she said softly, 'It hasn't made any difference, has it, me coming here and telling you the truth? Happen I might as well have stayed at home.'

He got down from the edge of the desk and came over to where she was standing. She looked quite pathetic standing there in those scarecrow clothes, looking at him out of eyes that stood out in their misery like a noosed rabbit's. He put a consoling arm around her shoulders as he led her gently towards the door. 'Listen, young 'un,' he said. 'Life isn't quite as simple as that. Telling the truth, while a creditable thing in itself, doesn't always change things the way we want.'

'But me Mam says they will end up in the Poor House. Don't let the Turvers end up there, Black Jack – don't!'

Jack Greville gave a smile. She was the only one to call him that to his face. 'Nobody ends up in the Poor House these days,' he said. 'Didn't you know we've got Socialists in the government now?' The last comment was made with his tongue firmly in his cheek for, like his father, the only kind of Socialism he favoured was the type that had National in front of its name – the kind being promoted across the Channel in Germany right now.

'But if your Dad puts them out then they will have to

face the consequences.' She was still not sure what exactly was meant by the phrase, but it sounded impressive and might just sway him.

They were standing at the door to the hall now, and he looked down at her, his hands resting on her shoulders as he said seriously, 'Listen, young Miss Baine. You can be a cheeky little devil when you like, but I admire what you've done in coming up here today and speaking up for your friends. And I promise you one thing, if I can do anything in my power to ease the lot of Tom Turver and his family, if the worst comes to the worst, then I will. Will that do you?'

She looked up into his eyes and they were not smirking or superior any more; she really believed he might actually be telling the truth.

Ned was sitting on the steps in front of the main door when she found herself outside a few moments later. He immediately reached inside his pocket and took out the crumpled paper bag of sweets once more. Bethany reached inside and extracted one from the sticky mass with difficulty.

'Ta again, Neddy,' she said gratefully. Then she paused before popping it into her mouth. Her eyes were serious as they looked into those of the young man on the step. 'Does your Jack tell the truth, Neddy?' she asked. 'If he promises to do something, does he stick to that promise?'

Ned looked back at her and his grin grew wider as he nodded vigorously.

It was good enough for her, and it was with a lighter heart that she descended the stone steps and ran, as fast as her booted feet would carry her, back down the long drive in the direction of the village.

Just being inside the grounds gave her a funny feeling, for no one from the village was ever invited through the great wrought-iron gates, or if they were it was usually to have the Riot Act read to them, according to her father.

And once in sight of The Row, the houses seemed incredibly small and drab in comparison with the huge place she had just left, with its black timbers and white walls. The whole street would fit into the Grevilles' house, and she wondered who it was long ago who had decided it was fair to have one single family living in a house twice the size of their whole row of cottages that had to house twelve families.

As she rounded the corner of The Row, she caught sight of her mother at the front-room window of Number Twelve. Betty Baine was dusting the precious Doulton vases that sat in pride of place on the windowsill and, seeing her, Bethany deliberately made for the narrow alleyway that ran along the back of the houses to avoid being spotted. There would be hell to pay if she was discovered out of school.

The narrow passage was dank and perpetually in shade, and had that sour, stomach-churning smell that she knew she would carry with her all her days. It emanated from the three brick-built, dry lavatories that served the twelve families in the terrace. Being only a small village, there was no municipal night-cart that came regularly to remove the waste; instead, it was left to each householder to take it in turns to empty the bucket regularly in the local midden. The result was an evil-smelling narrow path, on to which the vile contents of the overflowing pails were all too often spilt.

Along with the three other wives who shared their privy, Betty Baine was most particular about the regular weekly scouring of their closet, but it was still a place that her elder daughter liked to avoid as much as possible. This afternoon though, the excitement of the visit to Wolf Hall had proved too much. She would have to relieve herself before making her way back to school.

Bethany's booted feet slowed to a full stop as she reached the small outbuilding shared by all four of the families at their end of The Row. There was a strange snuffling sound, a sort of whimpering like an animal in pain, coming from within. She moved nearer, pressing her ear to the rough wooden planks of the door. Somebody or something was in there, and in quite a state at that. She held her breath then released it as the sound of a nose being blown noisily met her ears, then she jumped back guiltily as the latch began to move. The door opened and Tom Turver's stocky figure appeared. He had funny-looking smears in the dust around his eyes and he looked quite startled at the sight of the child.

'Bethany love, I didn't know you wuz waiting.'

Bethany stared at him. He had been crying. The thought shocked her, for she had never known a grown man to cry before. She felt she had to say something – anything – to help relieve his misery. 'I – I'm sorry about what's happened, Nancy's Dad,' she began. 'Are you awful mad at me?'

He looked surprised and gave a weary shake of the head. 'Nay, nay lass, I'm not mad at thee.' How could he be mad at a child for telling the truth?

Relief swept over her. 'Well, are you mad at Nancy's Mam?' The last thing she wanted was for Emily Turver to take all the blame for what was happening.

Again he shook his head as he attempted a smile. Was he mad at Emily? He thought for a second or two and gave a wistful sigh as he looked down at the child regarding him so intently. 'I tell thee, lass,' he said wryly, 'when we wuz courtin' I loved my Emily so much I could've cheerfully eaten her, and sometimes – like right now for instance – I wish to God I had!'

He grinned down at her until she was forced to grin back. 'That's better!' he said, then with a ruffle of her fringe, he headed back for the house.

She watched him disappear into the back door of Number Nine. He was a nice man; a truly nice, good man.

But it was not his little joke that remained with her as she made her way back to school a few minutes later, but the tears that had been wiped from his eyes. What she had just witnessed both puzzled and, in a funny way, angered her. It puzzled her because she could not imagine why he should feel like crying, when she knew if it had been her she would have been so wild at the behaviour of the Grevilles she would not have had any energy left for tears, and anger because it was not right that one family should ever have such power over another. Perhaps if a few more men in this village had the courage to stand up to the Colonel and his kind this type of thing just wouldn't happen. 'Power belongeth unto God,' the Bible said, but not in this valley it didn't. Power belonged to the folk who lived in Wolf Hall.

What was it that motto carved into the stone above their front door said? *Homo homini lupus* – Man is a wolf to man. They said that there were no longer wolves in England, but they were wrong. There were still wolves as long as there were folk like the Grevilles around.

Chapter Four

Bethany was at school the following Tuesday morning when they came to move the Turvers' belongings into the street. It was a day that began with more than an air of foreboding. Above the village – away above the crag itself – the Helm Wind was gathering. And there was no one born and brought up east of the Eden river who did not know what that meant. An ever-darkening roll of whirling cloud known as the Helm Bar would begin to gather across the tops of the fells, and the locals would watch its progress with fear in their hearts. They knew that for as long as three weeks afterwards the whole of the countryside could be laid low by its violent, north-easterly blast.

As the skies darkened over Utherby, Betty Baine stood with little Sammy clasped in her arms at the window of the front room of Number Twelve, The Row. A shiver ran through her spare frame, and she knew it was not only the gathering wind clouds hanging low over Uther Crag that gave the village at its foot its sense of foreboding. There was tension in the very air they breathed. Even the hens that scratched out their meagre pickings from the gritty earth of the back yards seemed to sense it as they paused in their constant scratching to cock their heads as if listening – waiting. And the scrawny cats that infested the dank alley at the back of The Row would slink closer to the brick walls, and the mongrel dogs would creep closer to heel as they followed their masters to the quarry every morning. Even the children had been on edge before they set off for school this morning.

A sigh shuddered through her as she lifted her eyes to the darkening grey sky above the houses opposite. It was a day that seemed eminently appropriate for her feelings, she thought, as she stood silently behind the glass of the sash window and watched and listened to the enactment of Tom and Emily Turvers' worst fears being played out three houses away.

It was not the first eviction that Betty Baine had been witness to, nor would it be the last, and there was a uniform awfulness to them all that the glowering sky seemed to echo. This could be a hard land, and the lives of its people, never easy at the best of times, could often be desperate.

The painful sounds from the street beyond made little Sammy Baine's bottom lip quiver, so his mother had to bounce him in her arms to pacify him. 'There, there now . . . It's all right . . .' But it wasn't all right. Never in all her thirty-six years had Betty Baine heard sobbing and wailing like she had heard over the past half-hour, as piece by piece each article of her neighbours' furniture was picked up from the place it had stood for the past thirteen years and carefully manoeuvred out through the narrow front door to lie on the pavement in full view of the neighbours and all who cared to pass by.

It made a pathetically shabby heap; no saleroom would give more than a few coppers for the few bits and pieces the Turvers had begged or borrowed from friends and relatives over the years. But it was their whole life in there. On that donkey's breakfast of a straw mattress perched so ludicrously on top of the kitchen chairs Emily had given birth to all her children, and that old pine table had had its top scrubbed religiously every morning. It might be just a worthless jumble to some, but it was all they had. And Betty Baine's heart went out to her neighbour as she stood helplessly by and watched the two men, specially hired by the Colonel for the occasion, methodically stack the family's meagre possessions against the side of the house, then, when each room had been emptied, lock the door behind them and prepare to take their leave.

It was a firm from Sedbergh that had been hired for the job, and the two men were obviously embarrassed by the task they had been hired to perform. No one likes to bear the brunt of a whole street's wrath. 'It's nowt to do wi' us, Missus. We're just here to do a job,' the smaller, younger one shouted back as one of the women from further down The Row called out that they ought to be ashamed of themselves.

Tom Turver stood alongside his wife and listened to the comments of their neighbours and friends, his shame complete. He could not even defend his own home.

'You'd better not attempt to regain entry to the premises, I warn you,' the bigger of the two warned the couple before they left. 'You'll be arrested for breaking and entry if you do.' It had happened before and would do so again, for folk would do anything rather than see their family on the street.

'That would be all we need now!' Tom commented bitterly. 'Bloody well arrested for trying to get back into our own home!'

He had been officially given his cards first thing the previous day when, despite a warning to stay at home, he had reported for another Monday morning's work with the rest of the men. He was also told he had twenty-four hours to vacate his home. Twenty-four hours to pack up a lifetime.

But it was no more than they had been expecting, for the whole village was buzzing with the news that young Amos Greville had at last been charged with the murder of Sarah-Jane Youdell.

The dead young woman's father, Isaac the baker, was beside himself and had to be restrained from laying siege to The Hall and physically attacking the remaining three Grevilles. Normally a mild-mannered man who had been able to exert no control over his wayward daughter during her lifetime, he was determined to bring her killer or killers to book. Unlike most of the village, he did not depend upon the Grevilles for his livelihood, and had no hesitation in roundly condemning the whole family to the friends and customers who rallied to his side.

The confirmation of the charge had put the whole village in a ferment. One of the Grevilles accused of murder. There had been nothing like it to set tongues wagging in living memory, but it also lent a feeling of great unease to the community. Too many people in Utherby, and the surrounding countryside, were dependent upon the Colonel for their bread and butter to be heard to say anything in public that might indicate a belief in young Amos's guilt.

But if the affair was a source of comment and excitement for the rest of the inhabitants, it was the beginning of the end for Tom Turver and his family. The quarryman had felt physically sick when the news was given to him on his arrival by Bob Hughes, the foreman. 'You know I'm only carrying out orders, Tom lad. It's certainly not my wish that this state of affairs should have come about,' the little Welshman had said, looking down at the metal toecaps of his boots to avoid the other's eyes.

Tom had clapped him on the shoulder. 'Aye, I know that.'

'Them bloody Grevilles,' Will Dearden put in. 'Kick one and they all limp – and mek damned sure whoever was responsible for their slight injury ends up wi' *his* legs amputated!'

'Aye, they never do things by halves in that family,' Cheevers Baine had added, coming over to shake Tom's hand. 'May God go with you and Emily in your hour of trial and sorrow,' he said, clasping his old colleague by the shoulder with his free hand. 'Any roads, Tom lad, you know we'll all be thinking of you on the day.'

And Tom knew exactly which day he had in mind, and now, a mere twenty-four hours later, it had arrived. If he lived to be a hundred there could surely never be a worse one, he thought as his arm tightened around the shaking shoulders of his wife. Emily's plump face was red and swollen with tears and her breath came in jerky gasps. She had almost cried herself out.

Plucking up courage to face the distraught couple, Betty Baine joined them on the front step, as they watched the two hired men disappear in the direction of the station. 'I've got the kettle on,' she said quietly but firmly. 'You're not going anywhere without a cup of tea.'

But Tom Turver could only shake his head as he tightened his grip on his wife's shoulders. 'Thanks, but no thanks, Betty love. There's a mate of me brother's will be along with his cart to pick up all this stuff later on this morning, and as for us, well, we'll be heading right on to Emily's Ma's with the little 'uns here.' He gestured with his head at their two youngest, the year-old twins Joan and Janet who sat, one each end of their old black pram, silently observing the proceedings through eyes large with apprehension at the state of their mother.

'But that's all of four miles!' Betty protested. Emily Turver's widowed mother lived in the next village of Butterslack. 'That pram'll never make it!'

Tom gave a wry smile as he looked down at the already buckled wheels of the perambulator. 'Aye, it's a bit like mesel', I reckon. There's no denying it's seen better days.'

'Wait there a tick!' Betty disappeared back inside her front door, to reappear a few seconds later pushing her own Sammy's much newer pram. 'Here – take this!' she said, shoving it at her neighbour. 'This young lad here'll be walking everywhere in a few weeks, and poor Emily'll not have the twins on their feet till after Christmas!'

The inadvertent mention of the festival now only some seven weeks away brought another wail of anguish from Emily. 'Don't mention that word to me!' she groaned. 'God only knows how we'll even survive till then, wi' not as much as a brass farthing coming in, let alone have anything extra to put by for Father Christmas!' She drew her shawl tighter around her shoulders and attempted a smile all the same. The first of the day. 'But thanks all the same, Betty love. I'm not so proud as I'd say no to that pram . . . It'll be a grand help in getting some of the small stuff over to me Ma's this morning.'

And so Betty helped her neighbour load the small vehicle with what little to eat there had been in the house and various other household articles they preferred not to leave to the expected cart.

After an initial reluctance to gather round in case of appearing nosey, quite a few of the neighbours had now come out to say their goodbyes and one or two were offering what little they could in the way of food for the desperate days they knew would lie ahead for the family. There were those too, however, who had been conspicuous by their absence. Not everyone in The Row, let alone the village, was filled with the milk of human kindness at a time like this. There were those who took a positive delight in the misfortunes of others, and Betty Baine had had a hard job biting her tongue in Wilks's the grocer's that very morning when, an hour or two before the Turvers' scheduled departure, several of their neighbours intimated that perhaps it was no more than the family deserved.

'She never could hold tongue, that Emily,' Hilda Capstick said, as she dropped her change back into her purse, and adjusted her basket over her arm. 'I'm not surprised her tittle-tattling has got her into hot water. I was just saying to my Joe t'other day she would land that man of hers in t'soup one of these fine days.'

She turned to Betty Baine as she left the shop. 'We can't be seen to bite the hand that feeds us, now can we? We're all beholden to them Grevilles whether we like it or not. She ought to have had more sense than go pointing the finger at young Amos there. Don't you agree?'

Betty Baine had stood her ground. 'No, I can't say as I do, Hilda. Emily Turver's been a good neighbour to me over the years and I can't see that it does anyone any good by adding to her troubles at a time like this by saying it's all her own fault. We're all human, you know. We all make mistakes from time to time. We should think ourselves fortunate it's not our belongings that are being piled on the pavement out there. There but for the grace of God, say I.'

It was not like Betty Baine to speak her mind in such a way, and Hilda Capstick had thrown a well-I-do-declare look to Hector Wilks, the proprietor, as she took her leave, and when the door had closed behind her, the shopkeeper had shaken his head. 'Well, I can only say, if time ever comes, like that man of yours hopes, when all men are created brothers, then all t'women will be created sisters – and, by God, that'll be awkward! Don't you agree, Mrs Baine?'

Betty Baine had been forced to smile, although she could cheerfully have run after Hilda Capstick and said a great deal more. 'Aye, we women can be a catty species, Mr Wilks,' she sighed. 'And some more than others, I think you'll agree!' It angered her beyond measure when people you had lived beside for years and had come to trust seemed to be actually revelling in a neighbour's misfortune. It was not in her own nature to do such a thing and she could not understand it in others. And now her own heart was fit to burst with sympathy for Tom Turver and his small family as she stood and watched them take their leave of their home.

'At least the young 'uns will have a roof over their heads

tonight,' Tom said, as he adjusted the hood of the twins' pram. He was always one to try to look on the bright side. 'At least we have their Gran Bowland to go to, that's more than my grandparents had when yon old bugger Greville's grandfather did t'same to them.'

Then a wistful look came to his eyes as he looked at Betty still standing there with little Sammy in her arms, and remembered. 'And do you know, Betty love, what saved them that night from sleeping in t'ditch?'

Betty Baine shook her head.

'Your Dad, that's what. Harrison Hetherington. He were just a young lad then, straight out of college, and he took them into his own home till they found somewhere to go. Christian charity on two legs, that were Harry Hetherington all right. A gradely fine man.'

'Thank you, Tom. I appreciate that.' How like him. How very like him still to find time to remember the good in other people at a time like this.

His words continued to ring in Betty Baine's ears as she waved her final goodbye as they set off on their long trek to the neighbouring village of Butterslack a few minutes later. The cries of 'Good luck' and 'God go with you' that followed their departure were whipped by the wind from the mouths of the small crowd that watched from their doorsteps, making it a sorrowfully mute farewell as the two figures, heads bowed into the wind, set off into their uncertain future, pushing their infant daughters before them in Sammy Baine's old pram.

As she watched them go, there was no doubt in Betty Baine's mind that the dale could do with another of her father's calibre at a time like this. He would have been up there making a fight of it with the Colonel on Tom's behalf, she had not the slightest doubt. Right up to the last minute he would have been speaking out. And knowing he was still remembered for his courage and his love of his fellow men gave her a warm glow for what was left of the morning as she prepared for her four eldest children coming back for their midday meal.

The man with the horse and cart ordered by Tom was just finishing loading up the last of the Turvers' possessions, to follow the couple on their long walk to Butterslack, when Tom and Teddy, the two Baine boys, arrived back home. They were usually first to reach the front door and they prided themselves in beating their sisters to the dinner table. They stood and watched for a moment or two as the few remaining sticks of furniture were stacked precariously high, then roped tightly so they would not topple off, or be caught by the wind, on the journey along the rough road between the two villages.

This time there was no embarrassed crowd of aproned women to see the cart off, as there had been to bid farewell to the owners of the furniture shortly beforehand. They were busy inside their own homes putting food on the table for their children returning from school. Along with Tom and Teddy Baine, only a few of those children now stood in silent witness as the cart eventually clattered and creaked its way down the road. Then they too turned and made for home.

Bethany and her small sister Libby were still battling into the face of the wind, holding tightly on to each other's hands, as they met the cart turning the corner at the end of The Row. Telling Libby to run on before her, Bethany stood watching it till it disappeared from view. The street seemed curiously empty after it had gone.

There was almost no one left in the street by the time she reached the Turvers' old front door. Already the house looked different. The curtains had gone from the windows, giving them a bleak, empty look like staring, accusing eyes.

She sat down heavily on the windowledge of the front room and kicked her booted feet against the wall. Despite Libby's entreaties that dinner was on the table, she continued to sit there, reluctant to move.

She stared in through the polished glass of the window into the room beyond. It seemed bigger now it was empty and she could see marks on the walls where the various items of furniture had stood. There was a light patch above the cast-iron fireplace where a picture of Captain Scott the explorer had hung, surrounded by the men of his ill-fated expedition. Nancy had told her once that her Dad would have liked to have been an explorer, 'but our kind can't be one of them'. Bethany had wondered at the remark. What exactly was 'our kind' and were there lots of other things that 'our kind' were not allowed to do? It seemed so unfair; Nancy's Dad, Tom, would have made a wonderful explorer.

It was hard to believe they had gone, for they had been in this house since long before she was born. Nancy, along with all her brothers and sisters, had been born in that upstairs front bedroom, just as she and her own brothers and sister had been born in the one three doors away. Yes, a whole generation of Turvers had first seen the light of day from that window up there, Bethany marvelled, and now there it was, staring back at her, unblinking and unforgiving, as she sat craning her neck on the sill of the window below.

Nancy had told her at school this morning that she would be walking over to Butterslack at four o'clock to stay with their Gran, and would probably be attending Butterslack school come the following week.

'Do you mind leaving here and starting a new school?' Bethany had asked, knowing that under different circumstances, she herself might actually find the prospect quite exciting.

Nancy had shrugged her chubby shoulders. Never one to be nonplussed for long by the ups and downs of her young life, she was philosophical about the whole business. 'It won't make much difference, really, will it? I'm due to leave school for good come next Easter any roads.'

The two friends had looked at one another in silence after that. In so many ways, life would never be the same again.

As they walked back into the line for reassembly after the break, Nancy had tugged at her friend's sleeve. 'Do you really believe in God, Beth?' she asked, her eyes serious. 'I mean really and truly believe that when you pray He actually listens and answers your prayers?'

Bethany blinked and thought hard as they nudged their way into the girls' line in front of the school door. She herself did not pray half as much as she knew she should. 'My Dad prays,' she said uncertainly. 'He prays a lot.'

Nancy's face retained its worried look. 'I'm only asking,' she said softly, 'because *my* Dad prayed last night. I could hear him behind the door in the back kitchen when I went down for a drink last night . . . He's never prayed before. Never. Not so's I've heard, any roads. It were funny listening to him. He didn't sound like me Dad at all. He sounded like a little kid who'd done summat wrong and was asking not to be smacked. I didn't like it. I didn't like it at all. It gave me a creepy feeling . . . Oh, I know it's not the end of the world us having to leave Utherby, and in some ways now that I'm more used to the idea I'm not that bothered really, but in other ways this carry-on's done awful things to our house. Honest it has.'

'Girls first . . . No pushing now! Single file if you please . . . And no talking there, Nancy Turver!' The shrill voice of Miss Bunter, the infant mistress, rang out over the heads of the jostling children, and so no more could be said. They had made their way back inside for the rest of the morning's lessons.

And now, as she sat kicking her heels against the front wall of the empty house, despite her friend's seemingly philosophical acceptance of her lot, Bethany felt a great sadness within her about what had happened, but a sadness tinged with anger at the injustice of it all.

'Bethany Baine, are you coming in for your dinner or do you intend sitting there all day?'

Her mother's impatient voice from the doorway of Number Twelve assailed her ears, and, heaving a sigh, Bethany slid down from her perch and made her way into her own home.

'We saw the cart, Mam!' Libby informed their mother in a piping voice as Bethany joined them at the table. 'Didn't we see the cart, our Beth?'

Bethany ignored the question and aimed one instead at their mother who was ladling the soup into four separate bowls, as usual omitting to put one out for herself. 'Did you watch them go, Mam? Did you see Nancy's Mam and Dad leave?'

A pained look came over their mother's face as she set a bowl of broth down in front of each child in turn. 'Aye, that I did,' she answered, replacing the soup pot back on the range. 'And a sorry sight it was.'

Then she went on to tell them of Tom Turver's last words to her before they set off on their journey to Butterslack. And her children listened, just as they always listened when their mother spoke of Grandfather Hetherington and how he had been revered by all who knew him. To them he seemed only slightly less exalted than the good Lord Himself. At any rate, degrees of goodness were always measured against their mother's father, and as Bethany listened she wondered exactly what her own father, Cheevers, made of it all. He was a good man himself, a God-fearing man, but even he in his goodness could never measure up to the white-haired man in the black coat and dog-collar who gazed down at them from the front-room wall.

'Eat up, our Beth!'

'Yes, Mam.' But Betty Baine's eldest child was finding it hard to finish her dinner as she thought once more of Tom Turver praying to a God he had barely believed in. In her head she could hear again the awful sound of that sobbing coming from the privy at the bottom of the yard. And, as she struggled with her soup, she felt a deep anger within her for the type of person who could do this to a fellow creature. To rob a man of his pride was to rob him of his soul, she had once heard her father say. And that's what they had done to Nancy's Dad all right. And the indignity of having to bow the head and give in to such behaviour – to go meekly to your fate like Tom Turver and his family had had to do. She shuddered as she put down her spoon. The Bible had it all wrong. 'The meek won't inherit the earth,' she announced in a loud and very definite voice.

As all eyes turned to her, she pushed back her chair and declared, 'The meek can't even keep hold of a rotten old house in The Row like this! No, the meek won't inherit the earth, our Mam. The meek end up in bloody Butterslack!'

And with that she ran from the table, with tears of anger and frustration stinging her eyes.

The other children round the table gasped, then looked at one another, their eyes large with anxiety at what their mother's reaction would be. Tom's freckled face betrayed his instant feeling of admiration at his sister's outburst and he stuffed another wedge of haverbread into his mouth as he fought to keep it from quirking into a smile. Libby, across the table from him, had no such feelings and immediately her lower lip began to quiver. 'Bethany swore, our Mam!' she gasped. 'She did. She said . . .'

A sharp dig in the ribs from Teddy sitting next to her avoided a repetition of the sin, as all eyes remained riveted on their mother.

It was the first time any of her children had sworn in front of her, but Betty Baine had hardly even noticed the profanity as she gazed in consternation after her flown daughter. She understood entirely what the child was going through. Life was a hard lesson when you lived it in bondage, and that was what it boiled down to for them all.

Each and every one of them who lived on The Row were here on the sufferance of the Colonel and his family.

'You four get on with your meal!' She put down the knife with which she was buttering the bread for the youngest, and followed Bethany up to her bedroom.

The child was standing, gazing out of the window with unseeing eyes. There was a set look to her pert features that her mother knew only too well. Whenever she felt there had been an injustice perpetrated on herself or anyone else in the family, that expression would surface. Yes, more than anything her eldest child hated injustice in any shape or form.

'Don't take it so hard, love,' Betty Baine said, as she stroked her daughter's auburn head. 'It's a tough old world out there, and there are two sorts of people in it — the Haves and the Have Nots. The Turvers, along with the likes of ourselves, just happen to belong to the latter, so we have to adapt and learn to make the best of things. To accept our station in life, if you like.'

Bethany rounded on her mother, her hazel eyes glittering in the pale November light from the window. 'But what if I don't like it, Mam? What if I don't want to be a Have Not all my life?' It seemed crazy just to accept that you were inferior to other people and not seek to do anything about it — not even object.

Betty Baine sighed. 'You just have to accept it, Bethany love. The only way out for a lass like you is to marry someone with money. Marry into a family like the Grevilles, for instance. But you might as well whistle for the moon as stand a chance of that.'

Bethany looked at her, aghast. Marry one of the Grevilles! Marry into a family that had people in it who would do something like that to Nancy and her family — into a family with a murderer in its midst! The grief that had been caused to Isaac Youdell and his family must be even worse than that of the poor Turvers.

Her friend Ellen Capstick had told her this very morning of the state that the baker was in. A widower with six children, three still under ten, he had relied on his eldest, Sarah-Jane, to help with the younger ones, and flibbertigibbet though she was, for the most part she had done so. And now Sarah-Jane, with the long fair hair, big breasts, and a liking for anything in pants, had gone. The baker's daughter might not have been the most chaste young woman in the dale, but she certainly didn't deserve that fate, and neither did her family deserve to suffer like this.

'I hope they hang Amos Greville, our Mam,' Bethany said vehemently. 'I hope they hang him, so that the Grevilles can know what it's like to suffer too.'

But they did not hang Amos Greville. The Colonel's second son never came to trial. His incarceration lasted only as long as the Helm Wind wreaked its havoc on the dale. The case was dropped through lack of evidence a week or so later.

The freeing of Amos was no more than most in the village expected. No one could really believe that a Greville could ever seriously be brought to trial – not with the Colonel on the bench, and on just about every other committee and public body that counted for anything in the North Riding.

As soon as she heard the news, Bethany wondered what the Turvers would make of it. Had all their suffering been for nothing? She was almost embarrassed to face Nancy on her friend's final day at Utherby village school on the last day before half-term, two weeks later.

She had chosen her moment carefully, waiting till there were no other children within earshot in the playground when she brought up the subject of Amos's release during the morning break. But, incredibly, her friend had only shrugged at the information she herself already knew. Nancy had tossed back her brown braids behind her shoulders and raised her eyebrows in a who cares? fashion. 'It doesn't really matter now, does it?'

Bethany stared at her. It was not the reaction she had expected. Nancy Turver had the same short, stocky body of her father Tom, but her mother Emily's plump, sweet-natured face. It was a face that was maddeningly inscrutable this particular morning, and she felt curiously cheated that her news had had such little effect. 'What do you mean, it doesn't really matter now?'

Nancy looked at her, then glanced around her shoulder. 'I'm not supposed to say,' she said, dropping her voice to a whisper.

Bethany moved closer. She loved secrets and quite obviously there was another in the offing. 'You can tell me. I'm your best friend.' Then seeing that had little effect, she added confidentially, 'Anyhow, I have a right to know, seeing as I was with your Mam when she first saw Amos Greville wi' Sarah-Jane.'

Nancy's lips pursed as she considered the matter. Would it really make that much difference if she told her very best friend? Bethany was looking at her as if she would burst with curiosity. She had never known her betray a confidence before. And her grandad was a minister, after all – a man of God, so that must make her a 'something' of God herself.

'Come on, Nan. You know I won't tell!'

'Cross your heart and hope to die?'

Bethany made the sign of the cross on her left breast as her heart pounded. 'Cross my heart and hope to die,' she said breathlessly.

Nancy gave another furtive look about her, then whispered, 'Me Dad's got another job.'

Bethany was amazed. They said he'd never work again anywhere in the dale. In fact, they said he probably would never work again ever, with half of Yorkshire out of work. This was the last thing she expected to hear. 'But where?'

'High Fellside farm,' Nancy informed her. 'T'other side of Butterslack . . . It were queer really, there were a note waiting at me Gran's telling him there were a job going there as soon as he finished at quarry.'

Bethany shook her head. This was truly astonishing, especially after all the fire and brimstone the Colonel had been breathing about the Turvers. 'You'd better not let on to anybody else, though, just in case them Grevilles get to hear of it.'

'Oh, don't you worry about that! Me Dad's already seen Black Jack up High Fellside way and he's keeping his head well down in case it gets chopped off again!'

Bethany nodded thoughtfully. 'I don't mind Jack Greville as much as some of the others . . . That Amos for one.' Her voice dropped as she sidled closer to her friend. 'Do you think he did it, Nancy? Do you think he actually killed Sarah-Jane?'

Nancy Turver opened her eyes wide and shrugged her shoulders. 'Me Dad says he wouldn't put anything past any one of them after this —after what they've done to us. And if you ask me, I reckon he did it — and enjoyed doing it! Some folk do, you know — they actually enjoy killing people. Me Mam says she read of cases in Germany where really nice, churchgoing men have killed dozens of women for the sheer enjoyment of it.'

Her eyes darted to the side then fixed on Bethany's face. 'There was one man — I forget whereabouts in Germany it were — but he used to invite all these women back to his house, then kill them.' She took a deep breath. 'Then he cut up the bodies and cooked the flesh, which he sold in his shop as smoked pork! And he did a roaring trade, by all accounts!'

The bell rang before Bethany had a chance to reply to this revelation and her friend scampered off to join the line. Somehow smoked pork — that twice-a-year treat — would never taste quite the same again.

Chapter Five

The winter of 1932 was a dank, dreary one in the dales; unemployment was high all over the country and at the quarry men had been on short time since just before Christmas. For workers like Cheevers Baine, the break-up of the Labour Government in August of the previous year had been a blow and they had very little faith in the coalition National Government that had taken its place.

Phrases like 'the Means Test' and 'the Poor House' came more frequently to ears hungry for good news, but it seemed neither the National Government nor anyone else had the answer. And in truth it was not just Britain that was suffering. It seemed to be the same all over. In America the Depression was reaching its height and President Roosevelt's 'Fireside Chats' to the nation were doing little to relieve the gloom. Only across the Channel in Germany did there seem to be hope, and those such as Cheevers Baine, who had given three years of their young manhood to fighting that country on the battlefield, looked on in some consternation as it began to rise again from the ashes of defeat.

'Never mind what's going on elsewhere,' Betty Baine kept telling her despondent husband. 'Just thank the Lord there's still some money coming in at all these days.'

But Cheevers Baine could not find it in himself to thank the Lord for very much at all these days as he continued to rise before dawn to expend his energies till nightfall for barely enough reward to keep the minimum of food in his children's stomachs.

And so the dark winter days dragged on, and on the surface very little had changed. The sounds that filled the narrow streets of the small North Riding village were those that had been familiar to its inhabitants for generations past. Very often Bethany would be awoken before daybreak as up and down The Row front doors began to slam, including their own, and her father's booted feet joined those of the other men as they made their way up the steep path, past the veins of worked-out stone and slag heaps, to begin yet another day's work at the quarry.

Just after first light the din would start and that private world that had been created around the great cavern that had been dug into the limestone of the crag began to groan, screech and creak into life. And despite the mood of gloom that pervaded life that winter, Bethany still found a strange sense of security in the very continuity that those familiar sounds brought. She knew them all: the sonorous clang of the crane, the sharp rap, rap, rap of the hammers, the ring of the picks, and that never-to-be-forgotten screech of the saw, whose engine throbbed into life at the crack of dawn each day, and whose blades sliced through the stone like a knife through butter.

On top of the mechanical noises, if the wind was in the right direction, she could even hear the shouts of the men and the whinnying of the shire horses as they were harnessed up to set to hauling their heavy loads down the hill and on through the narrow village streets. Past The Row, beneath her bedroom window they would go, sweating and panting under their loads, then on out of the village itself to their destination of Uther station over a mile away. Great lumbering, gentle beasts they were, with names like Flossie and Belle, their broad backs scarred and bowed through a lifetime of toil. Six tons apiece they pulled, six tons of hewn blocks of limestone, carefully stacked edge to edge by the loading lads on to the flat-bottomed, small-wheeled carts that rattled and creaked their way up and down the crag and backwards and forwards along the cobbled, rutted track that served as Utherby's main road.

For the first part of the way down the crag, the path was so steep that the carts had to have special steel bars called sledge-sticks fitted to the back wheels to act as a brake to stop them from taking off and careering out of control into the village. It had long been a favourite game of Bethany and her friends to sneak rides on the backs of the waggons. The sharp screeching sound the metal braking rods made as they bit into the stony surface of the road set their teeth on edge and made them screech at the tops of their voices in return and wish they could cover their ears with their hands as they clung on for grim death to the wooden backboards.

Deep grooves scarred the road surface all the way down in mute testimony to the ancestors of these same horses who had made the identical journey, pulling similar loads of worked stone over the generations. Bound for London most of it was, and for the other great cities of England: stones for the grand houses of the rich who knew next to nothing of the land from which it had been torn. Walling stones had gone from here for almost two hundred years; stones that had helped build the great mills and fine houses of Leeds and Bradford, and the equally grand buildings of the North Riding's elegant spa town of Harrogate, where the rich still went to take the waters.

But, young as they were, the children who clung to the backs of those carts knew that the nearest anyone from this village would ever get to any of those fine houses would be scrubbing the stone steps. And Bethany knew that would be her fate too come her thirteenth birthday next summer.

Despite the short-time working, over forty men and boys were still employed at the quarry and most had fathers, grandfathers and great-grandfathers before them who had toiled there. As soon as one gallery was worked out another would be opened up which, it was hoped, would see yet one more generation in employment for another thirty years. 'And it's not just the rock that gets worked out, lass,' her mother had once told her. 'It's the men themselves. There's ne'er a one reaches his three score and ten around here, I can promise you that.' And the words had chilled Bethany to the bone, for she knew it to be true. Grandfathers did not exist in Utherby — not among those families who lived by the quarry, at any rate.

But despite it all, young boys continued to follow their fathers up the hill, as had their fathers before them, and the hierarchy of the rockface was continued from one generation to the next. Quarrymen all, they were proud to call themselves, despite their grumbles. But once up there in their own world they were split into a pecking order that continued right down to village level, where the voices of the more skilled men held a greater sway whenever community affairs were discussed.

Although Bethany was aware that the most skilled work was undoubtedly done by the knappers such as her father, in the dressing shed, the hardest and most dangerous work was done by the men who worked on the rockface itself. These men had become something akin to folk heroes to the local children as they risked their lives daily on the great galleries that had been hewn out of the sheer face of the crag.

These galleries were like a gigantic set of stone steps, leading up into the grey clouds that so often shrouded the top of the crag. Cheevers Baine had once told his daughter that these steps led straight to heaven, but there was nothing celestial about the type of work that went on there. With consummate skill in the use of explosive charges, pick and crowbar, hammer and chisel, combined with sheer brute strength, the youngest and hardiest of her friends' fathers, uncles and older brothers blasted and coaxed the mountain to give up its stone. The children who often watched from down below, on their way to and from school, grew quite used to seeing their fathers suspended by hemp ropes around their thighs, hanging precariously over the edge of the rockface, in an attempt to lever the massive blocks free. And Bethany, along with all the others, accepted it as the most natural thing in the world for these men to be hanging there like flies from an invisible web that crossed the mutilated face of Uther Crag. It was an exciting backdrop to their childhood games that was as much a part of them and their lives as going to school or Chapel on Sundays.

'You kids get out of here, do you hear? Scram – the lot of you!' The cries of warning would go up when blasting was about to start, and then the blasting bell would be sounded – the signal for all to take shelter.

Minutes later the fuse would be lit, and crouching somewhere far below, Bethany and her friends would hold their breath and press their palms tightly over their ears as they waited for the earth-shattering explosions that were sure to follow.

Sometimes it was an awesome sight as the dynamite brought tons of limestone careering down the sheer face, then, several minutes later the all-clear would sound and they would rush out to investigate the results. The most exciting days – those that were worth braving their fathers' wrath to see – were the days when a giant rogue piece of rock known as a 'tumbler' would break free from an overhanging escarpment and come crashing with a mighty roar on to the rock below. These huge boulders were often up to three hundred tons in weight and provided an awesome sight and sound.

But those were the exciting days, and all too often there was very little to see. The massive slabs loosened by the blast would be simply prised from the face, then split into workable sizes, before, with the help of a giant crane, they would be loaded into the pony-led trucks that ran along the iron rails to the head of the gallery. There they would be offloaded by the bogiers into the dressing sheds, to be worked on by the knappers, such as Cheevers Baine.

A few of the men, like Cheevers himself, had had proper stone masons' training and took a real pride in their skills. At nineteen shillings a week they were regarded as rich compared with those such as the tip-men who had nothing but their brute strength to bargain with. Tom Turver had been a tip-man, one of those fated to spend their days clearing the waste rock from the galleries and depositing it on the giant tips that surrounded the foot of the crag. Theirs was a hard lot, for they were paid by the ton of waste removed. In hard times such as they were now experiencing, a lot of sweat and back-breaking toil went into a weekly wage packet that provided little recompense for their efforts.

It was a strange, incestuous world up there, where old affections and old rivalries alike were carried on from one generation to another with no thought to the passing of time. To Bethany, used to listening to her friends' gossip, only her own father seemed to be the exception, for Cheevers Baine had been neither born nor bred anywhere near Utherby or its quarry. He had come all the way down from the county of Cumberland, at least a day's walk to the north, in search of work after three years spent in the bloodied fields of Flanders fighting the Germans.

Down in London at the time, Lloyd George had been calling for homes fit for heroes to be built for the fighting men returning from the trenches, but all Cheevers Baine and his young wife got was the tiny terraced house of Number Twelve, The Row, and they were thankful for that. Many hereabouts had to begin married life imposing upon in-laws in already cramped conditions. But, thanks to his skill as a mason, honed in the northern limestone quarries of Shap, he had qualified for a company house and, luckily, there had been one available. The Grevilles valued skill. And it was a skill he was proud of, and even now his pale eyes would gleam with concentration as he hand-worked the stone with hands almost as hard as the grey limestone itself.

His tools were his pride and joy — from Brayshaws in Sheffield they were — the best money could buy and bought at a time when he could ill afford them. 'A workman's only as good as his tools,' an old journeyman had once told him, and a lifetime's work had proved that to be true. The precious implements, honed and tempered to a fine pitch by Joe Capstick the blacksmith, never left his side, and despite the rheumatics that plagued him from time to time, he could still execute a fine herring-bone finish with the best of them when called upon. It was a skill that had not changed for centuries and he felt sorry for the others, mainly the older, less able men and boys who spent their days on more menial tasks, barrowing the chippings to the tip and fetching and carrying for those assigned to the more difficult but infinitely more satisfying work. 'Stone is a living thing, lass,' he would tell his young daughter. 'Good stone in the hands of a good mason should be as easy to work as putty.'

And he was a good mason all right. His daughter knew that and was as proud of her father as any child could be.

But for Bethany that winter was not a happy one. The Turvers' forced move to Butterslack meant that she now saw her friend Nancy only infrequently, and even those occasions proved to be not the totally happy, intimate occasions that she so longed for. Already Nancy was distancing herself from her previous life and talking of boys, whose names Bethany did not recognize. They were lads she had come to know at Butterslack school, and Nancy's eyes would glow as she told tales of notes passed between the desks at school from her would-be Romeos, and Bethany would feel shut out from this new world into which her friend had moved.

It was a world of talk about such things as hairstyles and silk stockings, and boyfriends – things which for her held no interest, and she felt cheated that a move of only a few miles could have brought about this change in her old friend. But perhaps most curious of all was the fact that on the last occasion they had met, just before Christmas, Nancy had grown impatient at Bethany's professed lack of interest in the opposite sex, and had come out with a very odd remark indeed.

'I couldn't expect you to understand, Bethany Baine, seeing as you're a child still and I'm now a grown woman!'

Bethany had stared at her friend, who was standing preening herself in Isaac Youdell's shop window at the time. 'What do you mean, I'm still a child and you're a grown woman?' she demanded. Nancy looked exactly the same to her, except that maybe she took a bit more care about her personal appearance these days, and had taken to wearing her hair loose over her shoulders, instead of in the usual braids. And of course there was her bust. Her friend's bust had most definitely grown of late, while her own remained as flat as a washboard.

'Go on then, tell me! What do you mean, I'm still a child and you're now a grown woman?' she had repeated, even more indignantly this time.

Nancy had half-turned to give Bethany a pitying look. 'Happen you'll know soon enough,' she said mysteriously. 'It's something I've got and you haven't, and Mam says I'm not to tell anyone 'cause it's not something decent people talk about.' And she would be drawn no further.

Bethany puzzled on those remarks for days afterwards and was thankful that at least the chirpy Ellen Capstick had not mysteriously decided she too had become a woman. Ellen was still quite happy to play hopscotch on the road in front of their house and roam wild up on the fells. But even as they did so, Bethany knew that these precious days too were numbered. Ellen would turn thirteen at Christmas and as soon as the festival was over she would leave to go into domestic service with a family in Sedbergh.

And so Christmas came and went, and on the day after Boxing Day, Bethany went down to the station with the rest of the Capstick family to see her friend off on her new life. It was a bitter-sweet moment, for she barely recognized the young girl who stood there, brown cardboard suitcase in hand, on the edge of the platform, trying hard to look as if her insides were not quaking, and that there was nothing she longed for more than to turn and run for home.

'You look real nice, Ellie,' Bethany said, not quite sure if her tone was sincere enough, as she took in her friend's new look. Gone were the stubby braids from either side of the heart-shaped face, and in their place was a sedate bun at the nape of the neck, the straying hairs held in place with one of her mother's hairnets. She was wearing her mother's old coat cut down to fit and black stockings held up by garters above the knee had replaced the normal pair of wrinkled socks. They looked incongruously baggy on the short little legs. Her shoes were also second-hand and gaped at the side from feet far wider than Ellen's that had once had the pleasure of breaking them in. In truth she looked a fright and Bethany's heart went out to her as she leant across and pecked her on the cheek at the door of the carriage, as the guard further down the platform raised his flag. 'I'll miss you, El,' she said, and knew it to be the truth. Childhood was pulling out of that station along with her friend's train. Soon she too would have the worry of earning a living and making ends meet.

And so winter dragged on. With the wind that blasted the huddle of houses at the foot of the crag came the rain. Relentless and chill, it ran in sullied streams down the cobbled streets and flooded the narrow alley along the back of The Row. Bethany hated the rain and the skies of sodden grey that hung low and threatening over the village from morning to night. It was almost a relief when the frosts came at last, covering the bare branches of the trees that stood out in filigree relief against the gaunt skyline of the fell behind her home, and caused dragon's breath clouds to form from her lips as her booted feet crunched on the thick carpet of brown and gold beech leaves that edged the road to the schoolhouse.

But there was no one left now with whom to swap confidences as her breath billowed white in the frosty air, and she made slides on the icy slope of the road that ran down from The Row, past the post office and village hall, before flattening out as it reached the gate to the school playground. No more would either Nancy or Ellen walk by her side talking of boys and film stars, and everything that was exciting in the world of twelve-year-olds; now she had only Libby at her side and, with her little sister's hand clasped tightly in her own, she passed the quarter-mile walk pointing out to the child, just as her mother had once pointed out to her, all the wonders of nature that surrounded them.

On the bramble bushes where they had gathered berries for jam earlier in the year, a few leaves stubbornly clung to the bare branches, yellow and pale against the dark-green splash of the holly bushes next to them. In the days running up to Christmas, it was their fronds of red berries that she had taught Libby how to collect on the way home from school to decorate their front parlour for a festive season that had seen little in the way of gifts from a Santa Claus that only the younger children still believed in.

For the weeks immediately after Christmas the village seemed permanently shrouded in a thick blanket of frosty fog, with hoar frost clinging to every surface. But even that was preferable to those days when the Helm Wind blew down from the Eden valley to the north, causing the villagers to butt their way, heads down, against its fierce blast. On such days the roads became littered with broken twigs, loose tiles from the rooftops and household debris snatched from the dustbins in the alleyways behind the rows of terraced houses. Everything that was not battened down would be whipped into the air and Bethany would have to hold on tightly to little Libby's hand as with the other she attempted to keep the skirt of her gymslip from billowing up over her navy-blue knickers, while they tried and often failed to make headway into the teeth of the gale.

And through it all she waited impatiently for spring to come, so she could cast off her hated brown coat and run free once more up there on the fells, where the air was pure and came straight from heaven itself.

It appeared first at the foot of the hedgerows that bordered the road between her own home and the house once lived in by her Grandmother Hetherington at the edge of the village. There the primroses would push their little yellow heads through the carpet of rank dead grass and she would gather posies of them to take home to her mother who would sit them in a place of honour on the sill of the front-room window.

Then, come Eastertime, buds the size of pinheads would appear on the hawthorn bushes, giving the bare brown branches a delicate purple bloom. 'In the spring a young man's fancy turns to thoughts of love,' Ellen Capstick had once informed her, reading the words with slow deliberation from the first page of one of her mother's *People's Friend* magazines. But the only signs of romance they had witnessed with the longer evenings were the courting displays of the pigeons in the loft at the foot of the Capsticks' garden. And there was a sadness now in Bethany's heart as she reflected that Ellen was no longer there to watch the courting couples puff their feathers and strut their amorous dance steps on the warped wooden slats of the roof.

Life was changing now all around her, and just as nature was awakening after its long sleep, there were days too when Bethany would awaken after a night of pouring rain to see a washed-out sky filled with lace-white cirrus clouds whose feathery streamers pointed like warning fingers towards the north where the Helm Wind would be waiting to snatch the breath from one's lips and send the washing tangling round the clotheslines in the back yards of The Row. Such mornings brought a shiver of excitement as she snuggled down beneath the blankets to snatch a few more precious minutes before tumbling out of bed and into her waiting clothes. The promise of the coming day was always sweet at this time of year.

The air was milder now and in the hedgerows the sparrows had begun to chirp with their insignificant little voices. They too had endured the long winter months, in conditions only those bred in that bleak landscape could comprehend. Did they feel as trapped as she sometimes did throughout the long winter, Bethany wondered. On the whole she was happy with her lot, but just occasionally she longed for a kinder, more gentle place, where for months on end she would not always be cold and the skin of her hands and feet covered in painful red chilblains.

That there was another world out there vastly different from this, she had no doubt. Occasionally, apart from Ellen's mother's cherished *People's Friend*, which told stories of families much like their own, a different type of magazine, such as *The Lady*, would come into the possession of one of the women in the street and it would be passed round each home in turn. This showed another type of existence, far removed from their own. 'The upper crust' she had heard them referred to, or 'nobs' – these exquisite creatures that graced the dog-eared pages and seemed to come from another planet entirely alien to her own.

After her mother had finished with it, Bethany would

devour the stories with their pictures of high-born ladies in the latest Paris fashions. Often they would be featured inside their elegant drawing rooms, or admiring the flowers in their wonderful landscaped gardens. They were as proud as peacocks in their fine feathers, and she often wondered if they even guessed at the existence of people like her – the sparrows of this world, destined to live out their lives in the shadow of their splendour.

But she had her joys too. And these were to be found mainly on her beloved crag, where the passing of the seasons could be read in the beauty of the landscape as each day she walked the steep path to deliver her father's cold tea and haverbread.

At the edge of the path the early white clumps of January snowdrops would be replaced by the perky yellow primroses that burst forth in their thousands, to be followed in their turn in late spring by the bright golden daffodils that carpeted the ground beneath the trees on the lower slopes, nodding their trumpets in the breeze as she passed. She was looking forward to them most of all, for often she would wander up the crag before supper and bring back armfuls of daffodils – her mother's favourite flowers – to fill the two Doulton vases, inherited from Grandma Hetherington, which sat on the windowsill of the front room. Hand-painted with grazing Highland cattle, the vases were her mother's pride and joy, but from an early age Bethany had been told she need have no designs on them. As the eldest boy, they would be Tom's by birthright, as would almost everything else of worth in the house. And already she knew that would be very little indeed as, bit by bit, the few valuable items left by their grandmother had been sold over the years to provide the basic essentials of life. But it seemed very unfair nevertheless that boys should be deemed to be more important than girls in the eyes of the law.

'It's just the way of the world, love,' her mother told

her, one day when she had commented on the matter. 'And, anyway, it makes sense when you think about it. Boys are the ones who have to go out to work and set up a home for their wife and family when their turn comes, so it's only right and proper that they should be the ones to inherit.'

'And what do girls do?' she asked, puzzling over her mother's logic.

'Why, they get married, of course.'

Bethany's brow had furrowed. 'Do they have a choice?'

Her mother had smiled and shaken her head. 'Mercy, no! What would they want a choice for? It's every girl's ambition to get married and raise a family, isn't it?'

Was it? She had made no reply to her mother that day and had puzzled over the question ever since.

It was one of those fine evenings in mid-March that called for her to head for the crag, and she had not been gone half an hour when an unexpected knock came to the door of Number Twelve, The Row. Betty Baine was preparing the water and clean towels for her husband's nightly wash when she looked up in irritation at the sound. She glanced around her at the pile of unironed clothes in the wicker basket on the table and the un-washed supper dishes still stacked beside it. The place was a mess. She hurried through to the back kitchen with the basket of laundry and sat it on the stone floor. 'Who on earth can that be at this time?'

Cheevers Baine opened one eye, from where he was nodding off by the fire, but made no reply. He was too fagged out to care.

After a cursory glance in the mirror over the mantel-piece to see that her hair was in order, she made for the door and opened it to see a face she had never reckoned on seeing on her own doorstep. For a second or two she peered at the tallish, well-dressed figure with the smiling face beneath the trilby hat, just to make sure she wasn't wrong. But no, it was him all right. 'Why, Mr Greville, isn't it? Young Jack Greville, if I'm not mistaken.'

The Colonel's eldest son nodded in confirmation as he stood beaming down at her from a height of almost six feet, then he politely removed the grey felt hat from his head. He quite obviously expected to be invited in.

'Well, this is a surprise!' Flushing in confusion, Betty Baine took a step back to allow the young man to enter, and, holding his hat in his hands, he had to bow his head to get through the front door.

He followed her into the kitchen beyond, where she informed her startled husband, 'Look, Cheevers – it's young Mr Greville here.'

Cheevers Baine, not yet washed from his day's exertions in the dressing shed and dog tired, grunted in his half-dozing state, but remained, eyes closed, mouth half-open, and head slumped against the wooden back of the chair.

Betty Baine darted a look of apology at the young man by her side and repeated herself, louder this time. 'Rouse yourself, Cheevers. We have a visitor. Young Mr Greville's here!'

Reluctantly her husband opened his eyes, then the sight of the young man in front of him jerked him awake. What in tarnation was he doing here? Awkwardly, for his back was playing him up, he raised himself out of his chair and, after a moment's hesitation, extended a callused hand. 'Well, this is a surprise and no mistake,' he began, then his tone became more anxious. 'There's nowt wrong, is there?'

Jack Greville gave a reassuring laugh. 'Not in the slightest,' he said. 'I'm not here on quarry business, or any other kind of business as such, come to that. No, I'm here entirely for me today.' He glanced down at the rosette in his buttonhole. 'You might not have heard yet, but I'm a candidate at the local by-election in a fortnight's time.' He gave a slightly embarrassed smile. 'I've been doing the rounds tonight canvassing support, you might say.'

Cheevers Baine's face darkened. He might have known. You'd never see a Greville unless he were after something from you. 'Well, you're out of luck here, lad. I'm a Labour voter, as was my father before me, so I shall be voting nowt but Labour, I'm afraid.'

Jack Greville's face fell. 'But that's a poor argument,' he protested. 'Just supposing your father had been a thief, would that make you a thief too?'

Cheevers Baine pondered on the question for a moment, then looked pityingly at their visitor and shook his head. 'Nay, lad, happen that would mek me a Conservative!'

The prospective candidate had the good grace to smile. 'Well, thankfully, I'm not standing as a Conservative. I'm the new National Socialist candidate. Perhaps you've heard of the party? It's going great guns in Germany right now. In fact they say they will sweep the boards at the next election.'

Cheevers Baine looked sceptical. 'Aye, well them Jerries always were a bit funny like. I reckon we're more sensible over here. Folks like me know what side our bread's buttered on.'

Jack Greville gave a disappointed smile. 'So this is one more down for voting Labour, is it? Well, it's a free country and I can't say as I blame you for wanting a change from the same old Tory policies, for that's what this National Government is pursuing — that's why I'm standing for the National Socialists. We want to get this country back on its feet — get rid of unemployment like they're doing over in Germany. There's hardly a household in this country that's not got a member looking for work.'

'We'll be one of those ourselves come next month,' Betty Baine put in. 'Our Bethany leaves school then. You wouldn't happen to know of anybody that's looking for a young lass to help around the house, would you?' It was a long shot, but worth a try, for the Grevilles were acquainted with all the toffs in the North Riding.

'Well, not offhand,' Jack Greville began, then he paused. 'Unless . . .'

'Unless?'

He shook his head as if to clarify the idea that had just come to him. 'Well, it's just a thought, but Father is always complaining these days that Tabby – Miss Fleetwood, our housekeeper – just isn't up to the heavier household chores such as the laying of fires and carrying of coals, and that sort of thing.' He looked from man to wife. 'Your daughter, Bethany, she's a healthy enough little thing, isn't she?' With so much consumption around, it was as well to ask.

'Oh yes, she's healthy all right,' Betty Baine assured him. 'She might look like a breath of wind would blow her over, but she's as strong as a young heifer – and bright, too. In fact, to tell the truth they are not that keen for her to leave school at Easter. The headmaster was saying just the other day she's one of their brightest youngsters and would have no bother matriculating later on, if we could afford to let her stay on.'

'But that's out of the question, I take it?'

Betty Baine gave a mirthless laugh. 'Well, what do you think? With four other young mouths to feed behind her, it's completely out of the question.'

Jack Greville moved slowly towards the door and they could see his mind working. 'Just leave it with me, Mrs Baine,' he said. 'I'll let you know if I come up with anything.'

He gave a nod in the direction of her husband, who was standing with his back to the mantelpiece listening to all that was being said. 'A very good evening to you, then.' Then with a glance at the rosette in his buttonhole, he added, 'And remember, if it's good enough for the Germans, it's good enough for us!'

'Good enough for the Germans!' Cheevers Baine exploded as soon as he was out of earshot. 'I'll give him good enough for the ruddy Germans! Three long years in the trenches I fought against that lot, and now he wants us to take a leaf out of their book. Not flipping likely!'

'The lad was only trying to be helpful,' his wife said, lifting the singing kettle off the fire and carrying it through to the back kitchen where her husband was about to get washed. 'If Jack Greville can get our Bethany placed with one of his fine friends, then we will have a lot to be thankful to him for, and I'm sure Bethany will be delighted. She can't wait to grow up and get out there in the wide world like Ellen and the rest.'

But Bethany was not quite as delighted as her mother anticipated. With the Baines' house being the last in the street, Jack Greville paused on the stone wall alongside it for a much-needed smoke before heading for his car to drive the two miles back to The Hall. He recognized immediately the young girl skipping along the road in his direction. 'Well, if it's not the squirt – young Miss Baine herself!'

Bethany stared at the well-turned-out young man in his sharp three-piece grey, pin-striped suit and highly polished black shoes. 'Don't you "squirt" me, Black Jack Greville!'

She paused in front of him, eyeing critically the well-brushed head of dark curling hair and the rosette in his buttonhole. She noted that he didn't bother even touching his hat in her presence, let alone remove it. 'What are you doing down here, any roads?'

Jack Greville raised one eyebrow. 'It's a free country, isn't it? Anyway,' he laughed, 'don't forget we own most of this village –including all of your street, so I reckon that entitles me to be down here occasionally, don't you?'

'Aye, and you'd like to think you own the folks in it too, wouldn't you?' She shot the words at him accusingly and waited for the reaction. But to her annoyance, he merely laughed.

'Well, you are a little firebrand and no mistake. Heaven knows what Tabby would make of you!'

'Pardon?'

'Our housekeeper – Miss Fleetwood – I was just wondering what she would make of someone like you, if you did come and work for us at The Hall.'

Bethany's brow wrinkled beneath the auburn fringe. 'What do you mean, if I did come and work for you at The Hall?'

The young man opposite her shrugged and studied the glowing tip of his cigarette. 'Oh, it was just an idea I had when I was speaking to your parents a moment ago. Your mother informs me you will be looking for work shortly and . . .'

'I'm not going to work as a skivvy for you or anybody else!' Bethany cut in before he could get any further. 'I've got my own plans!'

'Oh really, and what might they be?'

'I'm going to be a nurse,' she announced firmly. 'I'm going to work at St James's in Leeds.' Ellen Capstick had a cousin who did just that and it sounded a wonderful occupation.

Jack Greville looked somewhat taken aback and slightly disappointed. This smart-Alec young brat amused him and he was beginning to think it might be fun to have her around up at The Hall. It would certainly liven up the old place, there could be no doubt about that. 'Well, if you change your mind, you know where to find me . . .'

'I won't!' she shouted after him, as he made for his car. 'You'll not see me in a skivvy's uniform, Jack Greville!'

And how those words were to come back and haunt her over the next few weeks. The negotiations that went on

117

behind her back between her parents and the Colonel's eldest son came as a complete shock. She had had absolutely no idea as she watched his sports car disappear up the road in a cloud of dust that he had already made up his mind he was going to convince his father they really did need a younger pair of hands and legs to help out Tabby, who was now well past her three score and ten. 'Decent help is hard to come by these days, Father,' he had insisted. 'And I can vouch that the girl in question comes from a respectable family. In fact, if I remember rightly, her grandfather was the local minister here once.'

The Colonel puffed on his pipe and considered the matter. 'Hetherington,' he said. 'Harrison Hetherington. I remember him well. A damned fine preacher — for a Nonconformist.' As Church of England himself the praise was grudging, but none the less genuine. 'And she'll make a good worker, you say?'

His son nodded vigorously. 'No doubt about it. She's quick on the uptake, all right. It's just a case of convincing Tabby she needs help.' And that was easier said than done, for the elderly housekeeper wanted none of it.

Her eyes, now faded to an indeterminate colour behind the wire-rimmed spectacles, looked askance at the young man who dared even to suggest that she might not be up to her job any longer. 'Well I never, young Jack!' she said in a shocked tone. 'It's a fine state of affairs we've come to when you have to come down here and tell me I'm no longer fit to look after you all!'

'It's not a case of that, Tabby dear,' Jack said patiently. 'Far from it. We think at your age you should be taking it a bit easier, that's all. Get someone younger to do all the fetching and carrying — all the donkey work, if you like.'

The housekeeper looked at him long and hard. Someone to do all the fetching and carrying, he said. There was no denying her knees were not what they once were and just getting up and down that big main staircase was becoming a bit of a nightmare when her arthritis was playing her up. 'You have somebody in mind, I take it?'

Jack nodded. 'The Baine girl. Her father works at the quarry. You know the family – her grandfather was the Reverend Hetherington.' He knew that should clinch it, for Tabby was as staunch a Methodist as they came.

The housekeeper's sparse brows rose behind the wire frames and her heart beneath the buxom frame, draped in rows of jet, beat faster than it had done for years. Harrison Hetherington had been the only man to set her pulse racing as a young woman. The fact that she had never missed a sermon in the thirty years up to his death had more to do with that fact than any great sense of piety. And the fact that he had married her old classmate, Edith Holroyd, remained a sore point to this day. 'Is that right now?'

Jack Greville could see her resolve visibly melting before his eyes. 'You can at least give her a try, Tabby. If she's no good, then there's no harm done, we can just revert to life as normal. You're the real boss in this house, you know that as well as I do.'

The housekeeper smiled as she nodded her grey head and picked up her knitting once more. 'Aye, young Jack, I know that,' she said, pulling more yarn off the ball in her lap. There had been no other female in this house for sixteen years and any that did come came on her terms or not at all. 'Well, there'll be no harm in giving the lass a try, then, will there?'

Jack Greville smiled quietly to himself as he patted the old woman reassuringly on the shoulder. It had gone easier than he had expected. But then there wasn't a woman on this earth who wasn't susceptible to a bit of flattery now and again.

But for Cheevers Baine and his wife it was not so easy. They watched in growing apprehension as their eldest child's face grew paler by the second as, less than a week after his original visit, her mother told her of Jack Greville's second appearance in their kitchen earlier that very day, and of how it had all been arranged. She was to start as housemaid at Wolf Hall on Easter Monday.

'No . . . No . . . I won't do it. You can't force me. I'll run away, that's what I'll do! You can't make me work for them Grevilles, you can't!'

'You have a better idea?' her father asked, his patience rapidly running out.

'I want to go to Leeds.'

'Leeds!' Her parents chorused the name of Yorkshire's biggest city in unison. 'What on earth do you want to go there for?'

'I want to be a nurse,' Bethany declared. Then, seeing the amazed look on both their faces, she added quickly, 'I want to work at St James's. They say it's the best hospital in the whole county.'

Her mother sat down heavily on her chair and looked across at her husband. Cheevers Baine's blood pressure was rising by the minute. 'That is just about the daftest thing I have ever heard,' he said. 'We haven't got the money to send you to Butterslack, never mind Leeds – and even if we had, there could be no question of you going off to some strange town to live and work at your age. Just think on, our Bethany. Have some sense, will you!'

And so it was decided. Instead of attaining her dream of donning the smart new nurse's uniform of St James's, with its starched white apron and cap, she would be putting on the clothes of a skivvy to go and work for the Grevilles at Wolf Hall. It was a depressing thought with which to welcome her next birthday.

Chapter Six

The other children in the bedroom were still fast asleep when Bethany rose at six on Easter Monday to prepare for the two-mile walk to Wolf Hall and her new life as housemaid to the Greville family.

Now fully dressed and ready to go, she crept back upstairs and stood silently in between the two beds for a last look at them all: tousle-haired Libby with her bare arm stretched across little Sammy's face, and Tom and Teddy both flat on their backs at either end of the single bed. The room was silent save for their steady breathing, and little Sammy's occasional asthmatic wheeze. Gently she lifted Libby's arm from his face, and suddenly realized how much she would miss them, despite all the times she had yearned for a bit of peace and quiet and a bedroom of her own.

As the eldest, she felt a great protectiveness for those under her. So often she was the one they would come to with their problems from school or other little worries. Even at that young age they knew there were days when they could not trouble their mother, for she had worries enough of her own. There would be no one now for them to turn to. A panic enveloped her – a feeling that she was deserting them, that they weren't ready for her to go. In her misery she had glanced up at the old 'Suffer the little children' calendar on the wall and whispered, 'Look after them, please, Jesus. Take care of them when I'm gone.'

She was near to tears as she tightened the knot in her bundle, then, wedging it under one arm, she made her way down the narrow staircase into the silent kitchen. She had never been up this early before and her eyes wandered fondly over the old range, with its permanently singing kettle, and Grandma Hetherington's Welsh dresser, with the best of the old lady's remaining china still proudly displayed on its well-scrubbed shelves. There was the distinct smell of carbolic about the place, and the stone-flagged floor was still damp from its first scouring of the day – a task undertaken by their mother as soon as their father had set off for work.

She could hear her mother moving about in the back kitchen, preparing the copper for the week's wash. Her father must already have gone. A stab of disappointment ran through her, but maybe it was just as well, she decided. He was never one for shows of emotion and she was sure she would only have made a fool of herself by breaking down in front of him . . . No, it was better that he had already joined the straggling line of men making their way up the well-worn track to the quarry. Already the probing fingers of dawn were piercing the night sky to the east over Butterslack and lending an eerie half-light to the village streets. Another day's work would be under way. But today she would not be trekking up the winding path of the crag to deliver her father's cold tea and haverbread; from now on that would be Tom's job.

So many things were to come to an end today, for childhood had been composed of a myriad different experiences and habits that had lent a security to life. And suddenly that was all being swept away. There could be no more meanders up the crag and over the fells after school; no more would she know the freedom of the birds and other small wild creatures who made those lonely, windswept places their own.

Yes, perhaps that's what she would miss most of all – the freedom; the freedom just to be herself. She had found that up there among the clouds. Down here in the world of human beings men had made rules and drawn boundaries around her life that had already mapped out her future. There were those for whom all things were possible – people like the Grevilles and their set – and there were the others, such as her own family and friends, whose lot it was to serve those others – make an already sweet and easy life infinitely sweeter and more easy for them. And what puzzled her most of all was that so many of 'her' people seemed simply to accept this as the way of the world. They used phrases like 'know your place' or 'getting too big for your boots' whenever she sought to question these things, and it made her wonder if she really was as peculiar as they tried to make out, or if it wasn't the case that *they* were the odd ones who mutely accepted a second-class ticket through life without ever questioning the reason why.

It was a strangely muted goodbye she said to her mother on the front step of their house a few minutes later.

'Be a good girl, for our sakes, Bethany love,' Betty Baine implored, fighting back the tears at the sight of her eldest child standing there on the doorstep, her few possessions tied in a cloth bundle clasped in her right hand. She looked so young, so very young. 'Do as you are bid. Keep yourself neat and clean. Don't answer back. And . . .' Her eyes sparkled with unshed tears. 'Well, just be a credit to your Dad and me, that's all.'

Bethany forced her mouth into a smile as her mother put her arms awkwardly around her daughter's narrow shoulders. Theirs was not a demonstrative family and neither was finding it an easy situation. 'I'll try,' Bethany said, as her mother's dry lips pecked her cheek. Then, as if by afterthought, Betty Baine reached into her apron pocket and took out a small, square cardboard box.

'What's that?' Bethany asked as her mother removed the lid.

Betty Baine reached inside and extracted a small silver

St Christopher medallion. 'My father gave this to me on the occasion of my twenty-first birthday,' she said proudly. 'He said it was to encourage me to seek fresh fields and protect me on my journey through life.' She gave a wistful smile. 'Had he lived longer, happen he might have been a mite disappointed I never got further than The Row in Utherby.'

It was the first time Bethany had heard her mother express the slightest shame or disappointment at her lot. 'You – you want me to have it?'

Betty Baine nodded. 'Somehow I always felt I let him down in that regard, and I've never had the heart to wear it. I reckon it'll do you more good than me from now on.'

Bethany stood still as her mother fastened the fragile silver chain around her neck, then adjusted the small medallion, with its picture of the saint carrying a small child on his shoulders. When it was sitting just right between the two white points of her daughter's collar, Betty Baine gave a smile of satisfaction. 'You remind me a lot of myself at your age, you know, Beth. I just hope you turn out to have more sense.'

Bethany looked at the strange, wistful expression on her mother's face and could not bring herself to ask what exactly she meant by that. In her heart she already knew.

She did not look back to wave as she turned the corner of The Row. She knew her mother would still be standing there on the front doorstep and she knew that the sight of her would surely bring tears to her eyes. She could feel them there already, lurking beneath the surface, and she was doing her best to keep control of herself.

A brisk wind was blowing, whipping the new black skirt her mother had made against her thin legs and sending strands of reddish-brown hair flying out of the carefully knotted bun at the back of her neck. She had begged her father to be allowed to shingle her hair before taking up her new post, but the answer had been an emphatic 'No.

Thou's got little enough in the way of assets, lass,' Cheevers Baine had said firmly. 'Thou'll look like nowt but a skinny little lad wi' your hair got rid of!'

So the hair stayed – long and thick and cumbersome – and as Bethany battled on against the wind, she wondered just how long she was going to remain looking like a skinny little lad, when already so many of the girls in her class at school had begun to display all the signs of young womanhood.

Young womanhood. She repeated the words in her head as she fingered the silver St Christopher around her neck. She was well aware that, like her mother before her, and like every other young woman who had ever left home, she was on her own now. For better or worse, what she made of her life would be up to her from now on. She had entered the world of adults, where she must learn to stand on her own two feet and do her best not to let her parents down. They had problems enough without her adding to them.

It was not yet seven o'clock and the countryside was still bathed in the grey half light of early morning. Ghostlike wraiths of mist lurked between the spreading branches of the ancient oaks as twenty minutes later she made her way up the gravel drive towards the old house that was her destination.

She found herself shivering with both cold and apprehension. At the end of the drive Wolf Hall was just becoming visible and it appeared even more grim and forbidding than she remembered it. There were no lights at the windows and she expected any minute to find a headless horseman dashing towards her from the row of ivy-clad stables that went off at an angle from the main building.

Still half-asleep, she yawned into the wind and doubted if she would ever get used to rising before daybreak, as she knew she would have to from now on. Long before she would normally have been out of bed, she had been told, she would have to set to and clean out grates, light fires and prepare breakfast for the Colonel and his sons. It was demeaning, that's what it was, having to serve the likes of Black Jack Greville and his brothers.

She thought of her own brothers and sister still tucked up cosily in their beds at home and tears, born of frustration and anger, once more pricked at the hazel surface of her eyes as she bent her head into the gusts and thought of the life that had gone and the one that now lay ahead of her. And to make matters worse, she had had the most dreadful ache in her stomach ever since getting out of bed this morning and it seemed to be getting worse with each passing minute. She would have given anything to have been able to turn back, but they would never believe her at home. Just one of her fibs to get out of going, they would say. So doggedly, fighting back the tears, she ploughed on.

There was not a sound to be heard, nor a sign of life anywhere as she reached the main door of The Hall and for a moment she panicked. What if she roused them all from their beds by ringing the bell? She gazed in mounting apprehension at the ancient bell pull, with its rusted handle and flaking black paint. Then, taking her courage in both hands, she pulled on it with all her might.

Old Carnforth, the odd-job man now assuming the role of butler, answered at the second pull. His thin, bent figure peered at her irritably from the dark depths of the great hall beyond. 'Aye?'

'I've come to work here,' Bethany said, getting straight to the point. 'Can I come in?'

'You should've come to the back entrance,' the old man informed her gruffly. 'This door is not for the likes o' thee.'

The likes o' thee indeed! Bethany bit her tongue with difficulty as she followed him through the main hall and on down a dark, dank-smelling passage into the kitchens

126

beyond. They passed several closed doors until they came to one that was open a fraction and she could discern a chink of light. She could feel her heart beating as Carnforth pushed it open further to reveal a large working kitchen, still lit by oil lamps, although the rest of the house was lit by gas. In a rocking chair to the side of the newly-lit range, Tabby, the housekeeper, was sitting drinking a cup of tea.

'It's the new lass,' Old Carnforth announced, before abruptly closing the door behind him and disappearing back down the passage.

Bethany hovered in the vicinity of the closed door, her eyes taking in the large room, with its huge, shining black range and tall pine dresser full of blue-and-white crockery. It was roughly four times the size of their kitchen at home. An enormous scrubbed pine table stood in the centre of the room and over it several flitches of curing hams hung from hooks in one of the enormous black beams that straddled the ceiling.

On either side of the range a dazzling array of highly polished horse-brasses hung on their brown leather straps and, on the mantelpiece above, a collection of pewter tankards vied for space with an array of biscuit barrels and tins decorated with the highly coloured countenances of various royal personages.

There were two chairs on either side of the fire, one a Windsor carver containing a marmalade-coloured cat curled up comfortably on a cushion, the other an ancient rocker from which the housekeeper now observed the new arrival. On the hearth rug a border collie gnawed at a bone Bethany knew her mother would have been only too glad of to make enough soup to last them a week.

'So you're the Baine lass.' The old woman picked up her wire spectacles from the table beside her and scrutinized the child-woman before her. 'Hmmm.' She was a pretty enough little thing, Tabitha Fleetwood decided, but not much of a specimen as far as physique was concerned. The cheeks could do with some colour and a bit of fattening out.

She got up with a sigh, easing her hefty frame out of the wooden rocker, and smoothing down her black skirts which came all the way down to a pair of bulging ankles and feet encased in misshapen tartan slippers. Everything about her seemed to come from another age: the high-necked black blouse that swathed the ample bosom; the long strands of jet beads that entwined the neck, to hang almost to waist level, if there had been a waist for them to reach.

The housekeeper was almost as wide as she was tall, but had curiously refined features for so large and cumbersome a body. The face that scrutinized Bethany from between the wispy white hair and treble chins had a small beaklike nose and a tiny, pinched mouth on which there was no semblance of a smile as she said frostily, 'I've said to the Master I'll give you a fair trial, my girl, and I'll keep my word. You'll be up at five-thirty to do the grates and be abed when the family turn in. That can be any time between ten and midnight. You get an hour off on Sunday to go to church and one day off a month. You get your room and board and the matter of your wages will no doubt have been settled between your folk and the Colonel . . . Any questions?'

Bethany had a million, but was on the point of shaking her head, when she heard herself blurt out: 'Can I have a cup of tea, please?'

The housekeeper looked at her, quite taken aback. The forward little monkey! 'I'm sure you *can* have a cup of tea, young lady. I'm perfectly sure you are well able to drink one, but whether you *may* have one is quite another matter.'

Bethany pursed her lips and stared at the enemy, for that was how she was already regarding the old woman. 'I were up too early to feel like anything to eat or drink afore I left and I've got an awful sore stomach.'

Tabby Fleetwood sighed. She would have her work cut out with this one and no mistake. 'I *was* up too early, girl – not *were*! Didn't they teach you anything at that school down there in the village? You're talking like a common street urchin.'

Bethany's ire rose. 'Happen then maybe that's what I am,' she retorted.

Miss Fleetwood rose to her full height of five feet five inches and her eyes, behind their metal rims, bore down on the child before her. 'No grandchild of Harrison Hetherington can ever be a common anything, my girl. You remember that!'

Bethany's eyes widened. Tabitha Fleetwood must have been a friend of her grandfather! Somehow the knowledge cheered her and she looked more closely at the elderly woman in front of her.

The housekeeper shifted uncomfortably under the steady hazel gaze. 'Did nobody tell you it's rude to stare, child?'

Bethany ignored the question, her eyes narrowing as a question of her own surfaced in her mind. 'Have you ever been married?'

'Mercy child, whatever next!' Tabby Fleetwood's multiple chins wobbled along with the teacup halfway up to her lips. Then her mouth broke into a wistful smile. If only she knew . . . But dignity must be preserved. 'There's been more than one would've been only too glad to get their feet under my table, I can tell you, lass! But I'd have none of it.' She shook her grey head quite emphatically. 'No, I can agree best wi' mysel'!'

The answer satisfied, for Bethany knew it would take a special kind of man to come up against Tabitha Fleetwood and come off best.

'Now about that cup of tea . . .' The housekeeper hobbled over to the dresser to fetch a fresh cup and saucer.

129

So Bethany got her cup of tea all the same, and a fresh bap with butter and home-cured ham to go with it, and she could not remember having ever tasted anything so delicious. It was over her throat in five mouthfuls. The housekeeper watched in amazement as the child licked her fingers, then with the damp tip of her index finger got up every last crumb off the plate.

'Are you sure you wouldn't like to lick the plate itself?' Tabitha Fleetwood asked with ill-disguised irony.

'Oh no,' Bethany answered in a shocked voice. 'That wouldn't be manners. I'd love another bap, though.' Then, seeing the look that came into the other's face, she added quickly, 'If you can spare one, that is.'

Shocked, but amused at the same time, the housekeeper rose from her chair once more to head for the pantry. 'Well now, young lady, Dickens's lad Oliver had nothing on you, I'll be bound! A real little Miss Twist you are and no mistake!'

But she got her second bap all the same and, as she downed it with as much relish as she had the first, she decided that perhaps Miss Tabby Fleetwood wasn't such a bad old bird after all.

After the family were up, washed, dressed and breakfasted, the Colonel called for the new housemaid to report to his study. It was the first time Bethany had actually spoken to the head of the Greville household and she found her natural confidence ebbing at the sight of the tall, raw-boned man, with the shaggy grey eyebrows, waiting for her in the library. He was dressed in full fox-hunting attire and looked a splendid sight in the dove-grey jacket, black jodhpurs and shiny black riding boots.

He carried a black riding whip in his left hand, and to her amazement he shook her hand with his right. His grasp was warm and firm and she felt immediately grown-up; it was the first time she had had her hand shaken by anyone in her entire life. But her initial favourable impression was shortlived for he did not invite her to take a seat, and he preferred to remain standing himself.

Leaving her standing just inside the door, he stood, legs apart, in front of the crackling log fire in the grate, the riding whip now clasped behind him. The dark eyes beneath the beetling brows looked her up and down as he might survey a new piece of livestock, then he pronounced himself satisfied with what he saw so far. 'You're not a bad-looking young thing, I suppose. Could do with a bit more beef, but that's easily seen to. This is your first post, so I hear?'

'Yes.'

'Yes – sir, if you don't mind, young lady.'

She stared across at him, but made no comment.

'Did you hear what I said?'

'Yes . . .' There was all of a ten seconds' pause before the 'sir' was reluctantly uttered.

'Hmmm.' Colonel Greville's lips twitched beneath the luxuriant moustache. An awkward, headstrong young filly he had here, he could see that. 'I knew your grandfather,' he announced, by way of finding common ground. 'Damned fine man.'

Bethany looked at the floor and could think of no suitable rejoinder. She herself had never met the man, although he had figured so large throughout her entire life.

'Yes, a damned fine man. He was sadly missed by this dale when he passed on, I can tell you. There was even talk of raising some sort of monument to him – you know, that sort of thing my own family have in the churchyard there.'

Bethany knew only too well the granite monstrosities the Grevilles had inflicted on the local population for their own glorification. It had been commented on enough in her family over the years. Her mother had told them in no uncertain terms how much her own father, Harrison

131

Hetherington, had disliked 'graven images', unless erected to the glory of God. Those that had money to spare should look to the poor, not spend it on such items of vanity. She frowned. 'Happen my Grandad wouldn't have liked that . . . sir.'

Her new employer raised his eyebrows in some surprise. 'How so, young lady?'

Bethany's small face was serious as it looked up into his. ' 'Cause he would've reckoned it a right waste of money, that's why. Me Dad says men were dying in t'war over there in France and their families were starving back home here in Utherdale when Grandad Hetherington died. Happen he would have said folk of t'dale couldn't eat stone statues or brass plaques. Why waste money on the dead when the living must do without?'

Colonel Greville's already ruddy cheeks reddened even further as he looked at this bit of a girl who had somehow contrived to make him feel a fool. He took a handkerchief out of his breast pocket and blew his nose for the want of a suitable reply. She was Harry Hetherington's grandchild all right, for he could be a cussed old bugger when the fancy took him — a bit of a Bolshevik too, if he remembered rightly.

He blew his nose noisily once more, then replaced the handkerchief in his pocket; all thoughts of what he had actually intended talking about had gone from his head. 'If you have any problems, child, go to Miss Fleetwood, not me.' The less he saw of this young lady the better for the time being.

The remainder of the morning was taken up with the housekeeper showing her around The Hall, and Bethany was amazed at the sheer size of the place: ten bedrooms in all, with four reception rooms, the main hall, a bathroom, and with the big kitchen, the tack rooms, the wine cellars and the rest of it, heaven only knew how many rooms in the kitchen and utility areas.

'We have a woman comes up from the village twice a week to help with the cleaning,' the housekeeper informed her, 'but the day-to-day running of the place is my job . . . And some of those jobs will be yours now you're here.'

It was in Jack Greville's bedroom that she was told exactly what her chores would consist of. 'You see that ewer there?' Tabby pointed to a marble-topped washstand on which sat a large earthenware jug with a blue floral design on it, inside a matching basin. 'Well, it will be your job to see the ewers in all the occupied bedrooms are filled with boiling water when the Colonel and the Young Masters are ready to begin their ablutions . . . But, of course, you'll have all the fires to clear out and get going again before that so that the rooms are warmed for them rising.'

The Young Masters . . . So the rooms are warmed for them rising . . . The words rang in Bethany's head. She looked at the old woman and frowned. Didn't she ever stop to think how demeaning it was, bowing and scraping to other people like the Grevilles? Obviously not, for the housekeeper was warming to the subject of the Young Masters as she gave a sigh and looked fondly round Mr Jack's bedroom, as she called him. The other two, not having yet reached their majority, were still Masters.

'Yes, Mr Jack is a grand lad – although I shouldn't really call him that these days, not seeing as how he's now twenty-one.'

She pointed to a delicately shaded watercolour above the marble mantelpiece of a beautiful, rather ethereal-looking young woman. Bethany's blood ran cold. It was the same young woman whose picture in the carved ivory frame she had once shoved down the arm of a chair. 'He's the only one who really remembers his mother,' Tabby's voice was continuing. 'Quite devastated he was when she died.'

'She was very beautiful,' Bethany said truthfully.

133

'Aye, she was that. Looked as beautiful and was as frail a flower as grew in any garden. But looks were deceptive, mind, for she was as brave a horsewoman as they come. Could ride like the wind, she could, and was determined her sons would do the same.' Tabby nodded proudly at the memory of the young woman in the immaculate red riding habit aloft her favourite chestnut gelding. 'That was why the Colonel has been so keen for the two eldest to excel as huntsmen – as a tribute to their mother.'

Bethany bit her tongue. It was one of the most common sights around the village, the Utherdale hunt, with the Colonel and his two eldest sons at its head. As a lover of nature and all wildlife, she never could understand what pleasure could be derived from killing fellow creatures such as the fox. It just didn't seem right, somehow.

'And look you here, little Miss Twist,' Tabby continued. 'It's not just at hunting young Mr Jack has excelled. These are all his trophies from school.' She hobbled over to a large, glass-fronted bookcase filled with all shapes and sizes of silver cups and shields. Out of politeness Bethany joined her for a closer look. 'John E. Greville, Junior Sports Champion 1921' and further along the shelf an even bigger cup that stated proudly: 'John E. Greville, Senior Sports Champion 1929'; and there were what seemed like dozens in between. 'Yes, young Jack is a son his dear mother would have been proud of,' Tabby said, with just the hint of a mist on the surface of her faded eyes. 'I shall miss him when he goes to Hergott Spring.'

'Hergott Spring. Where's Hergott Spring?'

'Australia,' Tabby answered with a heartfelt sigh. 'He'll be leaving us shortly to go out to his Uncle Hugh's sheep farm to learn the business. With times so hard here, the Colonel thinks it would be a good thing if he went down under to pick up some tips, you might say, on large-scale sheep rearing, so he can come back here in a few years' time and put all his knowledge to good use.'

A wave of disappointment swept through Bethany that surprised her. One half of her thought Jack Greville was a big-headed good-for-nothing, but the other half of her thought that he might just be her saving grace around here. He was certainly a lot less obnoxious than that Amos, who wouldn't even pass the time of day with you, nor even acknowledge your presence in the street if he tripped over you. 'I'm sorry Black Jack's going,' she said truthfully. 'He's the only one I reckon anything to, apart from Neddy.'

The housekeeper's spectacles slipped a good inch down her nose as her eyebrows rose at the candour of her young companion, and she shook her grey head. 'You're a one and no mistake, Bethany Baine. I can see I'm going to have some work to do with you, my girl, if that sharp tongue of yours is not to end up cutting your own throat!'

For the rest of the morning she was put to work sweeping and dusting the family bedrooms. 'Keep you out of mischief until I get your rota properly worked out,' Tabby informed her, as she handed her the brushes, pans and cut-down shirts that served as flannel dusters.

She began with Amos's, for that was the one nearest the staircase and she was only five minutes into the task when a sound behind her made her jump and gasp out loud. She turned her head, from where she was kneeling by the grate, to see Amos Greville himself standing inside the doorway. 'My, you gave me a start!'

The young man made no reply, but closed the door behind him and walked slowly over to the window, where he took a seat on the wide ledge. He sat there smoking a cigarette for a minute or so, swinging one riding-booted leg, but saying nothing as Bethany attempted to get on with her work. It was not easy with a pair of dark eyes boring into the back of your head. But, at last, he spoke. 'I was pretty mad with Jack, I can tell you, when I heard that you were the one who was coming to help out Tabby.'

Bethany knew just what he was referring to, and her heart missed a beat. She got up stiffly from her kneeling position and looked at him, feigning innocence. 'I beg your pardon, Amos Greville?'

'*Mister* Amos, if you don't mind – or even if you do mind, girl! . . . And don't come the innocent with me. We both know it was you along with that silly Turver bitch that just about got me hanged for that tart's death!'

Bethany stared at him, her colour rising. 'Nancy's Mam's not a bitch, *Mister* Amos,' she said, stressing the 'Mister' through gritted teeth, 'and I don't think it becomes you or anyone to speak ill of the dead. Poor Sarah-Jane didn't deserve what happened to her – and anyroads, you seemed pretty fond of her the last time I saw the two of you together!'

She saw the other's jaw clench. He had a more angular face than either Jack or Neddy. He looked more like their father, with strong aquiline features and much straighter hair; he also had much thinner lips that quirked into something resembling a smile as he regarded her thoughtfully. 'I could've put a stop to it, you know,' he said quietly. 'This job of yours, I could've objected. I could've said, anyone who had tittle-tattled to the police wasn't to be trusted working here.'

She straightened her back and looked him right in the eye. 'And why didn't you, then?'

He obviously wasn't used to having his questions thrown back at him, for he got up from the window and headed for the door. He turned as he clasped the handle and his lips barely moved as he vowed softly, 'You'll see, girl. You'll see . . .'

A shiver ran through her as she stared after him. Just what did he mean by that? She went to the door and half opened it, and she could hear his booted feet clattering down the staircase. And at that moment Jack Greville came out of his own room further along the passage.

He too had heard the clatter of boots and looked curiously at the young girl standing at the open door of his brother's room. 'Well now, if it isn't little Miss Baine!'

Bethany attempted a smile that didn't quite come off, and a look of concern flickered across the other's face. She was obviously upset about something. 'My brother Amos hasn't been having a go at you, has he?' He looked genuinely concerned.

Bethany shrugged. It seemed as if she was already getting something of a reputation for telling tales and she certainly wasn't going to add to it. 'I'm sorry you're going to Australia, Black Jack,' she said, changing the subject completely. 'Happen Hergott Spring must be a real nice place to make you go all that way to look at some sheep.'

Jack Greville laughed. 'Happen it must be, young Bethany!' he agreed, mimicking her good-humouredly. 'I'll let you know when I get back – whenever that's likely to be!'

She regarded him seriously. 'And just when will you get back, do you know?'

He shook his head. 'Could be a couple of years, could be several. Depends how much I like it out there, really.'

She nodded thoughtfully, trying to imagine life on the other side of the world. 'I wish it were your Amos that were going and not you.'

He gave a wry smile. He had no doubt there would be quite a few around Utherby who would express that particular sentiment. But he felt a curious sense of responsibility towards this skinny, serious-eyed child. 'I can send you a boomerang.'

She looked at him quizzically as she repeated the word. 'A boomerang? What's that?'

He laughed. 'Why not wait and see?'

Jack Greville sailed for South Australia two weeks later and almost six months to the day afterwards a most peculiarly-shaped package arrived at Wolf Hall, addressed to Miss Bethany Baine. It was covered in the most colourful display of foreign stamps that Bethany had ever seen. She stared at it in astonishment and mounting excitement, having completely forgotten the casual remark of several months previously.

'Well, open it then!' Tabby said, as curious as she was to find out what was inside. 'It's no good just sitting there staring at the thing!'

With trembling fingers, Bethany carefully undid the brown paper wrapping, taking great care not to harm any of the stamps. And when she had got to the final layer of tissue paper, she gazed in perplexity at the strange-looking object on the table in front of her. Gingerly she lifted it out and held it up to the astonished gaze of Tabby, who let out a gasp of recognition.

'Well, bless my soul, if it isn't a boomerang!' she declared. 'Well, I never did!'

'What's it for?' Bethany asked, still mystified by the peculiar wooden object in her hand. 'What am I supposed to do with it, Tabby?'

The housekeeper's ample shoulders shook with suppressed mirth as she surveyed the new arrival. 'I'm darned if I know,' she admitted. 'But I've no doubt any Aborigine would be glad to tell you.'

'Happen there aren't a lot of them around Utherby.'

'Happen not, lass.'

Chapter Seven

And so the seasons came and went in Utherdale, and as the weeks turned into months, and the months into years, the country, along with most of the Western world, continued to suffer under the worst Depression in living memory. At the quarry half the workforce had been laid off and the others, including Cheevers Baine, were still on short time. In the mean streets of the mill towns and villages of industrial Yorkshire, and in hamlets throughout the Dales, mothers like Betty Baine went without so that their children might eat. But still those children went to bed hungry, and it seemed life would never get better. That golden land with its homes fit for heroes that had been promised by the politicians to the young men who survived the trenches of the Great War – that new dawn of a fairer, more caring society – was still as far away as ever.

Only in Germany did things seem to be different, and in the dales, as elsewhere in the country, people read their newspapers with increasing unease. What had they fought the Great War for, they asked? Why were they and their families still starving when the nation they had defeated seemed to be going from strength to strength? Under the Nazis, Germany's terrible unemployment figures of the previous decade were being wiped out by the massive rebuilding programme being undertaken by the new government and almost everyone appeared to be caught up in the enthusiasm for the new National Socialist way of life.

In Britain, in November 1935, the National Government, now Conservative in all but name, was swept back to power – a fact that disgusted Colonel Philip Greville, who had himself stood as a British Union of Fascists candidate in the General Election. The owner of Wolf Hall was a great admirer of the new German government and was firmly convinced that what his own country needed was the same type of firm rule that the Nazis were providing in Germany. Any right-wing government that kowtowed to the Labour Party, in no matter how small a degree, he would have no truck with at all. This so-called National Government was a disgraceful creation that would do no one any good.

'We've seen what the likes of that Scotsman Ramsay MacDonald and his namby-pamby Socialists can do,' he declared. 'Absolutely nothing except fall out among themselves!'

And this was the message he took to village halls all over Utherdale. The fact that few agreed with him, resulting in a sound defeat at the ballot box, did little to blunt the old soldier's enthusiasm for the new Fascist cause he now espoused; rather it confirmed to him that his family was indeed the only one fit to rule their particular part of the North Riding.

'Numskulls, the lot of 'em!' he announced, as he read the election results over breakfast. 'I tell you, Amos, the British public don't deserve decent government when they vote the likes of this lot in!'

There were murmurs of agreement from the others around the table that morning. But not every mind was as firmly fixed on the election results as that of the master of the house. As Bethany piled up the dirty breakfast plates, ready for removal to the kitchen, she felt a hand reach for her leg behind the damask cloth that skirted the table legs. Insistent fingers caressed the back of her right knee.

'You'll be voting by the time the next one comes around, won't you, Beth?' Amos asked, his face and tone of voice giving no hint as to the actions of his left hand. 'If it's me that's standing then instead of Pa, you will be casting your vote in my direction next time round, won't you? I mean we have to make sure that the best man wins and all that.'

Bethany looked at him pityingly as she moved deliberately out of reach. 'Happen not, Master Amos, if what you say about the best man winning is true.'

She too was determined that the best man should win, and it certainly wouldn't be him. The smile on his face began to harden. Then she smiled, an open friendly smile, as if to assure the others around the table she was only joking. But she knew it had not fooled the young man who had asked the question, as he pushed back his hair and reached inside his jacket for his cigarettes. And she knew equally well that she would be made to pay for it.

'Well now, young lady, thank Tabby for another splendid breakfast,' the Colonel said, dabbing his moustache with a napkin, and pushing his plate, now emptied of its bacon, eggs and mushrooms, from him. 'And that reminds me – I promised Mosley I would send down a flitch of bacon for next weekend. You will see to that, won't you, my dear?'

Bethany nodded and smiled, but the order gave her no pleasure. One of those flitches of bacon hanging curing downstairs could be put to far better use feeding the hungry in their own village than being sent down south to grace the dinner table of Sir Oswald and his high-ranking Fascist friends.

But there would be little chance of convincing the Colonel of that – especially now that his political friends needed cheering up so badly. Things had not being going quite as planned recently for the proud wearers of the new black uniforms. The great British public did not seem quite so enamoured of the Fascist cause as the Grevilles most certainly were, and examples of that divergence of opinion were beginning to happen all too frequently for the Colonel's liking.

The marches that were being arranged in towns and cities around the country were being met with quite fierce resistance, but they were determined to carry on. They would not be deterred in their determination to carry their Fascist banners right into the heartland of working-class Britain. With the workers conquered, it would only be a matter of time before the middle and upper classes followed suit. 'Just think of it, Tabby,' Amos declared in the kitchen a few days before a particularly important rally in Leeds, 'before we know where we are, we could be the new government of this country! Just the new brooms that Britain needs to get back on its feet again!'

The housekeeper's eye glowed as she looked up from her mending. Her little boy in Parliament! She turned to Bethany, who was standing with her back to them, ironing by the side of the range. 'Well, listen to that, Bethany love! Amos here could be just the new broom our country needs!'

Bethany turned just enough to catch Amos Greville's eye and her expression was worse than scathing – it was amused, and that was something she knew her employer's son could not bear. 'So Amos here is to be a new broom, is he? Well, I can't say as I agree he'll be just what our country needs right now. New brooms rake up a lot more dirt than old ones, Tabby dear. We'd be well advised to remember that!' She continued her ironing with a quiet smile on her face. He and his Fascist cohorts were muckrakers, all right. From the Church down there was hardly a section of society that they hadn't tried to drag through the dirt. New broom indeed!

Amos's jaw set in its familiar fashion, and the look that passed over his face gave Bethany a quiet satisfaction. No matter how much he tried to impress, he knew he would not succeed with her, and it was a bitter pill for a proud young man to swallow.

Nothing she said or did, however, could blunt his enthusiasm for his trips to London to serve the Fascist cause. All the Grevilles had made frequent trips to the capital over the past few years. In fact they had been personally involved with Blackshirt business since 1933, when in the autumn of that year the fledgling British Union of Fascists bought the lease on Whitelands Training College in Chelsea and turned it into their own personal headquarters.

'Black House', as it came to be known, was created as an English facsimile of the German Nazi Party's 'Brown House' in Munich. The German arms manufacturer Fritz von Thyssen had supplied the funds to buy the old Barlow Palace on Briennerstrasse to serve as a base for the Nazi 'Brownshirts', and Sir Oswald and the other leading British Fascists felt it was high time there was an English equivalent. The Colonel was one of the first people approached to invest in the proposed project, and Philip Greville proudly brought home copies of the plans to which his money was contributing. Photos of the grandiose Senate Hall, in Hitler's Munich Brown House, were laid out on the dining-room table of Wolf Hall and even Bethany and Tabitha were called upstairs to admire the gigantic horseshoe table, surrounded by its sixty armchairs in red morocco leather, their backs emblazoned with the party eagle.

'Ours will be just as grand as that,' the Colonel told them. 'And it will be money well spent.' The last remark was aimed as much to comfort himself as to impress the others, for he knew that his finances were in no fit state to contribute to any cause other than his own. But these were difficult times, and the time, effort and money he and his family were now spending on his old friend Sir Oswald's new party would be more than paid back in the future. They were laying the foundations for a new and more prosperous Britain and what could be more important than that?

The goings-on at 'Black House' became a common topic of conversation at the dinner table after that, and Amos seemed to be forever attending courses there. He more than shared his father's hopes for a Fascist government, and he was determined that he would make the old man proud of him by rising to the top of the party as soon as possible. To have a Greville at the helm of the New Order in England, as he often referred to it, would be quite something. After several generations of genteel decline, the family was definitely on the up again.

Although not strictly a party member, for the Colonel was unsure how actually signing up for such a para-military organization would affect his army pension, as an honorary member of the BUF he was granted the privilege of a permanent office in 'Black House', alongside the other high officials. But such privileges did not extend to his son. When Amos went down to spend a few days he had to share a dormitory with the other young officers – a situation that did not always please him, for not all, he believed, deserved the honour of a commission, or were worthy of it. 'Riff-raff, some of them,' Bethany heard him complain to his father. 'Barely educated and can't even speak the King's English intelligibly. Should be marching behind that damned Red Flag, not ours!'

He also felt that as the son of one of the stalwarts of the movement, he was entitled to certain privileges, such as the use of his father's room when the Colonel wasn't using it and, like a dog with a particularly juicy bone, this was a problem he continued to gnaw away at. 'I'll be a Colonel myself before long, then there'll be no question of bunking up with such scum as I have to do now,' he told Tabby, and the old lady had not the shadow of a doubt he was speaking the truth. Young Amos had ambition and would go far.

With the magazine *Blackshirt* left constantly lying around the house, and the party the favourite topic of conversation above stairs, the affairs of Black House became almost as familiar to the housekeeper and her young assistant as life at Wolf Hall. And although there was still the estate to run, less and less was heard of the market price of cattle and sheep, or of the merits of the Blue-faced Leicester as opposed to the Hill Cheviot. Husbanding the land was deemed a crashing bore compared to the New Dawn they were witnessing in the history of their country.

Below stairs, they were called upon with increasing frequency to put in a special effort when the Colonel played host to the party bigwigs from time to time. Since his wife's death Philip Greville had done little in the way of social entertaining, but now the silver and best Sèvres dinner plates were pressed back into service for the small groups of black-uniformed men who arrived in their sleek black limousines to spend the weekend.

Amos began to receive more and more invitations to attend special leadership courses being held down in Black House and on his return Bethany would listen with a growing sense of foreboding as he regaled them all with examples of the supreme devotion to the cause demonstrated by those, like himself, who really deserved the honour of officer status and were being singled out for greater glory.

'I can understand why it's Amos who has taken so enthusiastically to Sir Oswald's party,' the housekeeper confided in Bethany one night as they sat over the mending. 'He always did like dressing-up best. I can remember how proud he was when he got his first riding habit in the colours of his father's Hunt . . .'

A mist came to her eyes as the years rolled back and she could see again that little boy sitting proudly astride Zephyr, his favourite pony, in front of the house, his sturdy little figure decked out in hunting grey, the black leather whip clasped tightly in the small fist. 'Yes, he likes to win, does Amos. Whether it's against foxes or folk. He's a stubborn little devil and once he gets his teeth into something he'll cling on to the very end.'

'Something or some*one*.' Bethany could not control her tongue and Tabby looked aggrieved.

'I wish you weren't always so agin the lad, Beth, I swear I do! He likes you, you know. For I've seen him looking at you.' She gave an almost embarrassed half-laugh, as she pulled more wool from the ball tucked into the side of her rocking chair and began another round of the sock she was knitting. 'Oh aye, I'm not that old that I can't recognize when a young man thinks a lass is worth a second glance now and then.'

Bethany made no comment. She knew exactly when Amos Greville was looking at her and the knowledge never failed to bring a cold sick feeling to the pit of her stomach. There was something about those brown eyes and that superior expression of his that chilled her. And it was particularly marked whenever he was in that awful BUF uniform. Somehow that black shirt and jodhpurs, and those long black leather jackboots, seemed to symbolize his character so well. There was something distinctly sinister about Amos Greville and the movement he espoused so enthusiastically. Some might say she was prejudiced, that she still believed him guilty of Sarah-Jane's murder, and that incident had clouded her judgement of him. But there was more to it than that; there *was* something evil in Amos Greville that this Fascist movement seemed actively to encourage, of that she had no doubt.

It was with just such a particularly uncomfortable feeling in the pit of her stomach that one day in October 1936 Bethany stood on the front steps of Wolf Hall, alongside Tabby and Old Carnforth, and watched her employer and his middle son prepare to leave the house for a major Fascist march in London. Thousands of them would be gathering in the nation's capital to take the message right into the heart of the East End. And with the workers of the Empire's greatest city won over, nothing and no one could stop them. Britain would march alongside Germany to capture the world for the Aryan race. The time of the *Übermenschen* would have arrived. The *Untermenschen* – or subhumans – such as Jews, Communists, Socialists and other such scum would be wiped from the face of the earth. Bethany had even seen literature in Amos's room explaining in great detail how this would be done. In fact, it had already started in Germany . . . Yes, there was something distinctly sinister about that black, military-style uniform, she decided. 'Satan's soldiers', her father had once called them, and he had been right.

She seemed to be the only one in Wolf Hall, however, who had such misgivings. 'Doesn't he look smart!' Tabby declared proudly, her eyes fixed on the young man in uniform as the pair made for the waiting black Bentley and they waved goodbye from the front steps. Bethany made no reply. The Colonel she could forgive; he was an old soldier who was relishing the opportunity to be of use to his country again, no matter how misguided, but the type of swaggering young man that Amos typified, who had made those black shirts and jackboots their own, were a different breed entirely. They were out to rule the world – beginning on their own doorstep. The few political meetings she had attended locally in the run-up to the election last year had almost always ended in a fight with other local youths if there had been Fascist supporters present. It was not an uncommon occurrence for Amos to come back from a political meeting nursing bruised knuckles, if not bruised pride.

On the morning of Saturday, 10 October 1936, however, such ill-mannered opposition was the last thing on their minds as they took their leave of The Hall for the streets of the nation's capital.

'Yes, I've not seen the Colonel so excited about anything in a long time,' Tabby continued fondly. 'And who could have failed to vote for him in any election, when he cares so much for the country and talks such sense into the bargain?'

Bethany could have added, 'My father for one.' But she didn't. She merely smiled quietly to herself as she thought of the difficulty Cheevers Baine had in retaining a dignified and non-blasphemous tongue when he talked of the Colonel and the cause he and his son had espoused. 'I'm no man of violence,' her father had declared on her last visit. 'But I have a hard job keeping control of myself at the sight of that swastika, I can tell you! They have taken the cross of Christ and made a travesty out of it. They have made it into the devil's emblem. Soldiers of the devil, that's what they are – soldiers of the devil, the lot of them!'

And she wasn't at all surprised that, once they arrived in London, the pair from Utherdale found that there were plenty of other people who felt that way too. Thousands had built barricades and thronged the streets of the capital in an effort to halt the march and there followed the biggest riot that London had seen for years.

Flagstones were ripped up and used as barricades along with anything else that came to hand as the citizens of the East End showed just what they thought of the men in black shirts who hoped to rule the world.

Sir Oswald Mosley's supporters were very soon both routed and humiliated, and it was a decidedly subdued Colonel Greville who returned to Yorkshire on the Monday morning, along with his son.

Amos had had his black shirt ruined by the contents of a flying paint pot, and was the not-so-proud possessor of a badly swollen left eye that was just beginning to turn from a livid red to a lurid black and yellow. He requested that Bethany be sent to his room to bathe it for him, but she had begged Tabby to go herself. 'I don't know anything about tending injuries,' she implored. 'Please, Tabby, you go.'

The housekeeper had looked at her over her glasses, with one eyebrow raised. 'You just won't give Master Amos a chance, will you, my girl?' she said, but took the matter no further.

A bond had been built up between the young girl and the old woman, during Bethany's first years at The Hall – a bond that was proving to be in many ways as close a one as she had with her own mother. She found she was learning much, both in the running of a large house and in personal etiquette, from the brusque elderly woman who had once been in love with her own grandfather.

Bethany had no doubt of that now, for Tabby took every opportunity to talk of Harrison Hetherington and those golden days before the death of the old Queen Victoria, and the glow that came into her faded eyes brought just a hint of the young woman who had had to watch from the sidelines all those years ago as the love of her life was claimed by another.

The fact that Harrison Hetherington and his new wife Edith chose to remain in Utherdale for the rest of their lives proved a bitter-sweet decision for the young Tabitha Fleetwood as she made her own life as an employee of the then young and dashing Major Philip Greville and his wife at Wolf Hall. She had watched with an almost unbearable ache in her heart as Edith became pregnant with Betty, their first and only child, and had wished with all her heart she could have been the one to present the handsome young preacher with a daughter. And a quarter of a century later, she remembered hearing from the now widowed Edith's own lips that she had been given the gift of a granddaughter, who was to be named Bethany.

Bethany knew that Tabby now looked upon her as the granddaughter she might have had if Fate and her beloved Harrison had smiled more kindly on her than on her own grandmother, Edith. But Tabby had always been a firm believer that it was never too late for anything, and now she had her true love's granddaughter under her roof she was keen to add the final polish to an upbringing that in itself had already been rather more refined than that of most children in the dale.

Conscious of her position as the Reverend Hetherington's only child, Bethany's mother Betty had been a stickler for correct manners and polite speech and behaviour, but the poverty of the Baine household had offered little chance for the practice of the finer points of etiquette or gracious living.

This was a fact of life Tabitha Fleetwood sought to do her best to remedy. Within months of her arrival, Bethany's speech had been polished, along with her manners; she had also been well advised on the inadvisability of speaking her mind to such a degree, and she had learnt most of the rudiments of the management of a large house like Wolf Hall. And there was much to learn. Even the ordering, storing and cooking of the food was a revelation in itself, for most of the ingredients that went into the Greville diet were totally new to her. Her mother's purse would never have stretched to a fraction of the fare that they seemed to take for granted at Wolf Hall, but within a very short time Bethany was not only learning new expressions, such as cheese soufflés, beef consommé and fruit fools, but she was more than capable of both cooking and serving them.

She was also learning far more about the world outside the confines of The Hall, and it was proving a revelation. Old newspapers and magazines, when finished with above stairs, were devoured in the sanctuary of her bedroom, once the chores of the day were behind her. She read with relish the scandals of the rich and famous, and of the glamorous lives of her favourite film stars, such as Douglas Fairbanks and Mary Pickford, and the wickedly dashing Clark Gable, whose dark good looks reminded her uncannily of Jack Greville. And, along with the rest of the world, she also read with increasing disbelief of the notorious love affair taking place between their future king, the Prince of Wales, and the American divorcee Wallis Simpson.

The small attic bedroom, hidden in the eaves of the great house, became her own private world, where she could create and live out her fantasies in complete privacy, and it had been there, almost one year ago, on one rainy Monday at the end of January 1936, that she at last become a woman. That day would be forever engraved in her memory, for it was when she crept downstairs at midnight to tell Tabby that something awful had happened – she had discovered the most terrible bloodstains on her nightdress and bedsheet, and she must surely be dying – when all thoughts of her impending death were banished from her mind. Another momentous event had just taken place, and because of it the housekeeper was sitting in her usual place by the side of the range, with tears running freely down her face.

She hurried to her old friend's side. It was the first time she had witnessed such a thing. 'Whatever's the matter, Tabby dear? Is something wrong?'

'It is, child.' The housekeeper dabbed her eyes, beneath the wire-rimmed spectacles; her handkerchief was a damp ball in the palm of her hand. 'The Master has been listening to the news on the wireless this evening and he just told me when I took up his last bite of supper, not five minutes since.'

'Told you what?'

'The King's dead. God rest his soul.'

Bethany was taken aback. Surely she couldn't be crying for an old man down in London whom she didn't even really know? But she was, and Bethany's heart went out to the old woman, who seemed to have spent her entire life adoring men who belonged to other women, be they King or commoner. She placed a hand on the housekeeper's shoulder. 'I'm sure the Prince of Wales will make a fine King,' she said softly, and Tabby nodded and snuffled once more as she stuffed her handkerchief into her apron pocket. 'I'm sure you're right, my dear. But I did so much admire his father – the Sailor King we called him when he was young. It seems like the end of an era somehow.'

So King George V passed away into the pages of the history books; his son, the popular playboy Prince of Wales, was declared the new King Edward VIII, and the world waited and wondered what would become of the little-known American woman who seemed to be constantly at his side these days.

And that evening became engraved on Bethany's memory, not only because it saw the end of a royal era, but because Tabby, in her own brusque, no-nonsense way, assured her that she certainly was not going to die, and the bright-red bloodstains that so alarmed her were not an indication of impending doom, but evidence that she had at last joined the ranks of womanhood.

'You have to be very careful from now on, my girl. And keep well away from the opposite sex. You let any of those village lads near you and you'll live to regret it. They have places they put young girls who get too familiar with men and get in the family way. Remember Madge Capstick.'

Bethany had stared at her in mounting alarm. Her friend Ellen's older sister had suddenly disappeared from the village the previous year. Having a baby they said she was – an illegitimate baby – and they had locked her up in Briar's Bridge, the local mental hospital, over by Hawes. Suddenly becoming a woman was quite an alarming thought. Just how exactly did one get an illegitimate baby? Just how did you get any baby, come to that? She was dying to ask, but daren't. The look on Tabby's face told her the subject wasn't really one for decent discussion, and no doubt she would find out in due course. After all, everyone had to, didn't they?

Things happened quickly after that, things that both disturbed and excited her. All her life she had hated her shape – the skinniness of her arms and legs, the thin white body that up till now had seemed to be more like that of a young boy than a fifteen-year-old girl. Shoulderblades that stuck up like chapel hat pegs, she had had, so her mother had once commented. But no more. The monthly 'curse', as Tabby termed it, brought with it rapid changes in her appearance. Within months her breasts and hips had rounded into soft womanly contours that brought both stares and increasingly embarrassing remarks from Amos Greville as she went about her domestic tasks. Ned's coy smiles and squeezes she could cope with, and even Amos's crude jokes she could handle – giving as good as she took verbally was always one of her strong points, despite Tabby's entreaties to bite her tongue on occasions – but what she found increasingly difficult to put up with were the other aspects of Amos's behaviour, which were beginning to get out of hand.

As the months went by, it became more and more difficult to avoid his stares and vulgar innuendo. He seemed to have two main interests in life: riding to the hounds and tormenting the life out of her. He even took to using the narrow back stairs to waylay her as she went up and down in pursuit of her usual household tasks. He would deliberately wait until she was halfway up or down and then come squeezing past, pressing his body against hers until she was so firmly squashed against the stone wall that she would be forced to cry out in pain. At such moments she could smell the whisky on his breath and would wonder if his father knew about the insatiable taste for strong liquor his son was developing.

After such encounters she would be on edge for the rest

of the day and Tabby would look at her intently as she went about her business. She was sure the housekeeper suspected something was wrong, but was deliberately playing the ostrich, and she herself did not dare mention it, for she knew that no matter how fond Tabby was of her, the old lady's first and last loyalties lay with the Colonel and his three sons. She had helped bring each one into the world and regarded the young men as the closest she would ever get to children of her own.

'Their own mother couldn't have thought more of those three lads,' she would say. 'And I'm just sorry she's not here to share my pleasure in seeing them all turn into such fine young men.'

Then she would shake her head as she thought of Ned. 'Poor lad, I doubt there'll be no betterment there, and it's such a pity that he'll never ride to the hounds like his father and brothers.' Tabby's eyes always gleamed with a special pride whenever she beheld her beloved young men dressed for the kill, on their favourite hunters.

For her part, Bethany was decidedly unimpressed. To her mind there was something faintly ridiculous about a posse of grown men dressing up to gallop after such a small creature as a fox. The sound of those baying hounds never failed to send a shudder through her, and she studiously avoided the kennels at the back of the house where the pack was kept in eager readiness for their next outing.

Alone among the others in the family, Amos even kept a trophy case in his room, containing several dozen foxes' tails, or 'my prize brushes', as he referred to them. Bethany would close her eyes as she ran the obligatory duster over the glass top of the case each morning. Some still had the dried blood visible on them, where they had been hacked off the dying animal to have the still-warm blood daubed on the cheeks of any 'virgin' hunter who happened to be present.

'There's nothing like the thrill of your first kill,' Amos once told her as he came in and saw her rub her duster across the top of the case. 'Anyone who hasn't been baptized with one of those brushes in there hasn't lived!'

Yes, the Hunt was all to Amos Greville. But what disturbed Bethany was not that he enjoyed the sport, for many fine, decent people in the neighbourhood did just that; no, it was the way his eyes would gleam and he would take such obvious pleasure in recounting the individual kills to anyone who would care to listen, on his return home. Foxes were vermin, or so all the farmers round here said, but the thought that anyone should take such undisguised delight in the hunting down of any creature to the point of exhaustion, then killing it, seemed to symbolize for her an aspect of Amos Greville's character that made her most uncomfortable in his presence. There was an underlying cruelty there – a certain harshness and uncompromising attitude to life that she had never encountered at such close quarters before. It was obvious in the way he both talked and acted, and that Amos loved to do a lot of both was made obvious from a very early stage.

On her occasional visits home Bethany sometimes recounted to her mother examples of Amos's deliberate cruelty, which often took the form of particularly cutting remarks aimed at his younger brother Ned, and Betty Baine listened with sympathy and growing unease. It did not come as a complete surprise, however, for it was said in the village that the Colonel's middle son was the spit of his great-grandfather in both looks and character. She remembered her own mother telling her of how Sir Harcourt Greville, survivor of Balaclava and part-time explorer when his soldiering days were done, was said to have whipped a pet dog to death in front of the servants when it failed to obey an order. 'You must learn to take your employers as you find them, Bethany love. It's not for the likes of us to sit in judgement on the ways of others,' Betty Baine would tell her daughter, with a resigned sigh.

But such a reaction did not satisfy the young girl, who wished fervently that Jack had never taken himself off to Australia, for she was sure Amos would not be half so cocky if his elder brother were still around. The boomerang she had been sent still had pride of place above the small cast-iron grate in her bedroom, but she had never told the Colonel or either of his other two sons of its existence, and they were never likely to know, for they never set foot in the attics . . .

Or did they? More than once recently she was sure she had heard the treads of the narrow wooden staircase that led up to her room creak shortly after she had gone to bed, but she had always been too afraid to investigate. The Hall was known to be haunted and she never could make up her mind if she would prefer to find Amos Greville or the ghost itself on the outside of her door if she opened it.

Her fears came to a head one Thursday in November, just after midnight. She had been late in getting to bed, for there had been a local election that day, with the Colonel standing as the Independent candidate for the local council, and Amos testing the water as a Fascist. Word had it that if Philip Greville hadn't been so shamed by his own performance in the past General Election he would have stood as the Fascist candidate himself. But trying your luck for the national parliament was one thing, bringing it down to local level and risking your own safe seat was quite another, so he put his son in to carry the black banner for him. It was a sound move. Amos was heavily defeated, with a mere twelve votes cast in his direction.

'I didn't know he had that many friends in the dale,' Cheevers Baine had commented wryly to his daughter as he walked her back part of the way to The Hall just after the count had been announced at ten o'clock. The Colonel was declared the winner once more, with a much reduced majority. But if his pride was wounded by the fall in his support, Bethany knew that Amos's pride would have taken even more of a dent. For a Greville to come bottom of the list in any count was humiliation indeed.

It had been an exciting evening. She was not normally allowed out of The Hall after tea on a weekday, but elections were special events, and, more importantly, the Colonel liked to have as many supporters as he could rally around him when the result was declared. It never seemed to dawn on him that not all his paid help hoped he would win, but that was the measure of the Grevilles, Bethany told herself – they truly believed themselves to be leaders of the community by divine right.

Several of her old schoolfriends had been there and she had listened in amazement as Nancy Turver, who had walked over from Butterslack for the event, commented on how handsome Amos looked in his black uniform. 'I know I hate the Grevilles and all that for what they did to my Dad,' she confided to Bethany, as they stood at the side of the village hall watching the candidates wait on stage for the results to be declared, 'but I always did think he were the best-looking of the lot of 'em.'

Bethany had looked at her friend in disbelief. Amos Greville, of the cocky manner and sly grin, good-looking? 'I reckon I'd rather go out with Adolf Hitler himself than that poor imitation!' she declared. 'All Amos Greville needs is that ridiculous little moustache and he'd be the dead spit!' And it was almost true, for along with the uniform, Amos had taken to wearing his dark hair cut short and brushed forward in the manner of the German Chancellor.

'Ssshhh – they're about to declare!'

And both girls tiptoed and jumped up with the rest of the crowd to try to get a better look as Henry Sutcliffe, now retired from the police force, stood up in the middle of the platform to announce Utherdale's choice for the North Riding County Council.

No one really doubted the Colonel would be returned, but it was exciting stuff nevertheless, and Bethany's mind was still ringing with the cheers of the crowd as the results were declared long after she had returned to her remaining chores back at The Hall later that evening.

She was in the kitchen having a late-night mug of cocoa with Tabby by the time the family all finally turned in for the night and she was told she was free to go to bed. 'But be a dear, Bethany love, and sit these riding boots outside Master Amos's door, will you? They came back from the cobbler's today, and I know he'll want them first thing in the morning.'

'I'll be glad to.' Bethany could see Tabby was all in, and was glad to save her the weary climb up the stairs so late at night. She bent over and patted the old woman on the shoulder, before lighting her candle for the even steeper climb to her own room in the attic. The gas lighting that lit the rest of the house did not extend to the upper reaches where she slept.

The house seemed deathly quiet and the longcase clock in the main hall struck a single chime for half-past midnight as she passed it and made her way up the curved staircase to the first floor where the family slept. The sound of snoring could already be heard from behind the Colonel's closed door, and as she reached Amos's room she noticed its door had not been properly closed. She bent down to place the boots neatly outside, then momentarily froze in that position. She could hear him talking. Was there someone else in there with him?

Slowly she straightened up and moved closer to the open crack. It was barely three inches wide, but there was space enough to give a good view of the fireplace. He had switched off the gas lights but the room was well lit by the fire of oak logs that still burned brightly in the grate. Amos himself was kneeling in front of it, with his back to her, and he appeared to be casting something into the flames. Whatever it was, it caused the fire to flame up and crackle even more, and then, as she watched, he slowly moved back from it on his knees, and raised his hands in an imploring gesture towards the ceiling.

She could feel the very hair on the back of her neck stiffen and gooseflesh cover the skin of her arms as his voice rose in the silence of the night: 'Come forth, O Great One of the black night of the soul and make thy presence felt by this your craven servant. Grant me the power manifest in you to call forth the messenger and granter of all desires so I may possess the object of this carnal lust which possesses me.

'Io Pan! Io Pan! I am a man: do as thou wilt, as a great god can. Io Pan! Io Pan! Hear thou the Voice of Fire! I am thy man, flesh to thy bone, steel to thy rod. And I rave, and I rape, I rip and I rend, everlasting, world without end. Io Pan! Io Pan! I offer you my symbols of worship; these I have laid at your feet, and I have cast my offerings into the eternal flame. I crave by the Great God Pan I am granted my vision so it shall become reality, and that you and your messengers of darkness may go forth into the night and claim the mind that refuses to submit. My loins are aflame with desire, my manhood aroused and a-ready. In the name of and by the flames of the Great Lucifer, the bearer of light and the living flame of burning desire, grant me this wish . . . Shemhamforash! Hail Satan!'

Bethany stood frozen with horror. Hail Satan! And those words . . . Io Pan . . . Io Pan . . . They were the same words she had first heard all those years ago at the Fire of Beltane. It was the same type of devilish worship she had witnessed then she was witnessing now.

Then, before her horrified gaze, he prostrated himself full length before the fire and lay there beating his fists into the thick pile of the rug, the lower half of his body undulating in a rhythmic, thrusting fashion in time to the groans that were being emitted from his lips.

She was not sure exactly what type of devilish incantation she was witnessing, but whatever was happening in there, it was certainly evil. Of that she had no doubt. And somehow it was all mixed up with sex. Ever since that drunken night of fire and death on the crag, somehow she had felt sex to be one of the motivating forces: sex and power; power and sex. They were perhaps the two most powerful forces known to man, and the two things those such as Amos Greville desired more than any others.

Out of the corner of her eye, she could just make out the outline of the black Fascist uniform hanging on the outside of the wardrobe door, and her eyes moved from it to the groaning, thrashing man on the floor in front of the fire. A Soldier of Satan indeed, for tonight, in this very house, she had heard the devil called upon. There was evil here this night. She could feel it in the air she breathed.

'BETHANY . . . !'

The loud groaning of her name made her jump back in shock and sheer terror, until she realized he had no idea she was there.

Then he began to sob – great heartrending sobs that seemed to shudder up through him and reverberate throughout the silence of the sleeping house, as his still prostrate figure writhed on the rug, as if wrestling with some intangible force.

She remained transfixed for several seconds – a frightened rabbit caught by the light – as her eyes remained riveted on the scene being enacted on the rug in front of the glowing fire. A mixture of panic and fascination held her rooted to the spot. He was invoking the devil in there and it had something to do with her. The power and sex he so craved – she was the object of that craving. He was calling on the devil to gain control of her! She went cold, then a sweat broke from every pore of her body.

Then, blindly, she turned and began to run.

The sudden motion blew her candle out and she continued running and half-stumbling through the darkness until she came to the narrow staircase that led up to her own attic room.

She was out of breath and physically shaking by the time she reached her bedroom door and for the first time since arriving as a servant at The Hall, she disobeyed orders and locked the door behind her. The old iron key creaked in the lock, then juddered into position.

Almost too tired to stand a moment longer, she staggered back to her bed and sank down on to the hard mattress. She lay there staring through the darkness at the closed door for several minutes, then just as she was about to take off her clothes, she sat up with a start.

There was a definite creak on one of the treads halfway up the stairs. She held her breath, feeling she would surely die of fright.

There it was again!

She recognized where it had come from. It was the third step from the top! She could feel her heart pounding painfully in her breast and she knew there was someone outside her door. And it could only be one person. It had to be him. Dear God, let him go away, she prayed. Please make him go away. Don't let him touch the door handle! Don't let the door handle move!

But it did. Before her very eyes, in the pale moonlight of the small room, she saw the cast-iron handle begin to bend slowly downwards. The scream she let out seemed to reverberate round the walls. She sat there petrified for several minutes, her terrified shriek still ringing in her ears. She hardly dared to breathe as she strained her ears, her eyes glued to the door. How long she sat there she was not quite sure. It seemed for ever, but was probably no more than a few minutes. But there were no more strange sounds or movements, and only when she was totally convinced it was safe to do so, did she finally remove her clothes and slip beneath the blankets.

Sleep took a long time to come that night, for in her head she could still hear the words that had been intoned in that room down below, and she knew that never again would she feel truly safe in this house. And in her dreams Amos Greville and his hero Adolf Hitler became as one, and as one they became the Devil Incarnate. Fingers, long and white, stroked the fur-covered neck of a helpless rabbit, then in turn the fur dissolved into the smooth pale skin of a young woman. And those long white fingers encircled the neck of that young woman and squeezed and squeezed. And the rabbit's scream became as one with the scream of the young woman, and both became mingled with her own scream until, just before dawn, she awoke still screaming and bathed in the cold sweat of fear.

Still half-asleep, she stumbled from her bed to the window and threw it open to breathe the fresh pure air of the night. A pale moon was gleaming in the dark heavens above Uther Crag, bathing the countryside below in its pewter glow. And she thought of the sleeping people down there, and of the generations who had gone before. Amos Greville was not the first to evoke the powers of darkness in this place and he would not be the last. It was true they had held no more Fires of Beltane since Sarah-Jane's death several years ago, but that did not stop the worship of the old gods. Their power was still as potent in this place as ever it was, of that she had no doubt. Christianity, even in the hands of such dedicated men as her own grandfather or the Reverend Barden, could not rid the hearts and minds of these people of their ancient inheritance. Their gods were as old as time itself, as old and cruel as this land that bore them, and in which they would be buried as their ancestors before them. Ashes to ashes, dust to dust.

She shivered in the cold draught and closed the

window, then made her way slowly back to bed to say the Lord's Prayer with more feeling than ever in her life before.

Chapter Eight

Bethany rose at six to face her usual morning chores in a state of near exhaustion. She longed to tell Tabby about her experiences of the previous night but dared not. Who would believe her anyway? Certainly not the old woman who regarded the Greville sons as her own kith and kin. So she kept her fears to herself as she set about her usual tasks, trying hard to put the evils of the night behind her.

Try as she might, however, in her round of grate cleaning and fire lighting, she could not face going into Amos's room first thing, so she asked Old Carnforth if he would do her a special favour by seeing to that particular fire. He had looked at her knowingly for a moment, then given an understanding nod of the head. The old man knew more and saw more than almost anyone in the household, but had had over fifty years of keeping his counsel. 'I reckon I can do that for you, lass,' was all he said, as he picked up the ashcan and brush and set off up the stairs.

Once breakfast was over, it being the end of the week, the next task was the topping and tailing of the beds in the Colonel's and the two other occupied bedrooms on the first floor. This time there could be no getting out of doing Amos's room, but Bethany waited till she heard the sound of horses' hooves outside the window, heading for the morning gallop on the moor, before she set to.

Thanks to Carnforth, the fire was already crackling merrily in the grate when she opened the bedroom door and in the clear light of day it was hard to imagine the happenings of the night before had actually taken place in such normal surroundings.

As she walked over to the bed to make a start, she noticed what she took to be a ball of paper left over from the old man's fire lighting lying inside the hearth. Rather than give Amos any excuse for accusing her of untidiness, she went over and bent down to pick it up, only to discover it was, in fact, not paper at all, but the white ball of a pocket handkerchief that lay by the side of the brass fender.

She knelt down to pick it up for depositing among the dirty linen, then stared in amazement at what she found in her hand. In the centre of the linen square was a thick ball of dark-auburn hair. Her hair. It had to be her hair, for no one else had hair anything like it in the house. But unlike her own hair, it felt as if it had been dipped or sprayed with something, for it was distinctly tacky to the touch.

A peculiar feeling came over her as she stood gazing at the curious bundle. He must have collected it from her room. But not just the once. He must have gone into her room and taken it from her hairbrush over quite a considerable period, judging from the amount of it here. 'Oh, my God!' Not only was the idea of him being in her room abhorrent, but the very fact that he should do such a thing made her feel physically sick.

As if it were contaminated, she picked it up and tossed the bundle into the flames of the fire. For a fleeting second it hissed, then crackled and blazed and was no more. And a sudden thought ran through her. Was this what he was throwing on to the fire as he chanted those devilish words on this very rug last night? Was it strands of her own hair that were going up in flames as she watched transfixed from the doorway? Was this all part of that loathsome ritual that his sick mind had conjured up because of this fixation he seemed to have for her? The thought appalled her.

It was no secret that black-magic rituals were still carried out in some parts of the countryside around here, and not just by the poor and ignorant and those who did not know any better. There were tales of the gentry being involved as well, with some very strange goings-on at weekend house parties in the district over the years. But this was different. This was one person directing his evil intentions at another. At her. The horror she had witnessed during the night came back to haunt her and she wanted to turn and flee as far away from this place as possible. But who would believe her? She could scarcely believe it herself.

Numbed by the awfulness of it all, she turned to direct her thoughts to the job in hand, and began stripping the bed with even more vigour than usual. She had her back to the bedroom door and had almost finished smoothing the gold satin coverlet into place several minutes later when she heard a soft click behind her.

Her breath caught in her throat. Someone had come in and had closed the door behind them. She froze as she bent over the bed, her hands in the act of smoothing the creases out of the shiny material.

'Amos, is that you?' She could scarcely get the words out; her throat and mouth had gone quite dry.

There was no reply.

In three bounds he was across the Persian rug and had swung her round, to pin her against the side of the mattress. This time his courage did not fail him. Unlike last night, there was no locked door here to thwart his desire. He was on his own patch and was king of all he surveyed. And what was more, he had more than mere human strength on his side. Courage surged through him, fanning the desire that had become an almost uncontrollable passion over these past few months. 'You've been avoiding me, haven't you, Miss High-and-Mighty?' His dark eyes were gleaming and his breath was hot on her face and smelt of whisky.

166

'I — I don't know what you're on about, Amos Greville, I swear I don't!'

He had her gripped by the shoulders now as his eyes bore down into hers. His voice was huskily low and accusatory. 'Yes, you do! You've been avoiding me all right, you little bitch. Deliberately driving me crazy for months. You've enjoyed seeing me stare, haven't you? I know all about the likes of you — forever on the tease. You've been egging me on, haven't you? Been asking for me to do something about it, for long enough.'

He could feel the excitement rising in him just to be touching her again, to feel his body against hers, to feel her breath against his face, and see the flush come to her cheeks as his eyes locked with hers. Inside that stubborn exterior she must be just as excited as he was. He was certain of it.

Bethany shook her head so violently that her cap came loose and he ripped it from her head, bringing her hair tumbling out of its loose knot. The sight of it falling freely about her shoulders seemed to excite him even more and she could see perspiration break out on the skin of his face, and felt his breathing become more rapid as he pressed himself against her.

'Come here . . . Come closer . . . Relax, will you . . . ?'

He was moving against her, willing her to melt, not to make it too hard for him. But the body trapped against his own remained rigid. If he tried coaxing she might respond quicker, he decided. Some of them preferred the softer approach. His right hand moved up and found her cheek. It felt soft to his touch and his other hand found the back of her neck, tangling itself in her hair.

She winced. 'You're hurting me! Let me go, please!'

'No chance!' His body was taking over now, urging him to hurry, to forget the gentle approach. He had waited months for this moment. 'You bitch . . . You little bitch . . .' She must know what she had been doing to him. But

167

they were all the same. Loved the power, they did. Loved to have men panting after them. Bitches on heat, that's what they were. Bitches on heat. His mouth found hers. It was just as soft as he had imagined. Soft and pliable. He was panting now as he pressed her lips apart, his tongue thrusting down her throat, so far that she found herself gagging as she struggled to break free.

The tussle served only to heighten his excitement. This is what he had been visualizing all morning as he sat in the stable with his bottle of Scotch. His father had gone out for his usual morning ride over the moors, but he had excused himself – had said he wasn't too happy about his own gelding's fetlock. If only he knew . . . If only anyone knew the agony he had been going through, or how close he had come last night to breaking into her room.

She gasped for breath. 'Please, Amos, no . . . !'

His mouth silenced her once more. They all protested at first, it was part of the fun. How many times had he lain in bed at boarding school and listened to friends tell of their conquests of serving maids in their households? How he had envied them! All he had had in his own home was an elderly old crone! Until he had left school, that was. And no one had been more surprised than himself at the gradual transformation over the past few years of that scrawny little kid into this desirable young woman he now held in his arms. Heaven knows what she was struggling so hard for, for none of the females at any of the house parties he attended ever put up so much resistance. Quite the contrary! And if the truth be told, none of them excited him half as much as this struggling, common little bitch. 'Hold still, damn you!'

But Bethany would not hold still. With one almighty tug she wrenched herself free, only to be grabbed by the wrist and swung back against the side of the bed. For a moment they stood staring at one another, both faces flushed, both chests heaving as they panted for breath.

'I've waited for this moment for so long, so very, very long . . . You're not going to deny me now, Bethany Baine. You want it just as much as I do. I know you do.'

She shook her head vigorously, pushing her hair back from her eyes as they locked with his and she implored him. 'No, Amos. Please. Please let me go . . . I don't know what you want of me, honest I don't.'

To her shame she was almost crying now. The situation was way beyond her control. What was he trying to do? What was he trying to tell her? Did he love her? Was that it? Was that what was behind all that mumbo-jumbo last night? If so, it was a funny way of showing it. All those strange goings-on . . . That bundle of hair . . . This attack . . . It was all quite beyond her. 'Maybe we can talk,' she pleaded.

He shook his head. There was nothing to talk about. He wanted her, more than he had wanted anything in his entire life. And he was going to have her. It was not love, for he had no desire to get to know her better – to talk to her, as she so pathetically begged. It was pure unadulterated lust. It was consuming him, scorching his loins, bringing the skin of his body out in a positive lather of sweat, making his very breath come in panting gasps that robbed him of his voice as he shook his head and grunted an unintelligible reply.

Then, before she knew it, he had grabbed her under the arms and behind the knees and hoisted her on to the newly smoothed cover of the bed.

The leap he made on top of her completely winded her for several seconds and she was aware, quite ludicrously, of thinking of the mess his muddy riding boots must be making of the satin cover as he lay on top of her, his face buried in the tangle of hair over her left shoulder.

Then, as he began to raise himself to gaze down at her, she opened her mouth to scream. His reaction was immediate as he pressed one hand over her open mouth and reached across to his bedside table with the other. 'One cheep out of you and you'll get this!' he said, brandishing his hunting knife in her face. The shiny steel blade glinted above the ebony handle. 'Just lie back and enjoy it, girl – so many have!'

Then his voice softened and became more intimate, more caressing in its tone, as he let the knife fall. 'Just close your eyes and enjoy it . . . It's what we're made for, after all. It happens all the time between young men and women like us. Just lie back and enjoy it . . .'

She was barely aware of what happened next, for she was not quite sure exactly what she was supposed to lie back and enjoy. His hands seemed to be all over her as he fumbled and struggled first with her clothing and then with his own. Then suddenly and quite violently a pain seared through her. Pain such as she had never experienced before. She drew in her breath in a half-strangled gasp, then felt a silencing hand cover her open mouth to muffle the long, prolonged scream of anguish that left her lips.

She kept her eyes tightly closed as the touch of his fingers on the skin of her throat sent shock waves through her every bit as great as those taking place below her waist. Beneath her closed eyelids the face of Sarah-Jane Youdell was merging with that of the dying rabbit as Amos Greville's long, lean fingers caressed their throats, just as he was caressing hers now. He had killed that innocent rabbit just as he had killed that innocent girl. Slowly, caressingly, with the tips of his fingers. Her nightmare had become a reality. Dear God, save her! I'm going to die! The conviction screamed through her brain. I'm going to die, and he will dispose of my body and no one will ever know. And if anyone suspects him there will be a cover-up just as there was over Sarah-Jane's death.

Tears sprang to her eyes beneath the tightly shut lids, and oozed out, hot and bitter, between the lashes. She could feel the sobs shuddering through her as her body was used as he would use any other animal. These past few months he had known the thrill of the hunt as he toyed with her, cornering her in dark passages and on the back stairs, and now he was in at the kill and enjoying every minute of it.

When it was all over, he grunted and half-collapsed on her, his panting mouth tasting the salt of the tears that streamed down her cheeks. The fact that she was crying seemed to bemuse him for a moment. 'That wasn't so bad now, girl, was it?' he asked, pulling himself up to look down on her. 'Tell the truth now, you really quite enjoyed it. All women do.'

She gazed up at him through her tears. The only enjoyment she felt was in the relief that it now seemed to be all over, and, unlike poor Sarah-Jane Youdell, she was still alive to tell the tale.

She avoided his eyes as he rose unsteadily from the bed a few minutes later. He continued to gaze down at her as he pulled up his trousers and fastened the broad leather belt around his waist. Looking down at her lying there spreadeagled and motionless, he had an almost uncontrollable urge to start all over again. She looked more desirable than ever in her state of *déshabillé*, her skin flushed and glowing, and her long hair spread out on the pillow behind her head like a radiant auburn halo.

But common sense prevailed. What if he was not up to it again quite so soon? Far better to go out on a winner first time round. Yes, far better to expend his surplus energy this morning on his second favourite occupation. He would head for the stables where his best hunter was still waiting for its morning's exercise. 'You're quite a filly, young Miss Baine, do you know that? Quite a filly!'

Bethany guessed where he would be making for after he left her and she waited in his room until she heard the canter of his horse's hooves across the yard beneath the window before she rose from the dishevelled bed to watch horse and rider disappear out of the gates in the direction of the moor.

She did not bother to smooth the crumpled satin of the bedspread, but left it there, in its stained and wrinkled glory, a mute testimony to the sin that had just occurred in this place. And sin it was, she had no doubt about that. Ignorant though she might be on matters of the flesh, she had no doubt in her mind that what had just occurred this cold November morning was what was known as rape. And whatever devilish practices Amos Greville was up to last night, what he had perpetrated on her body this morning was as great a sin as a man could inflict on a woman. Only poor Sarah-Jane had suffered worse at his hands.

The only person to witness her flight from the room was Neddy, who was standing just inside the door of his own room as she emerged, still dishevelled and distraught, several minutes later. He had a most peculiar look on his face as his eyes met hers for a fleeting second before she continued on her way along the corridor and down the main staircase, heading for the front door. Had he heard anything of what had just occurred? The question passed through her head for a moment and then she dismissed it. She neither knew nor cared; all she was concerned about was to put as much distance between herself and this place as possible.

It took her less than half an hour to run the two miles down the long drive and along the road that separated her old home in The Row from Wolf Hall. She was aware of passing several people on the way and of them looking curiously at the flying figure in the housemaid's uniform, with the tousled hair and ripped blouse. But she did not care who saw her or what they thought; her only thought was to get home. As far as she was concerned, if she had experienced hell in Wolf Hall this morning, then Amos

Greville was the devil incarnate who had inflicted it upon her, and there was no way she would ever go back and risk a second dose.

It was a dark, dank, drizzly morning and barely daylight, although she knew it must be just after nine o'clock when, red-faced and perspiring, she turned into The Row. She had heard the bell ringing in the school playground as she passed and had caught a glimpse of Libby at the tail-end of the girls' line. She knew her two brothers would be there somewhere too, in the long, straggling column of scruffy urchins who waited reluctantly for their turn to file in to the two-roomed schoolhouse.

She was relieved there would be only her mother and little Sam at home. The boys and Libby would ask too many questions. What she had just gone through at Amos Greville's hands was an experience that had left her both shamed and confused, but with every step she became more determined that nothing on earth would possess her to go back to work at that place. The thought of having to endure a repeat performance horrified her. She could not believe that painful degrading act had any connection at all to what men and women did when they were in love and getting married.

With every step she took she could still feel the pain of what had just occurred and the shame of it was almost more than she could bear. Could she bring herself to confess to her mother what had happened? Colour stung her cheeks, already flushed from her flight, at the thought. The nearer she got to her old home, the more unthinkable such a confession seemed to become. She would have to hurry and make up her mind for she was almost there.

But wait . . .

There was a crowd gathered on the pavement outside their front door. She recognized several of the men – Will Dearden, who worked alongside her father, and Joe Capstick, the blacksmith, were there, along with one or

173

two others she recognized from the dressing shed. They were huddled together, talking quietly among themselves, their faces grave. She paused at the end of the road and took stock, her own predicament suddenly pushed from the forefront of her mind.

Automatically one hand went up to smooth her hair, and the other tucked the ripped shred of cotton blouse back behind the white bib of her apron. This was the last thing she had expected. The quarry had begun work ages ago. What on earth were they all standing around there like that for at this time of day? And with such long faces!

Slowly she began to walk towards them, then just as she reached the Turvers' old front door, Dr Munro came out of their own house three doors down. She recognized him immediately, the tall, bent figure in the black coat, black homburg hat, carrying his brown Gladstone bag. He had been a familiar sight around the village for the past generation. After a cursory nod to the men gathered on the pavement, he turned to set off in the direction of his surgery.

'Doctor — wait!' She waved a restraining hand and began to run towards him, and recognizing her as one of the family he had just attended, the old Scotsman paused, then came to meet her.

His face was grave. 'Bethany, isn't it?' He had almost failed to recognize the Baines' eldest child, for she was quite a young woman now.

'What's wrong? What's happened?' She clasped him by the arm, as if to shake the truth out of him. 'It's not Mam, is it?' Her father had told her on their way home from the village hall last night that her mother was suffering from a bad attack of shingles. 'She's not worse?'

The elderly Scotsman shook his head. 'No, lass, it's not your mother.' He paused and glanced back at the group of waiting men. They were straining their ears for what he had to say. 'It's your father,' he said in a quiet voice. 'There was an accident at the quarry this morning.'

174

'An accident! What kind of an accident?'

Will Dearden walked forward and the doctor said, 'I think Will here can tell you more about what actually happened than I can.'

Bethany looked desperately at her father's workmate and Will Dearden shook his head. His face was drawn and his eyes had a dazed look to them. The memory would remain with him to his dying day. 'Just after eight o'clock it were,' he said, in a voice still betraying his shock. 'They were blasting this morning and had set the charges for eight, and they went off all right, but the bugger of it was, it weren't any of the rock from that as caused the trouble. It were a tumbler that did it. A right big 'un. Must have been all o' twenty tons. Came crashing down into t'back of shed where thy Dad was working.' The words came out mechanically as if he himself was still trying to come to terms with it. He shook his head as if to rid himself of the memory of that awful moment, for he had been the one nearest to Cheevers Baine when it happened.

Bethany's face drained. A tumbler! The very name of those huge boulders had sent a charge of fear through her from childhood. She looked from one face to the other, searching for a sign of comfort that it might not be as bad as she feared. All avoided her eyes, for none could bear the abject fear in her gaze. 'Is – is he badly hurt?' She could barely get the words out.

'Aye, lass, he is that.' Dr Munro took her gently by the arm and began to walk back in the direction of their front door. 'But I want you to be brave for your mother's sake.'

Leaving the others outside, the two of them entered the front room of Number Twelve and it took a second or two for her eyes to become accustomed to the dim light. Coming back to their small cottage always seemed like entering a doll's house after spending so much time in the spacious grandeur of Wolf Hall.

Her father was stretched out on the sofa, covered with a

grey blanket. His eyes were closed and his face was ashen. There was blood caked on the pillow behind his head, and traces of dried blood were still obvious round the edges of his nose and down the side of his mouth; a film of fine grey dust matted his brow and hair. He looked nothing like the man who had walked her home from the election last night, fussing and fuming about Amos Greville's brass neck in turning up in his black-shirted uniform, and impressing on her the need for the Labour Party to make up its differences caused by the split over membership of the National Government.

'This country can have a great future once again, our Beth,' he had said. 'We must have faith in the working man. Faith in ourselves. When we have that, the days of the Colonel Grevilles of this world will be numbered. We don't need folk like that to tell us how to run our lives. We're not babbies. We're grown men and women, with our own pride and dignity to uphold.'

But when they had parted company at the bottom of the drive to The Hall, his thoughts had all been for her mother. The stress and strain of life on the breadline was taking its toll. Betty Baine had never been quite right since Sammy's birth, with one ailment after another sapping what little strength she had left. 'These shingles are a terrible thing, so they are. And it's not just the itching. They run you down something terrible. I worry for her, Beth love, I really do. God knows what I'd do if anything happened to her. It doesn't bear thinking about.'

Bethany stared down at the face on the pillow and a great love welled in her heart for this man who had fathered her. Dour he might be – a hard man at times to love – but he had loved them, each and every one, no matter how much harder each successive mouth to feed had made his life. And he had loved her mother most of all. She had been his pride and joy: the Reverend Harrison Hetherington's beloved daughter who had deigned to love him — a man who had nothing to offer her but his love and a lifetime's toil by the sweat of his brow. And his daughter leaned forward now and laid her hand on that brow. It already felt cold to the touch.

Her mother, who had been sitting on a chair at the foot of the sofa, got up and came unsteadily towards her. 'Beth love, it was good of you to come . . . Good of them to get the word to you so fast.'

Bethany did not demur, but clasped her mother's hand and led her back to the chair. Betty Baine's pallor was as grey as that of the blanket that covered her husband, and her face was seamed with grief. Already a thin woman, her husband had been right in believing this recent illness had taken its toll and now this was the final straw. She appeared to have faded to a mere shadow of the woman she once was. She shook her head as she looked from her daughter to the prostrate figure of the man she had married, but her eyes remained dry. Tears would come, but not yet. The shock was still too great.

Sammy, who had been sitting solemn-eyed on the floor by his mother's chair, got up and rushed to throw his chubby arms around his sister's legs. Bethany lifted her small brother up and kissed his cheek, before turning back to the doctor. 'How bad is it, then?' It was important that they know the truth.

Hamish Munro shook his head. He had been a general practitioner in this dale for over thirty years and had never seen a worse case of a fractured spine. The middle vertebrae were smashed and he was pretty sure there were severe internal injuries to boot. He gave the man no more than a few hours at the most. 'Just about as bad as it could be, lass,' he said quietly.

Silence followed; a bleak emptiness that mirrored the feeling in all their hearts. The old doctor offered no words of comfort, for there was none to give. Cheevers Baine would not see the day out and he would leave a wife and

177

children as hostages to a fate worse than most could even imagine. 'Would you prefer I had him moved to the Cottage Hospital?' he asked.

Betty Baine shook her head. 'No, he stays here with us.' It was the right decision and they all knew it. If he had to die then he would die with dignity, his family around him.

Hamish Munro replaced his hat on his head and half-turned for the door. 'Aye, well I'll be looking back in myself later on. You know where to get me if you need me.'

Bethany followed him to the door and watched as he made off in the direction of his Main Road surgery. He had a shambling gait, the legacy of a shrapnel injury to his left hip at the Somme. Her father had had a lot of time for the crusty old Scotsman, for they had both known the horrors of those killing fields they called Flanders in the Great War. Hamish Munro had been a Captain in the Medical Corps then, Cheevers Baine a Private in the 'poor bloody infantry', but over there they had both been men doing a job no man should ever have been called upon to do. And those that had gone through it never forgot. It bound them in an unspoken comradeship that would last through life.

'If there's anything we can do, Bethany love, just say so.'

She had almost forgotten the others still waiting silently on the doorstep. She shook her head wearily. 'No thanks, Will. We'll manage.' She did not know how, but they would. She was determined about that. Anything she could do now to safeguard the future of what was left of her family she would do. Unless it meant returning to that awful place. That was one thing she could not contemplate.

She had not even given Amos Greville and what had occurred at The Hall a second thought since arriving back, and now it all seemed totally unreal.

She attempted a weak smile of thanks in the direction of her father's workmates as they reluctantly took their leave to make their way back to the quarry. She glanced up in the direction of the crag. A dark cloud the colour of Cumberland slate covered the top, shrouding the wild lonely places she loved with its dank, cloying mist. It was hard to recall now those happy times, the carefree green days of summer that she had known as a child up there on the fells. A child of the clouds, her mother had called her, for her love of those wild, wide-open spaces on the very top of their own small world that was Utherdale. But all that seemed a whole world away now, for childhood itself had gone, and she knew as she made her way back into the house that that part of her life had gone forever. If she had ever doubted it, there was no question of it now. If what Dr Munro said was true and her father would not recover, then they would be burying her childhood alongside him in that cold grave up there on the hillside, beside her grandfather's old church.

It took Cheevers Baine almost four hours to die. Bethany fetched her two younger brothers and sister from school so the family could be together when he drew his last breath, and they were sitting there, gathered around the sofa, aware that the end could not be far off, when the Reverend Barden appeared. Kenneth Barden, Utherdale's Methodist minister, had been a friend and support to the family ever since he had taken over the parish on the death of his predecessor Harrison Hetherington. The fact that Betty Baine was the great man's only child made the bond even closer, and the pain in the middle-aged man's eyes was genuine as he took the distraught woman in his arms.

Bethany made a pot of tea and they sipped it quietly, all seated in the positions from which they had barely moved for over three hours. Kenneth Barden did not sit, but stood with his back to the fireplace and struggled for some words of comfort that might prove adequate to the trauma that was facing the family.

'You must not think of dying as something dreadful,' he implored them. 'Dying does not mean entering into endless darkness. It is a door through which we leave the darkness of this world behind; it is the twilight through which we pass into the eternal light. We must not think of death as the destroyer of man, but rather as Christ coming to save. Let us not regard it as the end, but rather as the beginning. Let us not think we are having someone we love taken from us, rather that we are giving him up into the arms of our Saviour.'

His eyes softened as Betty Baine began to sob softly for the first time that day. Her two youngest children, Libby and little Sam, ran to their mother and clung to her, burying their faces in her aproned lap as silent sobs wracked her thin body and the tears ran freely down the pale skin of her cheeks. 'It is good that your mother should cry,' he said softly. 'God washes the eyes of his children with tears in order that we may see Him more clearly at times like this. Remember this, children – the soul would have no rainbow had the eyes no tears.'

He placed his cup and saucer on the mantelpiece and walked over and laid a comforting hand on Betty Baine's shaking shoulder. 'Have courage,' he said. 'And pray for his soul.'

When the minister had gone, Bethany gathered all the children around their mother and, haltingly at first, they said the Lord's Prayer together. They all knew they were nearing the end. She looked towards the motionless figure of her father on the sofa and her heart stopped. The eyes that had remained closed ever since he was brought from beneath the path of that giant stone this morning began to flicker open. And as the small voices chorused their 'Amen' at her feet, Cheevers Baine's eldest child whispered out loud, 'We love you, Dad.'

He heard. She would believe he heard to her dying day, for his eyes met hers, and a film of mist blurred his gaze, and as she watched, a single tear hovered on his lower lid to trickle slowly down the colourless skin of his cheek. It made a silent path through the limestone dust that caked his face. Then his eyes closed and she knew he had gone.

They buried him three days later, against the far wall of the Methodist cemetery, in the shade of a giant oak tree. It was in the plot next to Harrison Hetherington and his wife Edith. Out of respect, the quarry closed for the afternoon.

They were all there – all his workmates, and more besides. 'You never know the worth of a man until he's gone,' Will Dearden said, as he clasped the widow's hand at the cemetery gate. 'It'll be a long time before this village sees a turnout like this again. It was the measure of the man.'

Betty Baine nodded her head in thanks and managed a wistful smile. There had been nothing like it since the funeral of her own father, when the procession behind the carriage carrying his remains had stretched halfway through the village. And now most of them were back again, although a trifle older, to honour her husband. Her eyes took in the tall figure of Colonel Greville and his middle son, both in black ties and identical black overcoats. They doffed their hats as they shook her hand at the gate and the Colonel offered a few words of sympathy at her loss. 'He was a fine man, Mrs Baine. One of my best workers.'

'Thank you, Colonel.' Why couldn't he simply have said 'one of the best'? It was as if even in death a man was classified. She had never been one for the type of radical politics that had attracted her husband, but at times like this she was as fervently egalitarian as the best of them. Surely death was the great leveller, or so they said? But not to the likes of the Grevilles. As long as there were folk like them owning half a village and the people in it, there would be this Them and Us attitude. Class-consciousness was as necessary to the Englishman as the air he breathed.

She watched as the Colonel and his son went on to shake hands with Bethany in turn. Amos was last in the line-up and to her surprise her daughter turned from his proffered hand and deliberately looked the other way. The young man then took hold of her arm, but they were too far off to make out what was being said.

Bethany's pale cheeks flushed as she shrugged her arm free. 'Take your hand off me, Amos Greville.' The words were hissed out from between clenched teeth.

The young man looked unsettled. She had not been back to The Hall in three days. Not since that morning – that fateful morning, in more ways than one. 'Listen, Beth, I'm sorry – really sorry.'

'About what?' Her eyes looked straight into his.

'About your father's death, of course.'

She turned her head abruptly to the side. 'Is that all?'

He glanced nervously at his father, who was waiting by the side of their car, ready to return home. 'Are you coming back to work for us?' he asked, ignoring her question.

'I wouldn't come back within a mile of any house that had you under its roof!' The words were whispered but had a vehemence about them that quite took him aback.

'You're making a big mistake, you know,' he said, his face flushing. 'But maybe if I can't persuade you, then our Jack can.'

'What do you mean by that? Jack's in Australia, isn't he?'

Amos nodded. 'He is. But not for much longer. He's due home by Christmas.'

'You'd better be going. Your father's getting impatient.' The Colonel was now at the wheel of his Bentley and was revving the engine with his right foot as his fingers tapped irritably on the steering wheel.

182

'I'll be seeing you, then.' Amos replaced his hat on his head and then turned to nod for the last time in her mother's direction.

'Not if I can help it!'

And then he was off, hurrying across the muddy path to where his father waited. Bethany stared after him. The conversation, short though it had been, had left her unsettled. Just seeing him again, having his body that close to hers, his touch on her arm . . . A shudder ran through her and she had an awful feeling that she hadn't seen the last of the Grevilles or of Wolf Hall.

Chapter Nine

The premonition Bethany had at her father's graveside was more than borne out almost as soon as they got home that same afternoon. She was helping her mother wash the supper dishes when Betty Baine raised the subject of her daughter returning to The Hall. 'I know you've been staying off work to help me through the funeral and all, Beth love, but you can't impose on the Colonel's goodwill for too long, you know.'

Bethany's heart stood still. She had been waiting for this moment ever since that awful day she had run home to escape the horror Amos Greville had inflicted upon her. But just how much should she tell? What on earth could she say? She had never breathed a word of it at the time; her father's accident had put even that terrible experience in Amos's bedroom into perspective. And now – well, now it just seemed far too late. 'I – I'm not going back there, Mam.'

Betty Baine's hand paused in mid-air as she began to hand her daughter a dish for drying, then let the plate slip back into the soapy water. 'Not going back?' Was she hearing things? She turned to look askance at her daughter.

'That's right, Mam. I'm not going back.'

'What do you mean, you're not going back? That's your job. You have to go back. Especially now.'

'What do you mean, especially now?'

Her mother sighed as she plucked the dish out of the soapy water and placed it on the wooden draining board.

'Use your imagination, our Beth,' she said wearily. 'This is a tied house. We were only entitled to live here as long as your father was alive and working for the Grevilles. They could have us out tomorrow – and probably will, knowing them. But at least we have a chance of staying on a while longer, as long as you are at the Hall. I know you're thought of as a good worker there, for Tabby Fleetwood has told me so . . . But if you were just to up-tail and leave at a time like this . . .' She shook her head. 'Well, it doesn't bear thinking about. We'd be out on our ear in no time.'

Bethany was silent as her mother's words hit home. She had never thought of it like that. She had been so bound up in her own desire never to put herself at Amos Greville's mercy again that she had never given a second thought to her mother's predicament over the house. A feeling of shame engulfed her as she realized what her mother must have been going through, both before and after her father's death.

'Well, are you listening to what I said?' Betty Baine's drawn features took on an even more harrowed look as she waited for the reply.

Her daughter nodded. 'I heard,' she said, staring into space. 'Believe me, I heard only too well.'

Even her younger sister Libby added to Bethany's discomfort over the matter that same night by telling her in bed that both she and the boys thought she should go back to Wolf Hall. 'We heard our Mam telling Mr Barden, the Minister, t'other day that she hoped you'd be going back once the funeral were over. Why aren't you, our Beth?'

Bethany lay on her back on the hard mattress and stared up at the ceiling as the younger girl in the bed beside her waited for her reply. 'That's not an easy question to answer right now, Libby love,' she said at last.

'But you're thinking about it?' Libby was now at an age when she was acutely aware of what was going on around her. She had stood behind the kitchen door and listened on more than one occasion over the past few days when the Minister called to offer solace and she had heard her mother speak of her fear of being turned out of house and home. 'You *are* thinking about it, our Beth?'

Bethany sighed in the enclosed space and reached out to squeeze her sister's hand beneath the bedclothes. 'Yes, Libby love, I'm thinking about it.' It was the least she could say, tonight of all nights.

But try as she might, she could not bring herself to go back to Wolf Hall. The thought of a repeat performance of that awful morning was just too much to bear. And it was not merely the thought of another physical assault by the Colonel's second son that worried her – it was also all that mumbo-jumbo Amos got up – that devilish chanting in his bedroom that night was playing with fire in more ways than one. It made her blood run cold just to think about it. She had been brought up to believe in God, but that did not mean there was no such thing as the Devil. After all, the Old Testament was full of stories about him. Yes, and even the New, for wasn't Christ tempted in the wilderness by just such a being? Who knew what devilish powers were being brought into play up there in Wolf Hall right now? For all she knew, Amos Greville could be kneeling before the fireplace in his room at this very moment, chanting some weird spell and invoking her own name along with those of the other Powers of Darkness that he seemed to be in league with these days.

No, she decided. Wild horses would not drag her back to live and work in the Greville household. For once Amos Greville, and even Satan himself, would not get his way.

Instead, she got a job behind the counter, helping out at the local grocer's and general store. A world of drawers and jars full of blue bags, Zebo polish, senna pods, Fuller's Earth, balls of string and red sticks of sealing wax. A shop catering to children buying a ha'porth of liquorice root, tiger nuts and locust beans was to become her sanctuary. Hector Wilks, the proprietor, was inundated with volunteers for the vacancy as soon as it was advertised in his shop window, but the moment he heard Bethany was available, that had been it. Harrison Hetherington had been his father's oldest and dearest friend, and anything that could be done to help the Minister's family, even two generations on, was, he declared, 'both a privilege and a pleasure, my dear'.

She never even went back to The Hall to collect her few belongings that had been left there, before taking up her new post at the shop.

Bethany's decision to leave The Hall upset her mother greatly, for, as all her family were now well aware, Betty Baine lived in constant fear of losing her home. Eviction — that dreaded word — haunted her night and day. She had seen it happen so many times to other people and, despite soothing words from Mr Barden, the Minister, among others, her nervous disposition had her convinced the same fate would now await them.

'I can see it now — that cart at the door being loaded with our few sticks of furniture!' she would say, her face creasing with grief at the thought, as she sat by the meagre fire each night, her needles clicking endlessly as her fingers worked of their own accord, knitting new school socks for the boys.

But somehow Bethany could not bring herself to believe that the Colonel could be so cold-blooded as to force them to leave their home — not after what had happened. The accident had, after all, taken place in his own quarry. Surely not even a Greville would be as callous as that?

Despite the repeated reassurances she tried to give herself on that score, there was another reason for her to feel guilt at her decision to leave the Grevilles' employ. This was the disloyalty she felt regarding Tabby. Her reluctance even to set foot in Wolf Hall again had meant she had not been back to explain her decision to the old lady. When eventually the housekeeper paid a special visit to The Row to enquire about her young helper's health, Bethany more than willingly fell in with her mother's excuse for her leaving the post. 'It's nerves, the doctor says,' Betty Baine told the old housekeeper. 'The shock of her father's death, you see. The doctor recommends only light work for the time being.'

Tabitha Fleetwood had been understanding itself and had gone straight back to inform her employer. And Philip Greville had nodded gravely. His own beloved wife had suffered from nerves. It was, after all, the most common of women's complaints. Sign of a sensitive soul, Munro had told him, and he had not disagreed. 'Perhaps young Miss Baine will return in due course,' he said. 'When she has fully recovered. Can't see her reckoning much to a life behind old Hector Wilks's counter myself. Not a bright young madam like that. Bored out of her mind in no time, she'll be!'

He was not to be proved far wrong, for it very quickly became clear to Bethany that a whole day spent standing behind the counter of a grocer's shop, dealing out a few ounces of this and that to folk who could ill afford even the cheapest of diets, was not exactly the most interesting way to spend her life.

The shop, which stood on the corner of the Main Road and Chapel Street, had once been the front room of a private house and with its small, mullioned window and cramped interior, it was not a pleasant place in which to spend any length of time, let alone a whole day. As well as the drawers and screw-topped jars full of all manner of items essential to the daily life of the village, open tubs of different meals and flour, and various open shelves of butter and cheese gave the place a sour, cloying smell that stayed with her long after she had taken off her apron at six o'clock and locked up for the day.

Bethany also quickly learned that there was more to being a shop assistant than merely dealing with people's orders. You had to become a bit of a diplomat, too. There was a hand-written sign on the front of the counter stating 'No tick', but that did not stop people from begging for just the odd item to be put on the slate 'until pay day, Bethany love. I'll clear it then, as sure as God.' And Bethany had no doubt that most of them would have at least made an attempt to do so, but she was equally sure that there were those who would not. Like any village, Utherby had its fair share of scroungers, and it did not take her long to recognize who fell into which category. But 'No tick,' Hector Wilks said, and that was what he meant, be they honest as the day was long, or otherwise. 'If they know not to ask, they can't get offended when it's refused,' he declared firmly. 'There are far too many these days content to live in never-never land. If you don't have the money, you can't afford it. It's as simple as that.'

But Bethany knew it wasn't always as simple as that, especially for those like her mother who had no man behind them, and a mere pittance on which to bring up four children still of school age. It was the widows like Betty Baine she felt most sorry for, and there were a good many of them around. Many of the older women had been left husbandless a generation ago, as a result of the Great War, but there were also quite a few of her mother's age, for the quarry had claimed more than one victim over the past few years.

Yes, the local women had a hard time of it, and the talk in the shop was often of 'nerves'. It appeared to be the most common complaint among the housewives thereabouts, and it was something she knew her own mother had suffered from for as long as she could remember. And never more so than now.

Things were especially difficult at home just now, for with the restraining hand of their father gone, the boys

189

were playing up and often proving to be more than Betty Baine could handle. 'They need a man about the place,' she would say despairingly to Bethany as they sat up together knitting in front of the feeble fire during the long, dark evenings. 'They miss their father.'

There could be no reply to that, for they all missed the man who had been the mainstay of their lives. It was as if they had suddenly been cast adrift, to be buffeted by every ill wind that blew. And there were quite a number blowing that winter.

But none was so bad as the one that blew in with the postman one morning in early December. Bethany had not yet left for work, or the children for school, when the white envelope landed on the hessian mat behind the front door. She bent down to pick it up to hand it to her mother, then paused. The writing looked vaguely familiar, but she thought no more of it as she handed it over. 'Post, Mam,' she said as she reached for her coat.

'Mrs Elizabeth Baine.' Betty Baine took the letter and her brow wrinkled as she looked down at her own name on the front of the envelope, executed in copperplate spidery handwriting. Who could be writing to her? Outside the village very few people knew she was a widow and she was not used to getting mail addressed to herself in person. 'I don't know who this can be from,' she said a trifle anxiously, as she ripped it open and extracted the white sheet of paper. 'Who would be writing to me?' Then there was a sharp intake of breath. 'Why, it's from Wolf Hall!'

Bethany paused in the tying of her scarf and moved closer for a better look. She thought she had recognized the stationery and that distinctive handwriting. 'Here, let me see . . .' She stood looking over her mother's shoulder as they read:

190

Wednesday, 9 December 1936

Dear Mrs Baine,

I feel I must write to inform you that as your husband, the late Cheevers Baine, is no longer in my employ, the house you are presently occupying at 12 The Row, Utherby, will now be required by another employee. I assure you I have no wish to cause you undue distress at this time and will most willingly accede to your remaining in situ until the New Year.

May I wish you and your family my very best wishes for the festive season and the New Year ahead,

Yours sincerely,
Philip Greville (Col. rtd.)

'Until the New Year!' Bethany exploded, snatching the sheet of paper from her mother's hand. 'How noble of him! How very noble!'

Betty Baine took an unsteady step backwards and sat down heavily on the nearest chair. She had woken up this morning to her worst nightmare. Her face had gone quite white, her lips colourless, as she said quietly, 'I knew it. I just knew it would come to this before your father was cold in his grave.'

Bethany put a protective arm around her mother's shaking shoulders and her face hardened as she thought of the family up there in The Hall. All of them looking forward to Christmas, with never a thought in their heads about the misery they had just caused down here in the village. Tabby would be up there now, busy baking from her store of plenty for the festive season, but there would be no festivities for the small family Cheevers Baine had left behind.

Outside a steady snow was falling, and it was cold in the house. Coal had become a luxury on a widow's pension. Bethany looked at the miserable embers in the grate and thought bitterly of the huge fires she herself used to lay in almost every room of Wolf Hall, and a cold rage rose within her against the man who could do this to someone who had already lost almost everything.

She knotted the scarf around her head even tighter and said through narrowed lips, 'I'm off now, Mam. But don't you worry. There'll be nobody throwing us out on the street if I can help it!'

Betty Baine chewed on her lip, but made no reply as she watched her elder daughter make for the door. The fight had gone out of her.

A few minutes later, Hector Wilks watched in amazement from his front-parlour window as his new assistant went sailing past, with not even a glance at the shop door, instead of using the key he had given her to unlock it and beginning preparations for the first customers of the day.

'Well, I'll be . . .' His first thought was to run out into the street after her, but something about the set of her face told him that somehow this would not be such a good idea, so he contented himself by craning his neck to see which direction she took when she got to the end of the road.

Bethany knew exactly where she was headed. She had sworn she would never set foot in Wolf Hall again, but that was before this had happened. Her fingers curled round the sheet of paper in her coat pocket. 'Until the New Year indeed!' She spat out the words into the cold air as she dug her hands deeper into the patch pockets of her coat and hurried on in the direction of the moor.

Once in sight of The Hall she found herself in two minds as to which door to use. Should she go round the back and see Tabby first? But no – the housekeeper would only try to defuse the situation and she was in no mood for letting the Grevilles off the hook. Even if it made no difference to the outcome, she would let them know just how low this type of behaviour really was.

Despite her simmering rage, however, her heart pounded as she stood on the front step and reached for the old iron bell pull. It was one thing rehearsing her speech on the way here, but quite another delivering it when the time came.

She could feel herself tense as she waited and she held her breath at the sound of approaching footsteps behind the front door in response to her ring. Then came the clink of the chain being slipped and the massive iron handle began to turn.

But it was not Old Carnforth who answered the bell as she had expected. The face that stared down into hers she did not even recognize at first. It was deeply bronzed and much leaner than she had ever known it. But if she herself was momentarily thrown, then so was the possessor of that enviable tan, who had been disturbed from his book-keeping to act as his own servant until Warton Carnforth got back from the village. 'Yes? Can I help you?'

'I – I've come to see the Colonel,' Bethany began. Then her expression began to change and a look of disbelief crossed her face. She moved her head to one side, as if to scrutinize the features better. Then she gasped. 'It's not Black Jack, is it? You're not Jack Greville?'

The Colonel's eldest son gave an amused smile. 'Guilty, I'm afraid,' he said, looking even more closely at the young woman on the step.

'Well, don't you recognize me?'

It was the voice that did it. He edged a fraction closer, his dark eyes peering at the face beneath the tightly knotted headscarf as realization dawned. 'Good Lord! It's not the Squirt, is it?' He had a quite distinct Australian accent that made her smile, despite her fury at his father. 'It's not little Bethany Baine?'

'It is.' She pulled the headscarf from her head and ran a hand through the mass of auburn hair that suddenly found its freedom and tumbled around her shoulders. 'Only not so little now.'

'Well, I'll be blowed!' He stepped back to allow her to enter, gazing in some astonishment at the attractive young woman before him. A right corker was what they would call her back in Australia, and they would be right!

193

'Little Bethany Baine! And you're dead right – not so little nowadays, I'll be bound!'

He closed the door and shook his head in bemusement. Had he really been gone that long? 'And to what do we owe this pleasure, may I ask? I heard you had had a go at life over here in The Hall for a while, but had given it up.'

Bethany gave a polite but noncommittal assent as he led the way in and then headed in the direction of the library, holding the door open for her to enter. There was a huge log fire burning in the grate and the room was filled with a warmth that she had not known since she had left Wolf Hall all those weeks before.

'It's your father I came to see,' she said, anxious to get her business over with before any more pleasantries took the wind from her sails.

But Jack Greville was already acting the perfect host he had been brought up to be. As she spoke he had his back to her and was in the act of pouring two sherries from a crystal decanter on a side table by the window into two matching glasses.

He handed one over and kept the other for himself. 'Sorry to disappoint you,' he said. 'But you'll have to make do with me. Pa's ill. It's the old ticker playing up again, I'm afraid.'

His words made Bethany's heart sink. She was about to say she was sorry, then checked herself. That would be a platitude. She wasn't sorry at all. 'Not too ill to write letters, though,' she said stiffly, placing her glass on one of the bookshelves as she dug into her coat pocket.

He watched her curiously as she extracted the letter and handed it to him.

'Happy Christmas from the Grevilles,' she said bitterly.

He read the contents with a puzzled look on his face and stood staring down at the familiar handwriting for a moment, then his colour heightened perceptibly beneath the suntan. 'I didn't know about this,' he said.

Bethany gave a shrug. She hadn't imagined he did. She hadn't even known he was back in this country yet. 'You're acting for your father, I take it – when he's ill?'

He nodded as he handed her back the sheet of paper. He was searching desperately for something to say – some excuse for the inexcusable. 'I'm sorry about your father. It was a terrible thing to happen.' He deliberately did not refer to the contents of the letter. She was standing only a few feet away and staring at him, waiting for him to say the words she wanted to hear, and his mind went back to that day he had met her outside her home in The Row, after he had spoken to her parents about her coming to work at The Hall. There had always been something about her, even as a child, that disconcerted him. There was something about the way she looked at you – an independence of spirit that bowed to no one. And it was still there.

He downed his sherry in one and went to pour himself another. 'You – you've caught me unawares over this, Squirt,' he said. 'You'll need to give me time to look into it. I'll probably find it's company policy . . . You know, written into the tenancy agreement on the houses – that sort of thing.'

Bethany remained silent. She was determined not to pretend to understand – to let a Greville disavow any personal guilt, just because it was 'company policy'. Damn it all, they *were* the company!

He downed the second glass in one gulp and cleared his throat as the warming liquid found its way to his stomach. She was still standing there staring at him as if he had personally committed some mortal sin. 'Look here, I can see you're upset. And quite rightly so. I'll look into this as best I can, I promise you. But there's nothing I can do right now. I'll need time. Can you come back this evening?'

'This evening?' Her heart sank. She had hoped to clear this up and be able to ease her mother's mind long before then.

Her annoyance was obvious and he flushed slightly once again as he toyed with the glass in his hand. He was embarrassed. He was actually blushing out of embarrassment. It was funny how she had never noticed that habit in him before.

'I'm really sorry if it's not convenient.'

'It's hardly convenient being thrown out of your home on to the street either, is it?'

He glanced down at the empty glass in his hand, then looked up to meet her eyes. 'I've said I'll do what I can. If you don't mind calling back later.'

She shrugged, and her frustration was evident in her face and tone of voice. 'If I have to.'

'Well, say around seven-thirty, then. If that suits?' He held out his hand and there was a plaintive look in his eyes.

'Around seven-thirty.' She ignored the proffered hand and turned and made for the door, leaving her drink untouched on the shelf beside her.

Hector Wilks was not at all amused that his new employee had taken an hour off without warning, but he let the matter rest when Bethany assured him it was important business connected with her father's death and wouldn't happen again. The truth was, he liked the young woman with the ready smile and bright, perky manner. Never a one for chit-chat himself, his customers seemed to enjoy passing the time of day with her, and there was laughter to be heard in his shop for the first time since his wife had passed away four years before.

They were a mixed bag, his customers, he would be the first to admit – as ready to pull a body to bits as to praise them. But this young woman he had hired wasn't like that and she seemed to have a way of keeping them all sweet without kow-towing to the gossips or antagonizing them. Aye, she was a real asset and no mistake.

'Happen, you'll be asking for quite a bit of time off

before long, Miss Baine,' he said, during one of the quieter moments that morning. 'For I can't believe there's no young man around hoping to monopolize your time.' He had never as much as looked at another woman, either before or after his dear wife passed away, but there was no denying his new assistant was a comely lass. With her trim figure and well-turned ankles, and that mane of auburn hair of hers, she must have broken quite a few hearts before now, even though she was still only a young thing.

Bethany laughed and shook her head as she cut the oiled wrapping from a new cheese. 'There's no one special yet-awhile, Mr Wilks, so you've nothing to fear in that regard.'

'Happen you're on the lookout, though,' Hector Wilks volunteered. 'Although there's barely a lad in t'village that's up to much, if you ask me.'

Bethany did not contradict him as her thoughts turned to the youths of the village who were now all young men. Of the dozen or so of eligible age she had gone to school with, it would be a trial to consider spending even an evening with any one of them, never mind a lifetime. In fact, there were quite a few she would not even give the time of day to – they were the ones who had hung around with Amos Greville, in years past, whenever the Colonel's second son was on holiday from his boarding school. At least half a dozen of them there would be, always off to the woods to pursue their deadly games with the area's wildlife. And not just wildlife, for once Nancy Turver's kitten had been found dead, with its eyes put out. Of course no one had claimed responsibility, but she had seen the gang of them that very afternoon the kitten had gone missing. Larking about in that den of theirs in the wood they were; she had heard them chanting that same chant she had heard so many times just before the dead corpse of some poor creature would be found over there in the elm wood that bordered the foot of the fell:

197

'Demons of the nether world,
By our magic hither hurled,
Do your work again tonight,
Take us now to yonder height;
Maker of the bad and good,
Creator of stone and wood,
Take this creature young and free
And invest its power in me!'

It all came back to her now. Suddenly everything was falling into place, and things she had long preferred not to think about swam to the surface of her mind – nasty, devilish things that all had one thing – one person – in common: Amos Greville.

Even today, years later, her flesh would creep when she thought of those goings-on. That there was an undercurrent to life here – an evil undercurrent – she had no doubt. It had always been here, since time immemorial. She was sure of that. The Christianity that had been brought to these remote parts from the monks of Lindisfarne had simply been grafted on to a much older faith, that still today some in the dale referred to as 'the Old Religion'. And it wasn't just the messing about of misguided youths as the likes of the Reverend Barden tried to imply; it was something much older than that. It was a kinship with the elements, a harnessing of the lifeforce itself, and if the honouring of this great Spirit meant the offering up of a life, be it human in the past, or animal in the present, then it would be done with as little thought as was given to the breathing of the very air around them.

There was a continuity to the evil that lay buried in men's souls and Amos Greville with his Fascist creed was simply a new outlet for it. Soldiers of the devil, who walked behind the banner of Satan, her father had called the German Nazis and the Fascist Blackshirts in this country. And she truly believed that to be the case. That dark, frightening underside to mankind's character was coming to the fore more and more these days, both at home and abroad. And certain people were revelling in it. Certain people like Amos Greville and his like. *Homo homini lupus* – Man is a wolf to man. There was nothing new on the face of this earth and it was a fearful, awesome thought that in the past two millennia, in many ways, Man had progressed no further than his ancient ancestors.

Perhaps it was a result of the depression she felt just now that her mind dwelt so much on such dark thoughts, she decided, as she tried to turn her concentration back to shop matters. So much seemed to have gone wrong in her life lately that maybe her fear of Amos Greville was becoming irrational. She would have to do her best to keep things in proportion, and she had at least made a start this morning by attempting to thrash out her mother's eviction notice up at The Hall. At least she was doing something positive, and not just standing here worrying about it.

She had little time to dwell on the darker side of life throughout the rest of the day, for the shop was busier than usual and there was much gossip among the customers about the King and Mrs Simpson. It seemed to be the only thing that interested the female population of Utherby at the moment, and all were keen to take sides. It was plain that the new King Edward's love for the American divorcee was splitting the nation into two camps.

'I can't see as it would make a ha'porth of difference who he married as long as he were happy,' Ellen Capstick's mother declared. 'There have been those who have married out of their class before now and got away wi' it, and there will be again. Why there were tongues wagging when your Mam married your Dad, God rest his soul, Bethany Baine, I can tell you! A right to-do there was among the congregation. Not good enough for her, they said. Just a common quarrier, he were and not good enough for the likes o' the Reverend Hetherington's only lass. And now they're saying much the same thing about yon American lass and the King. A right bitch they say she is. Not good enough for him, they say. Well, bitch or no bitch, go right ahead, I say and good luck to 'em! If he makes his bed he'll have to lie on it same as the rest of us — and mine's not the only one that's been pretty lumpy in its time, I can tell you!'

Bethany smiled. If her father had still been alive he would have had a wry comment to make about being lumped together with the glamorous Wallis Simpson, she had no doubt. Nor had she any doubts that Joe Capstick would have as much to complain about regarding the lumpiness of his marital bed as his wife.

'By the way, you *have* heard that our Ellen's getting married, haven't you?'

'Married? Ellen? Well no . . .'

'Oh yes, I'm surprised she's never been in touch. Marrying a chap from over Kirkby Lonsdale way she met at a dance t'other week. All very sudden and romantic it is. Only set eyes on him last month and now it's all official like, with a ring and all.'

'I'm very happy for her.' Bethany handed her friend's mother her order and accepted a half-crown in payment. 'Tell her that when you next see her, won't you.' She rummaged in the till and came up with the sevenpence-halfpenny change and had to force the smile to her lips as she handed it over. Her friend was getting married. It was a cause for celebration. Why, then, did she feel so suddenly depressed by the news?

She pondered on her old friend's forthcoming marriage for the rest of the afternoon and could not quite decide why it unsettled her so much. Perhaps it was because Ellen was one of the lucky ones who had escaped Utherby and its closed little community. It wasn't that she would ever wish to spend her life away from here; the fells and wild, lonely places were as vital to her as the very air she breathed, but she did wish occasionally for some new companionship. Male companionship. Even a lad from Kirkby Lonsdale would do, she thought wryly. Someone not too bad-looking; someone intelligent, for stupid people had always bored her; and someone with a little bit behind them. He didn't have to be rich, just comfortable, so she would never have to go through what she had seen her mother go through. There was no dignity in poverty – none at all, and those that said otherwise were simply mouthing platitudes about a condition they themselves had obviously never endured. Yes, just comfortable would do fine, for, more than anything, she was conscious of the fact that as the eldest of the family, and with her father now dead, she had a great responsibility for her mother and her younger brothers and sister. It was a burden that was weighing heavily on her soul, especially when it meant having to meet with the likes of the Grevilles to fight her family's corner. It was downright demeaning to have to go crawling to the likes of them.

It was a relief when six o'clock finally came round and she could help Mr Wilks lock up and get home. 'You'll be having a quiet night in tonight, then lass?' her employer enquired as he removed his apron and hung it in its usual place on the back of the stockroom door.

Bethany glanced across at him and smiled. She was well aware of his interest in her personal life, but had no wish to enlighten him as to her real intentions this evening. 'Aye, Mr Wilks, I'll be having a quiet night in.'

Hector Wilks sighed as he waved goodbye to her from behind the counter. If only he were twenty years younger . . .

Betty Baine had the evening meal on the table as usual for her daughter coming in and Bethany did her best to look grateful for the slice of bread and the plate of thin soup that looked and tasted as if it had had merely the most passing acquaintance with any vegetable.

'You're looking tired, love,' her mother said, as she poured her cup of tea. 'An early night would do you a power of good.'

Bethany glanced at the clock on the mantelpiece and sighed. It was almost six-forty. 'I can't Mam. I have to go out tonight.'

Betty Baine looked surprised. 'Am I allowed to know where?'

'Oh, I thought I would take a walk over to Butterslack to see Nancy. Her mother was in the shop today and suggested it.' Bethany avoided her mother's eyes as she spoke. It was not comfortable telling a lie, and she was not even sure why she did it. To protect her mother, perhaps? She gave a mirthless half-smile to herself as she sipped her tea. It was funny how the generations changed places without either really realizing it. She was not yet out of her teens, yet already she felt the elder of the two – the one responsible for taking care of her mother. It was a lonely, decidedly bleak thought.

She decided to make no special effort with her appearance before setting out for The Hall, for she had no intention of even taking her coat off once she got there. It was to be no social occasion. She was going to transact some business on her mother's behalf, that was all. She did, however, allow herself an application of lipstick and a smear of powder that she had bought with the little she had had left from her first wage at the shop, after paying her mother her board. She felt immediately cheered. Somehow adding the extra dash of colour to her face seemed to enliven her spirits too and give her that extra degree of courage she knew she was going to need.

'I shouldn't be too late, Mam.'

'Enjoy yourself, love.' Betty Baine looked up from her

knitting and gave an encouraging smile. Perhaps an evening out of the house, away from the problems of home, might do her daughter even more good than an early night. All too often when she had tried that remedy herself, all it had resulted in were a few extra sleepless hours going over everything in her head that was worrying her. 'Give Nancy my love.'

'Nancy?'

'It is Butterslack you're off to, isn't it?'

'Oh, yes – Nancy ... Of course!' Bethany gave a sheepish smile as she made for the door. Her father always said she never made a good liar.

Chapter Ten

Bethany pulled the collar of her winter coat up around her ears as she closed the front door behind her and set off in the direction of the Grevilles' home. The snow of earlier in the day had turned to rain and a fairly stiff breeze had got up, so the long walk to Wolf Hall proved more tiring than usual as her umbrella was buffeted by the wind and she had to battle head down into the gusts for most of the way. What exactly she was going to do if Jack Greville did not come up with the answer she was hoping for, she had not a clue. She could only hope that his time in Australia had invested him with some of the humanitarian instincts so obviously absent in his father and younger brother.

She had always quite liked the Colonel's eldest son and felt sure her life at Wolf Hall would have been a whole lot easier had Jack not taken himself off to the other side of the world when he had. But now he was back, and not a moment too soon, she told herself, as her fingers closed more tightly around the letter still in her coat pocket.

She arrived at the end of the long gravel drive just after seven-thirty, and to her surprise the young man she was due to meet was not in the house at all, but waiting for her at the foot of the front steps, seated at the wheel of his father's Bentley. Even in the half-darkness, from outside the car she could see that he was very smartly dressed, in a fine black woolcloth coat, with a fashionable astrakhan collar. His grey felt hat lay on the seat behind him. Was he just on his way out to some other engagement that had cropped up? Had he forgotten their meeting? She gazed anxiously into the car window.

Her anxious expression was countered by a relaxed smile on his part. 'Get in,' he said, leaning across to throw open the passenger door.

Bethany stared at the open door of the car, quite taken aback.

'Please . . . Get in. It's far too cold to talk standing out there.'

That was certainly true and she shivered as if in response as she dug her hands deeper into her coat pockets.

'Please, Bethany,' he begged. 'Just get in.'

She obeyed, a trifle uncertainly. This wasn't at all what she had expected. She sank awkwardly into the plush leather upholstery as she looked curiously at him. 'We had an appointment,' she began in an accusatory tone. 'You asked me to come back at seven-thirty.'

'So I did.' He threw her a grin as he jerked the car into gear, swung it round with an expert turn of the wheel, and they set off immediately down the drive. He knew this would surprise her. In fact he had surprised himself by his sudden decision less than half an hour ago to make up for the embarrassment he had felt over his father's insensitivity towards her family by inviting her out to dinner. Of course it wouldn't really make up for all the anxiety that had undoubtedly been caused, but it was a gesture in the right direction, nevertheless. And besides that, he was more than a little hungry himself. Having to make his own meals these days was as good an incentive for eating out as he could wish for.

'Ever been to Paddy Corrigan's?' he asked, naming the Dubliner who had taken over the Old Fleece Inn, an ancient hostelry on the the other side of Butterslack that now had an unrivalled reputation for good food.

'Oh yes, I go there every other day!'

For a moment he almost believed her, then he laughed. 'I haven't been there myself since the Irishman took it on, so it'll be a new experience for me too. But I've heard good reports on it though, since I got back. Amos has been there several times and anything that takes my fussy young brother's fancy must be all right!'

Bethany tensed at the mention of the name she now detested more than any other, and a momentary panic set in. She turned in her seat to look at her companion. Even in the darkness she could see that he still had a smile on his face, but it was a genuine, friendly smile, with no side to it. Not like Amos's at all. If they hadn't been related – if Jack had not been a member of that family – she could almost bring herself to like him, she thought.

Then common sense got the better of her. All this talk of a restaurant was quite ridiculous. She had come here for a purpose, not to eat. She felt cheated by having the wind taken out of her sails before they had even begun to talk. Anyway, Grevilles just did not entertain their hired help in expensive hotels, and that was how she would still be regarded, even though she had now left their employ. And for another thing, she certainly wasn't dressed for eating out. Unconsciously, one hand reached down to cover the worn tartan skirt she was wearing with the edges of her coat. In fact, even if she had had prior notice, she would have found it difficult to come up with something suitable to wear. Dinner in smart hotels such as the Old Fleece Inn was not something that had ever figured in her life before. Nor were rides in cars such as this. It was the first time she had ever been inside the Bentley and the smell of the fine leather upholstery and the polished walnut trims lent an added dimension to the comfort and smoothness of the ride as the limousine sped along the narrow country lane. 'Listen,' she said, turning in her seat to face him, 'I came back as you suggested this evening to discuss my family's eviction, nothing else.'

'And so we shall, my dear girl,' he smiled. 'So we shall. In fact, we can talk about nothing else all night if it pleases you!'

'It may be a great joke to you, Jack Greville, but it is no joke to me – or my mother, I can assure you!'

He reached across and took hold of her hand. 'Listen, Squirt,' he said seriously. 'I invited you back tonight because I genuinely want to help, but I also felt the need for a proper meal. Now you can't deny a fellow that, can you? Fending for oneself in the kitchen is no joke – even after a couple of years in the Outback!'

She was still nonplussed. 'What's wrong with Tabby's cooking?'

He let go of her hand to change gear and glanced round. 'Didn't you know? Tabby's been gone these past ten days. She had a bad fall just before I arrived back and has left for her sister's in Sedbergh to get over it. But, if you ask me, by the sound of it, I'll be surprised if she ever comes back. You don't get over broken hips and wrists very easily at that age.'

Bethany received the news in silence. She felt terrible that she hadn't known – that she hadn't even written to wish her old friend a speedy recovery. But that was what came of severing ties with her old job so abruptly and so completely. 'I'm really sorry about that,' she said quietly. 'I liked Tabby a lot. In fact, she was the best thing about working at The Hall as far as I was concerned.'

Jack Greville gave a rueful grin. That he could believe. 'Well, at least you're honest!' She always did tell the truth, even as a small kid, whether the recipient liked it or not.

The Old Fleece Inn, or 'Paddy Corrigan's' as it was now becoming known locally, was situated several miles out on the Sedbergh road and they were given a warm welcome by the portly Dubliner who combined the best of British and Irish cooking with a sparkling line in the blarney. This particular evening, though, Jack Greville was in no mood to be upstaged by any Irishman and he quickly ushered his guest to a quiet table in the farthest corner of the room, as far away from the bar and their host's cheerful chat as possible. 'Paddy's a real card from what I hear tell,' he informed Bethany. 'But you have to be in the mood for it. According to Amos, the fellow's not only kissed the Blarney Stone, but has made love to the darned thing!'

Bethany feigned a polite smile and tried not to let her distaste at the mention of his brother's name show.

'May I, madam?'

She glanced round to see a black-tied waiter waiting to take her coat. 'Of course.' As she slipped it off, she was immediately aware of the shabbiness of her blue twin set and tartan skirt.

She watched as the garment was hung on a stand already containing a positive warren of coney skins and other even more expensive furs. She could feel her face colour beneath its dusting of powder. 'I'm not exactly dressed for the occasion,' she told her companion in some embarrassment as they sat down at their table. 'You'll just have to take me as you find me.'

Jack Greville smiled across the three feet of white damask, with its array of silver-plated cutlery and fresh winter flowers. 'My dear Miss Baine, I have never dared do anything else!'

He ordered the best house claret with the meal, and they had polished off almost two bottles by the time the dessert course was at an end. Having inherited a taste for the fruit of the vine from his father, Jack began to explain to his guest the subtle differences between the produce of different regions, but seeing Bethany's eyes glaze over, he cut that particular conversation short. 'But why talk about it when we can just enjoy it?' he said, raising his glass to hers once more. 'And I can see by the colour of your cheeks that you're enjoying it too!'

Bethany flushed an even deeper pink. She was indeed. And quite apart from the wine which was giving her the most delicious inner glow, she had never tasted a meal like it. Brown Windsor soup – hot and thick, and much, much tastier than the soup she had had at home at teatime, followed by roast sirloin, elaborately garnished and served with chipped potatoes and peas, and finished off with a concoction consisting of fresh cream laced with Irish whiskey and poured over a particularly delicious piece of hot treacle tart. She had to refrain from gobbling the whole lot down far more quickly than she knew would be regarded as decent and she truly felt the waistband of her skirt would give way, as she pushed the empty dessert plate from her and sat back in her chair with a satisfied smile on her face. 'That was quite the most tasty meal I've ever had in my entire life!' she declared honestly, feeling no praise was too good for what she had just enjoyed.

Jack Greville laughed. 'Then you don't eat out often enough, I can see.'

He meant no offence, but Bethany was only too ready to take it from the likes of him. 'Your father did not exactly pay the type of wages that would go far in a place like this,' she bit back, then added ruefully, 'But I can't honestly say Hector Wilks pays that much better.'

Her companion looked suitably chastened. 'I didn't mean it like that,' he said, putting his hand in his pocket and extracting a silver cigarette case. He opened it and offered it across. She shook her head. 'You don't mind if I do?'

'Go right ahead.' She watched as he took a matching lighter from his pocket and held the flame to the tip of the cigarette. 'It's another world, you know,' she said as he drew the smoke deep into his lungs. 'All this . . .' She gestured around the room with her head. By now the other tables were filling up with well-dressed couples she knew must live locally, but most of whom she had never set eyes on before. They lived on another plane of existence from that of The Row and its inhabitants. But almost all seemed well acquainted with her companion, with many coming across to exchange a few words before taking their places at their own tables. Several old farming friends were keen to hear about life Down Under, but Jack made it very clear that that could keep for another time. His main interest this evening was in his companion, who herself was receiving more than her share of curious glances.

'This life . . . Is it one you would like to know better?' He looked at her curiously, once they were alone again. His eyes were fixed on her face as they had been for most of the meal.

'Would a cat lick cream?' She gave a scoffing smile as she toyed with her wine glass. 'You do ask the daftest questions, Jack Greville.'

'Do you always have to do that?'

'Do what?'

'Call me by both my names. Couldn't you bring yourself to call me just plain Jack?'

She smiled. 'All right – Just-plain-Jack. But you must call me Miss Baine!'

Now it was his turn to smile. 'To me you will always be either Bethany or Squirt. Take your pick.'

She sighed. 'I reckon the former is a bit more dignified for a place like this, don't you?'

'I do, Bethany. I certainly do.'

They touched glasses and he sat back in his chair, as the smoke from his cigarette rose lazily in the lamplight. For over two hours he had been sitting watching her and listening to her tell him of how mean and low his family was – how uncaring and insensitive to others less fortunate, and if she had been telling him how entirely wonderful they all were he could not have been more entranced. Even after all that time in Australia, he had never met anyone quite like her. There was something about her that was unique. She was a totally free spirit, despite the chains of poverty that bound her to a life that it hurt him even to think about.

She was aware of him looking at her far more intently than was merited and her eyes flashed in the soft light of the lamps as she chided quietly, 'You're staring at me again, Just-plain-Jack. You've been staring at me all evening and it's rude to stare.'

He had the good grace to blush as he dropped his eyes to his cup of coffee. But he knew he could go on staring for ever. There was something about this creature – this child he had known almost all her life who was now as beautiful a woman as he had ever laid eyes on –that totally captivated him. To his surprise he had thought about almost nothing else all day but seeing her again this evening. He had even tried to convince himself he should feel ashamed to be thinking along these lines, for the real reason for their meeting tonight was far removed from a social occasion. He even wondered if subconsciously he had asked her to come back at this time simply so he could ask her out. Certainly he could have made enquiries into the eviction order long before lunchtime, never mind seven-thirty in the evening, and in fact had done, and his father had required little convincing that he had acted in haste. There would be no question now of simply throwing the Baines out on to the street.

'Tell 'em they can stay as long as they need to, Jack lad,' Philip Greville had said over a slice of game pie that lunchtime. 'God knows, I didn't mean to cause the woman any distress.' It had been a pure formality, that letter, and he had barely given the matter a second thought. 'Maybe I should have enquired into their circumstances a bit more but, God knows, I've enough to do around here without concerning myself with the personal affairs of every employee. I'd be nosey-parkering into the half the village, if that were the case.'

Then he had given a dry chuckle as he reached for the pickle. 'Maybe that's something you might care to address yourself to now you're back.'

'Nosey-parkering?' Jack had laughed. But he knew exactly what his father was getting at. And it might not be such a bad idea after all.

So here he was on his first case – Knight Errant to the rescue, ready to assure the fair maid there was nothing to worry about. Her family would be safe in his hands.

He reached across the table and touched Bethany's hand. For a moment she began to draw back, but there was something about the look in his eyes that made her leave her fingers in his.

'I want you to know you have nothing to worry about. Not now. Not ever,' he said softly.

Maybe it was the wine, but there was something that told her for the first time this evening that things were beginning to get out of her control. She was looking back at him through that rose-coloured haze brought about by lamplight, good food and a plentiful supply of fine claret. Memories were crowding in on her – reminiscences of the Jack Greville she had known as a child, coupled with a heart-quickening recognition that that Black Jack of old and the good-looking young man sitting opposite her were one and the same.

He was dismissing her fears over her mother by telling her there was nothing to worry about, but she needed more than that. Her mother's situation required more than platitudes. She needed concrete assurances to go back home with. 'We came to discuss things properly,' she reminded him gently. 'To talk through a specific problem. A problem that is causing my mother a great deal of anguish.' It was best they got back to basics as quickly as possible. So far this evening had been pure pleasure and now a feeling of guilt was beginning to creep into the mellowness the meal and the wine had produced. She must not let it end without getting his firm promise that her family would be safe in their home for the foreseeable future. 'You do understand?' she implored him. 'I need to know there really is nothing to worry about.'

Jack nodded, his dark eyes grave in the lamplight. 'You want me to do or say something concrete that will allow your family to go on living in the house they are in now.'

'You know I do.' It was difficult to keep the impatience from her voice.

He was silent for a moment. He had deliberately put off discussing the real reason for their meeting till the very end in case she were to get up and walk out as soon as she got what she came for – as soon as he put her mind at rest on the subject. That was the last thing he wanted.

'Well?' she insisted.

He gave a half-smile as thoughts formed in his head. Dare he? On setting out for here tonight he had fully intended simply to put her mind at rest over a nice meal by telling her there was nothing to worry about. But it was obvious that was not going to satisfy her. She needed something more.

He leaned back in his chair as the ghost of a smile began to play around the corners of his lips. Was it the wine or a pure madness in him that was prompting him to consider the idea now forming in his head?

He reached forward to clasp her hand once more and as his fingers tightened on hers he said quietly, 'Would you agree that in every transaction there has to be give and take – one has to strike a bargain that is agreeable to both parties?'

'Of course.' She had expected something like this – a tit for tat. The Grevilles were the living examples of the old Northern saying that 'you don't get owt for nowt'. They would want their pound of flesh for allowing her mother to stay on in the house. It had even crossed her mind in the car that he might try to persuade her to take on Tabby's post as housekeeper now the old lady was indisposed. 'We are not asking for charity – merely justice.'

He looked pleased by her emphatic reply. 'Right then . . . What would you say to my allowing your mother an unlimited tenancy of Number Twelve, The Row, in exchange for you doing me a favour?'

Bethany's eyes narrowed suspiciously as she tensed and drew back her hand. 'How big a favour?'

'Mmm . . . Pretty big.'

She took a deep breath. 'You can only ask.'

He paused. And the pause grew longer as his thoughts crystallized. She wanted something from him and he wanted something from her. He was sure of it now – more sure than he had ever been of anything: he wanted to see her again. And soon. This evening had been special. He had not enjoyed himself so much in years. So for both of them to get what they wanted out of this evening, he had to come up with a suggestion that she was almost certain to accept – an idea that would mean all personal contact with her would not be lost after tonight. 'Come with me to visit Tabby next Wednesday,' he said. 'I haven't seen her since I got back and I owe her a visit. From what I hear, she'd love to see you too. Will you come?'

Bethany gave a relieved smile. If that was his favour, he could ask as many as he liked from her! 'There's nothing I'd like more. But I'll have to ask Mr Wilks for some time off. Wednesday is one of our busiest days.' She could just hear her employer's comments, after their conversation of earlier today!

He beamed across at her. 'Good. That's settled then. Given the good Mr Wilks's approval – I'll pick you up at ten.'

He looked so pleased as he poured what remained of the wine into both their glasses that it disconcerted her and doubts began to set in. 'He won't mind, will he – your father?'

'My father? Why should he?' He looked surprised as he raised his glass to his lips.

Bethany shrugged. 'Oh, I don't know . . . Us going off to Sedbergh together and that . . . After all, you hardly know me.'

He laughed out loud. 'My dear girl, I have known you all your life, remember. I watched you grow up.' His eyes softened as he remembered that little scarecrow he had first known all those years ago. It was impossible to relate that scrawny little figure to the beautiful young woman sitting across from him now. 'And I liked what I saw.'

Bethany passed a hand over her brow, pushing back the fall of hair that half-covered one eye as she forced herself to meet the gaze of the young man now looking at her so earnestly from the other side of the table. Black Jack Greville . . . Who would have believed it? Certainly not herself as a child. This evening had not turned out at all as she had expected when she left her mother's house for The Hall to have it out with him. 'This – this outing on Wednesday,' she began. 'It *is* only to visit to see Tabby . . . It won't be like us going out together purely socially.' She wanted there to be no misunderstanding over that.

'Purely a visit to the sick,' Jack replied primly, trying hard not to smile. 'A business arrangement, if you like. Just like tonight.'

Bethany nodded in satisfaction as she reached across and took another sip of her wine. 'I'm not trying to be awkward or anything. It's just that I don't want there to be any talk . . . Tongues to wag in the village and that sort of thing.'

'Is there any reason why they should – even though it *were* purely a social outing?'

'Don't be daft. You know as well as I do it'd cause as much gossip in the dale as has the King and Mrs Simpson affair. We're from two different worlds, you and me, Jack Greville. Two completely different worlds.'

215

He shook his head quite emphatically as he stubbed out the end of his cigarette into the ashtray. 'Even that's not totally true. For a start we both come from this dale – from Utherby itself, in fact. We were both born and bred here. And we both love this place.' She had never actually spoken of her love for Utherdale, but he had known all his life that the small child he had so often seen roaming the wildest parts of the fells felt just as passionately as he did about this strange ancient land they called the North Riding.

Bethany fell silent as she looked across at him. It seemed he had no qualms whatsoever about them spending Wednesday together and a procession of different thoughts danced through her head. She was certainly glad of the opportunity to see Tabby again, but was not at all sure what either her mother's reaction, or that of other people, would be to her going off with him in the car like that. But did she really care what other people thought or said?

She found herself smiling across the table at him as she toyed with the glass in her hands. There was no doubt about it, he was just about the most attractive young man she had ever laid eyes on. Was it really only the wine, or was she simply softening through the look of undoubted admiration there was in his eyes as he sat there less than three feet across the table? There was no real way of knowing. All she was aware of was of thinking how really nice he looked, how pleasant his voice sounded with that touch of an Australian accent, and how genuinely understanding he could be when there were just the two of them alone like this. She could not think of him as a Greville at this moment. He was purely the good-looking, very nice young man with whom she was enjoying the best meal of her life, and whom she knew she would be seeing again, in the not too distant future.

He raised his glass to hers. They touched across the

empty plates that now cluttered the tabletop. 'Here's to a lovely day out on Wednesday,' he said, then added quickly, 'And a very speedy recovery by dear old Tabby. I'm sure it'll be a real tonic for her seeing the two of us!'

His eyes were looking deep into hers and he was aware how much more greener hers looked in the soft light of the lamps. In fact, she had quite the most beautiful eyes he had ever seen. And the way her brows arched over them . . . 'Did anyone ever tell you how much you look like that French film star . . . ? You know, the one that's just starred in that film with Clark Gable – Claudette something or other . . .'

'Claudette Colbert?'

'Yes, that's the one . . .' Her eyes seemed to swim as they gazed into his. If he was drunk, he was a happy drunk. 'Here's to Claudette Colbert, Tabby, the King and Mrs Simpson, and old Uncle Tom Cobbley and all . . . But 'specially US!' Then he hiccuped. It entirely spoilt the moment, but they both laughed.

'I think it's time we were going, don't you?'

They were making their way out in the direction of the car when Paddy Corrigan, the landlord, called to them from the kitchens. 'The King is about to make an announcement on the wireless – do you young folks want to hear it?'

Jack raised his brows and looked at Bethany, who shrugged her compliance with the suggestion, and they both followed the proprietor back through the hallway, wondering what on earth the fuss was about.

There were already several others gathered around the brown bakelite radio that sat on the oak dresser in the hotel kitchen, as the two new arrivals took their places at the back of the listening group. 'It's going to be something important,' a woman in white overalls informed them. 'The announcer said so earlier.'

The reception was not too good at first, with a lot of

background crackling. 'Come on now, ye old beggar –
don't let us down at a time like this!' Paddy Corrigan
muttered under his breath, then he swore in Irish. There
were ladies present after all. Then after half a minute or so
of further knob-twiddling, the unmistakable voice of
Edward VIII came over loud and clear, filling the kitchen
with its high-pitched, slightly nasal tones. Everyone
tensed and moved closer as the message of his announcement became clear.

'At long last, I am able to say a few words of my own . . .
I want you to understand that in making up my mind I did
not forget the country or the Empire which as Prince of
Wales and lately as King, I have for twenty-five years tried
to serve. But you must believe me when I tell you that I
have found it impossible to carry the heavy burden of
responsibility and to discharge my duties as King as I
would wish to do without the help and support of the
woman I love . . .'

He was abdicating! The King was giving up the throne!
A gasp ran through the huddled group, with mutterings of
'Oh no!' from one or two of the women.

Bethany half-turned and caught Jack's eyes. He was
watching her with that same intense expression he had
had throughout the whole of the broadcast.

When it finished a silence fell in the room as everyone
present let the gravity of the message sink in. There was a
peculiar poignancy in the words, and for the first time in
the whole of the crisis that had been gripping the nation's
attention Bethany felt sympathy for the American
divorcee Wallis Simpson. Whether her own planned
outing with Jack Greville was purely a visit to the ailing
housekeeper or not, there would be a lot of people in this
dale with something to say about the Colonel's eldest son
and heir taking off in his car and spending the day with
someone like herself. For princes or paupers in this life,
there were certain social barriers that one just did not

cross. Wallis Simpson had tried it and it had cost the man she loved the highest position in the land. Bethany knew Jack was aware of it too as, grave-faced, he took her arm and they left Paddy Corrigan and his kitchen staff to themselves to discuss the matter of the King and his lady love well into the night.

They walked in silence to the waiting car, then, in a quietly fierce voice, as he opened the passenger door for her, Jack said, 'No one has the right to dictate to any other person who they should or shouldn't fall in love with. It is and can only be a matter for the two people involved.'

The words hung in the air between them and Bethany paused and turned her head to face him by the car door. Their eyes were only inches apart. 'Whether King or Colonel's son,' she added softly. Then she cursed the devil in her for taking control of her tongue.

He looked at her in the glow of the carriage lantern hung outside the hotel door. 'Whether King or Colonel's son.'

Then he kissed her. It was only the second time in her life she had ever been kissed by a man. But the horror of that first time with his brother Amos went right out of her head as she half-heartedly began to resist, then gave in to one of the most pleasant sensations she had ever experienced.

'I suppose I should apologize,' he said a minute or so later as she smoothed her dishevelled hair and leant back against the Bentley for support. 'But I'm not going to.'

She found herself smiling back at him. She liked a man who stood his ground. 'I suppose you could say you were claiming payment in kind,' she volunteered.

'For the meal?'

'No, for that boomerang that's been gracing my bedroom wall for the past few years. I never did thank you for that.' The fact that she had left it with her other belongings at The Hall when she fled was neither here nor there.

219

He laughed aloud as they got into the car and he switched on the ignition. The engine purred softly into life as he shook his head and the memories came flooding back. He had almost forgotten, it was so long ago. 'The boomerang for the Squirt! You know, I had completely forgotten about that!'

'You mean apart from that one kind gesture you never thought of me again out there in Australia?' she teased as she made herself comfortable in the seat beside him.

He paused and thought for a moment, then shook his head.

'Well, did you, Black Jack? Did you ever think of me over there in the Outback?'

He glanced round at her beside him in the darkness as they took off back in the direction of Utherby, and he shook his head once again. Oh, he had thought of her all right. But he had thought only of that scrawny little kid who would stand her ground and answer him back as good as she got on every occasion. That scrawny little kid with arms and legs like matchsticks who had suddenly turned into this quite unbelievable creature sitting right here beside him. 'The Squirt . . .' he mused in incredulity. 'The Squirt . . .' He would never have believed it.

Chapter Eleven

The road from Utherby to the little market town of Sedbergh wound through some of the most dramatic scenery in all England. Here the soft fertile land of North Lancashire and Westmorland's Lune Valley merged with the bleak outreaches of Yorkshire's northern Pennines. All England's history had marched along this road. The Romans, whose mighty legions had built the Emperor Hadrian's Wall, designed to keep out the marauding Scots; the Vikings, who had arrived off the Cumbrian coast in their longships and given the town its name; the Normans, who had built many of the fine old churches in the little villages they passed. And most of all the Scots, whose Bonnie Prince Charlie was forced to hide in a chimney in the town and then escape trussed up in the panier of a pack-horse, under the eyes of the notorious Duke of Cumberland's troops.

'See that old farmhouse over there?' Jack Greville said to Bethany, as his right hand left the wheel of his brand-new Duesenberg sports car to point to a tumbledown ruin by the side of the road. 'The locals call that Africa because of the black faces that used to peer out through the windows in the time of the slave trade. The poor blighters used to be housed there before being taken off to their new masters up north.'

Bethany shuddered as her companion swung his new prize possession into one of the blind hairpin bends with an abandon that made her grip the edges of her seat in panic.

'Hard times in a hard land, my dear,' her companion said. 'But we're headed down into civilization now . . . Old Sedbergh town, where beneath its flat-topped hill the sons of gentlefolk learn to rule the Empire and look down their upper-class noses at their fellow men.'

'I thought you liked it at school there.'

'I did, I did, dear girl. But let's just say I much preferred my open-necked-shirt days in the Australian Outback to the dark-blue blazer, shirt and tie of public schooldays here.'

She could understand that. 'Will you go back to Australia?'

There was a moment's silence and Jack Greville's almost permanent smile faded to a look of resignation and he sighed. 'That I doubt very much – in the short term at least. It depends on Pa's health, really. He isn't up to running the whole show on his own for that much longer, and from what I can gather Son Number Two, who should have been shouldering most of the work of the estate, has been much too busy playing blackshirted soldiers to have been of much good while I was away.'

'If I remember rightly, you were pretty keen on the BUF yourself before you left the country.'

He acceded the point with an embarrassed grimace. 'You could say that, but I've grown up a lot since then. Australia does that to you, you know. Knocks off the edges. Lets you know there's more to life than you think. It brings you into contact with people from all walks of life and cultures. Some of the finest people I met out there I probably wouldn't have passed the time of day with before, back here in England.'

Bethany gave a wry smile. At least he was being honest. 'You mean there are actually some decent types among the "lower orders"?'

He gave a sheepish smile. 'Maybe that did sound a bit snobbish. I didn't mean it to. I suppose what I'm really

222

trying to say is that I never realized what a sheltered life I had led until I went out there and met other people from all sorts of backgrounds. The experience did me a lot of good. From then on I resolved not to be so one-dimensional when I got back home – not to judge people purely by their station in life.'

Bethany turned and looked at him curiously, if a trifle sceptically. This was certainly a Jack Greville quite different from the one who left England several years ago. Life down under had obviously agreed with him, both mentally and physically. And, more than that, it had broadened his horizons. At least one of the Grevilles now recognized there was worthy human life beyond their own County social set. And, who knows, in the future, as Master of Wolf Hall, he might even think of doing something tangible for his fellow dalesfolk not quite so fortunate. 'I take it you won't be joining your brother on the Fascist platforms any more, then?'

Jack laughed as he threw the sports car into a higher gear. 'Lord, no! I'll be far too busy for that. I was sent out there to learn all there is to know about animal husbandry – well, sheep-rearing, actually – in the hope of rejuvenating the family fortunes. And that, my dear girl, is a task I still have to accomplish. If the Grevilles are to thrive and prosper well into the twentieth century, then something will have to be done, and I'm afraid it looks as if I'm the one who is expected to work that particular miracle.'

'I wish you luck. But poverty's a relative thing, you know. Most folks in this valley would think the Grevilles were the next thing to millionaires.'

'Is that what you think?' He sounded surprised.

She thought for a moment, remembering the shabbiness of much of the furnishings, and the bare patches on the walls where valuable paintings had hung for generations, before being sent, along with other valuables, to auction to help pay the mounting bills. 'No, I can't

223

honestly say that's what I think – not after having worked at The Hall for so long.'

Jack gave a wry smile. 'Aha – you discovered all our murky secrets, is that it? And that's the reason you left in such a hurry.'

It was the first time that her leaving the Grevilles' employment had come up between them and she tensed as she stared ahead of her out through the windscreen of the car. She had no wish to taint what might just turn out to be a most enjoyable day by delving any further into his family affairs. 'Let's just say I think I know your family pretty well by now, Jack. Warts and all.'

Detecting a slight testiness in her voice, he had the good sense to leave it at that and changed the subject to one much more amenable. 'It's Wednesday today,' he said brightly. 'Sedbergh market day! If we can get near it, we'll buy some cream cakes for Tabby from the Women's Institute stall. They are always delicious.'

'That sounds lovely.'

They parked the car just before the junction of Main Street and Finkle Street and made their way through the thronging crowds to the church gate and the covered market stalls where all manner of goods were laid out for sale. Among the crowd was a generous sprinkling of older boys in blue blazers, short trousers and knee-length blue socks and Jack gave a sheepish grin as he nodded in their direction. 'Can you imagine the indignity of wearing those short pants when you're already a lanky six-footer?' The memory haunted him still.

'I bet you were a really insufferable little prig as a schoolboy.'

'Wrong. I was an insufferable *big* prig. You may remember, I was taller than Pa by the time I was fourteen.'

She looked at him quizzically and tried to remember at just what age she could first remember Black Jack. Then she shook her head. It was impossible. He had simply always been there. He had been part of her childhood. Part of the life of the dale. Black Jack and the Grevilles in so many ways *had been* Uthcrdalc as much as her beloved crags and fells. She shook her head. 'You were always just part of the scenery to me.'

He looked at her in surprise and then grinned. 'I'll settle for that.' After all, he knew just how much that scenery meant to her.

They set off for Tabby's sister Martha's small terraced cottage in Bainbridge Road, armed with a paper bag full of the most delicious-looking cream cakes that Bethany had ever set eyes on. She carried them carefully so as not to squash them as they made their way along the cobbled main street. She could hardly wait to see her old friend again.

The living room Tabby shared with her sister was small but cosy, with comfortable oak furniture and an inglenook fireplace in which a stack of pine logs blazed merrily. On the mantelpiece above stood two framed school photographs of Jack and Amos, resplendent in their blue blazers and school ties, their hair specially combcd for the occasion, above well-scrubbed smiling faces. Next to them sat a much humbler, framed family snapshot of Ned and a pang of pity pierced Bethany's heart. How he would have loved to have been able to come here to this town and be the proud wearer of one of those uniforms.

They found Tabby herself sitting in a straight-backed armchair next to the fire, a lace woollen shawl around her shoulders. She looked older and more shrunken than when either Bethany or Jack had last seen her, but there was no mistaking the delight in her eyes as the two young people came into the room.

'Well I never!' She held out her left hand in welcome and Jack hurried over to take it. Her right hand lay motionless in her lap, the plaster cast still visible on her wrist beneath the edge of the shawl. 'I never expected this!

Mister Jack *and* Bethany! Well I never did!' Her voice too seemed frailer than either of them remembered as she gazed from one to the other in obvious delight.

'Here we are – do be sitting down, the pair of you!' Martha Fleetwood brought two dining chairs from the table by the window and sat them side by side in front of the fire, between her sister's and her own. 'You two young folk make yourselves right at home now while I put the kettle on.'

After taking off their coats as Tabby insisted, Bethany and Jack made themselves comfortable under the housekeeper's delighted gaze. 'Both of you here to see me. It's better than any medicine the doctor can come up with, I can assure you of that! . . . And my, you do make a lovely couple!'

That was a comment Bethany knew would never have been made had the old lady any thoughts of ever returning to work at Wolf Hall; it would just not have been thought at all seemly. She gave a rather embarrassed smile in return as Jack Greville flashed her one of his wide grins.

'She's turned into quite a young lady, hasn't she, Tabby – our little Miss Baine?'

'Bethany was as good a young housekeeper in the making as ever I saw,' Tabby said. 'And it grieved me when she left, I can tell you that.' Her faded eyes fixed on Bethany. 'You have gone back, Bethany love, haven't you? You haven't left the Colonel to cope all alone after I took bad?'

Bethany felt herself flush and she shifted uncomfortably on her seat. But her embarrassment was immediately sensed and alleviated by Jack, who cut in with, 'Oh, don't you worry yourself about that, Tabby dear. There are others who know the value of this young lady just as well as you do – and I'm one. There's no way we would let her off the hook, don't you worry . . . But never you mind bothering yourself about worrying over us. It's you we're concerned about. Just you hurry up and get over this. We miss you, you know.'

Tabby's eyes misted behind the wire spectacles. 'Eh, Mister Jack, there's nothing I'd like better than to return to The Hall, you know that. But I reckon Our Lord has other ideas. Wouldn't you agree, Martha?'

Martha Fleetwood regarded her older sister with a wistful smile and sighed as she put down the tray with the tea things on top of a small folding table in front of them. 'Make a long arm now, you young folk. Them's fresh-baked scones and butter with this dish of tea.'

She handed a brimming teacup and saucer to each in turn, then turned back to her sister. 'They say the Lord works in mysterious ways, Tabby dear. But to my mind there's nothing mysterious about him deciding it was time you had a rest. And knowing you'd never do it of your own accord, He's forced you to retire. That's all. He's made the decision for you.'

Jack beamed as he sipped his tea. He couldn't have put it better himself.

They spent over an hour with the old housekeeper and her sister while Jack told them of his time in Australia and brought Tabby up to date with affairs at The Hall. She was keen to hear all about her other two 'boys', as she called them, and was much concerned to learn that their father's heart had been causing him problems again. 'It's right glad I am that you're back to take care of things, Mister Jack, I can tell you!' she said, shaking her head. 'Young Amos never did spend enough time on the estate, and . . . Well . . .' She paused. She could go on, but had no real wish to air Amos's failings in front of anyone, let alone his elder brother.

She held out her good hand and Jack squeezed the frail fingers in his own as she sighed and shook her head. 'He's a gradely lad at heart, is Amos. And I'm glad for Neddy's sake too that you're home. Amos hasn't had a great deal of time for him of late. Poor Ned's been left out in the cold over this Blackshirt business, you know, and he feels it.'

'I know. Pa did say he thought of having a uniform specially made for him – not a real BUF one, of course, but similar. But Mr Fisher, the tailor in Kirkby Stephen that he's used for years, turned out to be Jewish, so that was the end of that idea. Almost had a fit, the poor man did. Said he'd rather make a new black cloak for the devil himself than sully his hands on a Fascist black shirt.'

Tabby gave a strained smile. 'It seems they have made more enemies than friends since they came out in support of those Fascists,' she sighed. 'It's a pity, really; I'm sure if people knew more about it they would understand. All they want is what's best for Britain, like we all do.' She shook her head as she let out a heartfelt sigh. 'I don't know what this country's coming too, really I don't. All this political unrest and the poor new King abdicating like that. All I can say is, I'm glad I'm not young any more. Things weren't like this when I was your age. People knew their place and there was none of this argy-bargy about how to run the country.'

Jack patted the old lady's hand. 'It's the way of the world, Tabby dear. One day these will be the good old days to my generation. An amazing thought, but true nevertheless.'

His old housekeeper sighed once more. 'Aye, and it's a relief I won't be here to see it, I can tell you.'

Jack got up off his chair. He could see she was tiring. They had talked long enough for one day. He leant over and pecked the dry skin of her forehead. 'You'll give us all a run for our money in this Wilson Race of a life,' he assured her fondly.

He glanced down at Bethany and gave an imperceptible nod of the head for her to take her leave also.

'Goodbye, Tabby dear. I promise not to leave it so long the next time.'

'I'll see to that,' Jack butted in, as he took Bethany by the elbow and began to usher her towards the door as Martha went off in search of their coats. 'It won't be long before we're back, I can promise you that.'

It was just on lunchtime when they found themselves out in the street again and Jack suggested a meal in the Red Lion, the fine old sixteenth-century hotel opposite the church. Bethany gladly accepted. It was one of the coldest days of the winter so far, with a thick hoar frost still shining silver on the walls and cobbles, despite the pale sun that appeared from time to time in the pewter-coloured sky. The prospect of a blazing fire and a plate of the home-made steak pie they were advertising was too good to miss.

There were few other diners in the restaurant, for even on market days few people dined out midweek in small dales towns such as this, and Jack looked around appreciatively as they waited for their meal to be served. 'This was one thing I did miss out there in Australia,' he said with feeling. 'A good old English inn, with real English grub, as they called it. It's hard to beat.'

'I'm surprised to see you looking so healthy since you seem to have been fending for yourself up at The Hall,' Bethany mused.

He wagged an admonishing finger across the table at her. 'You women are all the same. Think us men will starve to death left to our own devices, don't you? Well, let me tell you, Miss Baine, I am a cook to be reckoned with! You come to dine at my place and you can have your pick of anything in the larder – as long as it's a boiled egg!'

She laughed. And was to laugh a lot more throughout the next hour. There was no denying Jack Greville was good company as he regaled her with tales of his life in the Australian Outback. She was not sure if she believed the half of it, but it really didn't matter. Never had she enjoyed a meal so much or the companionship that went with it.

At least, not since their meal on the night of the Abdication. The thought gave her quite a jolt.

Afterwards, Jack took her to see his old school, but after climbing Loftus Hill to reach the fine old buildings where he had spent so much of his childhood, they did not linger for long, preferring to wander further out to gaze through the freezing mist that had descended upon the great fells that surrounded the small town.

'This is the part of Sedbergh that I like best to remember,' he said, with a sweep of his arm in the direction of the snow-covered hills. 'Cautley Fell, Calf Fell and Winder Fell,' he informed her, pointing out each of the great, white-coated mounds in turn. 'And they do say, it's Cautley, Calf and Winder that make a Sedbergh man.'

'What on earth do you mean?'

And he went on to tell her of how as schoolboys they would don their running shorts and go haring up Howgill Lane, racing one another to the summit of one or other of what they regarded as their own special mountains. 'But March was really the month for the fell runners among us,' he said, with more than a touch of nostalgia. 'For it's then that all the boys take part in a special ten-mile race on the Tuesday nearest to Lady Day. The Wilson Race they call it. Off they go at the stroke of three, up the slopes of the fell, along the skyline ridge, across the rocky gills, and then down the notorious "Muddy Slide", to arrive back filthy and exhausted.'

'Sounds fun,' Bethany said, with more than a touch of irony.

'Puts backbone into 'em, young lady!' Jack declared, taking off his old form master to a T. 'Rulers of the Empire we're building here. The best of the breed!'

She raised an eyebrow and shook her head. 'You'll excuse me if I vomit, won't you?'

He grinned as he linked his arm in hers and they continued on past the fifteenth-century belfry tower, now resounding with the sound of student bell-ringers practising their peals. 'Does nothing impress you, Bethany Baine? Is there nothing I can say will make you think . . . Ah, what a fine young man this is! How lucky I am to be keeping his company on a cold and frosty winter's day like this, when half the girls of the North Riding would give their eye-teeth for just one wink of his eye!'

'Just half the girls?' she laughed. 'Why, Jack Greville, your modesty quite becomes you!'

It was already dark before they arrived back in Utherby and, reluctant to allow the day to end, Jack suggested they head for Corrigan's to finish the evening with a quiet dinner.

Bethany shook her head. 'I really think it's time I was going in,' she said, as the car pulled up outside Number Twelve, The Row. She saw the Capsticks' curtains move and smiled across at him in the semi-darkness. 'Whatever will the neighbours think?'

'Do you mind what they think?' His voice was serious.

She shrugged, then gave a quiet laugh. 'Do you?'

He was silent for a moment, then answered quietly. 'No, no I don't. In fact, I want them to know. I want everyone in this whole gossipy little village to know what a good time we had today, and what a good time we're going to have tomorrow, and the day after that!'

'Hey, hang on a minute!'

'I thought you didn't care what they thought.'

'I don't.'

'Well, then, did you or did you not enjoy today?'

'I did.'

'Then what's wrong with us repeating it tomorrow, and the day after, and the day after that, if we want to?' He was well aware he was getting carried away by his own enthusiasm, but he really didn't give a damn. He had not enjoyed a day so much in years.

Bethany shook her head in confusion. 'Well, there's

231

nothing wrong with it, I suppose,' she began uncertainly. 'But . . .'

'But nothing!' he cut in. 'You enjoyed today and I enjoyed today. So I'll call for you at seven-thirty tomorrow night. Be ready.'

And she was.

And she was ready the following night and the night after that, until the whole gossipy little village, as he had termed it, knew that she, Bethany Baine, the quarrier's daughter, was seeing Jack Greville, the Colonel's eldest son and the heir to Wolf Hall.

'Eh, Beth love, you've landed a right 'un there,' Hector Wilks said one morning after an unexpected visit from Jack just before Christmas to present the shopkeeper with a bottle of vintage Scotch malt whisky, for allowing his assistant so much time off over the previous two weeks.

'A small liquid token of my appreciation, kind sir,' Jack said. 'A drop of Christmas spirit to enable your good self to be even more full of good cheer than otherwise!'

Hector Wilks had been delighted. 'A real gentleman Jack Greville has turned out to be. A real gentleman, and there's few enough of them around these days.'

Bethany glanced out of the window and raised her hand in return to Jack's wave as he put his sports car into gear and roared off down the road. She had to admit her boss was right. But their growing relationship still troubled her, nevertheless. It also appeared to trouble the village as well, for by no means all their customers were as happy as Hector Wilks was at the knowledge that Cheevers Baine's daughter was walking out with a Greville – and the eldest son into the bargain. What had just been the odd comment in the beginning had now turned into some very cutting remarks deliberately made within her hearing. And what hurt most of all, many of them had been voiced by people she had regarded as her friends.

Even her own mother felt uneasy about them seeing so

much of each other. Although she had voiced no real objection to Bethany herself, Betty Baine had made her qualms known to the Reverend Barden, who of late, Bethany had noticed, seemed to have taken on the role of her special adviser on practically every issue under the sun.

The cleric lost no time in passing the older woman's fears on to her daughter. He was the shop's last customer on the afternoon Jack delivered the bottle of Scotch to Mr Wilks, and Bethany looked at him in some surprise as she wrapped his quarter of Cheddar cheese and listened to him ask if she knew just how worried her mother was about the developing situation.

'What do you mean, "worried"? What on earth has Mam got to be worried about?' As far as she was concerned, her mother was confiding far too much to the clergyman these days. From what Bethany could gather, he seemed to be popping in for cups of tea and a chat every other day. 'I don't know what you're on about.'

Kenneth Barden looked distinctly uncomfortable as he accepted the wrapped cheese and placed it in his overcoat pocket. This really wasn't the sort of job he was best cut out for – telling young people how to run their lives. 'You're a sensible young woman, Bethany. You must know that some things are acceptable in this world and some things are not . . .'

He was struggling for the best way to put it; the last thing he wanted to do was to alienate Betty's daughter. But someone had to make the young woman face facts, nevertheless. Her mother was certain no good would come of it and that Bethany would end up with a broken heart and injured pride, despite her protestations they were 'just good friends'. Kenneth Barden cleared his throat as his eyes met those of the young woman across the counter. 'Well, you must know that a fellow like Jack Greville will never be at liberty to – to – well, to . . .'

'Make an honest woman of me? Is that it?' Bethany's stare was unblinking.

Kenneth Barden coloured and looked the other way. She wasn't going to make this easy for him, that was for sure. 'I wasn't going to put it quite like that.'

'No, but that's what you were thinking, all the same.'

There was no point in lying. The girl was nobody's fool. 'If you want to put it like that . . . Well, yes. They marry their own kind, do folk like the Grevilles.'

'Not ordinary mortals like us.' Bethany deliberately turned away and began brushing crumbs from the counter.

He sighed. This was not going the way he had intended it at all when he had promised Betty he would have a word with her elder daughter. 'Look, my dear, we — your mother and I — we just don't want you to get hurt, that's all. We want you to realize before things go any further that there can be no future in it. Jack Greville is a healthy young man. That he's taken with you is plain for all to see, but I know for a fact it won't go any further than that.'

Bethany looked up sharply from tidying the counter. 'Oh, you know that for a fact, do you?'

'Yes, I do.' Should he be honest or not? Tell the truth and shame the devil was a motto he had always practised and preached. He took a deep breath. 'Young Amos told me.'

Anger flared in Bethany's eyes. 'You mean you discussed Jack and me with Amos Greville?'

Kenneth Barden put out a pacifying hand, but it floundered in mid-air as Bethany took a step back from the counter and glared at him. 'Now, now don't go getting yourself all het up,' he protested. 'It came up in conversation, that's all.'

'And Amos said there would be no future in it.'

'Aye, to be perfectly honest with you, he said exactly that. And went on to say that if I cared at all for your feelings I'd have a word with you before things got too serious on your part.' He looked increasingly uncomfortable as he added, 'In fact, he said I'd be doing you a favour, seeing as you were such a romantic at heart.'

'I beg your pardon? Amos said what?'

The minister looked quite taken aback by the ice that had come into both Bethany's voice and eyes. But he had gone this far, so he might as well continue. Not only Amos Greville, but Betty expected it of him, and she was the very last person he wanted to let down. 'Aye, well, you might as well know, Amos confided in me that when you worked at The Hall you had had this . . . well, this infatuation you could say, for him, but that when you saw it wasn't getting anywhere you transferred your affections to Jack when he arrived back from Australia.'

Then, seeing the effect his words were having, he added quickly, 'It's simply that he wants to protect you, Bethany love, that's all. His brother Jack's always had the reputation of being a bit of a ladies' man. He doesn't want to see you hurt, that's all.'

Amos Greville didn't want to see her hurt, that was all! Bethany took a deep breath. It was taking her all her time to control herself. Her hands were two clenched fists behind the counter as she fought to keep her voice steady. 'So Amos Greville doesn't want to see me hurt, is that it? Now there's a noble human being for you!'

And Kenneth Barden almost believed her, until she lifted the flap of the counter and pushed past him to stride across the floor and throw open the door of the shop in a clear invitation for him to leave. 'I would be very grateful if you and the other nosey parkers in this village kept your long snouts out of other folks' affairs. I will not have my life discussed by you or anybody else – particularly that dirty beggar Amos Greville!'

'Bethany, really!' The Minister looked quite shocked.

'I mean it,' she continued, her voice rising. 'And I'd be

obliged if you would pass that message on to the others who have taken it upon themselves to pass judgement on whatever there is or isn't between me and Jack Greville — particularly that loathsome toad of a brother of his, Amos! It's our business, do you hear? Ours! And no one else's!'

And with that she turned and rushed past him into the back shop, leaving an astonished Kenneth Barden staring after her retreating figure and looking straight into the eyes of an equally astonished Hector Wilks, who had emerged from the back shop, where he could not but help overhear what had just passed between them.

The shopkeeper immediately rose to his assistant's defence. 'Eh, I think thou's gone a mite over the score there, Mr Barden. There was no call for that. He's a nice young fella, is Jack Greville and there's no harm in them keeping company as far as I can see.'

The Reverend Barden pulled the collar of his coat up around his neck as he prepared to leave. 'Perhaps that's half the trouble, Mr Wilks,' he said solemnly. 'Perhaps some of us are not far-sighted enough to see beyond the length of our own noses. Young Bethany there is flouting the conventions of respectable behaviour in this village and it won't be tolerated by some. I'm not saying I'm one of them, mind, but it's as well that she knows it. You don't go breaking conventions and get away unscathed, you know. There's been talk and there'll be lots more before this year is at an end, mark my words. I just hope she has the stomach for it, that's all.'

From her position behind the curtain that separated the front from the back shop Bethany could not help but hear every word as she took off her apron and reached for her coat. Her face was set, as was her resolve, as she stood before the chipped wall mirror and pulled on her hat. Let them talk! Let them all talk till they're blue in the face, she thought bitterly. She had done nothing to be ashamed of in keeping company with Jack Greville, and if she had had any doubts herself about the wisdom of their relationship before, they were now dispelled in a firm resolve to rub all their gossipy noses in it. Particularly that loathsome Amos Greville's. How dare he insinuate what he did! How dare he!

But despite her resolve, and try as she might to put the clergyman's warnings behind her, she brooded over the conversation during the next few days. It did not help any that Jack was up in Scotland for the week. He was combining a stock-buying visit to Perthshire with a friend's wedding and Bethany tried not to read too much into the fact that she had not been asked to accompany him. Her anxiety was heightened by a meeting with Ellen Capstick's mother two days after Jack had left for Perth. Her neighbour informed her that she had been taken on on a daily basis by the Colonel to act as a part-time housekeeper at The Hall and, seeing the interest in Bethany's eyes, she lost no time in enlightening her as to another reason behind Jack's visit north of the border.

'From what I've heard, young Mister Jack's expected to come back from Scotland with a rather special front-seat passenger in that new sports car of his,' she said knowingly. 'According to Amos, the lad whose wedding Jack is best man at has got a sister who Jack's been sweet on since their schooldays. Met her on a holiday up there, he did, when they were about sixteen, and she's been writing to him in Australia. She's chief bridesmaid at the wedding . . . And you know what they say about the best man and the bridesmaid . . .'

Bethany listened until she could bear to hear no more. She did not even bother to make her apologies for turning on her heel and making off down the road in the direction of The Row. Her neighbour had aimed her darts good and true and they had hit the target.

She could not think of anything else that night, although she knew equally well that the words had been uttered with the sole intention of causing pain. After tea she sat silent and sullen in the armchair by the front-room window, watching the rain fall on the cobblestones and run in dirty rivulets into the overflowing gutters. On her lap lay a copy of the *Daily Mirror* that Hector Wilks had given her to take home for her mother. The newspapers were full of pictures and stories of the new King George and his pretty Scottish queen, Elizabeth, but somehow she found no comfort in reading about royalty or anyone else in the public eye. Her thoughts were hundreds of miles away, north of the border, and would remain there until Jack came back, with or without a front-seat passenger.

The following day she deliberately avoided getting into conversation with old friends and neighbours whenever possible, but one person she did not spurn a friendly chat with was Warton Carnforth. She saw the Colonel's old retainer at least once or twice a week and always found time to pass the time of day whenever he popped into the shop for his few purchases. He had been a quiet but comforting presence during her difficult first days at Wolf Hall and she remembered him fondly for that and knew he still harboured a soft spot for her.

It was late on Friday afternoon, there was no one else in the shop, and she was just in the act of preparing to lock up when he came in for his usual ounce of tobacco and packet of roll-your-own cigarette papers. She knew he was well aware of the fact she and Jack were the main topic of conversation of the moment around the place, but both studiously avoided any mention of the Colonel's eldest son or his trip up north as they passed the time of day and she asked after the rest of the family.

The old man's brow furrowed as he stuffed the purchases into his jacket pocket. 'Oh, there's nowt much to complain about up at t'Hall, Bethany love – not wi' t'Colonel and young Ned at any rate. Amos though, I'm not so sure about. The lad's gettin' his sel' too deep into things he shouldn't, if you ask me . . . Not that anybody ever does, mind!' He scratched the day's growth on his chin and gave a weary smile. 'I'm nowt but an owd bit o'furniture around the place, you know that.'

'What's Amos been up to now, then?' She did not really want to know, after the trouble he had been trying to cause, but she felt she should show an interest; the old man was obviously worried about something.

'It were bad enough wi' all those Blackshirt friends o' his around the place in the past,' he said confidentially. 'But, if you ask me, this lot he's got entangled wi' now are a darn sight worse.'

Bethany's ears pricked up. 'And what lot are they?'

Old Carnforth shook his head and scratched the stubble of his chin once more. 'The White Knights of Britain, they call themselves. Wear white cloaks with hoods and all that type of stuff. Based on yon American Ku Klux Klan they are. Hate half the human race, it seems – Jews, Negroes, Catholics . . .'

He leant forward and his voice dropped even more. 'Got all sorts of secret passwords and magical mumbo-jumbo they recite,' he informed her, in a voice almost of awe. 'Their patron saint is the first King Edward, who expelled the Jews from England hundreds of years ago, and they have to swear to the death to carry out his policies once again. Weird it is, Bethany love, I can tell you. Scares the living daylights out of me at any rate!'

'But how do you know all this?' Bethany asked. It certainly didn't surprise her, after what she had witnessed before at The Hall, but it gave her a great sense of unease nevertheless.

' 'Cause I've seen it with my own eyes, that's how. In Lot's Barn, it were.' The old man glanced around him nervously, then when he was satisfied there were no other prying ears he leant even closer and continued, 'Know that old barn t'other side of the stable at t'Hall?'

She nodded.

'Well, they hold their meetings in there. Every Friday they have them. Eight o'clock on the dot, and they go on till about nine. They'll be having one tonight – all prancing around in them cloaks and hoods and stuff and chanting their rubbish and saluting their swastikas. I tell you, lass, it's sick. I know it's sick, for I've seen things there wi' my own eyes I couldn't tell a soul. Even you.'

Bethany felt that same shiver of fear she had felt so often in the past as she nodded her head slowly. 'I understand, I really do. I'd keep well away from them if I were you. If there really is such a thing as the devil and dark forces in this world, then they are the ones capable of conjuring them up, I'm sure of that.'

The old man nodded and sighed as he turned for the door. 'Things have come to a sad turn when we have that kind of thing happening in our own village, wouldn't you say, lass? God knows what we fought the last war for. It certainly wasn't to end up with this type of thing in our own back yard.'

Bethany stood motionless for a long time after he had gone. That Amos Greville was a malign influence in this village she had no doubt and, worse than that, she felt herself a personal victim of his malevolence. There was no doubt in her mind he was doing his best to destroy her relationship with Jack and that if she did not do something about it, he would go on sowing his seeds of doubt and destruction until he succeeded. There was nothing else for it; she would have to have it out with him. And not only that – it might just give her a better idea of exactly what was going on in this village. Were there really dark forces at work here, or was it simply Amos up to his old tricks? There was only one way of finding out. Eight o'clock at the old barn, Old Carnforth had said. She would be there.

Chapter Twelve

The moon had a halo of pale silver in a sky already bright with stars as Bethany made her way up the drive of Wolf Hall. Despite the darkness, she kept well to the side of the road, beneath the canopy of bare branches of the gnarled trees that lined the drive like aged sentinels, stretching their bare limbs towards the starlit heavens. She could see a light at only one window of the big house; it seemed to be coming from the Colonel's bedroom, and she imagined the elderly man lying there in the big four-poster bed, a pile of books and newspapers littering the elaborately embroidered quilt, and a fug of tobacco smoke hanging in the air. Since his first brush with heart trouble several years previously, he had increasingly used his bedroom as a study, and his bed as his favourite desk.

But she knew she was not headed for The Hall on this occasion and her eventual assignation was not with the retired soldier but with his second son, although she was the last person she knew Amos Greville would be expecting to meet tonight.

She still could not bring herself to think of that particular young man without emotion, and nerves tightened their grip on her stomach as she turned off the main drive to make for the track that wound round the back of the stables and other outbuildings that lined the courtyard at the rear of the house.

As a child she had often sneaked into this area at the back of The Hall in the conker season with a few of the other most daring children from the village. Some of the finest horse-chestnut trees grew along this old road, and half the fun had been in outwitting Old Carnforth, who would lose no time in chasing them off, invoking a stream of blasphemous curses upon their heads as he did so. It seemed ironic that she should now be traversing this very road with what amounted to his blessing to spur her on.

She could see quite well, for the moon and stars lent a silver glow to the surrounding countryside, and the old stone outbuildings that littered the area at the back of the big house loomed large and strangely unfamiliar as she passed. Although she was moving as silently as she could on the icy ground, some slight sound must have given away her presence to the pack of fox hounds the family kept in the kennels about twenty yards to her right, and to her dismay one of the dogs began to bark as she passed, then several others joined in. She shivered. She had always hated that sound – a cacophony of barking and baying hounds that seemed synonymous with Amos Greville and his way of life.

Her nervousness calmed slightly as she left the restless animals behind and continued her way along the old drove road that led across the edge of the moor to the village of Butterslack, some five miles beyond.

Lot's Barn, to which Old Carnforth had referred, stood on its own about half a mile from Wolf Hall itself, on the road to the old disused farm of which it formed part. No one could remember the Lot who had given the farm and its barn their names, and with the place no longer tenanted, both it and its barn had been out of use for as far back as Bethany could remember. Although they belonged to the Wolf Hall estate, the Colonel preferred to utilize the more convenient buildings nearer to hand and had let many of the outlying places sink into a quiet decay.

As she rounded the last corner of the road, its stone bulk loomed out of the darkness about fifty yards ahead. It stood back about twenty feet from the edge of the road, amid a tangle of nettles and a generation or more's undergrowth. There were no lights visible at all and at first she thought she had been led on a wild goose chase; it looked as if it had not seen a human being near it for decades. An owl hooted from somewhere up near the roof and made her start and catch her breath as it took flight at her approach, swooping down just above her head, to disappear with a flap of wings into the night. As she drew nearer she could see that the windows of the barn appeared to have been boarded up, but wait . . . a chink of light was just visible from the one furthest away from her.

Her heart began to pound. Old Carnforth was right. There must be someone in there.

It was not until she was within a few yards of the building that she heard the first sound from inside the old stone walls, and it chilled her blood. It was like the strange melancholy incantation of monks she had once heard on the wireless as she sat in the kitchen with Tabby one Saturday night. The sound rose and fell on the night air and sent a physical tremor through her body, causing the skin of her arms to turn to gooseflesh. Through the thick stone walls of the barn it reverberated like the hum of the universe itself. But she could not believe whatever was going on in there had anything to do with any God she knew.

The long grass was full of tangled briars and nettles and was damp and slippery underfoot with the thick hoar frost that lay like icing sugar across the night landscape. She cursed beneath her breath as the thorns pulled at her coat and she felt her stockings tear as the prickly branches ripped into her legs.

When finally she emerged on to the shorter grass around the building, she could see that the large swing doors at the gable end of the barn had been closed from the inside and there was no possibility of getting even a peek at whatever was going on inside. Then her eyes lighted on the old stone steps that climbed up the outside of the building to what had once been the hayloft above. Dare she? If she could get in that way, it would certainly give her a grandstand view of whatever devilment was going on beneath. They must be almost finished now, for she had timed her arrival for just before nine o'clock. What she had already heard had both horrified and intrigued her and she wanted to get an idea of exactly what was going on in this place, before she confronted Amos Greville on his own. Old Carnforth had said that as Grand Master of these so-called White Knights of Britain, or whatever Amos liked to call himself, he was always the last to leave, and that would suit her just fine. She did not particularly want an audience for what she had to say tonight.

She could feel her heart pounding as she picked her way over the icy ground and put a tentative first foot on the bottom step. The barn must have been all of three hundred years old and the treads were worn smooth and slippery underfoot with the night frost. She began to edge her way up the side of the building slowly, one step at a time, until she reached the top, and there she pressed herself against the wall and breathed a great sigh of relief.

There was now what sounded like singing coming from down below as, in the moonlight, she searched for the handle to the wooden, ramshackle door that faced her. It was missing, broken off generations ago, by one of the marauding children from the village such as she had once been, no doubt.

Her fingers pushed tentatively at the wooden planks of the door but it refused to budge. She doubted if it had been locked from the inside however, so, summoning all her courage and strength, she leaned her right shoulder against it and pushed with all her might. It began to topple inwards under her weight, but she was saved from its total collapse by one rusty hinge which, thankfully, still held.

She landed painfully, half on top of the edge of the collapsed door and half on what felt and smelt like a pile of ancient sacking.

'What was that?'

She froze as a male voice barked the words from what seemed only inches away, beneath her.

'Oh, just the rats,' someone replied. 'The bloody place is full of them.'

Bethany held her breath. They were only a few feet below her, and all that prevented her from tumbling down into their midst were the rotting planks that straddled the ancient rafters. They had once made up a perfectly sound floor, but now, from the feel and the smell, they were riddled with woodworm and every type of wet and dry rot imaginable.

The timbers at her side of the floor nearest the door seemed to be in a worse state than those at the far side, so if she could possibly manage it without being heard, she decided she would attempt to get across to the other side. The middle of the floor seemed particularly bad, for there was a crack of almost a foot wide between two of the planks. It would be ideal for her purposes, however, for if she could crawl over to that and edge her way round it to the other more sound part of the floor, she would have an excellent bird's-eye view of the proceedings.

She manoeuvred herself on to all fours, slowly and painfully, for she had banged her knee in her unceremonious entry. She began to inch her way across the floor. It made unnerving progress, for so clear were the voices that floated up to her from down below, it sounded as if she was crawling in their midst.

Moving only an inch at a time, she edged her way forward, skirting the gap in the floor by at least a foot, at last to find a safer perch across the other side of the loft. And when she found the courage to lean over, the sight that met her eyes through the gap in the floorboards made

245

her breath catch in her throat. It was pure theatre down there, but theatre of the most diabolic kind. There were at least thirty people present, all dressed in long white cloaks and hoods similar to those worn by the Ku Klux Klan in America's Deep South. She could not make out the identities of any of them, for their faces were totally obscured, save for slits cut out of the material for their eyes. Their voices, however, it was impossible to disguise, and there was no doubt who was leading the proceedings. She would recognize that voice anywhere, for it had haunted her dreams since childhood. It was Amos Greville.

He was standing in the middle of a circle painted out of whitewash, which had what appeared to be various magical symbols inset in triangles all pointing towards the centre. From her vantage point Bethany could see at least five or six quite clearly; these included the sun, the moon, the swastika, and the already notorious Double S lightning flashes of Hitler's SS. From the lighted candles and other items that lay around what looked like a makeshift altar, it seemed as if the main ceremonies had already taken place. Amos was about to give the assembled company their final, inspirational, winding-up speech of the week.

As she watched, Amos Greville stood there, arms outstretched, holding aloft in his right hand what looked like some sort of mace with a bird's head on the end of it, and in his left, a book. He was surrounded by the group of hooded figures who stood holding hands as if ready to begin some crazy dance around their human totem.

After appearing to bless the assembled group, Amos began to speak in that same familiar, almost ranting style he had used on public platforms around the dale during election time. It was a poor imitation of the style of oratory used by his two heroes Oswald Mosley and Adolf Hitler, but it did not lend itself to the English language and sounded so ludicrously theatrical to Bethany's ears that she wondered how those others down below could stand there and take it seriously.

'True brothers of the blood,' he began, 'once more before we take our leave, we are gathered here within the most sacred circle to pledge allegiance to the cause of our country and our race. We know that at home and abroad there are enemies to this cause; they have been identified by our leader across the water, Adolf Hitler himself.

'In this book, *The Protocols of the Elders of Zion*, we have the final and ultimate proof that cannot be denied that the hydra-headed conspiracy of World Jewry is at work to take over our world for their own greed and self-gain. This must never happen, and we, along with our brothers across the water, are pledged to work against that conspiracy with body and soul. As we leave this place tonight, we must be aware that there are those who wish to thwart our sacred task – there are those, such as the "slobbering, bastardized, mendacious triumvirate" of Churchill, Eden and Cooper, referred to by our brother William Joyce, who wish to use the House of Commons to prevent true patriots such as ourselves from enlisting in the British Army. This must not be allowed to happen. We must do all in our power to rally to the flag and save our nation from the infidel.

'We know that, to aid us in this fight, we must call upon every power at our command, both of this world and beyond. In Germany our brothers in the National Socialist Party have already done this and are reaping the rewards for all to see. We know that it is no coincidence that as their symbols they have adopted the *Hakenkreuz* – or swastika – that ancient crooked cross that has been the most potent occult symbol since time immemorial, or that they have chosen the double S of the "sig" rune, that sacred symbol of racial purity, to identify the members of that elite band of brothers, the SS. Those two tools of the

Ancients have been used by practitioners of the Old Religion since time immemorial and are with us now as we stand here and pay them homage in this our own most sacred inner circle.

'We know that our esteemed brother across the water Heinrich Himmler has created his elite band of SS brothers by basing their most sacred principles on the ethics of the Ancients which were recognized and utilized by the Order of the Jesuits in the service of the prophet Jesus Christ. These ancient and revered statutes of service, first presented by Ignatius Loyola, are now called into service again to form the pattern which will lead us and our SS brothers forward to the New Dawn.

'What we are now entering, brothers, is the Age of Horus, the Age of War. Let every man here prepare himself for service. Our SS brothers have been instructed to prepare for their glorious mission, to create a New Age, a New World, a New Man, and they have already embarked on that most sacred mission. And in co-operation with the divine laws of the Cosmos, they have sworn vows which proclaim their allegiance to our irreversible human destiny. Let us salute them now, and pledge once more to join them in that fight . . . Hail the SS!'

And to a man, the company that surrounded him raised their right hands in the Fascist salute and proclaimed: 'Hail the SS! Hail to the Brotherhood! Hail Hitler! Hail to the New Dawn!'

From her perch above the proceedings Bethany watched in both fear and fascination. It was all there – Fascism and what they called the Old Religion, but what she knew to be Black Magic. It was all mixed up just as it had been ever since that night when as a child she had witnessed her first Fire of Beltane, and then, years later, had relived that same uncomfortable feeling when she had happened upon Amos kneeling before his bedroom fireplace in Wolf Hall. She felt as if she was bearing witness to something that was as old as this land of the North Riding itself. All those figures down there were simply a manifestation of something that had been practised here for centuries. But, despite that, she could not help feeling there was a new urgency to their rituals, and that it was all bound up in this new political creed those such as Amos were propagating. Those were British Fascists down there, there was no doubt about that. But were they really planning to take over the world, and to vow its allegiance to the dark forces that had hovered over them all since before Time itself?

A shiver ran through her. Surely folk around here were too down-to-earth – too straightforward and God-fearing to be taken in by all this mumbo-jumbo? Then her mind raced back once more to her very first introduction to this black underside to life – to that ceremony on top of Uther Crag she had witnessed all those years ago as a child. Was it really so far removed from reality to believe that at least those same people who had spent the night worshipping the ancient god Beltane could also be persuaded, like the German people across the Channel, to throw in their lot with leaders such as Adolf Hitler and his SS who, through the harnessing of these ancient forces and rituals, had promised to lead them through this dark age of Depression to the brightness of that promised New Dawn?

Suddenly Amos Greville, with his silly chanting and love of dressing up, was no longer just a posturing, harmless, fanciful creature. He and his kind were a real threat to their very way of life – to the way of life of everyone who cherished all that was decent and good in this country.

Bethany sank back on the rotting sacking that littered the ancient timbers and took a deep breath. That must have been his closing speech, for they were preparing to leave down below. She could hear what sounded like their paraphernalia being packed away amid the hum of male voices.

She half sat up and, pulling herself a few more feet across the loft floor, she leaned against the stone wall of the barn. It had all become too much and she wished she had never come here tonight to bear witness to what was happening right here in her very own village. If England was to go the way of Germany, she did not wish to know. It was both an awesome and a frightening thought. And suddenly she felt tired. It was as if she had found herself in some terrible nightmare from which she would surely soon awaken.

She closed her eyes and the hum of voices down below throbbed in her ears then gradually faded. The smell of the ancient beams and floor timbers and decaying sacking suffused her senses, and it was mingled with another scent – a cloying perfumed scent that had floated up from down below. She had been aware of it as soon as she entered the loft. She had never actually smelt incense before, but felt that it must surely be that exotic substance.

The concoction of smells, distant sounds and the darkness that surrounded her seemed to have a soporific effect so that she was finding it more and more difficult to stay awake as her eyelids grew heavier and heavier . . . Perhaps she could speak to Amos Greville tomorrow . . . Perhaps what she had to say could wait those few hours at least . . . Perhaps . . . Perhaps . . .

'In the name of . . . !'

The male voice jerked her out of her momentary loss of consciousness and she scrambled to sit up. In front of her, bathed in a pool of flickering blue light from a lantern held in his right hand, a tall shape loomed above her out of the night.

'Amos!'

Amos Greville, now divested of his cloak and hood, was standing about fifteen feet from her, on the other side of the loft floor, his right hand holding aloft the lantern, and in the crook of his left arm a collection of furled flags. A cold panic gripped her as her eyes focused on the tall, bulky outline of his figure. She had totally forgotten that these old barns also had inside steps up to the loft area. This was obviously where they stored their devilish trappings. His sudden appearance threw her into an almost blind panic, but the sight of her sitting there had had a similar effect on him. He was staring down at her as if he had seen a ghost.

'What in tarnation are you doing here?' He did not even wait for her to answer the question as he placed the lantern on top of an old chest then threw the flags he was carrying down on to the floor of the loft and answered his own question. 'You little bitch – you've been spying on us!'

Bethany shook her head vehemently. 'No . . . no . . . I haven't . . .' But her excuses ran out there. They both knew that was exactly what she had been doing.

'How the hell did you know to come here?' he demanded.

She stared up at him through the darkness. Her mouth had gone quite dry, but nothing would possess her to tell on the old man. 'I don't owe you any explanation,' she said, with far more confidence than she felt.

'But I think you do.' She could sense rather than see him begin to smile in the darkness as he began to walk towards her. 'I think you owe me one hell of an explanation, Miss Baine!'

She scrambled to her feet and pressed herself against the wall in a vain attempt to put as much distance between herself and the advancing figure as possible. She now knew exactly what a trapped fox felt like when Amos's beloved, baying hounds were rounding in for the kill. 'I came here to speak to you,' she said quickly. 'That's all.' She must get him talking. If she could only keep him talking, she might be all right. 'I wanted to talk to you about Jack.'

'Aha – my dear big brother!' He snorted in derision as he moved closer still. 'And what can you possibly tell me about your affair with my big brother that the whole world doesn't already know? There's not a man, woman or child in the whole of this dale who doesn't know that you've been doing your whoring best to trap him.'

She stared at him through the darkness as she felt the blood surge to the cheeks. How dare he . . . ! Just how dare he . . . !

'Yes, when it didn't work with me, you thought you'd try out your tarty little ways with him, didn't you?' he mocked. 'Just because I wouldn't come the lovey-dovey stuff with you, you thought you'd have a go at him, didn't you? You thought he might just be soft enough to fall for it.'

He moved even closer until his face was only inches from her own and she recognized the familiar smell of whisky on his breath. It brought it all back, every awful moment of that morning that would live in her mind for ever.

'Was he good, then, bitch?' he taunted. 'Was my beloved big brother any good as a stud – or did he treat you just the same as he treated those poor bleeding sheep he's been buggering for the past few years out there in Australia?'

Revulsion filled her as she pressed herself so hard against the old stones of the wall that it hurt. 'You're a pig – you know that, Amos Greville? You're nothing but a revolting pig of a human being . . . And if you must know, then, yes – he was good. Damned good. A darned sight better than you, at any rate, but then that would not have been hard to beat!'

The sound of the slap that stung the side of her face resounded through the darkness and would have sent her reeling backwards had she not been already hard against the wall. It brought tears to her eyes as her right hand flew to the stinging skin of her cheek. She knew she could not retaliate in kind, but she could with words. All the hurt, all the anger that had been festering in her since that awful morning came tumbling out as she spat at him, 'You think you're so big and clever, don't you, Amos Greville? You and your stupid dressing up and marching around like some silly toy soldier – and all that childish nonsense you get up to. I saw you that night, you know, sitting there in front of the fire in your bedroom, prostrating yourself on the rug to a grate full of coals.'

She began to laugh, a scoffing, scathing laugh that bordered on hysteria. 'I found it, you know, that pile of my hair you collected. Did it give you some sort of cheap thrill going up to my room and pulling it from my hairbrush? Is that really how a grown man – a blood brother of the SS – gets his thrills, Amos Greville? Would the great white *Führer* Adolf Hitler himself be impressed with that?'

His face was in almost complete darkness, but she could hear from his breathing, which was becoming faster and more harsh, that she was getting to him. The knowledge spurred her on. 'There is one man who doesn't need to creep about collecting my cast-off hair, you know. He can run his fingers through it any time . . . Like this . . .' She moved slightly into a shaft of moonlight that beamed down in a silver pool from a gap in the roof. And when she knew she was fully visible she pulled off her hat and ran her fingers through her hair, letting it trickle seductively through her fingers. 'Unlike you, your Jack can have any part of me – freely given – any time . . . Because unlike you, he is a real man, not a clockwork, toy soldier who . . .'

'You little bitch!'

She got no further, for he grabbed her by the hair and swung her off her feet. She landed heavily on top of a pile of sacking and he fell on top of her.

'Bitch!' he hissed into her face. 'You scheming little bitch!' He had her by the shoulders and was banging her head up and down on the sack-covered floor. 'This family has been cursed since you wormed your way into it . . . But don't think you have it all your own way. I had you before my beloved brother, remember. You were mine before you were ever Jack's – and will be again!'

'I was never yours, Amos Greville!'

'Oh, yes, you were! And you will be again . . . And again . . . And again . . .'

He was pulling at her clothes now with his right hand as his left hand pinned her to the floor by the neck. She could hardly breathe, but was determined he should not win a second time. If it took every ounce of strength in her body, she would not submit again.

And suddenly she was fighting like a wildcat. Hands and nails, legs and feet were all lashing out in every direction, until he was forced to relax his grip on her throat and she succeeded in throwing him off her with one almighty heave. He made to get up, but had only got as far as his knees when she lashed out again with her right foot and caught him in the groin, sending him flying backwards with a sharp yell of pain.

They were in almost total darkness now and she was aware of him scrabbling on the floor. She knew she had hurt him and was determined to take advantage as she got to her feet and, grabbing the end of one of the banners he had thrown down earlier, she lashed out in his direction.

By the sound of the crack, it seemed to catch him on the side of the head, for he went sprawling back on the floor, then let out what was more of a groan than a scream as the rotting area around the hole in the floor began to give way beneath him.

Bethany listened in a mixture of horror and relief as the groan turned into a cry and he tumbled helplessly into the darkness below.

She could still hear the clatter in her ears, then the dull thud as he hit the stone-flagged floor of the barn, as she made for the upper door through which she had first entered the loft. In her panic she forgot how icy it was outside and her shoes slid on the top step, to send her crashing down the remaining fifteen steps to the ground below.

The fall winded her, but beyond a painful back and hip, which she knew would be badly bruised come morning, she was relieved to find she was not seriously hurt as she pulled herself to her feet. Her first inclination was to run as fast as she could away from this place, then her thoughts returned to the man still inside the barn. Should she help him, or just leave him there? If she left him to rot it would be no more than he deserved.

But, slowly and very reluctantly, she began to walk towards the barn door. It creaked on its hinges as she pushed it open and peered inside. 'Are you all right?'

'I need help.' The voice that answered was faint and quite unlike itself.

She ventured in further, but went no closer than twenty feet away from the crumpled figure in the middle of the floor. 'Are you badly hurt?'

The figure moved slightly, then let out a long groan. 'It's my left leg. I think it's broken.'

'Stay there,' she began to say, then realizing the ridiculousness of the comment, she added quickly, 'I'll get help. I'll send someone as soon as I can.'

Then she turned on her heel and ran out of the barn, just in time to see another figure disappearing round the corner by the outside steps. For a moment she almost froze with fear, then a thought occurred to her. It was probably Carnforth checking to see that she was all right. He must have guessed she might come here tonight and felt responsible for her.

'Stop!' she shouted. 'Stop or I'll shoot!' She had no idea

why she gave such a stupid order, for she had never held a gun in her life, let alone possessed one.

But the cry had its effect on the fleeing figure. It slowed down and turned round, then slowly began to walk towards her.

She stared at it in amazement. 'Why, Neddy, whatever are you doing here?'

Chapter Thirteen

Amos Greville escaped from the fall in Lot's Barn with nothing more than a badly broken leg. 'Broken in three places, Dr Munro informs us,' Jack told Bethany, the day after his return from Scotland. 'And it might take quite a while to heal.'

Bethany looked across at him from the passenger seat of his sports car and tried to sound as concerned as possible. 'That's too bad. He'll miss not being able to ride.' She had no idea how much Jack had heard of her own involvement in the incident, so it would be better to let him do most of the talking, she decided. She made herself comfortable in the bucket seat of the car and brushed the melting snowflakes from her coat as she glanced across at him. Just to be sitting here again was quite a surprise after what she had heard from Ellen Capstick's mother.

Jack slid the car smoothly into first gear and they moved off down the road. 'To tell the truth, I've been expecting something like this to happen for long enough. I knew it was only a matter of time before he took a tumble from that darned horse of his, and now it's happened he's moaning like mad about it. If he wasn't on that darned thing chasing foxes, he was marching around in that black shirt of his – and now he can't do either. Serves him damned well right for being out riding at that time in the evening. Any fool knows this hasn't been the weather for gallivanting across the countryside on horseback. If he hadn't been the one to get his leg broken it would have been that poor horse.'

'Did – did he tell you where it actually happened?' Bethany ventured.

Jack nodded. 'Over on the old drove road by Lot's Barn it seems. That track's positively lethal at this time of year when there's ice around. All those pot-holes and ruts simply fill up with water and make it a virtual skating rink when the temperature falls below zero. Thank God, Ned was around, that's all I can say, or Amos might be lying there yet!'

Bethany breathed a silent sigh of relief. He obviously didn't know she had borne witness to the accident. Heaven only knew what she would have done if Ned hadn't been hanging around. What excuse would she have used to explain having found Amos way out there in that old barn at that time of night?

She had told Neddy not to mention she had been there when he ran back to the big house for help, and he had understood all right. His eyes had narrowed and he had placed a finger to his lips and made a conspiratorial shushing sound, then shivered with either nervousness or excitement, before running off in the direction of The Hall.

She had watched him go with a strange feeling of unease. Poor old Ned; he always seemed to be hanging around whenever she had her altercations with Amos, and she wondered just how much the poor lad knew. More than most folk realized, she felt. She could remember how, even as a child, when the other children would run after him shouting their favourite taunt of, 'Ned, Ned, daft in the head!' she would watch the look that came over his face as he walked through the village streets pretending not to notice, and her heart would go out to him. He noticed, all right, and it hurt. She knew it did. Poor old Ned was not half as daft in the head as folk liked to make out, and he would prove it to them one of these fine days.

'Horses and women – we men make fools of ourselves over both!'

Jack's voice broke into her thoughts and she gave an understanding smile. 'I expect Amos won't be of too much help around the estate for some time to come then,' she sympathized. She knew this was a sore point with Jack.

He gave a derisive snort and cursed under his breath as he missed a gear. 'A fat lot of help he's been in the past anyway! I can't see that him having his leg in plaster is going to make a ha'porth of difference to running Wolf Hall or any of the estate, come to that!'

He reached into his jacket pocket and, after feeling around for a moment, extracted a packet of cigarettes which he threw into her lap. 'Be a love and light one for me, will you? The matches are in the pocket nearest you.'

She took one of the Capstans from the packet and placed it between her lips as her right hand delved into the pocket of his tweed sports jacket. 'I'm not very good at this,' she apologized as the first match went out on her, and she choked on a mouthful of smoke at the second attempt.

He grinned as he took the cigarette from her and drew deeply. 'I seem to have spent a good deal of my time since I've been back in this country crossing swords with my dear little brother. Funny really, because we used to get along so well when we were younger. Used to follow me around everywhere, did Amos. And time can't really change that, you know. When you've been that close as children, the bond remains. I'd do anything for him, he knows that – although he also knows he drives me to distraction at times.'

'But would he do anything for you?' Bethany did her best to keep her tone light-hearted, for she already knew the true answer to that particular question and wondered if her companion did.

Jack shrugged as he swerved the car into a corner to avoid the last bus of the evening from Kirkby Stephen. 'That's immaterial, really. I'm the eldest, and for the rest of my life, once Pa's gone, I'll be the surrogate father to both of them. I suppose Amos, in particular, has always felt a certain rivalry towards me – pitting himself against Big Brother and all that sort of stuff. But it doesn't mean anything. I know he must feel the same way I do at heart. I'd do anything for either one of them and woe betide anyone who does or says anything agin either of them, for I'll be the first to be in there gunning on their behalf.'

So there she had it. It was said in a light-hearted tone, but there was no mistaking the seriousness of his statement. Bethany gave a bitter smile in the darkness of the car. What was it they said about the Grevilles? 'Kick one and they all limp.' If she had ever doubted the truth behind those words, she would no more. It was no ordinary band of brothers who lived at Wolf Hall; the blood tie that bound the Grevilles was as strong as ever it had been in generations past. And perhaps that was what had kept their family such a force in this land for so long. Great families rose and fell with the generations all over England, but some seemed to go on for ever. And the family that had spawned two such different men as Jack and Amos Greville was one of those.

As if reading her thoughts, Jack said softly, 'It's quite a responsibility, you know, being the firstborn in a family like ours – knowing that, come what may, I will be the one responsible for the upkeep of the family home and estate – such as they are nowadays. And for the continuation of the family name.'

The last sentence was said so softly Bethany almost missed it, but it brought Amos's taunts of the previous night back with a vengeance as the words sank in. 'I suppose that's what took you up to Scotland the other day,' she said, fighting hard to contain the tightness that had come into her throat. 'Rumour has it you have a girlfriend – the future Mrs Jack Greville – up there.'

Jack looked round sharply, causing the car to veer

dangerously near the side of the road. 'Who's been telling you that?' he asked testily. She had obviously struck a nerve.

'Oh, word gets around,' she said mysteriously. 'Is it true?'

He ground the car to a halt so abruptly that she had to bring both hands up to stop herself from going through the windscreen. He stubbed the remainder of his cigarette out in the ashtray by his side as she rubbed a painful knee that had struck the glove compartment. They had stopped almost in the centre of the main thoroughfare of The Row, although they had been headed for Corrigan's.

'What did you do that for?'

He ignored her question as he turned to face her, his face more serious than she had ever seen it. 'Have I ever lied to you, Bethany?'

She shook her head. 'Not that I know of,' she answered, more light-heartedly than she felt, and she moved uncomfortably in her seat, nervous at what might follow.

He did not return her smile as he continued earnestly. 'I never have and I never will — God willing.' He paused, as if wondering just how much to say, then added quickly, as if to get it over with before he changed his mind, 'There is a girl up there in Perthshire. Molly Malcolm her name is. She's the sister of a very old friend of mine — Gordon — from my schooldays at Sedbergh . . . It was Gordon's wedding I was best man at the other day . . .'

'Look, Jack,' Bethany said, laying a restraining hand on his arm. 'You really don't have to tell me this — any of it. It's really none of my business. In fact, I'm sorry I brought the matter up.'

'I'm not sorry. In fact I was going to bring it up myself tonight.'

She looked puzzled, and he continued, 'You see, the idea *was* that Molly and I might announce our engagement at Gordon's wedding. At least that's what her family

– and old Gordon – were hoping for. We've all been so close for so long, and Gordon and Moll even flew out to see me in Australia last year. I'd been writing to both of them, you see, and it was no secret that her parents – not to mention her brother – would have liked to see us hitched. A good match, that's what we would be. She is a good sort, is old Molly, and the poor thing has had the misfortune to have been quite soft on me for ages now.'

Bethany sat silently by his side as he told his story, oblivious of the cars that hooted in annoyance at his sports car parked so inconsiderately in the middle of the road. Her spirits were sinking by the second as he unburdened himself over this Molly person, who sounded far too good to be true. 'And, you – what about you?' she asked quietly. 'Did you think it was such a good idea, too? Did you want to marry her as much as she so obviously wants to marry you?'

He remained silent for a moment or two, then said slowly, 'I suppose I hadn't ruled the idea out entirely. It had been the accepted future for so long, I suppose – by both our families. At any rate I felt I at least owed it to her to go up to Scotland this month armed.'

'To go up to Scotland armed?'

'With this.' He dug his fingers into the right-hand pocket of his sports jacket and pulled out a small red leather box. He had not even been aware it was still secreted in the pocket of this, his best tweed jacket, until his search for his cigarettes a few moments ago. It lay in the palm of his hand as they both stared down at the object. 'This has belonged to the wife of the eldest Greville son and heir for at least four centuries,' he said, finding it difficult to disguise the pride in his voice. 'Tradition has it that it doesn't get buried with the last owner, but as a family heirloom it gets passed on to the next in line . . . So you see it doesn't get given away lightly.'

He prised open the lid and sat the small box on the ledge

by the gear lever as he lit a match. In the light from its flame Bethany gave an audible gasp. Inside, embedded in a bed of blue satin, was the most beautiful emerald ring she had ever set eyes on. It was a single stone, the size of the nail of her little finger, set in a gold band. 'Family legend has it, the first Mrs Greville-to-be to own it was from the Emerald Isle – hence the stone . . . That may or may not be true, and anyway I'm much more concerned about the next Mrs G-to-be.'

Bethany's heart was beating much too fast as she continued to gaze at the gem. 'But why bring it with you tonight?' she asked with difficulty, for her mouth had gone quite dry.

He snapped the box shut and replaced it in his pocket as his eyes met hers. In the semi-darkness he could sense rather than see the mixture of nervousness and expectation on her face. There was a unmistakable tenseness in the air between them as if the unthinkable was suddenly thinkable. Their thoughts were racing across the enormous divide their backgrounds had created and were building bridges that neither was even sure were there to cross. Should he have left it where it was, safely in his pocket? What perverse impulse had made him bring the ring out into the open like this? Was it that same impulse that had made him ask her out to dinner that first night? He really had no idea. It was as if some strange exterior force took control of his actions when she was around. But it was too late for regrets now.

'Why show it to me like this?' Her voice was tremulous. 'Why bring that ring with you here tonight?'

He could not be too literal with the truth and tell her its finding was accidental; her pride was a fragile thing. He sighed as he ran a hand through his hair. 'I suppose I wanted you to see it, that's why. I wanted you to see the evidence with your own eyes that I did not place it on anyone's finger – that I am still a free man. That I didn't go to Scotland in search of a wife – no matter what you might hear to the contrary.' His voice was tight as he spoke and he realized he was telling the truth. And it was important to him that she should know that – very important.

Bethany sat staring out of the windscreen as he finished his cigarette. His words hung in the air between them. There was so much she wanted to ask, but was too fearful of what the answers might be. It was as if they both knew he had said too much too soon. All these excuses. All this talk of marriage and a ring. Did he really have to tell her all about this Molly person in such great detail? Yet the real anxiety for her was more in what he had not said over the past few minutes. She felt as if they had been indulging in some strange sort of double-talk that left her both confused and mentally exhausted. She was getting out of her depth and it was not a comfortable feeling.

She glanced towards the closed door of Number Twelve, behind which her mother would now be sitting down with her knitting for the evening. 'It seems we've arrived back home. Would you care for a cup of tea?' The question came out much more primly than she intended.

Jack gave a rueful smile. 'The good old British cup of tea . . . To tell the truth, I'd love one.'

That cup of tea was to be the first of many Jack Greville drank in the small family kitchen of Number Twelve, The Row, over the next few weeks. That strange, oblique conversation in the car had somehow acted as an un-spoken bond between them. Bethany no longer felt vulnerable about what interpretation other people might put on their growing relationship, or worried about his feelings for other young women; for her part she was simply glad to have him around. If in any way she was 'on trial', as some in the village cruelly put it, he never let her feel it. He treated her as a lady as much as any young woman could have wished.

He was fun to be with and he got on well with her

mother and younger brothers and sister, despite Betty Baine's continuing reservations about the relationship. He also took her to places Bethany had never dreamt of visiting in her life before. Places like Leeds, with its fine Victorian buildings, and Harrogate, with its grandiose hotels frequented by the rich and famous, who came to 'take the waters'. The fact that she was far more humbly attired than any of the other females they mingled with seemed not to bother him one jot. 'You're the best-looking girl in the place,' he would assure her at every opportunity, until Bethany almost came to believe it. There was no question he was doing wonders for her morale.

As far as Jack Greville himself was concerned, there was never any question of the young woman he took such a delight in squiring around being on trial as a possible wife. She was quite simply the one person he enjoyed being with above all others. His years in Australia had given him a taste for 'females with a bit of spunk about them', as he put it to his father. 'I want someone I actually look forward to spending my time with. Someone I miss when she's not there.' And Bethany was certainly that. She now filled all his waking hours, whether they were together or apart. And it was not just her looks, although heaven help him, they played a part. It was simply that for the first time he had met someone with whom he could discuss almost anything – someone who had her own set of values and a way of looking at life that he totally respected, although he might not always agree with it.

A few years ago his father might have objected to him spending so much time with 'a village girl', but the Colonel was changing along with the times. His heart condition and the growing awareness of his own mortality had convinced Philip Greville that there were more important things to life than the 'good breeding' which he used to set so much store by in the past.

'Plucky young miss, that Bethany Baine,' he told his

oldest son. 'Gets her looks from the good Lord and her brains from old Harry Hetherington. I can see why you seem to have taken such a shine to her, Jack lad, but what do you intend to do about it, that's what I'd like to know?'

And Jack knew there were more folks around than just his father who wanted to know the answer to that particular question. By now Bethany herself must be wondering. They had been seeing each other regularly for weeks, and it was becoming increasingly evident he must 'do the honourable thing and make his intentions known', as his father put it, before much longer. The fact that they were from such different backgrounds made this even more important, if Bethany was not to risk 'getting a name for herself', as her mother, Betty Baine, had once told her.

The ring he had inadvertently left in the pocket of his best jacket after his return from Scotland, he now left there permanently. He was not particularly superstitious by nature, but it seemed it would be a bad omen somehow if he now removed it and secreted it away in a drawer of his dressing chest. So there it still lay, burning a hole in his pocket as he tussled with his feelings over whether to 'do the decent thing' or not.

Christmas came and went, as did New Year, with the snow lying deep and crisp all over the dale, and Betty Baine doing her best to make it as memorable as possible for her small family. The fact that Hector Wilks presented Bethany with a small Christmas box packed full of special treats, and that Jack himself appeared on the doorstep of Number Twelve on Christmas Eve carrying a five-pound hen, did wonders to ensure the family had the best festive season ever. The only sad factor was that their father was not there to enjoy it with them.

On Boxing Day Bethany was invited up to Wolf Hall for dinner and accepted with reluctance, wondering how she would cope with a meal eaten in the malign presence of

Amos Greville. Her apprehension she tried successfully to keep from Jack, so well that he apologized to her with real feeling on their way up to The Hall that evening for the fact that Amos would not be able to attend. 'Gone down with a temperature of 102,' he informed her. 'Poor lad. The doctor says it'll be at least a week before he's up and about again.'

'That's a real pity.'

Jack agreed and added, 'By the way, Bethany, if you notice any difference in Pa, I'd rather you didn't let on, all right? He really hasn't been himself for some time now, but he gets quite worked up if other people notice it.'

But even those words of warning could not prepare her for the change she found in the Colonel as he held out his hand from his seat by the fire in the drawing room of Wolf Hall. The fact that he no longer appeared able to rise or walk unaided came as a great shock. But his obvious pleasure in seeing her again was real enough.

'Why, you're as pretty as a picture!' Philip Greville exclaimed at the sight of his visitor in a new rust-coloured velveteen dress her mother had helped her make up specially for Christmas. 'It's a long time since I've set eyes on you with proper clothes on!'

'Pa, really!' Jack exclaimed.

But Bethany merely laughed. 'I think what your father means is he's used to seeing me in my old uniform,' she said quietly. The old man had not meant to remind her quite so early in their meeting of the gulf that she knew still yawned between them, but it was there all the same – just waiting for one or other of them to put their foot in it.

And so the festive season came and went and, apart from Bethany and Jack's obvious growing pleasure in each other's company, for most of their friends and neighbours in the dale there was little joy to be found in the cold dark days of December and January. If not exactly accepting them as a couple, Betty Baine was beginning

267

gradually to come to terms with the fact that her elder daughter was living her own life as she wanted it, not as others in the village might choose.

'The Lord will decide on the outcome, just as He holds all our fates in His hands,' her friend and counsellor Kenneth Barden told her, and Betty Baine accepted this. There was nothing to be gained by nagging where Bethany was concerned. She was her own woman and no one was going to tell her how to live her life.

For Bethany herself, however, her innermost feelings were not quite as cut and dried as her mother imagined. That she was falling in love with Jack Greville, she had no doubt, despite all her initial reservations, and that he loved her in return she was also quite sure. But what then? Did they just drift on like this for ever? And matters might indeed have drifted on for several weeks more if fate had not intervened in the form of a letter requesting Jack to spend a weekend as a guest at Altreoch, the Malcolms' Perthshire home, to celebrate Molly's birthday.

Jack showed the letter to Bethany, a trifle uncertainly, as they sat parked outside her home, late one early February evening.

She could not read the writing in the semi-darkness, but she was well aware of the implication. Her heart lurched. 'Will – will you go?'

He took the letter from her and, folding it carefully, put it back in his pocket. 'Do you want me to?' It was a stupid question, but he wanted to hear her say it – tell him with her own lips how hurt she would be if he went back to Scotland. For weeks now they had studiously avoided any mention of long-term intentions or serious commitments to each other, but he knew in his heart they could not go on like this much longer. Even if this letter had not arrived, as far as he was concerned the strain was beginning to tell. The sheer physical attraction he felt for Bethany and the strain of keeping that desire in check was beginning to make him irritable by the end of an evening in her presence. 'Would it really upset you if I go?'

She shrugged. 'Maybe.'

'What's that supposed to mean?'

'Do you want to go?' She wasn't exactly making it easy for him.

His fingers drummed on the steering wheel. 'They always have a whale of a time up there whatever the celebration.'

She half-turned towards him. 'Then there's no reason why you should deny yourself the pleasure, is there? I mean, who am I to deprive you of all that fun?'

'Yes, just who are you?'

They stared at each other in the dark confines of the car, then Jack gave a bitter shake of his head. Enough of this double-talk and fooling around. 'I'll tell you who you are, Bethany Baine. You're the woman I love, that's who you are. And it's something I should have told you ages ago. God only knows what stopped me – except that I wasn't sure – am still not sure – that you feel the same.'

Bethany had caught her breath as he began to speak and she let it out in a long sigh, half of relief, half of shock when he finished. Did he really mean it? Did he really not know?

'Well?'

Her insides were churning. She had not expected this tonight and for once was lost for words. She turned and stared ahead of her down the dark street. 'Wh – what do you want me to say?'

'You could start by telling me you love me.' He reached out, and with the index finger of his right hand, he tilted her chin and turned her face towards him. 'You do love me, don't you?'

She nodded mutely as, to her own amazement, tears flooded into her eyes.

Jack's heart was beating faster. 'And what you want

most on earth is to marry me – be my wife . . . Say it, Bethany, say it!'

She sat gazing back at him as the tears streamed down her cheeks, then slowly, hesitantly, she began to nod her head.

But it was not enough. 'Say it, my love, say it . . . Say: I love you, Jack, and want to be your wife.'

He was pleading with her, begging her to say the words he longed to hear more than any others. He reminded her of her small brother Sammy pleading for the puppy he had wanted for Christmas. 'You've never asked me what I really wanted for Christmas,' she said softly.

He thought of the gold bracelet he had given her and, bemused, he replied, 'Well, what did you want, Bethany? Tell me?'

She reached out and touched his cheek. 'You, Black Jack . . . More than anything on earth, I wanted you for Christmas. And for the rest of my life.'

His relief was obvious in the whoop of pleasure and relief he let out. 'Let's tell your Ma!' he shouted, not caring if the whole street could hear. 'Let's tell everyone you're going to be the next Mrs Jack Greville!'

Half-dazed, Bethany staggered after him as he ran towards Number Twelve and, totally out of character, for he was a stickler for politeness, he threw open the cottage door and shouted, 'Mrs Baine, where are you?'

Betty Baine came running through from the kitchen, drying her hands on her apron, her eyes wide with anxiety. 'What is it? What's happened?'

'I've got engaged, Mam, that's what,' her daughter told her, as she brought up the rear, her face flushed. 'I've got engaged to Jack. I'm going to be Mrs Jack Greville!'

Betty Baine stared from one to the other in turn, as if not quite comprehending what she had heard. Then she slowly began to shake her head. 'No, no . . . Beth love, you can't be serious.'

270

'She most certainly is,' Jack butted in. 'And I've got the ring here to prove it!' His hand delved into the right-hand pocket of his jacket, only to find a crumpled handkerchief and a half-empty packet of cigarettes. Disappointment flooded across his face. He had on his suit tonight, and the ring – that precious ring – still lay in the pocket of his favourite sports jacket back up at The Hall. 'Well, if it's not right here, it's certainly safe and sound and waiting patiently for its new owner!'

Bethany's eyes sparkled almost as much as the emerald she knew would soon be glittering on the third finger of her left hand. 'And it's beautiful, Mam. Really beautiful – a family heirloom, in fact!'

Betty Baine's lips pursed as she looked into her daughter's radiant face. Beautiful – it would be that all right. And worth a small fortune, no doubt. More than Cheevers could have earned in a lifetime, most likely. Then her eyes moved to Jack Greville's face. 'Have you really asked our Beth to marry you?' she said, in a voice faint with incredulity.

The young man by her daughter's side nodded in confirmation as he slipped his arm around Bethany's shoulders. 'Yes, I have. And what's more, she's said, "Yes." She has made me the happiest man in the world tonight, Mrs Baine.'

Betty Baine listened, but could barely comprehend. She had been discussing Bethany's continued 'walking out' with Jack Greville and what to do about it with the Reverend Barden only this morning, when he had called. They were both of the opinion that all that could come of it was a broken heart before the year was out. 'Well, if you're the happiest man in the world tonight, then that makes me the most amazed woman,' she told the young man before her. 'I really didn't think it would come to this.' Then she turned to her daughter. 'But if that's what you want, Bethany love, then I'm happy for you.'

But there was no real warmth in her voice and no lightness in her step as Betty Baine turned and walked through to the back kitchen to put the kettle on for a cup of tea.

The smile that had been on Bethany's lips ever since leaving the car died as her eyes followed in her mother's wake. She was well aware that the Grevilles were not the most popular people in this dale, and that in throwing in her lot with them by marrying Jack, she would be fair game for all those who chose to sit in judgement on 'them at t'Hall', and that included her own mother. 'Wait there a sec,' she told Jack, slipping free from his arm.

She followed her mother through to the back kitchen and put her hand on the older woman's arm as Betty Baine held the kettle under the single cold tap of the sink. 'What is it, Mam? What's wrong? I want you so much to be happy for me.'

Betty Baine turned her head to meet her daughter's beseeching gaze. 'I'm sorry, Bethany love. I just wish I could believe your father would have been happy for you at this moment. If I could believe that I would be the most contented woman in Utherby this night . . . But I can't, and I think you know why.'

Bethany looked away as she withdrew her hand from her mother's arm. It was as if that cold water that had just gushed into the kettle had been poured over her happiness. She stared out of the small window into the darkness of the back yard. Her father had lived and died in the Grevilles' pay and he had had no love for the family of the man who now stood through there in the front room waiting for her; the man who had just asked her to be his wife.

'This land will never be free, nor the people in it free men or women as long as there are those such as the Grevilles to play God over us,' her father had once said.

And now she – his own daughter – was to be one of them.

Chapter Fourteen

The wedding could have been one of the social events of
the North Riding's year, but neither Bethany nor Jack
wanted a lot of fuss. 'I don't know about you, Squirt, but
I'd be just as happy with only the two of us,' Jack told his
bride-to-be, once they got down to the serious business of
discussing the details. And Bethany agreed, but added that
that perhaps might be a bit drastic and leave quite a few
people disappointed, particularly her younger brothers
and sister, who were gaining quite a lot of mileage at
school by having an elder sister who was marrying into
'them at t'Hall'.

'Will you get to wear a fur coat when it snows like this?'
Libby asked her, as they sat by the window one Friday
teatime in late February and looked out at the thick white
coating, like icing on a wedding cake, that lay on the tiled
rooftops of the houses opposite. 'And will you get to eat
jam and cakes whenever you like?'

Bethany smiled as she looked up from the pile of
darning on her lap. Her younger sister was now at an age
when other people's lifestyles were a never-ending source
of interest, particularly when they were far removed from
her own. And Bethany recalled wistfully how at almost
the same age she had first begun to read copies of *The Lady*
passed on from a neighbour who worked in one of the big
houses in the area, and realized that there was a whole
world out there about which she knew next to nothing.
'Jam and cakes?' she mused. 'Happen so, our Libby. And
there might even be some left for you.'

'And for me!' little Sammy shouted, from the rug by the fire, where he was colouring in with the crayons and colouring book that Jack had bought him for Christmas. 'I love cake, our Beth! You know I do! 'Specially tipsy cake.' Tipsy cake was another rare treat introduced to them by the young man from The Hall whom they had now come to regard as some sort of all-the-year-round Father Christmas.

In a way, Jack had been a very real Santa Claus this Christmas, for along with the basket of goodies he had come armed with on Boxing Day, he had brought something even more special to the inhabitants of Number Twelve, The Row: he had brought laughter and joy to a household which had known very little of either since Cheevers Baine's death. For the first time in years they even played Forfeits, with each child having to do a personal little party piece before claiming his particular gaily-wrapped parcel from the basket on the table. There had hardly been a dry eye to be found when young Sam stood up in the middle of the floor, and in his piping voice recited:

'It is Christmas Day in the Workhouse,
And the cold bare walls are bright
With garlands of green and holly,
And the place is a pleasant sight:
For with clean-washed hands and faces,
In a long and hungry line
The paupers sit at the tables
For this is the hour they dine . . .'

No one had clapped louder than Jack when at the end of the poem Sammy had breathed a huge sigh of relief and scampered back to his seat.

The question that then followed from Libby, however, had brought a momentary embarrassed halt to the proceedings. The child looked curiously at her mother and asked in a loud voice, 'Is the Workhouse the same as the Poor House where you said we'd all end up if we didn't get to stop here, Mam?'

Betty Baine had gone the colour of the berries on the holly above the fireplace and was at a complete loss for words. It was their visitor who came to the rescue. 'Yes, it is, young Libby,' Jack informed the child. 'But that's a place you'll not have to trouble your head about ever again.'

Then to change the subject entirely, he had jumped up and, grabbing the toy banjo he had brought Tom for Christmas, he declared it was request time. Mayhem followed as the children all shouted out their special favourites, and it was only after several encores of 'Yes, We Have No Bananas' that he was allowed to catch his breath and accept another cup of tea.

'Will we be having Jack every Christmas from now on, our Beth?' Sammy asked, as he painstakingly coloured in Humpty Dumpty's red waistcoat and remembered that happy time. 'Will he still come round and see us when you live at t'Hall?'

' 'Course he will, stupid!' Libby cut in. 'They're getting married, that's what. He'll be part of the family, will Jack, even though our Beth's a Greville.' The last part of the sentence was said with just a trace of wistfulness as the young girl looked across at her elder sister. How she envied Bethany marrying a *Greville*! But then she envied Bethany in so many ways and despaired of ever growing up to be half as pretty or half as lucky as she was.

As Sammy pondered on his sister's words, Teddy and Tom, the two older boys, looked up from the table by the window where they were doing their homework. 'They say at school you'll go all posh and won't want to speak to the likes of us again when you marry Jack,' Tom put in and his brother nodded in agreement.

'Aye, they say you'll go all la-di-dah and won't buy your things from the Co-op or from Mr Wilks no more. Instead you'll get stuff sent up from *Leeds*!' Teddy breathed the name of Yorkshire's biggest city as if it were the moon.

Bethany laughed as she glanced across at the two earnest faces at the table opposite. Both boys were now approaching puberty and had that gangly, gauche air about them that belied the air of worldliness they attempted to convey. On Tom, in particular, the occasional pimple was beginning to appear on a chin already sprouting the odd stray hair, and that caused no end of anguish, particularly on Saturday nights when hops at the village hall meant half an hour spent in front of the kitchen mirror slicking reluctant thatches into place and pulling their father's old cut-throat razor over virgin skin. The fact that their elder sister was about to become 'one of the nobs' had created a new interest among their female schoolfriends, always avid for the latest gossip, so Bethany was regularly squeezed for any drop of information that might sweeten their relations with the opposite sex.

'Aye, and they say you'll be having your picture in the *Yorkshire Post* when you get wed an' all,' Teddy added, chewing the end of his pencil.

'Oh, that's what they say, is it?' Bethany gave an amused half-smile as she pulled her darning needle through the heel of a school sock. It didn't surprise her that the local gossip was taking all sorts of funny turns. Utherby, in fact the whole of this dale, was just about the nosiest place in creation. You couldn't even have as much as a ticklish cough without the whole village having you dying of consumption. She could just imagine the field day they would all be having now at the news that Jack Greville hadn't been just 'playing around' but was actually going to do the decent thing and marry the daughter of one of his father's old workers. But, even more interesting to many of the older inhabitants, it was Harrison Hetherington's granddaughter marrying the Colonel's son. Now that was something to write home about indeed, for there were those still alive who could remember the old clergyman and the young Squire, as Philip Greville then was, having more than the occasional spat over village affairs, and to their delight the old man usually won.

Bethany gave a wry smile as she pulled another strand of darning wool off the ball in her lap and snipped at it with the scissors. They had a habit in the dales of identifying folk by reciting the family pedigree as part of the name, and she still recalled with some amusement, as she queued in the post office one day early in her engagement, hearing one of the old women in front of her ask Miss Wright, the postmistress, if she had heard that Harrison's Betty's Bethany was marrying one of the Grevilles – John's Philip's Jack, to be exact. Miss Wright had smiled sweetly and said, 'Oh yes, I have most certainly heard and the young lady in question is right behind you.'

A flustered eighty-year-old had spun round in some confusion and Bethany had then had her hand clasped as warmly as it had ever been and congratulations poured over her. 'Eh, lass, he's a fine young man is Jack Greville. You'll do all right there, I'll wager.'

But that old woman had been the exception. Very few had actually found it in themselves even to come up to her and wish her luck, and it hurt. Those from whom she at least expected a kind word, such as the Capsticks, never mentioned the fact, although she saw both of Ellen's parents several times a week.

One of the few villagers to appear genuinely delighted, however, was Hector Wilks, her employer. 'You've done all right for yourself there, Bethany love,' he said, the first morning she appeared wearing her engagement ring. 'He's all right, is Jack Greville. You've got a good un there.'

277

Bethany had given a weak smile in appreciation. That's what they must all be thinking: she had 'done all right for herself'. But, in truth, that was not the reason she had agreed to marry Jack. In fact, she could have squared it with her conscience a great deal more easily if it hadn't been one of the Grevilles of Wolf Hall she was marrying. Somehow that fact had made her feel almost a traitor in the midst of some of the people around here. Even to her own family, in fact, for despite the delight of her brothers and sisters, she knew her mother would never quite come to terms with her daughter marrying into a family that her husband had detested so much. Yes, it would have been a darned sight easier if Jack's surname had been Smith or Jones, or just about any name under the sun other than Greville.

They had decided on the last Saturday in April for the wedding, and she really had nothing to reproach herself for, Bethany kept telling herself as the big day grew nearer. She was marrying the first man to make her feel special; the first man with whom she had ever felt like a woman; a man who had opened the door to a whole new way of life. From a child she had known only poverty and service, and she knew as well as anyone the misery of being one of life's Have Nots. It had not been easy coming to terms with the knowledge that out there in the world, beyond the grey, narrow streets of Utherby, there was another world where people did not have to worry about where their next meal was coming from, or if they would be put out of their house if they could not pay the rent, or if their husband died . . . And there was the crunch. No matter how happy she might be with Jack personally, nothing could change the fact that it was his family who had almost put her own out on the street.

But, despite her reservations about what she knew Jack's family represented locally, she found she could not feel too much resentment towards the Colonel himself.

Jack had told her, with relief evident on his face, that Philip Greville had reacted to the news of his son's forthcoming marriage like the gentleman he was, and for that Bethany was more than grateful. It would have been only too easy for him to have thrown a spanner into the works and announced he was cutting off his eldest son for marrying 'beneath him'. Such things did still happen these days. But, on the contrary, when he had received the news, Philip Greville had clasped his son by the hand and said, 'So it's little Bethany Baine, is it? I had suspected as much, and I must say I admire your taste, lad. I always thought that one had spunk. Pretty with it too – a rare enough combination these days.'

He had sat back in his chair and a look of quiet satisfaction had come over his face as he mused thoughtfully, 'Aye, that one should bring an infusion of good red Yorkshire blood to pep up the old bloodline and, God knows, this family could do with it.' What this old house needed more than anything was the sound of youngsters around the place again, and a woman's touch to add light and colour to the drabness that had descended over the past two decades, since his beloved wife died. The old man's recent heart trouble had reminded him quite forcibly that his own days as Master were numbered and he had found himself thinking more and more of the future of Wolf Hall once he had gone.

Then he had sucked thoughtfully on his pipe and added, with a wry smile, 'I've said it before, and I'll say it again: somehow, I never could see you ending up with one of your own set – damned pretty though some of them might be. You never were one for that type of hot-house flower, were you, Jack lad?'

He could have added, neither had he been in his youth, for he had sown his wild oats far and wide across the North Riding, and, if the truth be known, there had been one particular young woman over Kirkby Stephen way he would have dearly loved to have wed and brought back as Mistress of Wolf Hall. But her father was naught but a farrier on one of the big estates over that way, and the young Philip Greville had lacked the courage even to contemplate such a match. He had run into her once many years later at the horse fair in nearby Appleby, one hot June day. She had married the local doctor, and seeing her on her husband's arm he had felt cheated somehow, even though he was by then happily married himself. It could have been him walking there by her side, an upright pillar of the community. But he had lacked the courage. A man who had won the Military Cross for valour on the field of battle had lacked the courage to marry out of his class.

Philip Greville's eyes misted as he puffed thoughtfully on his pipe. He had to hand it to the lad, he had had the guts to know what he wanted and damned well go out and get it. 'I'm proud of you, son,' he heard himself saying softly. 'Damned proud of you.'

Jack Greville looked puzzled and gave an embarrassed smile. He had not the faintest idea what exactly his father meant by that remark and would never know.

'Give me a hand up, will you, lad?'

Jack took his father by the arm and led him in the direction indicated, towards the drinks table by the window.

'Aye, Jack, you could have done a lot worse. By God, you could!' Young Bethany Baine would be an asset to this family in more ways than one. She had looks, she had brains, and wasn't afraid of a bit of hard work, which was more than could be said for quite a few young women these days. And, most important of all, the future of the Greville line would be safe in her hands. After all, she had that old bugger Harrison Hetherington's blood in her veins, hadn't she? The Colonel smiled to himself as, leaning heavily on his son for support, he poured them both a celebratory glass of Scotch. 'Only man to ever get the better of me in an argument,' he said, speaking his thoughts aloud. 'Stubborn old devil, Hetherington — if I can say that about a man of the cloth. Cantankerous into the bargain. But a doughty fighter for what he believed in. I'm just sorry he's not still around to see his first great-grandchild born!'

'Hey, hang on there!' Jack laughed. 'We're not even wed yet!'

His father handed his son a glass of his best malt whisky, then raised his own in a shaky salute. 'Here's to my first grandchild!' he declared. 'Old Harry Hetherington would have been a proud man this day!' Then he gave a rueful chuckle as he downed the golden spirit in one. That perhaps might be a moot point, he thought to himself. But the old blighter wasn't here to argue with him, so for once he himself could have the last word.

For Bethany herself, the last few weeks before the wedding proved to be one tiring round of the writing of thank-you letters after work as presents poured in from Greville family and friends far and wide. If there was surprise, or even shock at Jack's choice of bride among the County set they moved in, it was not obvious from the letters and cards expressing good wishes for their future happiness that poured into The Hall, although Bethany had her suspicions that this did not necessarily reflect the gossiping that might be going on behind the scenes.

There was no room for all the gifts to be displayed in the small front parlour of Number Twelve, The Row, as tradition decreed, so they were arrayed for all to see in one of the guest bedrooms of the groom's home, where the dalesfolk were given an open invitation to call and view. From what they heard there could scarcely have been a single man, woman or child locally who did not take up the invitation. The forthcoming wedding had captured the imagination of the whole of Utherdale, and had brought out into the open almost every conceivable reaction, although most were careful not to air their views within the hearing of either of the families in question.

But if the opinions of their friends and neighbours still worried Betty Baine, they certainly did not bother her elder daughter, who was happier than she had ever dreamt it possible to be. Bethany had accepted from the beginning that there would be those who would have dearly loved to have seen her romance with Jack run aground on the rocks of social prejudice and, in this regard, the esteem in which she now held the Colonel was far higher than in previous days when as a worker at Wolf Hall she had often found the old man a rather irascible employer. But there could be no doubt that now he was doing his very best to make his prospective daughter-in-law feel welcome and part of the family.

He even went out of his way to invite her own family up to The Hall on several occasions before the wedding to view the growing array of gifts that were now spreading over three long trestle tables in the first-floor bedroom.

To Betty Baine and her younger children the room was a veritable Aladdin's cave which seemed to become even more amazing with each visit. The rows of fine table linen, silver and crockery on display were beyond their comprehension.

'You could open a shop, our Beth,' Teddy breathed in awe on his first viewing, his eyes on stalks as he gazed around him. 'You'll need a heck of a big house for this lot, I reckon.' Then he turned to his sister. 'Where are you gonna live, anyroads, when you're wed? You haven't told us yet.'

Bethany drew in her breath and glanced across at Jack, who could not pretend he hadn't heard. The question, innocent in the extreme, had been heard by all in the room, so could not be ignored. But for those on the Greville side it was still a very vexed issue indeed. Philip

Greville's dearest wish was for Jack and his new bride to take up residence in Wolf Hall itself. 'Only right and proper that would be,' he had told his son. But Jack had remained noncommittal. He had Bethany's wishes to take into account and he knew only too well what they would be. Wild horses would not drag her up here to live. Just why she was so set against moving into the big house he was not quite sure, and up till now he had refrained from pursuing the subject to any great degree, hoping that she might come round of her own accord in time.

But now it had been raised in all innocence and all eyes were on the young couple.

The Colonel coughed diplomatically and eyed his eldest son. 'The lad deserves an answer, wouldn't you agree, Jack?'

Jack cursed inwardly but attempted to maintain a calm exterior. 'Well now, young man, I think that's something that still has to be decided upon.' He could feel himself flush as he offered round a fresh plate of cream-filled brandy snaps. 'It requires a lot of thought, that does. But when we have come to a decision, you will be the first to know.'

Teddy beamed. That made him feel very special indeed. 'I hope it's here in The Hall,' he said truthfully, gazing round the comfortably furnished room, with its array of shabby, but still valuable antique furniture, and family portraits on the walls. 'I like this place.' Never in his life had he been in such a grand house. It was even bigger than the school and the church put together. Even the village hall itself was no bigger than the main hall downstairs. 'Say it's gonna be The Hall, our Beth. Say you want to live here.'

Bethany gave her brother a fixed stare as she bit into a brandy snap. She could cheerfully have strangled him. But how was he to know that he had in all innocence touched on the one thing that was causing so much friction? She was well aware of the pressure the Colonel was putting on Jack for them to move into Wolf Hall. Not only did his father need him here, it was the duty of the eldest son to live in the home he would one day inherit. To do any other was tantamount to treachery; it would be an insult that would not be easily forgiven.

'Insult to whom?' she had asked despairingly, the first time Jack had brought the subject up. 'To your father? To the house? It's quite ridiculous!'

'It may be quite ridiculous to you, my love,' Jack had sighed. 'But these things matter in families like ours.' Then his voice had softened as he looked at her imploringly. 'Would it really be so bad living in the old place?'

Would it? She had stared past him, out of the car window. They seemed to do so much of their heart-to-heart talking in the car. She didn't know why. It was most uncomfortable, and made it almost impossible to disguise one's true feelings.

'I honestly can't see what real objection you have to it. It's a lovely old place, and the family are not that bad, surely?'

She had listened with mounting despair. How could she tell him that nothing on earth would persuade her to share a house with his brother Amos? The very thought of being under the same roof as that young man made her feel physically ill. The fact that she was Jack's wife and had a wedding ring on her finger would not matter a jot. As long as she was around him, Amos Greville would regard her as fair game. He had this grotesque idea that somehow he had had her first, and that somehow that had created some sort of mystical tie between them that transcended her betrothal and marriage to Jack.

Her first meeting with him after his accident in the barn had been just as bad as she had anticipated, for she had had Jack at her side, and the Greville heirloom emerald ring on the third finger of her left hand.

Amos had stared at the gem from the depths of the

chaise longue by the library window and his normally ruddy face had gone quite pale in the morning light.

'Well, aren't you going to congratulate your big brother?' Jack had asked, proudly putting his arm around his bride-to-be's shoulders.

At that moment Bethany had been grateful indeed for the plaster cast that kept Amos seated on the chaise, his injured limb stuck out in front of him; to have him embrace her in some hideous, phoney display of good wishes would have been more than she could bear. 'I think poor Amos is too down on his own luck to enthuse too much on other people's,' she said charitably. 'But I'm sure he wishes us well.'

Amos grunted and waved a hand towards the door and said to Jack, 'And just to prove it – be a good chap and fetch that new bottle of Glenlivet that's sitting on my bedside cabinet. There's no better excuse for cracking a new Scotch malt than an engagement!'

'Good idea!' Jack had smiled in relief at his brother's response and Bethany had watched anxiously as he disappeared out the door to fetch the drink.

She turned to Amos lying on the chaise. He was looking at her with that same mirthless smile that had first curdled her blood all those years ago. 'Well, well, well . . . You've actually done it! Little Bethany Baine has landed a Greville – and the biggest fish in the family pond to boot!'

'Don't say any more, Amos!' she warned him. 'Don't you dare say one more word! Whether you like it or not, you will be my brother-in-law soon and you had better just make the best of it!'

'Oh, but I will, Bethany, I will! I will not only make the best of it – I will make the most of it, never you fear! I will be so full of brotherly love, you'll wonder what's hit you.' He laughed, that oh so familiar laugh. 'In fact, I think you'll know only too well what's hit you, for you and I go back a long way, don't we? A very long way . . .'

But even the thought of Amos in the congregation could not blight the joy Bethany felt when the day of the wedding finally arrived. Nor could the knowledge that they would indeed be setting up home in The Hall as the Colonel wanted. Sensing the tension it was causing between father and son, she had finally agreed to begin life as a married woman under the same roof as her brother-in-law, although she resolved to make sure she had as little to do with Amos as possible.

The actual ceremony was attended by very few guests, as both bride and groom wanted it, and was conducted by the Reverend Kenneth Barden in her grandfather's old church. There was only the immediate family on both sides present, except for Tabby and her sister, who were brought over from Sedbergh by Jack especially for the occasion.

The service was simple and the small church had never looked more beautiful, with displays of hot-house flowers ordered specially from Harrogate's biggest florist for the occasion. There was only one hymn, 'Oh Perfect Love', Bethany's favourite, and as the last bars faded into silence and Jack's eyes met hers, she thought her heart would burst with happiness.

She laid her bouquet on her father's grave in the small churchyard beyond, and asked to be left alone for a moment or two before joining her new husband in the car waiting to take them up to The Hall for the reception.

As she stood by the plot with its simple wooden cross, a wind was blowing from the direction of the crag and as she raised her eyes she could see the familiar cigar-shaped clouds massing in the pale blue of the sky, and she thought of the years her father had toiled on that stony hillside. Hard years that had claimed his youth and then cut short his manhood. He had never had the chance to live. And now he was gone, like so many before him who had lived and loved in this ancient place. And just as the Helm Wind had blown down this valley throughout the years of his life, so it would continue to blow throughout the coming years of her marriage to Jack.

And tears came to her eyes as she thought of the years of poverty that had been her parents' marriage, and of the love that had endured that hardship, to survive after death. 'To live on in the hearts of those we love is not to die,' Kenneth Barden had told her mother the day that they buried her father in this unforgiving earth. And she knew that to be true. 'I love you, Dad,' she whispered. And the wind took her words and swept them up into the pale blue of the heavens as she closed her eyes and said a silent prayer for the man who lay beneath this sacred earth.

Jack was waiting for her at the gate of the churchyard, in the back seat of his father's Bentley, which was specially decked out in white ribbons for the occasion. He leant over and placed a kiss on her cheek as she slipped into the seat beside him. 'You look absolutely beautiful,' he said proudly. 'Your father would have been a proud man this day.'

Bethany squeezed his hand and knew it to be true, for despite any reservations he might have had about the Greville family, Cheevers Baine had wanted nothing but the best for his own.

She glanced down at the dress she was wearing. Jack had insisted she took her pick of the very best that Carleton's of Kirkby Lonsdale had to offer. She had settled for a simple cream satin affair, with a slim body and skirt, and a white fur cape that slipped over the lace shawl collar, for standing in the church. Parishes such as Utherdale could not run to special heating for their places of worship, even for the wedding of the Squire's son, and it had been a cold, cold start to the springtime that everyone said was just around the corner. 'Thank you, husband,' she said. 'You don't look so bad yourself.'

They settled back in their seats as Old Carnforth, dressed

in his Sunday best, turned the car into the main road. 'Happy?' Jack asked, then laughed at the total super-fluousness of the question.

'I'm so happy I could burst.'

'What could make you happier?'

'Nothing. Absolutely nothing.'

He gave a quiet smile. 'You haven't seen your wedding present yet.'

'Wedding present?' She looked genuinely amazed. She had never given such a thing a single thought. 'What wedding present?'

Jack leaned forward and tapped Old Carnforth on the shoulder. 'Before we go back to The Hall, I think we might just show Mrs Greville her wedding present, don't you?'

The old man was obviously in on the secret, for he slew the limousine round and began heading off back the way they came. The drivers and passengers of the wedding cars that were following looked on in amazement as the bride and groom passed them, going back in the opposite direction.

Bethany gazed out of the window in some confusion as the Bentley purred about a mile along the road between Utherby and Butterslack, past the barn where his brother Amos had had his accident, then turned off up a side road that skirted the back of Uther Crag. They pulled up outside the old stone dwelling known officially as Cragside, but always referred to locally as Lot's Farm.

'Let's get out,' Jack said.

He rushed round the car and opened the door for her, and she looked about her in bemusement as he led her down the overgrown path towards the door.

Most of the front of the old stone walls was covered in the deep rich red of Virginia creeper throughout the summer, but now only the skeletal outline of the ivy traced itself against the pale grey of the limestone, although the first signs of buds were beginning to appear.

Bethany shivered on the stone step and glanced back towards the car. The old man at the wheel was sitting with a quiet smile on his face. Did he know something she didn't know?

Jack took down a big iron key from its hiding place above the lintel and slid it into the rusty lock. It creaked loudly as the old mechanism was forced into action. Then he pushed open the door with his hand, before turning back to his bride. Before Bethany had time to say a word, he had swept her off her feet and was carrying her over the threshold.

He put her down gently on the York stone flagged floor of the entrance hall. 'Welcome home, Mrs Greville,' he said proudly as she gazed around her. 'Welcome home.'

'Soars still thy spirit, Child of Fire?
Dost hear the camps of Europe hum?
On eagle wings dost hover nigher
At the far rolling of the drum?'

Laurence Binyon

Book Two

CHILD OF
FIRE

Horst

Chapter Fifteen

'Himmelhof',
THE OBERSALZBERG, BAVARIA,
Germany,
Summer 1938

The rain that fell that summer was warm and endless, running in streams down the windowpanes of the great house and filling the ornamental birdbaths that flanked the stone steps leading from the terrace down to the lawns in front of what had once been the nursery wing. It was unusual for the summers in this most favoured part of the world, on the border of Germany and Austria and only the echo of a Mozart minuet away from the city of Salzburg. Here they were known for their hot dry spells, when the gardeners of the Himmelhof would go round with their watering cans refilling the birdbaths and sprinkling the lawns so that *Der Hausherr* would have no cause for complaint on his return from the industrial North.

The eighteen-year-old boy, who sat at his desk in front of that old nursery window, looked out at the moist green carpet of land through the haze of fine rain, then yawned, stretched his arms above his head, and got up to toss a soft ball at the kitten that romped at his feet.

'I'm bored, Nikko Zwo,' he sighed. 'Bored and boring in return. Everyone's fed up with me here. "Get on with studying for your *Abitur*, Horst," they say. But what they really mean is "Get lost – don't bother us. Go back up North with the rest of the family." When all the cats are away, the mice will play . . . And you know all about mice, don't you!'

He gave a wry smile as he bent to throw the ball once

293

more and sent the kitten scampering across the fine Persian rug in pursuit. It was hard to think of fat Frau Winkler, the cook, or Oskar, the seventeen-stone odd-job man, as mice. But, be they fat or thin, young or old, one thing was for sure – the staff of the Himmelhof breathed easier when the family were not in residence. 'One von Karsten left here when the others have gone is one too many for them . . . I wish I were back in Berlin or Essen – anywhere but here!'

There was a gilt-framed mirror on the wall opposite the window and he caught sight of himself and gave a rueful grimace. How he hated what he saw: the tall, lanky frame, with the crop of short light-brown hair that topped a tolerably decent face made intolerable by a skin still in the throes of teenage acne. Neither Otto nor Elsa, his elder brother and sister, had ever been plagued with such a thing, and he leant forward to prod disconsolately at one of the worst spots on his chin. His interference made it bleed. '*Scheisse!*' He swore under his breath as he dabbed at it with the corner of his handkerchief, before sitting down with a sigh at his desk once more.

His slim fingers drummed in frustration on the desktop. He felt as if he were waiting for something to happen, but quite what he had no idea. Perhaps that's what being bored was all about: waiting for things to happen; waiting, waiting . . .

The kitten was now lying on its back on the rug, balancing the ball between its paws, and he smiled fondly at it before his gaze travelled to meet the eyes of the figure on the wall above the fireplace. He could do nothing in this room without those eyes following him. 'It's worse than the *verdammte* Mona Lisa!' he muttered at the large oil painting of the grand old man, with the bushy white whiskers and gold watch chain strung out across the ample stomach. They had even hung a portrait of his great-grandfather in here – the nursery; to inspire future generations, no doubt. From the cradle to the grave, remind them of their heritage! Everywhere he went he was haunted by old Otto von Karsten. '*Der Alte*' – the Old One – as they still referred to him in the family; the ten-years-dead, venerable head of the House of Karsten. Second to none, not even to the great Alfred Krupp himself, when it came to forging the steel that had made Germany great in the days of the Kaisers and was now, three generations later, arming Germany's growing war machine, under its new leader Adolf Hitler. '*Der Kanonenkonig*' – the Cannon King – they had called Krupp, but old Otto had been known throughout the land as '*Der Kanonenkaiser*' – and everyone knew that an Emperor was far greater than a mere King.

Even the real King himself, the old Kaiser Wilhelm I, had paid homage to the man whose portrait now gazed down from the nursery wall. On the day of his coronation as Emperor of the newly-united Germany, in 1871, in the magnificent Hall of Mirrors in the Palace of Versailles, he had raised his glass to the head of the House of Karsten and said, '*Ich auf meinem Thron und Du an deinem Amboss, Otto*' I on my throne and you at your anvil, Otto. Then the old monarch had slapped his friend on the shoulder and declared: 'Together we can make Germany great again!'

And they would have succeeded, if his impulsive grandson, Kaiser Wilhelm II – poor old Willy – had not got into a war with the Allies and almost lost the lot, including his own throne.

Even the great von Karsten works on the Ruhr had been reduced to a mere shadow of its former capacity when the Americans, British and French had finished with it. That month of May 1920, would live on in the family folklore for ever, for not only was it the month that an Allied Control Commission had set up business in the von Karsten home, Talhof, just outside the city of Essen, to oversee the dismantling of the family's great iron and steel works, but it was also the month that Getrud von Karsten, wife of the owner's grandson and heir, gave birth to Horst, her younger son.

'Your father did not know whether to rejoice or weep the day that you were born,' Horst's mother told him years afterwards. 'For that was the day they told him that half our factories must be dismantled —destroyed by our own workers, whom we must pay for the privilege!' Nearly a million tools were to be scrapped and plant weighing almost 10,000 tons was to go. And according to the Allies, it was all perfectly legal, for Article 168 of the Versailles Treaty, drawn up after Germany's defeat in the Great War, had said so.

Der Alte had wept that day. In his huge works on the outskirts of Essen, he had almost 150 acres of factories, with steam plant, electrical plant, coking plant, with almost 300 blast furnaces, devouring annually one and a half million tons of iron ore and regurgitating five hundred thousand tons of forged steel: the world-famous Karstenstahl. And now half of it must go.

The old man had returned from his meeting with the Commission that day and sat down at his great oak desk and put his head in his hands and wept. *Der Alte* – the man who had created it all – had wept like a baby in front of his grandson Otto, the Third. Only once before in his long life had he done such a thing, and that had been at Christmas 1916 when he had heard of the death of his only son, Otto the Second, on the battlefields of the Somme.

His grandson had stood and watched in stunned silence as the old man, the rock on which his own foundations were built, began to crumble, then he had gone to the hospital and told his young wife as she lay with her new baby in her arms: for the first time in his life he had seen his grandfather weep. 'May I never live to see such a day again, *Liebling*,' he had said. It had shocked him to the core.

'German men do not weep,' Gertrud von Karsten had told that baby when he was old enough to understand, 'especially Prussians. Our enemies had humiliated us, just as they had humiliated our country and our Kaiser. The tears shed by your great-grandfather were shed for the Fatherland as much as for the House of Karsten. But the day will come when those tears will be avenged, *mein Kind*, and I pray to God it will be in my lifetime, but, if not, it will certainly be in yours.'

The young Horst's thoughts had often dwelt on those words as he grew from childhood into adolescence. They seemed to make up an unwritten law that had ruled his life. One day Germany would be great again, and it would be up to the von Karstens to do all they could to bring that about. The family that had forged the steel of the sword of victory of Bismarck and Kaiser Wilhelm I would rise again and avenge the humiliation of the Great War. They had been Kingmakers once and would be again, even if the man who led their country was no longer a King, or a Kaiser, but an Austrian by the name of Adolf Hitler.

The young Horst often wondered what his grandfather would have made of the new German Chancellor, for old Otto had died before Hitler came to power in 1933. But although he had been dead now for almost a decade, nowhere the *Kanonenkaiser*'s great-grandson went in this his Bavarian estate could he escape the great man's presence. The giant mausoleum built for *Der Alte* by the family was here in the middle of the smooth green lawns that swept from the front and sides of the house down towards the road that wound into the valley below. The old man was buried there beneath the black marble tabernacle in a leaded, brass and walnut coffin so heavy, they said it had taken the strength of eight of his devoted estate workers to carry it to its final resting place.

A choir composed of singers from the State Opera in Berlin had given a soul-stirring rendition of '*Preussens*

Gloria' as they had finally slid the casket into its marble tomb.

Although he had chosen to be buried in Bavarian soil, the old man had been a Prussian born and bred. And no one could have taken greater pride in the fact that under his old friend Otto von Bismarck, it had been with the Prussian sword that German unity had been forged. And there was an even greater pride in knowing that most of those swords had been forged in von Karsten steel. Yes, Germany had a great deal to thank 'the two Ottos' for, as he liked to refer to himself and the Iron Chancellor.

Some of his great-grandson's happiest childhood memories were of sitting on the old man's knee and listening to stories of 'the old days'; tales of how he had ridden in the next carriage to the great Bismarck in the enormous military parade down the Unter den Linden, after the Prussian victory over the French at Sedan, in 1871. That great victory had opened the door for the unification of all the German states under one Emperor, the old Prussian King Wilhelm I, and one Chancellor, the old warhorse himself, Otto von Bismarck.

But greater still than the thrill of the victory parade had been the invitation to attend the declaration of the new German Reich in the spectacular Hall of Mirrors at Versailles.

'Your great-grandpapa stood there among the greatest of them all, young one,' the old man said, his blue eyes growing moist at the memory, as he sat with the small child on his knee and puffed on his beloved *Meerschaum* pipe. 'It snowed that day, as I remember . . . January 1871. It will go down in the annals of German history as the most momentous date of all – and the von Karstens played their part to the full in bringing it about.'

And in that deep, husky voice of his he went on to describe how in the mirrored splendour of the *Galerie des Glaces*, in Louis XIV's magnificent palace of Versailles, the seventy-four-year-old Prussian King, his whiskers gleaming as white as the snow outside, and wearing the uniform of the First Regiment of the Guards, had slowly passed between lines of his victorious soldiers to mount the great staircase and enter the huge gold and white hall, with the beribboned retinue of crowned German heads and princelings and other dignitaries shuffling slowly behind him.

'And you know what happened then, little one, don't you?' his great-grandfather would ask, and the young Horst would nod his head as the old man gave a broad smile and waved the *Meerschaum* pipe in the air like the pendulum of a clock. And 'Dong! Dong! Boom! Boom!' the child would sing out and the old man would beam with delight. '*Jawohl, mein Kind!* You know it well! Clocks all over the palace struck noon as he passed through those doors and outside in the snow the cannons — *my* cannons — thundered their salute as we who had made Germany great once more followed in his wake.'

It was a story he never tired of telling, or the child of hearing. And the old man's voice would break with emotion as he went on to describe how the old King had mounted the dais at the far end of the Hall and there had been tears in the pale blue of the royal eyes as he surveyed the briliance of the scene before him. This was the moment he had never dreamt he would ever see; the greatest moment in Germany's history.

Cuirassiers, in gleaming helmets and breastplates stood, with drawn swords erect on either side of him, and on his right stood his only son and heir, the thirty-nine-year-old Crown Prince Frederick of Prussia, husband of the British Queen Victoria's eldest child, Victoria, the Princess Royal. Around the dais, in a huge semi-circle, stood the other Kings, Princes, Grand Dukes and Dukes who were now about to throw in their lot under Prussia to create the new German Reich.

'But among all those great men,' his great-grandfather

said, his voice dropping to an even huskier, even more reverential tone, 'was the one man who had done more than any other to bring this moment about . . . We stood together, Otto von Bismarck and I . . .' And his eyes would focus on the far horizon as he continued softly, 'I can see him now, that mighty figure in his white Cuirassier's uniform. And do you know what he said to me, child, as that great moment of the Coronation arrived, can you imagine what he said?'

The old man's white whiskers would quiver as he leant back and brimming eyes would meet those of his great-grandson. And the young boy knew how to play the game. 'No, Great-grandpapa,' he would say, although he knew the story off by heart. 'What did he say?'

And the old man would look past the child on his knee into the distance once more as he relived that precious moment, and his voice would break with emotion as he said softly, 'He turned to me – your great-grandfather, Otto von Karsten – and he said, "Otto, my man, it has been on our shoulders – yours and mine – that we have carried our King to that imperial throne this day." '

There had been great celebrations all over Germany after that, and when the victorious Prussians had returned to Berlin, there had been banners flying from the station roof proclaiming: 'HAIL KAISER WILHELM OF A UNITED GERMAN EMPIRE!' and 'ALL GLORY TO PRUSSIAN VICTORY'. 'It made me proud to be a Prussian, child,' *Der Alte* went on to say. 'Proud to be a Prussian, and from that day, through blood and iron, and steel forged in my own furnaces – a German!'

Then his great-grandfather would blow his nose noisily into an enormous white handkerchief and dab his eyes, and the small child on his knee would wonder if old people always cried when they remembered the past.

And now he had gone. He was lying there in that great black monstrosity, as he had so often heard his mother refer to it. And his great-grandson had often imagined him lying there, resplendent in the medals and honours that had been bestowed upon him by the grateful monarchs he had served so well: Prussia's Cross of Merit for War Aid and Order of the Crown First Class; Saxony's Commander's Cross of the Order of Albert First Class; Bavaria's Military Order of Merit of St Michael First Class; Mecklenburg's Grand Commander Cross of the Order of the Griffin, to name but a few . . . Who else could claim to have been so *Kaisertreu* over so many generations, or been so amply rewarded for his loyalty?

Of all Germany's past monarchs, Horst could only remember poor old Willy, the ill-fated last Kaiser, to whom their family had once paid a courtesy visit in his exile in Holland. But he knew, for *Der Alte* had told him himself so many times, that the von Karstens had served the royal house of Prussia for three generations. Yes, the united Germany owed more than it could ever repay to the giant fiery furnaces of the Karsten works of the Ruhr valley.

The fact that the old man had chosen to go to his grave with those honours still around his neck, or pinned to the breast of the new evening suit they had buried him in was a source of great pain to the family, who would dearly have loved to have retained them as treasured family heirlooms. But it was typical of the man, as was the gold-lettered inscription he had chosen for his tomb: '*Der Kapt'n ist in den letzten Hafen eingelaufen*'. 'The Capt'n has put into the last harbour' was hardly the epitaph for a man who had spent the whole of his long life as head of Germany's greatest steel works. But old Otto had loved the sea and some of his happiest days had been spent sailing on the Baltic, with Kaiser Willy as honoured guest, aboard his beloved yacht *Wellenreiterin*. And he had had the even greater honour of accompanying his Emperor aboard the royal yacht itself for the prestigious and hotly contested Kiel Regatta and Cowes weeks, where the Kaiser's magnificent *Hohenzollern* would be in contention with the yacht of his uncle, the portly English King Edward.

Almost all the old man's memories he shared with his great-grandson, until the young boy felt he had experienced them himself. And Horst's own personal last memory of his great-grandfather was a remarkable occasion indeed. They had gone as favoured guests of the Wagner family themselves to a special performance of *Götterdämmerung* in Bayreuth and the young boy had been fitted out in a specially tailored new sailor suit for the occasion. He had also had the special privilege of sitting between *Der Alte* and Frau Winifred Wagner, who was kind enough to slip the small child next to her a sweet just before the grand finale of the opera.

He could still remember the impact of that moment on stage when before his startled eyes the citadel of the gods collapsed in flames amid a musical climax that was positively spine-chilling. He had physically jumped out of his seat at the initial shock, and to the consternation of the illustrious adults on either side of him, he had almost choked on the mint, so great was his excitement at the musical avalanche of sound in his ears and theatrical ferment on stage. And to add to his shame, in the car going home, instead of having the pleasure of mentally reliving what had been the most exciting evening of his life, his great-grandfather had lectured him on the rudeness of eating sweets in such a hallowed place.

'But Great-grandpapa,' he had protested. 'Frau Wagner gave it to me!'

The old man had looked down at him from his great height on the back seat of the Mercedes and the white whiskers above his top lip had trembled with disapproval. This was one time the truth did not pay. 'A von Karsten does not betray his friends, young man – especially if that friend is a lady. It would be advisable for you to remember that.'

Old Otto had died in his sleep that night, no doubt with the music of his favourite composer still ringing in his ears. He had been quite a man, and it was not easy for a young child growing up in the shadow of such an illustrious forebear to forget his heritage, or the importance of his family in the fortunes of the Fatherland.

But he had another more tangible reason for remembering his birthright and it was branded across the palm of his right hand. At the age of four, on his first ever visit to a Karsten steel works, he had been so dazzled by the sight of the white-hot spitting flames that in an unguarded moment he had slipped the hand of his Scottish nanny, Miss Nellie, and before any one of the small visiting party could stop him, he had grabbed at the end of the bar of white-hot metal being worked beside them on the factory floor.

He could remember nothing of what happened next, or of being rushed to hospital in nearby Essen. What stuck most in his mind was being told by his father when he came to visit him in his hospital bed that he had now been branded by the fires of Karsten Steel as much as any of their famous products.

'Von Karsten born and von Karsten branded,' his father had said, taking the small boy's bandaged hand in his. 'Fire has made us, child, and fire can consume us all. It is the most useful element in our world, and the most dangerous. You have learned that lesson at a tender age. Some never learn it and perish.'

The hand that now drummed its fingers on the ink-stained desktop was never quite the same again. Almost all lines on the palm were obliterated, including the lifeline and, as the small fist had begun to clench around the white-hot metal, the skin from his fingertips had also melted away, to leave them, like the palm, a smooth, shiny reminder of that day, and the element on which their empire was founded.

Horst von Karsten bent to scoop up the kitten and it mewed as he held it to his cheek. 'Nikko Zwo . . . my furry friend . . .' He made a purring sound in its ear and it purred in return; it was a game that they often played together. Then it wriggled to get down as he stroked the pure white fur. 'Even you are bored with me!'

He loved the small creature with a passion felt for little else in his life at present. It had been a Christmas gift from his sister Elsa and he had named it Nikko as its long white fur had reminded him of St Nicholas's beard, and Zwo because it was the second such object of his affections and had been given to replace an identical one killed in the forest the previous summer. Elsa had given him the first one too, six years previously, and had tried to tell him then that the Christmas Saint's servant, *Knecht Ruprecht*, had personally delivered it on his sleigh inside the basket tied up with red ribbon where he had found it beneath the Christmas tree at the end of the dining hall. Horst had groaned out loud and told his sister not to be so silly. Didn't she know he was not a child any longer and was long past the age of believing in fairy tales?

He had been twelve then, but little had changed in the intervening years. He was sure that was how they all still thought of him here – a naïve child. Yes, all of them: his mother, Gertrud; his father, Otto the Third; his twenty-one-year-old elder brother Otto the Fourth, and Elsa who at nineteen was one year older than himself. Little Horst – the baby of the family. Horst, who had had to spend so much time in bed as a child because of that terrible cough and weakness in his lungs that they spoke of him in hushed tones and sent for specialists from Berlin to pronounce upon him as if he were some laboratory specimen.

They said he had been lucky, the TB had been only a

304

very mild case and that his lungs would get stronger as he grew into manhood, but that did not stop his parents from incarcerating him here. Yet, despite all his mother's professed worry and concern, his illness was not deemed life-threatening enough for her to insist upon being near her youngest child. The lovely Gertrud von Karsten was first and foremost a social animal, and that meant that she, along with the rest of the family, spent most of her time in the north of the country, in either their Berlin or Essen homes, while Horst remained stuck down here in Bavaria 'for the air'.

'Himmelhof', their grand, turreted Bavarian *Schloss*, was certainly a beautiful place. Built in the last century by Horst's great-grandfather, in the manner of the one built by the mad King Ludwig himself for his mistress the notorious and wayward beauty Lola Montez, it sat high on the Obersalzberg, amid the tall green pines whose scent came wafting in on the breeze through the open windows at this time of year. It filled the whole house and was regarded as much more beneficial to his weak lungs than the smoke-filled air of the Ruhr, where his father had most of his works, or the stale, big-city air that wafted through the windows of their Berlin house on the Wannsee, or their apartment on the Unter den Linden.

Not that Horst minded being here too much, especially in summer. From the window of the old nursery that he now used as a study, he could see the massive bulk of the Untersberg mountain across the valley. Legend had it that the twelfth-century Emperor Frederick Barbarossa himself was asleep in a cave there, deep in the mountainside, ready to spring to life when needed badly enough in Germany's defence. His sign would be the circling overhead of the black ravens sent to summon him and warn him that the sacred soil of the German Reich was in danger. It was a story that had appealed to the young boy almost as much as those of his great-grandfather.

But there was another famous German leader now to be found in the area — and this one was very much alive. Adolf Hitler himself had built a new home not far from here, just above the small village of Berchtesgaden, some seventeen hundred feet down below in the valley. It seemed appropriate somehow for the Führer to be so close by, for the von Karstens had always been near at hand, ready and able to answer their leader's call. All his life Horst had been imbued with the notion that as a von Karsten his first duty was to serve the Fatherland and its leader, be it Kaiser or Chancellor. To serve the Fatherland was to be a hero in the greatest German tradition, and part of that fight now seemed to be to save the Fatherland from those deemed to be its enemies, like the Jews, the Socialists and Communists, and others regarded as enemies of the new state.

And somehow this very place, this beautiful, peaceful land of the Obersalzberg was part of that heroic fight. It seemed symbolic somehow that not only the legendary Barbarossa had his final resting place here, but so did the von Karstens, from old Otto onwards. And now Herr Hitler had chosen to live among them.

Horst had heard his father say that the 'Berghof', the Führer's mountain home, had one of the best sites in the whole area, and undoubtedly some of the finest views.

'But obviously not as fine as ours, *Liebling*, otherwise *Der Alte* would surely have chosen that part of the mountain to build on!' his mother had insisted. And the point was conceded. Old Otto never settled for second best in anything.

The Berghof, however, continued to fascinate the teenage boy growing to manhood in its vicinity. The house was hidden behind tall trees, with a nine-feet-high barbed-wire outer perimeter fence encircling the whole of the estate for nine uninterrupted miles, and an inner fence measuring two miles around the actual house itself.

'What do they need all that stuff for?' Horst had once asked his father, pointing to the lethal-looking fencing, stretching as far as the eye could see, as they drove past the estate in the family Mercedes.

'Herr Hitler likes to feel safe,' his father had replied, and his son's brow had furrowed as his eyes moved from the miles of barbed wire to the black-uniformed SS guards who spent their days and nights patrolling the property, machine guns at the ready.

'Why does he need protection from his own people?' he had gone on to ask, truly puzzled. But to that question his father could make no reply.

And on returning home from that drive, Horst had thought of his brother Otto, who now so proudly wore the distinctive uniform of an SS officer. The Nazi Party was his brother's whole life. 'I hope one day soon you'll join me in uniform,' Otto Junior had told his younger brother. But Horst had made no reply. If what the Nazis were doing was really so good for the Fatherland, why didn't everyone think so? What were they so worried about, that they needed all this security for a man whom it was claimed had the love of all the German people?

That all was not well with his country Horst had sensed from the very earliest days of National Socialism. Politics, in all its forms, had been the staple table-talk of his family over dinner throughout the whole of his life. And while his parents and elder brother appeared to have little doubt these days that the Nazis were leading their country on the road to recovery, Horst could not help feeling there was something wrong in this land, something that he could no longer question his own family about. And he had so many questions he wanted to ask. Questions without answers. So many questions that came back to haunt him more and more as he hovered on the brink of manhood, and could not fail to notice how one by one familiar faces were beginning to disappear from the neighbourhood.

Why, for instance, were they having to lock away such people as his friend Anna Marie's father and old Doctor Rosenbaum and his family?

Anna Marie Zimmermann was the daughter of one of the foresters on his father's estate – a jolly man who read a lot and liked to theorize on everything at great length. He had been imprisoned in one of the government's new concentration camps for almost two years now, as an enemy of the state. It had sounded a very grand thing to be when Anna Marie had first informed him of the situation, but Horst could not quite believe Herr Zimmermann to be the dangerous villain they made him out to be; he was far too much fun; he was the one who had taught him how to yodel and he could make a penny whistle from a hollowed-out twig better than anyone he knew. But Manfred Zimmermann was an active Socialist they said, maybe even a Communist. Such people could not be tolerated in the New Germany.

'I wouldn't waste your sympathy there, if I were you. They make trouble for the likes of us,' his mother stated firmly over the dinner table one evening, when he had dared to bring the subject up. 'Or they would if they got away with it. They resent our . . .' She searched for the right word.

'Our wealth. Let's not beat about the bush, Gertrud,' her husband had interjected. 'They resent the fact that people like us have got the power and money in this world and they don't, it's as simple as that!'

But was it as simple as that, Horst wondered? He had known Anna Marie's father all his life and he knew that Manfred Zimmermann resented no one. On the contrary, he was the happiest, most well-balanced person he knew. 'I liked Herr Zimmermann,' he had found the temerity to say.

Two pairs of eyes regarded him coldly from either end of the dinner table. 'Herr Zimmermann is a Socialist,' his father stated, spitting the word out as if it might contaminate his tongue. 'An enemy of the state.'

Horst had continued his meal in silence. But he could not remain silent when he heard later that not only old Doctor Rosenbaum, but his entire family had been deemed such. The elderly family practitioner had been the mainstay of the district's medical care for over two generations, and had been the one who had attended Horst almost daily during the worse spells of his illness. But no more. Dr Rosenbaum's licence to practise had been taken from him and he had been shipped off recently, along with his family, to somewhere in the East, where they said Jews were being resettled so they could no longer pose a problem for good decent Germans like the rest of them.

'It will be better for us all in the long run,' his mother had assured him when news of the transportation of the Rosenbaum family had first reached them and Horst had protested vehemently over lunch one day. Gertrud von Karsten had dabbed the corner of her mouth with her napkin and smiled reassuringly across the table at him. 'I'm sure the good Doctor will be happier over there in the East tending to his own kind and it means there will be more opportunities for our own pure Aryan doctors to make a good living.'

The word 'pure' was one that was used a lot these days, and despite parental assurances it was all for the best, Horst still found the whole thing distasteful, and he often told Otto so in no uncertain terms. But his elder brother had no such difficulties with the new philosophy. 'Germany is marching on to greater things these days,' he informed his younger brother. 'We should feel privileged to be part of it. You should be proud that one day soon you too can wear a uniform like this and will be able to repeat the Dagger Words and the honoured Oath that will make you a member of our Führer's most elite band, the SS.'

Otto had donned the black shirt of the *Schutz Staffel*, in the *SS Fördernde Mitgliedschaft* – that elite organization's even more elitist subdivision – and had taken real pride in displaying the new tools of his trade to his younger brother. His specially numbered swastika armband, with the circular inscription around its perimeter: *'Dank der SS fur treue Hilfe in der Kampfzeit'* – 'Thanks to the SS for faithful assistance in time of struggle' was passed round for inspection and admiration by all the family, as was his brand-new membership book containing a special dedication written for them by Reichsführer Heinrich Himmler himself, leader of the Blackshirts:

> *Es ist eine Ehre, SS Mann zu sein,*
> *Es ist eine Ehre, Fördernde Mitglied zu sein,*
> *Tue jeder weiter seine Pflicht,*
> *Wir SS Manner und ihr Fördernden Mitglieder,*
> *Jeder an seiner Stelle,*
> *Und Deutschland wird wieder gross werden*

> It is an honour to be an SS man,
> It is an honour to be an FM,
> Let each of us continue to do his duty,
> We SS-FM men at our posts,
> And Germany will become great again.

That might well all be true, Horst decided, but he did not want to be a member of that elite band and, in truth, he found all their marching and chanting of oaths and pledges faintly ridiculous. It was all right for some, he admitted that, for there were those who revelled in such things. Those such as Otto who had spent his childhood doing battle with battalions of toy soldiers right here on the nursery floor, and who knew all the great German victories off by heart, from Charlemagne's to Hindenburg's.

But Horst knew he was not like that. Battles and the thought of killing other people sickened him; he had always preferred quieter, more reflective pursuits. He was never happier than when he had the chance to talk to those such as Father Kroll who knew such stories from the Bible that he used to hold the young boy enthralled for hours, and now, as Horst approached manhood, there were even more interesting topics he was keen to discuss. In many ways what was happening in Germany today was far more disturbing than anything ever got up to in the days of Charlemagne. But Father Kroll rarely had time to visit these days and only seemed to make the effort when the rest of the family were at home, and with so much happening in the North, that was less and less these days. Even his mother and Elsa seemed to spend as little time as possible at Himmelhof.

Elsa, in particular, was a proving a great disappointment to her younger brother. An extremely pretty girl with ash-blonde hair like her mother, wide blue eyes that seemed to look permanently surprised, and a rather petulant rosebud mouth, she seemed to have no interest at all in things of the spirit. In fact, Horst could not remember her even opening a book since she left school two summers ago. 'Books are for bores!' she declared one day, seeing him engrossed in yet another tome from their father's library. 'And I shall never be a bore!'

To everyone's surprise, Papa had kicked up almost no fuss at all at her decision not to stay on and take her *Abitur*, which would have gained her entry to University. 'The finest thing a young woman can do these days is to marry and raise a family of fine sons for the Fatherland,' Otto von Karsten had declared over breakfast one morning, on hearing of his daughter's desire to put book-learning behind her. 'The Führer has the right idea in awarding gold medals to such mothers of the nation who succeed in producing more than their expected quota of children.

311

That is what Germany needs more than even my steel – fine, sturdy youngsters to take her from strength to strength for generations to come.'

'Papa made women sound like fat sows this morning,' Horst had told his sister afterwards. 'Do you really want to be a pig, Elsa, and get a medal for producing fine litters for the Führer? If Herr Hitler is so fond of children let him get married and produce some of his own!'

His sister had been quite shocked. 'Why, Horst von Karsten, I do declare you should be locked up for speaking such nonsense – and wicked nonsense at that!'

Horst had looked at her with that grave-eyed stare of his and said nothing. It seemed to him they were locking up far too many people these days, and had been for far too long. Where it would all end he had really no idea, but one thing was for sure, he didn't want to be part of it. And the longer time went on, the more convinced he became. The last thing he wanted to do was to leave school and don a fancy uniform like Otto, and go around arresting good people like Anna Marie's father and old Doctor Rosenbaum and his family. There was more to life than that and he would make sure of it.

And so the summer of '38 that passed so slowly was a peculiarly lonely one for the young boy on the brink of manhood. There were few people of interest around to talk to, and about the only time the rest of the family came to visit was when they knew that the government's top brass were to be in the area. Then a grand party would be thrown at the Himmelhof for their benefit.

Horst knew that even if he were invited to attend any of these illustrious gatherings, they would hold little interest for him. No matter how hard he tried, he found it impossible to share his family's love of high politics. While they were all taken up completely in the excitement of building this New Germany that they talked about so constantly, his thoughts dwelt much more on the land he knew first as a child; a land without marching black-uniformed soldiers and friends who disappeared overnight.

He wished fervently that Herr Hitler had not decided to build his holiday home so near their own, for just being able to glimpse that barbed wire and those lookout posts from his window gave the landscape around Himmelhof an entirely different feel. And having all those Party officials around so much, and all the security people that shadowed them, made his beloved part of the Obersalzberg seem like a prison camp. He could not bring himself to believe it was the 'honour' that the rest of the family claimed it to be to have the German Chancellor as their nearest neighbour, for his coming had replaced the peace and tranquillity with the throb of official Mercedes and motorcycle outriders, who constantly sped up and down the road that skirted the Himmelhof and led down to the village of Berchtesgaden far below.

The rain had stopped now and a pale, watery sun was piercing the clouds that hung low over the Untersberg in the distance. 'I think it's going to clear up, Nikko Zwo,' he said to the kitten on the carpet. 'It might even be fine enough for a walk very soon.'

He walked to the french window and threw it open, breathing the pine-scented air. It always seemed particularly pungent after rain. In the distance he could see a small animal scamper across the immaculately cut lawn. At first he thought it was a hare, for it was too big for a rabbit, but it lacked the long legs . . . No, there was no mistaking it – it must be Papi, Anna Marie's little dachshund. That meant that she must be around somewhere, for the animal was never allowed to roam far from its young mistress. There were too many employees on the Himmelhof estate eager to take a pot-shot at anything that looked like a rabbit for that.

He stepped out on to the terrace and closed the door

behind him so the kitten could not escape. He squinted his eyes into the weak sunlight. Yes, it was Papi all right. Poor stupid Papi had been the last present bought for Anna Marie by her father before he had disappeared into the hands of the SS that awful night two years ago. Her father had named the dog, calling it after the ex-Head of State Franz von Papen, whom he had blamed for opening the door to allow the Nazi Adolf Hitler through into the highest office of government.

'Physically there is no lower type of dog than a dachshund,' Manfred Zimmermann had declared to his daughter and Horst as they shared a pot of coffee in the family kitchen. 'And morally no lower statesman than Franz von Papen for allowing that Austrian Corporal to take over this country.'

His detestation of the Nazi leader had been well known in the area and the naming of his little daughter's dog had been symbolic of that. It had also been the beginning of the end of the forester's freedom, for someone had reported him for 'treacherous remarks against the state' and his family had never seen him since.

Ever since that cold autumn morning two years previously when he had heard the forester had been arrested, Horst had suspected the culprit in naming him to be none other than his own elder brother Otto. There had been a peculiarly satisfied smile on Otto's face over lunch that day when the subject of Herr Zimmermann's arrest had come up.

'People like that, who set themselves up as enemies of the Fatherland, deserve to have their freedom taken from them,' Otto had declared, in that pompous voice he reserved for such declarations. 'Pass that dish, if you don't mind.'

'Aren't you mixing up the Fatherland with the Government?' Horst had asked, as he handed the plum jam to his brother. Somehow he could never bring himself to believe that Manfred Zimmermann did not love his German homeland as much as any one of them gathered around that table. It was he who had taught him all he knew about nature, and the forest that surrounded the Himmelhof, and all the wild creatures that inhabited it. Yes, and who had taught Otto too, if only he cared to remember.

But that thought seemed to have escaped his brother's memory entirely as he answered stiffly, 'In the eyes of all good Germans, the Fatherland and the Nazi Party and Government are one, *Dummkopf*!' And that had been the end of that particular conversation.

He had not seen either Anna Marie or Papi for weeks, for although his father had allowed Frau Zimmermann and the children to go on living in the cottage, Anna Marie had left school that summer and had taken a job in one of the cafés down the valley in Berchtesgaden, so he had seen very little of her. But perhaps today was one of her days off.

He began to run across the lawn in the direction of the dog, which disappeared for a time in the undergrowth of one of the paths that led off into the forest, but he whistled that special whistle that both he and Anna Marie had taught it to respond to and it paused and ran back a few yards in his direction.

'Come here, Papi, that's a good dog!'

But the animal took off again with the boy in hot pursuit.

He followed it for almost half a mile down the rough forest track, often losing sight of it for a minute or so, and having to keep placing his two fingers in his mouth and make that special whistling sound which would bring it back into sight, only for it to take off again. Obviously it knew exactly where it was headed, and Horst decided to follow in the hope of finding Anna Marie at the other end.

The forester's daughter had been as close a friend as he had ever had, either here, or in Essen or Berlin. They were almost the same age and had known each other all their lives; they laughed at the same things, and she was the one person who did not seem to find him boring. The silences that fell between them were comfortable silences; there was never any need for excuses or explanation.

Papi had come into sight once more and seemed to be headed for an old forester's hut situated in an overgrown glade deep in the heart of the forest. It had been out of use for generations, but he and Anna Marie had often used it as children, until one day he had had quite a severe fall from the slippery shingle roof and had been made to promise never to go near the place again.

For some reason he did not shout her name as he neared the dilapidated door, for he could not really believe her to be in there. She was quite the young woman now, after all. Days of playing 'house' in old disused buildings were long gone.

Tentatively he pushed open the door and entered, his feet sinking into the soft earth of the floor. The constant rain throughout the summer had made even old packed-earth floors like this susceptible to the dampness that pervaded everything.

It was quite dark inside, for being so deep in the forest very little light penetrated even outside the small narrow windows of the hut. It smelt dank and musty from the hay that he knew used to lie on the raised bed platform above his head. Although only one storey in height, the one room of the hut could be used as both living and sleeping accommodation, by climbing the rickety wooden ladder that led up to the platform with its bed of ancient, smelly hay.

Although this had once been an enchanted place for him in the past, for on top of that very platform above his head he and Anna Marie had shared their first kiss, and down below they had often sat at that rickety old table and played cards and other board games to their hearts' content, now with its dank musty interior, the place merely depressed him. And for some reason he felt nervous.

'I think I'd better be going, Papi, old thing,' he said to the small animal at his feet. 'You've led me on a real wild goose chase this time.'

The dachshund pricked its ears and cocked its head to one side as if it was listening and understanding every word, then it rushed over to the wooden steps leading up to the platform and began to bark. And it kept on barking until Horst was forced to come over and look curiously at the old ladder that seemed to be the object of all the noise.

'What are you trying to tell me, old boy?' he asked. 'She's not up there, is she?' It seemed inconceivable that the now grown-up and sophisticated Anna Marie was up there in that musty old hay.

He glanced again at the ladder. It had been almost two years since he had last trusted his feet to those rotten treads and it was all of ten feet to the platform above. Dare he?

The dog was still barking, but not so loudly now, as if to encourage him in his decision.

'All right, old thing, you talked me into it!' he sighed.

He clung on to the sides as if for grim death as he climbed slowly up, one rung at a time, then when he had got two-thirds of the way up, he paused, for he could now see safely into the hay-strewn platform. '*Um Himmels Willen!*'

Two eyes were staring back into his from out of a face that was patently petrified.

He almost fell back off the ladder in shock, and his first instinct was to turn and flee. Then it registered it was no vagabond, or mere tramp. It was no one who would pose any threat. The face that stared back into his was that of a young woman of about his own age.

317

Chapter Sixteen

'Who are you?' Horst demanded, peering through the gloom. His fingers were gripping the top of the ladder as if his life depended on it. 'And what are you doing here?' He struggled to keep the nervousness from his voice. It was smelly up here, smelly and dank, and the last thing he had expected to find was another human being, and a female one at that.

The figure in the hay shrank back, obviously even more afraid than he was. By the time he had climbed a rung further up for a better look, she was pressed hard up against the hut wall and was staring at him like some petrified animal.

Recognizing her state of terror, his own confidence grew. 'You had better tell me, for you are on private property, you know. My father owns this estate and everything on it.'

'Everything and everyone.'

The cynical observation came from the open door down below, and Horst swung round in surprise to see none other than Anna Marie herself standing there, silhouetted against the light.

But instead of the usual smile of recognition he expected, his old friend's face wore a look of both anger and consternation. Her cheeks were flushed and she was breathing heavily. She must have been running. He might have known she wouldn't be far behind her little dog. 'What brought you here?' The words were almost snapped up at him. 'How did you find out?'

Horst looked down at the small dog now up on its hind legs pawing at his mistress's dirndl skirt. No, he wouldn't get poor Papi into trouble. 'Oh, I was just out for a walk and thought I'd revisit some old haunts,' he answered as casually as he could. Then his brow furrowed as he jerked his head in the direction of the loft. 'Who on earth is that up there?'

Anna Marie came into the hut and closed the door behind her, almost blotting out what little daylight there had been. But there was still enough light to see that her face was grave. She did not answer the question directly, as she took a portion of bread and small piece of sausage from her jacket pocket and placed them on the table in the centre of the hut. He could see that she was thinking, considering the situation carefully in her mind, and he waited for her to speak.

'We are old friends, aren't we, Horstchen?' she said eventually. There was almost a pleading in her eyes as they met his.

'Ja. Very old friends.'

'And just as you must know you could trust me with your life, and I could trust you with mine, could I trust you with someone else's?'

A shiver ran through him at the thought of what was about to come next. 'Of course. You know I would never let you down.'

Anna Marie came further into the room until she was standing right at the foot of the ladder and her voice was strained as she looked up at him and said quietly, 'You know strange things are happening to our country these days, Horst. Very strange things. Terrible things. People are disappearing from their homes – taken in the night by the SS, never to be seen again, like my own father. Or rounded up like the Jews and put on trains to the East, to end up God knows where.'

Horst listened to his friend, the apprehension growing

319

within him with each word she spoke. It was not like Anna Marie to be so serious, to be taking on the troubles of the world like this. Suddenly his friend seemed older, much older. He could almost hear her father Manfred's voice behind her words. But Manfred Zimmermann was locked up and had been for two years for saying just the type of thing his daughter was now telling him.

Horst took one hand off the ladder and ran it anxiously through his hair. His mother's placatory words of how it was all for the best rang in his head, but he knew in his heart that Anna Marie was speaking the truth. There were terrible things happening out there right now. Really terrible things. And, worst of all, his own family was party to it.

Anna Marie's eyes were grave in the darkness of the hut as she continued quietly, 'You know those camps they are taking the Jews to in the East – to "resettle" them as they say? You have heard of them?'

Horst nodded, a trifle uncertainly.

'Well, if I told you we have evidence they are not going to simply "resettle" them there as the government claims, but that they intend killing them? Killing them, Horst. By shooting or gassing, and God only knows what other fiendish methods they can dream up.' Then seeing the shocked look on his face, she continued quickly, 'Yes, men, women and children. It makes no difference – they intend putting them to death just because they are of the Jewish faith, or gypsies, or whatever.'

Horst could not believe his ears. 'But that can't be true!' he exclaimed. 'This is Germany, Anni! Things like that just don't happen. Not in our country. Not in the twentieth century.'

His parents would have heard tell of it, or Otto most certainly would. They would certainly never be supportive of anything like that. And if Anna Marie knew, there must be others who knew – good people, responsible people, people in authority who would never allow such a thing to happen. She must have gone mad. Quite mad. Taken leave of her senses.

But Anna Marie had not gone mad and she was shaking her head at his innocence as she said impatiently, 'I can't expect you to believe it – not just like that. It took me days to accept the truth of the stories myself. But now I have no doubt about them. None at all. I have seen and spoken to people who have escaped from those hell holes. They have actually experienced what is going on in those places in the name of the German nation – that's you and me, Horst. They are locking up good people like my father and intend killing people like Doctor Rosenbaum in the name of you and me!'

Horst let out a sound as if he had been kicked in the stomach and, indeed, it felt just like that. What he was hearing was so terrible that somehow he felt it just had to be true. Nobody, especially not Anna Marie, would just make up something like this. There would be no reason to; on the contrary, she risked being locked up herself for saying such things. That she was in touch with people who would make it their business to find out such information he had no doubt. Manfred Zimmermann had had many such friends before he was arrested. People his own parents might call Socialists – or even worse, Communists – but he knew to be, for the most part, decent caring human beings, many of whom belonged to no political party.

His eyes moved nervously back up to the wooden platform above his head. 'Who – who is that up there, then?' he asked quietly, almost afraid to hear the answer.

'Didn't you recognize her?' Anna Marie asked in some surprise.

'Well, no . . . Should I?'

'It's Geli – Geli Rosenbaum.'

'It's Angelika?' That haunted, petrified face belonged to

Doctor Rosenbaum's youngest daughter? But Angelika Rosenbaum was one of the prettiest girls in the area. Two years older than Horst and Anna Marie, she had broken more than her fair share of hearts before she had even reached her mid-teens.

'It surprises you?' Anna Marie asked, with a bitter smile. 'And so it should, for that's what weeks in hiding does to a person. It dehumanizes them, Horst. It makes them little better than a hunted animal. But at least she's alive. And while there's life there's hope, as they used to say.'

Horst leant back against the ladder and let out a deep sigh. In the space of a few short minutes he felt as if he had said goodbye to childhood and adolescence for ever. Whatever vestiges of it there had been left in him this summer, they had gone for good right here in this old wooden hut with what he had just seen and heard. Yes, he felt as if he had been kicked in the stomach all right — by one of his father's best stallions. And it hurt.

'How long have you known?' he asked Anna Marie. 'How long has Geli been here?'

'Since they took her father and mother and two older sisters away,' she answered simply. 'She was one of the lucky ones, she was spending the night away from home when they came for them. She was staying at our house.'

'Aah . . . Heidi . . .' It was beginning to make sense. Anna Marie's older sister had been one of Geli Rosenbaum's best friends at school. 'And you've hidden her here ever since?'

'It seemed like a good idea. No one ever comes here.' She gave a wry smile. 'Until today, that is.'

Horst made a dismissive gesture with his hand as if to banish the thought that somehow his coming here had made any difference. 'You can trust me, Anni. You know that. I will never give Geli away. Ever.'

His friend looked at him gravely for a second or two, then nodded her head in reply. 'I know that,' she said softly. 'You may be a von Karsten, but unlike most of them, you are also a human being.'

It was over an hour before he left the hut, and what he heard during that time both shocked and disturbed him profoundly. Up at the Himmelhof he led a life on a completely different plane from the workers on their estate, or even from those of the villagers down in the valley below. The policies of their National Socialist Government were having a profound effect on even the most ordinary citizens and their families – and not always to the good, as both Anna Marie and Angelika Rosenbaum could testify.

But there was never any mention of the dark side of Nazism over the dinner table in the von Karsten household. Whenever he was with his family all he ever heard was of the good that was being brought about, and how much more prosperous the country would be once it had been cleansed of its enemies. The word '*judenrein*' was one of the favourites on everyone's lips these days – Germany must be 'Jew-clean' – cleansed of the Jewish race. No member of that race, be it man, woman or child, must be allowed to remain a free and equal citizen of the German state.

He left the hut in a dazed state. His mind was in turmoil. He could hardly think straight. It was as if he had just had the security blanket of goodness and truth that one presumed one's family stood for, ripped from him. All that he was left with was the cold – icy cold – realization that things would never be the same for him again. Whom could you trust when you could no longer trust your own family? It was a question to which right now he knew he had no answer.

Over the next few days there were times when he found himself wishing fervently that he had never followed Anna Marie's little dog into that hut in the forest. It would have been so much easier not to have been personally

323

confronted with all of this. He could have suspected things were happening around him that should not have been happening, certainly; he had already been doing that for quite some time. But to have the evidence dumped on your own doorstep in the shape of an old friend and neighbour. Well, that was something else entirely.

For days afterwards the thought of that pale, petrified face haunted him and no matter how hard he tried he could not get that initial glimpse of Geli Rosenbaum cowering there like some frightened animal out of his head. So great was the turmoil within him that it took him almost a week before he could pluck up enough courage to go back to the hut. Somehow he felt partly responsible for Geli being there. As a von Karsten, he was part of it — part of the Establishment that had helped Hitler to power and was keeping him there.

But he knew his feelings of guilt wouldn't help his friend's immediate predicament. The last thing she needed was to have to cope with his own personal angst over the situation. What she needed most of all was food, and perhaps almost as important, companionship. He knew he could offer both — plucking up the courage to do so was quite another matter.

That courage came to him on waking up one morning. As he lay in the oak four-poster bed and watched the sunlight streaming through the open window of his room, he found himself thinking of that fugitive — that pathetic, petrified creature he had once known as a pretty young girl called Geli Rosenbaum — waking up in the dank, evil-smelling darkness of that old hut less than a mile away. Did the sun's rays ever penetrate that gloom? There was certainly a window in the shingled roof, but it was so encrusted with dirt barely any light could get through.

Despite the sunshine, there was the first suspicion of frost in the air this morning and the sky was the colour of opal over the mist-shrouded mountains as he got out of bed and opened his bedroom window to gaze out over the landscape that would never be quite the same again. His eyes narrowed as he shaded them with his hand and gazed out in the direction of the forest. There was someone in there – in that dense green world of tall firs – hidden from the prying eyes of their own world was a girl not much older than himself; a girl now totally alone in the world, except for a few staunch friends who were willing to risk their all that she might live . . .

He had dithered quite long enough, he decided. In fact, it was quite shameful it had taken him so long to do what in his heart he knew to be the right thing. And the right thing, he reminded himself, required certain practicalities.

It was not unusual for him to pay the odd visit to the kitchen. In fact, as a child it had been his favourite part of the house, even though he knew his mother frowned on him spending time there. So none of the staff going about their usual morning chores thought it at all odd to see him making his way down below stairs immediately after breakfast.

He deliberately waited until the coast was clear, then when he was sure the cook was busy elsewhere, he slipped into the pantry. How those cold stone slabs with their mouth-watering flitches of home-cured pork, wedges of home-produced cheeses, butter, and row upon row of carefully labelled preserves, used to make him drool. But now there was no time for that and he allowed himself the luxury of popping just one pickled egg into his mouth as his fingers reached into the tall jar to pick out two more to drop into his pocket for Geli Rosenbaum.

He then took a clean handkerchief and, lifting half a cooked chicken from a plate, he quickly wrapped it and squeezed it into the opposite pocket of his jacket. It made an unsightly bulge that he hoped would not be noticed on his way out as, into the other pocket with the eggs he squeezed two apples; any more he felt sure would be noticed.

'*Morgen! Morgen!*' He seemed to meet everyone on his way back upstairs, but happily none of the staff appeared in the least interested in his bulging pockets as he hurriedly made his way towards the back door.

It took him only a few minutes to run across the lawns and enter that part of the grounds where the forest reached its evergreen fingers along the edges of the beautifully cultivated herbaceous borders.

Once out of the formal gardens it was a different world entirely. It had been raining throughout the night and the forest was a dripping mass of branches and pungent smells as he wound his way along the path, through the dense undergrowth, towards the hut. There was a strangely melancholy feeling in the air, with signs of the dying summer all around him. Despite the occasional rays of sunshine that penetrated the trees, the forest had that tired faded look to it that signified the end of the long golden days that one felt would go on for ever. Among the evergreen firs, here and there already leaves of flaming red and gold were evident on the branches of the deciduous trees; leaves that soon the autumn winds would fan into the full glorious blaze of colour that was September in the Obersalzberg.

The path to the hut that sheltered Geli Rosenbaum was bordered in one part by bushes laden with wild black-berries, and he gathered handfuls on his way, only to find that he had absent-mindedly eaten most of them by the time he had reached his destination. The hut was situated in what had once been an open glade and the midday sun splashed the gently steaming grass as he moved nervously towards the closed door.

The door creaked on its hinges as he pushed it open. It was much darker inside than out and it took a second or two for his eyes to grow accustomed to the dim light. It smelt just as foul as it had the other day and he wondered how such a clean and particular young woman as Geli

Rosenbaum had been could put up with such a place. It was odd how he always thought of her in the past tense, as if, by being an official non-person now in the eyes of the law, she had somehow ceased to exist in reality.

'Don't worry, Geli, it's only me – Horst!' he called softly, to put her mind at rest as he neared the ladder. For all he knew, Anna Marie had a secret call or something so she would know not to worry when the hut door opened unexpectedly.

There was no reply from above, so he shinned up the ladder, more confidently this time, to investigate. 'I thought you had gone!' he exclaimed, in as quiet a voice as possible. 'You didn't answer me.'

Geli Rosenbaum was crouched at the far end of the platform and regarded him with large dark eyes alive with anxiety and suspicion as he swung his legs on to the hay-strewn boards and crawled over to join her.

His silent reception discomfited him somewhat, but he pressed on regardless, forcing a cheerful smile to his lips as he said brightly, 'Here – I brought you these.'

He dug into his pockets and produced the chicken, eggs and fruit, and what was left of the blackberries. He laid them carefully on the hay in front of her. But still she made no move. Her face was quite expressionless. 'I'll bring more next time I come,' Horst promised quickly, wondering if perhaps his first offering was too meagre. 'I would have brought more today but I was afraid of getting caught.'

But Geli still made no attempt to touch the food. She remained silent, crouching there with those big eyes of hers fixed on his face.

'You don't mind that I came – that I brought you this, do you?' Horst asked, by now more than a little unnerved by her silence. 'No one knows I've come and no one saw me – I made sure of that.'

Then, to his consternation, the dark eyes that had never

left his face for a second began to brim with tears that spilled slowly over her lower lashes and ran in rivulets down her face.

'Look here, I'm really sorry if my coming has upset you,' he blustered, not quite sure why she was crying. 'I didn't mean to cause any problem for you . . .' His voice tailed off as he reached inside his pocket for his handkerchief. It still smelt of chicken, but he handed it across, nevertheless. 'Here, take this.'

She shook her head as she accepted the linen square and dabbed at her brimming eyes. 'Forgive me,' she said thickly. 'It's a funny situation, that's all . . . You're the first human being I have seen for weeks – except for dear Anna Marie and Heidi, of course. It's becoming hard to relate to people, that's all. I'm almost beginning to feel I'm no longer a member of the human race.'

Horst stared at her through the gloom. Hearing that familiar voice coming from this scarecrow-like creature unnerved him. His heart went out to her. The first human being for weeks, except for Anni and Heidi! The thought of what that must be like horrified him, just as much as the sight of this pathetic creature who had once been a lively and very pretty young woman horrified him. And there and then he resolved to do something about it.

'You don't really mind me coming, though?' he asked, picking up one of the apples and handing it to her.

She shook her head as she sank her teeth into the ripe, firm flesh. 'No, I don't mind,' she said, through a mouthful of the fruit. 'I don't mind at all.' Then she laughed – it was something she had not done in weeks – as she recognized the understatement. 'It will be wonderful to have someone else to talk to.'

Over the next few days all thoughts of being bored, or boring to others, vanished as Horst made it his task to smuggle as many things as possible into that foul-smelling little hut that was now Geli's world. If he could not make her life exactly comfortable, then he could certainly do his best to make it as bearable as possible. What he could pilfer in the way of food from the Himmelhof's kitchens was supplemented by the occasional cream pastry he bought with his own money from Schindeldecker's, the baker's, in the village.

Now they were both working for a living, neither Anna Marie nor her sister Heidi could get up to the hut very easily, so they were only too relieved to have Horst to help them out. Horst made it a habit to call as often as possible into the coffee houses where they worked and usually managed to have the odd private word to keep them up to date on his visits to their friend.

'You will surely go to heaven, Horstchen!' Anna Marie smiled, on one of his first visits, as she placed his cup of steaming brown coffee in front of him and Horst had grinned in return, before biting into the wedge of golden *Sandkuchen*. 'Not for some time, I hope!' It was his firm desire to outlive even *Der Alte*. But what kind of a world he would find himself in by then he could not imagine. The way things were going, none of them might even survive the next few years.

For her part, Geli Rosenbaum began to look forward eagerly to the daily visits of the young man she had known only slightly before her family's arrests. Horst, she decided, was an exceedingly nice young man, but his brother Otto now, that was another matter entirely, for she had offended that particular young man deeply more times than she cared to remember over the past few years. That the von Karstens' son and heir had had a crush on her was a fact known to almost no one else in the area, for Otto would wait until the doctor's youngest daughter was quite alone on one of her many favourite walks through the forest before he made his play. The fact that he was rebuffed each time only seemed to increase his ardour, and Geli had breathed more than one sigh of relief three years ago when she heard he had joined the SS and would no longer be spending the long summers at the Himmelhof. The thought of having the forest to herself to walk through quite unmolested was wonderful.

And now she found it a curious quirk of fate that his younger brother was giving her all his attention, although as no more than a good and trusted friend, in what was a quite bizarre situation. It was a very odd world indeed.

But she was more grateful than she knew Horst could possibly imagine as he came smiling up the ladder each day, with always something new to eat, or some little extra to take her fancy. But more even than the food, perhaps what delighted her most of all as the days went by were the small feminine things he thought to bring, such as soap, a new comb and a mirror. And books. Books were the one luxury Geli could not get enough of. 'Time hangs so heavy on one's own here for hours, day out and day in, Horst,' she said, as her hands stroked the well-thumbed copy of Remarque's *The Way Back* that he had brought her.

'I think actually that's one of the books they have banned,' he said apologetically. 'But it's my own copy and I think Germany will be proud of it one day.'

He had been there that day, 10 May 1933, in the Kaiser Franz Jozeph Platz, in Berlin, when they had burned the books. His mother had taken him, along with Otto and Elsa, to witness what she had called 'an historic occasion'. Under Nazi orders, all writers deemed to be 'enemies of the state', such as Heinrich Heine, Thomas Mann, Erich Maria Remarque, Emile Zola, Marcel Proust, H.G. Wells and many others – alive or dead, it made no difference – were thrown on to a massive bonfire, so big that the pouring rain had made no impression on the dancing, crackling flames, which soared heavenwards far into the night.

Even as a young child, Horst had felt there was something disturbing about the way the Nazis and their supporters had danced around the flames, their ritualistic chanting filling the air as book after book was tossed into the burning inferno.

'Heinrich Heine — for writing works which defile and undermine the strength of the German people, we consign you to the flames!'

Volumes of German literature's revered literary giant were thrown through the air into the heart of the fire. And they, in turn, were followed by the works of their country's most popular modern author, Thomas Mann. And he, in turn, by those of the French Jew, Marcel Proust, then countless others from across Europe and America. And all the time they were cheering, cheering.

Then Dr Goebbels himself had arrived in his official limousine to declare that 'the phoenix of a new spirit would arise from the ashes of the books'.

'Why are they so afraid of books, Mother?' Horst had asked on the way home. And Gertrud von Karsten had looked perplexed for a moment, then composed herself to say nobly, 'Because these books are enemies of the state, child, and must be destroyed.' It was the first time he had ever heard the phrase and it had stuck in his head. What a funny state they were living in that had books as its enemy, he had thought.

He had recounted his feelings on the spectacle he had witnessed that night to Anna Marie's father on his next visit to Himmelhof, and the forester had nodded sagely as he listened, grave-faced, to the young boy relate his experience. 'What do *you* think, Herr Zimmermann?' Horst had asked. '*Can* books really be enemies of the state?'

'Have you never heard Heine's own words on that very issue, *Junge*?' the middle-aged man asked in return.

Horst shook his head.

'Over a hundred years ago, the great man wrote: "Where they burn books, soon they will burn people." '

331

Herr Zimmermann's face, as he recounted the great writer's prophecy, was as sombre as the words he spoke. And they were words that had had a profound effect on the mind of the young boy who heard them. Horst knew from that moment that there was at least one other person in his life who thought as he did; who considered it wrong that the works of those regarded as the greatest writers of their age should suddenly be deemed unacceptable. But he had little imagined then – if Anna Marie's claims were to be believed – just how true Heinrich Heine's words might turn out to be, and the thought was a horrifying one indeed.

But Geli Rosenbaum knew little of the memories that crowded her friend's mind as she cradled the book he had just given her in her hands. 'I hope it's as good as *All Quiet on the Western Front*,' she said. 'Heaven knows why they banned that one. They said it was anti-war, but how can that ever be a bad thing?'

'Nowadays, it can,' Horst replied gravely, for so much had happened even over the few weeks of her incarceration. 'In this country, war is something to be looked forward to now. They talk of it all the time when my parents are at home. Germany's divine destiny they are calling it. We must avenge the terrible deed done to the Fatherland at Versailles. They say the Führer claims the dead of the Great War will never rest in peace until we do. I'm beginning to think he's mad, you know. Quite mad.'

Geli gave a wistful smile. 'The whole world is mad. It must be, to let things like this happen.'

But Horst was insistent there was more to it than that. And as Geli listened, Horst told her of a conversation he had heard between his father and brother Otto on the family's last visit to Himmelhof. 'Father told him about a set of Articles the Führer has commissioned to be drawn up for the suppression of Christianity. I heard him say he actually saw them with his own eyes, Geli! And the last article states that the Bible will be replaced by Hitler's own holy book *Mein Kampf*, and the Christian cross must be removed from all churches and be replaced by the only unconquerable symbol, the swastika . . .'

Horst's voice faded as his mind turned to a visit his great-grandfather, *Der Alte*, had once made to the old Kaiser in exile on his estate at Doorn in Holland. There the proud but embittered old man who had once ruled Germany had shown his guest the vast collection of books he had gathered on the Occult. He was utterly convinced that certain secret Occult orders had been the direct cause of Germany's defeat after the Great War and of his own humiliating abdication. 'They all believe in it, Geli,' Horst said, shaking his head in incredulity. 'They all believe the way to the New Dawn, as they call it, is through the Powers of Darkness. We are entering a New Age when these powers will be harnessed for good or evil.'

Geli shivered as she listened, for she already knew which of the two that would be. And what she was hearing was beginning to make sense – to explain the inexplicable. Ever since the Nazis came to power she could not begin to understand the changes that were taking place in her homeland. How could whole sections of society, such as the Jews, the Socialists and Communists, Jehovah's Witnesses, Gypsies, Freemasons, and many more, suddenly become classed as subhuman? What evil had taken over the land that people such as her father who had spent his life healing the sick could suddenly be regarded as *Untermenschen*? For weeks now she had remained a virtual prisoner here in this old hut, deep in the forest, because to venture out was to risk her very life. It had all seemed so incredible, but now it began to make sense. As she sat here in the darkness and listened to Horst tell her of the hopes and dreams, the perverted beliefs of that man who had claimed their country for the forces of darkness, it all began to make perfect sense. Horst must be right in his assumption; Adolf Hitler was in league with the Devil, and if she had ever doubted it, then here was the proof, she was listening to it with her own ears.

'Take the swastika flag,' Horst was saying. 'Did you know that it was designed by a member of a German Occult society and that Hitler rejected the first design because the swastika faced to the right, which for Occultists symbolized Light, White Magic and Creation? Adolf Hitler himself had it reversed to face the left, to evoke the Powers of Darkness, Black Magic and Destruction.'

And over the next few visits, Horst and Geli would spend long hours on the platform discussing this depressing state of affairs and what could be done about it. He even persuaded his brother Otto, on one of his infrequent visits to the Himmelhof, to share with him some of the doctrines of his beloved SS, on the pretext that he, Horst, would soon wish to volunteer.

Otto was only too delighted to impart his knowledge of his beloved organization to his younger brother, whom he hoped was now beginning to see sense and take a proper interest. And Otto's blue eyes gleamed and his chest seemed visibly to swell with pride as he began an impassioned speech on what he saw as his own divine role in their country's destiny. 'In the SS,' he told Horst, 'we are taught that the only living being that exists is the Cosmos. Everything else, and all other beings including Man, are only various forms of the living Cosmos that have multiplied through the ages. As part of this living force, it is our divine destiny to create a New Age, a New World, a New Man. And this New Dawn that we are now approaching is the natural evolution of the Cosmos towards our Superhuman destiny – the *Übermenschen* destiny that our leader Adolf Hitler has been called to lead us towards.'

Horst had listened with a growing sense of both fear and awe. It was every bit as bad as he had suspected. They all believed it. It was not just some crackpot slur that the Führer's enemies were throwing at him, this Power of Darkness thing; this crazy, supernatural, mystical nonsense was real. He had heard it from the mouth of his own brother. It was a frightening thought.

And, as the autumn days grew chill and the evenings grew dark and long, a darkness seemed to descend on Horst's soul. The prospect of being able to engineer Geli's escape as he had at first hoped was becoming more and more remote, yet the thought of her having to spend the coming winter alone in that terrible place was unbearable, especially if he had to return to Berlin for the winter with his parents, which was certainly on the cards.

He knew that she was aware of his fears and her increasing anxiety at the possibility of him leaving was having a depressing effect on both their spirits. It was a subject that they could never bring themselves fully to discuss, for it was a situation without hope, and without hope how could one live?

With each passing week, he knew that his health was becoming stronger and that once his parents returned to the Himmelhof he would be considered quite well enough to return to the family home in Berlin. In their letters to him they were making it clear that, all being well, they would grant him his wish to return to Berlin in the autumn to begin studying for his *Abitur*, the state examinations that would allow him entry into university.

It was funny how quickly things could change. From a state of eager impatience to leave the Himmelhof, he now found himself making up every excuse in his letters back to remain. To leave here would not only be to desert Geli, which in itself was unthinkable, but it would also mean leaving this most beautiful part of the world to return right into the centre of what he now regarded as the black heart of Nazism itself – Berlin.

Chapter Seventeen

Werdet stark wie Stahl, und der deutsche
Volksblock, zu Stahl zusammengeschweisst
soll dem Feinde seine Kraft zeigen

'Be strong as steel, and the solidity of the German people,
welded into a single steel block, shall show the foe its
strength.' Horst gazed unblinkingly at the embroidered
sampler on the drawing-room wall and reread the familiar
words as Gretel, the maid, put the finishing touches to the
flowers cut specially for the arrival of his parents, who were
expected any time now. His grandmother had done the
embroidery during the Great War. It had been a direct quote
from the Kaiser that had appealed greatly to the whole
family. So there it still hung, Old Willy's brave words
captured for posterity in threads of black, red and white, the
colours of the old German flag. Only, Old Willy, the Kaiser,
himself, was long gone – banished to chopping wood on his
estate at Doorn in Holland, while Germany's new leader,
Adolf Hitler, was now in his mountain retreat only a few
miles from here, preparing to meet their prospective enemy,
the British Prime Minister, Neville Chamberlain.

The newspapers had been making much of what the
British were terming 'the Czech crisis', and the announcement a few days previously of the impending arrival of the
British leader at the Berghof, Hitler's Obersalzberg home,
had brought hundreds of people rushing to the area.
Along with the dozens of journalists, film and radio crews
and the like who had converged on the small community
over the past few days, Horst had not been at all surprised
to learn that his parents were also on their way back. Otto,
Senior, always liked to be where the political action was,

336

even if he was not asked for his advice as often as he would have liked.

That his father's political philosophy was at one with National Socialist thinking was something that Horst had long known; Otto von Karsten had more than proved his right-wing credentials back in 1928 when, along with the other steel barons, Krupp and von Thyssen, he had imposed a lockout on over quarter of a million workers in an effort to break the power of the unions.

The 1920s had been a decade of real suffering for the whole country as the German mark became worth less than the paper it was printed on. Millions of businesses went to the wall and among his father's friends Horst could remember at least one suicide.

It was during the period of the lockout in 1928 that Horst first encountered his mother in tears. She had been standing by her bedroom window, twisting a damp handkerchief between her fingers, and had looked at him with brimming eyes as he tentatively entered her room to tell her lunch was ready. 'What will become of us, my boy?' she asked bleakly. 'What will become of us if your father does not win this battle?'

The young boy had made no reply, but the incident had shocked him and remained in his memory, for up till then he had never thought of his mother as capable of such a display of real emotion. But the normally cool and collected Gertrud von Karsten had had good reason to feel depressed. The family stood in dire risk of losing everything if something wasn't done, and done soon, to bring about a reversal in their country's fortunes.

'Harsh times demanded harsh measures,' Otto von Karsten had told his nervous wife and confused children. It was a make-or-break time both for themselves and for their country as a whole; a trial of strength between the bosses and unions was required that would determine the future of the Fatherland for generations to come.

337

'You must have faith, *Liebling*,' Otto told Gertrud. After all, she had married into one of the most powerful families in Europe, and while others might be going under in the Depression, it was not in a von Karsten's nature to admit defeat.

Horst had never seen his mother in tears again after that, and Gertrud von Karsten's faith was well rewarded, for in the decade that followed her husband had been in the forefront of Germany's economic recovery. He was determined that all his grandfather had striven for would not be lost. Karsten Steel would rise again from the rubble of the Great War and, along with it, so would the Fatherland.

In 1931, with other leading industrialists, he had proposed a new economic programme in which the wages of the workers would come virtually under the control of the bosses: there would be an immediate cutback on social welfare policies, combined with a series of economic reforms beneficial to big business. The deal, thrashed out in part over the huge rosewood dining table in the von Karsten Berlin home, proposed that they, the capitalists, would work for the benefit of the Nazis, providing they were given a free hand over the unions and economic planning in any future Nazi Government.

'The country's military dictatorship,' Otto declared, 'will be married to the economic dictatorship of big business – a formidable combination indeed!' The listening Nazi leaders had been impressed, and they were even more impressed when, after their first year in government, they found their coffers sixty million marks the richer, thanks to contributions from their newfound allies.

'Our partnership with the Nazis will make this country the envy of the world,' Otto told his family. 'Together we will produce a new generation of Germans, untainted by Jewish blood, and ready to assume our natural role as world leaders.'

There was nothing that the head of Karstenstahl liked more than to philosophize on the past, present and future of the German people, particularly to his family over their evening meal. 'What nation has contributed more to civilization?' he would ask, his blue-grey eyes moving round the dinner table at each member in turn. 'What nationality was Beethoven? Was Bach? Was Schubert? Was Goethe? Was Hegel, Heine or Nietzsche?'

'But Heine was a Jew, Papa,' the eleven-year-old Horst had piped up on one memorable occasion. 'Aren't the Jews *Untermenschen*?'

Otto von Karsten had glared at his younger son. 'The Jews are indeed subhuman, *Junge*,' he had said, his face reddening. 'Papa was merely testing you. It is advisable to identify the enemy at all times. We Germans – real Germans – are a nation of *Denker und Dichter* – thinkers and poets, and as such we lead the world.'

'*Denker und Dichter*,' the young Horst had mused. 'But Anna Marie Zimmermann's father says we are now becoming a nation of *Henker und Richter* – hangmen and judges!'

Horst's father's brows rose a good half-inch and he laid down his knife and fork with a clatter at the side of his plate. The boy had been listening to that *verdammt* forester again! 'That man had better watch his mouth,' he said angrily, 'or it will dig him an early grave! The country's full of subversives such as him and they won't be tolerated much longer!'

That conversation had taken place in early March 1932, just before the first general election that made any impression on the young Horst's life. It was also the time when he first began to read the newspapers, and these appeared to reinforce everything his father was so keen to point out: to vote for a Nazi Government would guarantee that the Fatherland would go from strength to strength.

'We are at a watershed in our country's history,' Otto

declared as they eagerly awaited the results coming in. And in his mind he could visualize his grandfather, *Der Alte*, when he too was called upon by his leader Bismarck to act at just such a crucial time in the fortunes of the Fatherland. Otto von Karsten the Third's chest would swell with pride as he remembered the honours that had been bestowed upon the old man and the family name. And just such a moment in history had come round once more. Perhaps now the family would have no reason to mourn the honours that had gone to the grave round the neck and pinned to the chest of the old man, for, if he played his cards right, there would be more honours to follow now than even *Der Alte* had ever dreamt of in those far-off heady days of the *Kaiserzeit*.

It was during this time, too, that Otto chose to have what he called 'a proper man-to-man talk' with his younger son. He had been concerned for some time that young Horst had not been showing what he termed 'true German spirit' in his outlook on life now that he was leaving childhood behind.

'If you don't be careful, Papa will send you back to Berlin and enrol you in the military academy at Potsdam to put some stiffening into that backbone!' his brother Otto had warned Horst. 'Weak lungs or no weak lungs, that's where you'll end up.'

Otto Junior's words had sent a chill through Horst. He had always been aware he was something of a disappointment in his father's eyes – too dreamy a personality to be a real von Karsten.

'That boy has obviously inherited many of the failings of your side of the family,' he had once heard his father tell his mother. Gertrud von Karsten had, in her husband's eyes, the misfortune of having one uncle who was a painter, and a late father who had liked to write poetry in his spare time. Weak links indeed in the genetic chain. 'Something will have to be done.'

Horst's insides had quaked as he waited outside his father's study for the command, '*Herein!*' to be given. He entered tentatively, almost tiptoeing across the Indian carpet to stand in front of the large oak desk behind which his father sat lighting his Havana cigar.

Otto von Karsten's pale eyes fixed on his younger son as he took his first draw on the rich tobacco smoke. 'Stand up straight, young man!' he commanded. Then, 'How old are you now?'

'Almost thirteen, Papa.'

'Almost thirteen,' his father repeated. 'Old enough to take an interest in what is going on around you . . .'

Was it a question? 'Yes, Papa.'

'Here . . .' Otto von Karsten picked up a copy of *Bergwerkszeitung*, the newspaper of German heavy industry, and tossed it across the desk. 'Pick it up!'

Horst did so, holding it awkwardly in both hands in front of him. Was he meant to open it or what?

'From now on that will be part of your weekly reading matter. When I am here I will question you on the main articles at regular intervals, and when I am in Essen or Berlin you will write to me at length with your opinions on the same.'

Horst's spirits sank as he gazed down at the densely printed prose. He could barely understand half the words, let alone pass opinions on them. 'But, Papa . . .'

'No buts!' His father waved the hand with the cigar. 'Your brother was taking an interest in such things of his own volition at your age, while you . . .' He shook his head. 'You, it seems, will have to be dragged along by your ears.' He gazed unblinkingly across the desktop at his son as the cigar smoke rose in a long white column to the ornate ceiling above. 'You do understand what I am trying to say, don't you, boy?'

'I – I think so, Papa.'

'I am trying to make you understand that you are no

341

ordinary child. You are a von Karsten and as such you have a duty to fulfil, not only to your country but to your family name. Are you ready to fulfil that duty, Horst? Are you?'

Horst stared back at his father. Was he? He was not even sure what was meant by his 'duty'. Was reading this boring old newspaper every week part of that duty? Obviously it was. But at least that wasn't quite as bad as being sent off to Potsdam to some ghastly military academy such as his brother had warned him about. Slowly he began to nod his head. 'I'm ready, Papa.'

'Good! From now on I will expect you to make your own contribution to the conversation round the dinner table each night. You will be our personal reporter on the state of German industry and the nation's future!'

Horst left the room with a sinking heart. His father was determined to make a real von Karsten of him, as he liked to put it. He looked at the newspaper in his hand and grimaced, before throwing it in the air and aiming a disconsolate kick in its direction. It flew through the air and landed on a small Louis Quinze table, knocking off a delicate Meissen figurine. It smashed to pieces on the floor in front of him. He gazed at it in horror; it was one of his mother's favourites. Then, hearing movement in his father's study behind him, he bent quickly to retrieve the newspaper and the remnants of broken china which he stuffed into his pocket.

Three days later the young downstairs maid who was responsible for that particular part of the house was dismissed on suspicion of having stolen it. Horst immediately confessed, only to be told the incident was closed and a new maid had been hired. People, it seemed, were expendable, along with principles, if the situation called for it. It was a hard lesson to learn for a boy barely into his teens.

Reading the *Bergwerkszeitung* from cover to cover each

week taught him many things over the next few months, including the fact that principles could be changed at whim, depending on whichever government was in power. For the previous decade under the Weimar constitution, democracy had been deemed to be the fairest form of government, but now his father and all the other major industrialists were agreed that, with Russia firmly in the grip of Communism, the future of capitalism and families like theirs could be guaranteed only when democracy had been destroyed and a strong, right-wing government installed in its place. His own father was not only party to the destruction of democracy in their country, he was playing a leading role in its demise.

Along with his fellow industrialists, Otto von Karsten had promised Adolf Hitler a total of one million of the estimated three million marks required to secure victory in that election. 'It was no more than our duty,' Horst listened to his father tell his family as they waited for the results to be declared. 'Fatherland first, family fortunes second for the time being. The two go hand in hand. If Germany falls to Communism, so does the House of Karsten. It is our duty to make sure our country prospers, and to do all in our power to bring that about.'

Gertrud von Karsten had beamed across at her husband, who was now proudly playing the role of their country's saviour. Within the von Karsten household it was taken for granted that the head of the family was also a father-figure to the nation. Whenever the Fatherland called, the head of Karsten Steel would be there to offer his services to its leader, just as *Der Alte* had done in days gone by.

Would his great-grandfather have embraced the Nazi cause as enthusiastically as his father had done? Horst could not help wondering. And the answer in his own mind was usually, No. The men who paraded through their streets in their black and brown shirts were propounding an ideology that seemed to Horst totally at odds with the sense of justice and respect for his fellow men that had been the bedrock of his great-grandfather's life. To the young boy trying his best to come to terms with life around him, bearing the name von Karsten had never seemed a greater burden.

On the bitterly cold night that Hitler was appointed Chancellor at the end of January 1933, Horst had watched the celebrations with the others from the window of their Unter den Linden apartment in Berlin. But the thoughts that disturbed his own heart were not shared by his elder brother. Otto Junior's heart filled with pride at the stirring sight of columns of delirious Nazi supporters marching down their famous old thoroughfare singing the 'Horst Wessel Lied' at the tops of their voices, as they held their lighted torches aloft in the cold night air. 'One day I will wear one of those uniforms,' Otto Junior vowed to his family. Then he turned to his father by his side, 'And you will be so proud of me, Papa.'

Otto Senior had smiled in satisfaction and then turned to his younger son. 'And what about you, *Kleiner*?'

'They make a fine sight, Papa,' Horst had replied. Even at that age he was already the diplomat.

'*Kommt, Kinder*,' their father said, laying a hand on each of his sons' shoulders. 'We will go together to see history being made.'

And leaving their mother and Elsa behind to watch the festivities from the window, together they had joined the milling crowds to head for the Presidential Palace itself, where the great bulky figure of old President von Hindenburg, his bewhiskered face ashen in the torchlight, stood looking down at them from the balcony next to the smaller, more insignificant figure of Adolf Hitler.

'Tonight you see the Old Order give way to the New,' Otto von Karsten told his sons with pride. 'It is not given to many of us to live through such moments in history.'

But all that was more than five years ago now, and in the gracious, echoing rooms of the Himmelhof this afternoon, the eighteen-year-old Horst von Karsten was awaiting the arrival of his parents from Berlin with mixed feelings. While glad to be seeing them again, his life had taken on a completely new meaning over the past few weeks. It now revolved completely around that wooden hut deep in the forest with its fugitive inhabitant – a fact that he knew would land him in deep trouble if his parents ever found out.

But that was a possibility he preferred not to think about right now. It was enough that Geli appreciated what he was doing. And that Geli Rosenbaum was grateful he had no doubt. But now, with the imminent arrival of his parents, he had also become aware that a quiet desperation was setting into Geli's attitude during his visits to the hut. She was becoming more and more convinced that, just as Anna Maria and her sister Heidi did not come quite so often now they knew that Horst was making regular visits, so Horst himself would soon tire of coming so frequently or, worse still, would leave altogether and go back to Berlin with his parents. She was now in such a state of agitation that on his last visit she had even spoken of giving herself up. The thought had horrified Horst.

'Oh no, you must never do that!' he had exclaimed. 'You know what would happen.'

They had looked at each other in the semi-darkness of the hut and Geli had sighed, a long, despairing sigh that seemed to come from the bottom of her very soul. 'They would take my life if I did, I know that. But can't you see, they have already done that, Horst? They have destroyed my family, and what sort of life is this?'

She had waved a hand around the musty straw of the platform that was now her home. 'Is this living? And what of the future? Do I stay here until the Nazis are no longer in power?'

Her hollow laugh had echoed within the wooden walls. 'How old will I be when that happens . . .? Eighty, perhaps, or even ninety?' Then her eyes had looked straight into his and even in the gloom he could see the pain and despair in them. 'Can't you see, *mein Freund*, they are indestructible? The Nazis will never give up – and who can defeat them? They have the most powerful men in Germany behind them. They have men such as Otto von Karsten.'

It had been the most shaming moment of Horst's life.

He had done his best to revive her flagging spirits, even almost convincing her that there was a real chance of him being able to remain at the Himmelhof. It had been less than the truth, but he had almost convinced himself of the possibility as he awaited his parents' return with more than a little trepidation.

When the sleek black Mercedes finally rolled up at the front door, Horst was on the steps to greet them before they were even out of the car.

'*Liebling*, what a surprise! And my – how you've grown!' Gertrud von Karsten proffered her cheek to be kissed and Horst obeyed, pecking at the scented, powdered skin as he murmured, 'Hello, Mother. It's good to see you.' She always commented on his height, even if only away for a fortnight.

'Papa.' He shook his father's hand politely and studied the older man's face as they climbed the stone steps together. He could usually tell what sort of mood his father was in by the set of his mouth, but today he had a large, newly-lit cigar clenched between his teeth.

'It seems our little part of the world is the centre of the universe right now, doesn't it, *Junge*?' Otto von Karsten commented to his son as they entered the front door. 'All those reporters and other nosey parkers. Why, there was almost a traffic jam in the village as we arrived – and that's something I've never known before!'

From those first minutes of their arrival, there was only one subject of conversation – the fact that the world's press had descended on the area in their hundreds, if not thousands. It seemed as if there wasn't a country on earth that wasn't abuzz with speculation about the Führer's forthcoming meeting with the British Prime Minister. 'That poor, weedy little man', as his mother insisted on calling Neville Chamberlain.

Gertrud von Karsten looked across at her younger son as she sipped her first cup of coffee after her arrival home and sighed. 'I fear poor Mr Chamberlain will be no match for Herr Hitler, and for that we should be eternally grateful. If only we had had a leader capable of standing up for us in 1919 things would have been so very different!'

Horst had always considered his mother a shrewd judge of character, particularly where politicians were concerned. Be they British Prime Ministers or leading members of the Nazi Government, to her they were simply men and she judged them accordingly. Most were found wanting. She would run a hand through her naturally blonde hair and give one of her well-known sighs, and her aquiline features would assume an expression of complete scepticism whenever her husband would refer to them with what she regarded as more respect than they were due.

She now went on to complain bitterly about 'the summer season', as she called July and August in Berlin, which had left her with a wretched cold that would not go away. Then Horst found himself required to listen to her relate a catalogue of disasters that had been her washed-out succession of garden parties on the broad lawns of their Wannsee home, just outside Berlin.

And now, as she sipped her coffee, came the indiscretions of the rich and famous, related with her usual delicious, biting wit. Horst perked up immediately, for although his father always went hot under the collar at such tittle-tattle, he loved these bits. He had no interest whatsoever in the Berlin social scene that was so crucially important to his mother's whole existence, but the odd insight into the private lives of the leading Nazis made for entertaining listening indeed.

She was still on the same theme when they sat down to their first evening meal together for weeks and she poured herself another glass of mineral water and took a disconsolate sip, before dabbing delicately at her nose with her handkerchief. 'It's just as well I'm not one of those invited to entertain Mr Chamberlain while he's here. It would do no good at all for international relations if his hostess were to greet him with a cold in the nose!'

Her husband snorted as he gestured for Horst to pass the *Remoulade*. 'I would have thought a handkerchief held to the nose would be just the thing in that wretched Englishman's presence!'

He spooned a dollop of the oily yellow dressing on to the side of his salad and turned to Horst. 'I expect you've been plagued with security men crawling all over the estate these past few days. I understand their orders have been to leave no stone unturned over the entire Obersalzberg, just in case there's some scoundrel lurking beneath it who might take a pot-shot at the politicians!'

He gave a sardonic smile as he took a mouthful of *Kartoffelsalat*. 'If you ask me, it's not madmen keen to take a pot-shot at the leaders meeting here they are bothered about as much as English spies, who think they might use the opportunity to do a bit of reconnoitring on the sly! The English are like that, you know. Perfidious Albion and all that. Can't trust them an inch. We learned that in 1914.' He swallowed the forkful of cold potato and looked at his son, 'You haven't come across any of them recently, I take it?'

Horst, who had been looking puzzled, shook his head. 'English spies?' he repeated, with some incredulity. 'No, I can't say that I have. Where are they likely to have been?' He stifled a grin, for he was already imagining hordes of bowler-hatted, mysterious-looking individuals searching through the tomato plants in the greenhouses with their rolled-up umbrellas for possible threats to their leader, and driving old Schulz the head gardener mad.

His father shrugged as he helped himself to another slice of Westphalian ham from the platter on the table in front of him. 'Well, if there's been no one snooping around from British security, then I'm damned sure there will have been plenty of SS. But I'm not surprised you haven't noticed them. They'll have been concentrating on the forest area, no doubt — seeing that that's the part where our land meets that of the Berghof, and that's the part most likely to offer cover for any intruders. I expect it'll be old outbuildings and suchlike they'll be checking up on mainly, so it won't really bother us.'

Horst froze, his fork halfway to his mouth, which had suddenly gone quite dry. 'Old outbuildings, you say? They'll be checking on old outbuildings and suchlike?' He did his best to keep his voice steady as a cold sweat broke under his armpits.

'Don't worry, *Liebling*,' his mother put in. 'Papa doesn't mean the likes of the summerhouse.' She knew her younger son still had boxes of precious old toy aeroplanes and old kites and things stashed away there. 'It's those ramshackle old places in the forest he's talking about, so it needn't bother us.'

But Horst couldn't care less about the summerhouse, or his old kites. He looked from one to the other in mounting panic. But they were concentrating on their food and quite oblivious to the fear welling within him. His heart pounded. Geli — they would be sure to find Geli!

'I'm sorry, I don't feel very well . . .' It was the first time in his life he had left the table in the middle of a meal, and

349

he was aware of his parents' concerned gazes following him as he rushed from the room.

'Horst!'

He could hear his mother's voice ringing out behind him as he closed the dining-room door, but he did not wait to reply. He could not wait. To delay even a minute could mean the difference between her being found or not.

Despite the rain, he did not even stop for a coat as he sped along the corridor and headed for one of the back doors, almost knocking over Gretel, the maid, in the process. She staggered backwards, the tray in her hands wobbling precariously, as she gazed, open-mouthed, after his disappearing figure.

He knew he could not take his usual route to the hut as that meant using the path in front of the house and they would see him from the dining-room window. So he was forced to take a much longer path that wound round the back of the stables and entered the forest from the opposite direction.

How long had they been searching the grounds? The question plagued him as he ran through the dense, dripping undergrowth, and he cursed his stupidity for not realizing such a thing could happen. Why had it taken his father so long to mention it? Was he himself so stupid he hadn't realized there would be increased security for the British Prime Minister's visit? 'Damned fool! That's what I am, a damned fool!' he groaned out loud as his feet slid on the soaking leaves that covered the forest floor in a soggy carpet of rotting vegetation.

Because of his parents' imminent return from Berlin, he had not seen Geli since yesterday and had been hoping to make his daily visit directly after dinner tonight. Never for one moment did he imagine he would be making it *during* dinner.

As he turned what was almost the last corner of the path before he reached the clearing in which the hut was sited, he was met by the blazing headlights of a car. They seared the darkness and almost blinded him as the vehicle skidded to a stop only yards in front of him. His heart lurched, for he had never seen a motorized vehicle of any kind this deep in the forest before.

It was already too dark to make out much, other than that it was a black limousine – a Mercedes, most likely – and he was still trying to decipher the number plate when two men in the long black leather coats of SS officers jumped out from opposite sides of the car.

'*Hande hoch!*' The order was barked by the man who had been in the driver's seat.

Horst froze on the spot and held both hands in the air. You did not argue when two guns were pointed at you.

The men began to walk forward in unison, then the taller one, who had given the order, spoke again. 'Who are you and what are you doing here?'

Horst cleared his throat and tried to sound as casual as possible. 'My name is Horst von Karsten. My father owns this land.' He forced himself to assume a deliberately superior tone. 'I didn't realize I required permission to take a walk on our own estate!'

'No cheek, brat!' It was the smaller of the two this time. 'No one takes walks at this time of the evening in the forest in pouring rain. Identify yourself and explain your reason for being here.'

Horst felt in his trouser pockets. He had nothing on him to say who he was. '*Tut mir leid,*' he said apologetically. 'I came out in a rush . . . It's my pet kitten, you see. It escaped . . .'

The two men looked at one another and he could see from the scathing smiles that there was little chance they might actually believe him. But then, their expressions changed slightly. Maybe he was telling the truth. He would surely have to be genuine to come out with such a ridiculous reason for being here.

'You will get into the back of the car,' the one nearest him said, 'and we will verify your story back at the *Schloss*.'

In no position to argue, Horst got into the back of the limousine with the smaller of the two men, while the taller got into the driving seat.

'You are lucky you weren't shot out of hand, young man,' his new companion in the back of the car said, as they drove off in the direction of the Himmelhof. 'There has already been one suspicious character found round here today.'

Horst felt physically sick as he stared through the darkness at the man beside him. 'Really? Who was that?'

The officer shrugged his black leather shoulders as the wheels of the car bumped over the rough ground. 'Oh, no one of consequence, thank God. And not anyone meaning to do the Führer or Herr Chamberlain any harm, we reckon. Just some Jew bitch who has been hiding out in one of the old foresters' huts . . .'

He had no idea of the effect his words had on the young man beside him as he continued in a bored voice, 'But if you really are one of von Karsten's sons, then I've no doubt you'll hear all about it later on. Your brother was at headquarters when she was brought in. I understand he recognized her immediately.'

From sitting tensely on the edge of his seat, Horst went quite limp. 'Otto identified her, you say?' He had no need to ask her name, and he managed the next question only with great difficulty. 'What – what will happen to her?'

The man beside him shrugged once more and stifled a yawn as he said, 'Oh, the usual, I expect. She'll be resettled in the East with the rest of her kind. Personally, I don't know why they bother going to all that trouble.'

'You mean you'd let her stay?'

The man let out a guffaw that left no doubts as to what he thought of that question. 'Tell me, young man, have you left school yet?'

'Not yet,' Horst answered truthfully.

'It's just as well. Believe me, you still have much to learn!'

The following half-hour proved one of the most embarrassing of Horst's life as his parents were asked to vouch for the fact that he really was their son and that he had been telling the truth – he really had gone rushing off into the forest in search of a kitten. And the fact that Nikko Zwo had been in and out of the dining room throughout the meal and was now playing before them on the carpet did little to help matters.

Luckily, his father had the presence of mind to agree that that was indeed the reason for his son's flight in the pouring rain and the two SS men exchanged looks that left little doubt as to what they thought of the story. They also knew that it would be more than their jobs were worth to take the matter any further. One did not antagonize people such as this. It was no secret that Otto von Karsten was not only one of the most powerful men in Germany; he was also reputedly one of the Führer's most trusted advisers.

'We apologize for disturbing your evening, Herr von Karsten,' the taller one said as they prepared to take their leave. 'But I'm sure you will understand. We must take no chances at a time such a this.'

'Of course. Of course.' Otto von Karsten removed his cigar from his mouth and laid it in a nearby ashtray as he shook hands with each in turn. 'I wish you a very good evening, gentlemen, and a safe journey back to headquarters.' He retrieved the cigar and made a gesture with his right hand towards the door.

Horst watched as his father showed the two officers to the main entrance and then stood watching as the limousine disappeared back down the drive.

As the tail-lights of the Mercedes dissolved into the darkness, Otto von Karsten threw the stub of his cigar on to the gravel drive and strode back into the house.

Still soaking wet and shivering now, as much from shock as from cold, Horst waited anxiously just inside the drawing-room door as his father swept in, immediately to turn to his son and demand in a voice that betrayed both his exasperation and anger, 'What in heaven's name was that all about? And what did you think you were up to, dashing off so rudely like that during dinner? What on earth's been going on around here?'

Horst had no answer as he looked from one parent to the other. Both were standing there, the looks on their faces demanding an explanation, and a *good* one. What on earth should he say?

He straightened his back and looked first his mother in the eye and then his father. The truth was as good an explanation as any. 'I went to warn a friend of mine,' he said, trying to keep the nervousness out of his voice. 'A girl I know has been hiding out in one of our old foresters' huts and I wanted to warn her before the SS found her.' His voice dropped, 'But I was too late.'

At first there was complete silence, then his mother gave a delayed gasp. It was the catalyst for his father to explode, 'There has been someone hiding from the law in *our* property and *you* knew about it?' The boy had to be joking!

Horst nodded miserably, his determination to brazen it out waning by the second at the looks on both their faces.

'Who was this girl?' his mother demanded.

'Geli . . . Angelika Rosenbaum.'

His mother gasped once more. '*Du lieber Himmel*, I had heard tell one of the Rosenbaum girls had escaped resettlement, but never, never in my wildest dreams did I imagine my own son was harbouring her — was harbouring a common criminal!'

'Geli's no criminal!' Horst protested. 'She has done nothing wrong, except be born a Jew.'

'It's not up to you — or any of us — to define what

354

constitutes a criminal these days,' his father said sharply. 'The fact remains you were harbouring one in the eyes of the law, and that makes you an accessory after the fact, whether you like it or not. You could go to prison, do you realize that? Or worse!'

Horst looked down at his feet. It was useless arguing with them; they were on two different wavelengths entirely. Anger and frustration burned within him, along with mounting despair. He had never felt more impotent. But he also realized he had been playing with fire and that that fire, should it get out of control, could consume them all. The Nazis were deadly in their reprisals on those they suspected of aiding the Jews.

'I appreciate your concern,' he said, choosing his words carefully. 'And I know what I did might well have been against the law, but I don't regret it. Not for one minute. My only regret is that she was found – and that it was my own brother who identified her.' His voice choked on the final sentence. That really was too much to bear.

Gertrud von Karsten passed a hand through her immaculately groomed blonde hair and gave a sigh that was half frustration, half impatience, as she looked at her younger son. Now Otto was somehow involved, was he? But at least with him one could rely on sanity prevailing. How could two brothers be so different? There had never been this kind of trouble from Otto. But then Horst had always been something of a problem. Even his health had been such a blight on family life over the years. And perhaps that had been half the trouble; he had been left to his own devices far too much down here. A stint at a first-class military academy in Potsdam, as his father would have preferred, would have made all the difference. It had done Otto the world of good, but poor Horst had never had the chance, with those weak lungs of his. What he had done was inexcusable – and downright dangerous, but she must try to understand, she told herself. An education in the best *Mädchenschule* in Berlin had taught her that a soft tone often won far more arguments than a harsh one.

She reached for a cigarette from the small lacquered box on the table in front of her, and lit it with a flick of her gold lighter. She inhaled deeply, then threw back her head to emit two thin streams of white smoke down her delicately flared nostrils and said in a voice that transmitted an infinite patience that she certainly did not feel, '*Was nicht biegt mag brechen* – what does not bend may break – Horst. You would do well to remember that. All of us must compromise our so-called principles at some time or other for the greater good, or face the consequences. We will not attempt to convince you of the wrong-headedness of your actions tonight, for in many ways you are still a child – an impetuous child who believes only what he wishes to believe.'

She glanced at her husband, who was standing stony-faced a few feet away. 'Your father and I would like you to go to your room now and reflect on what could have been a great shame brought upon the von Karsten name. In keeping the whereabouts of that Rosenbaum girl a secret you did a great wrong, and you must realize that. As a von Karsten you have responsibilities not only to yourself and your family, but to the Fatherland itself.' She turned from him and made a sweeping, dismissive gesture towards the door with her hand. 'Go now, before you vex us any more tonight!'

Horst did not require a second telling. In three strides he was out of the room, closing the door behind him with an enormous sigh of relief. He felt as if he was leaving behind him two beings from another planet, so far apart were they in their beliefs these days. In keeping the whereabouts of Geli a secret he did a great wrong, did he?

He gave a bitter smile as he climbed the great sweep of the main staircase to his room, for his mind had gone back to that last car ride he had shared with his great-grandfather that night in Bayreuth. 'A von Karsten does not betray his friends – especially a lady. It would be advisable of you to remember that,' the old man had said. And he had remembered it down all these years. And he had remained true to that piece of advice. His parents might not be proud of him, but he had no doubt, if *Der Alte* had been here tonight, he most certainly would have been.

It was almost midnight before Horst heard his brother Otto enter the bedroom next door to his own. Although officially billeted in the village of Berchtesgaden for the duration of the Führer's visit, as a senior SS officer no one queried it if he chose to spend the night in his old home, but Horst had almost given up on him returning when the sound of the door closing roused him from his doze. He pulled himself up on the bed where he had been lying on top of the quilt, clad in pyjamas and dressing gown, and blinked the sleep from his eyes. He was really in no fit state for an argument, but he could not let this evening's happenings go past unchallenged.

Summoning up all his courage and energy, he slipped out of his own room to give three sharp taps on the door next to his.

'*Herein!*' Otto's voice sounded tired and irritable.

Horst opened the door and stepped inside, closing it behind him. His brother was lying fully clothed on top of his bed, his black-booted feet crossed on the blue satin quilt, a lighted cigarette in his hand. He raised a curious eyebrow at the sight of his younger sibling. 'What do *you* want at this time of night? Come to borrow money as usual?'

'I don't want your money. It's your conscience I'm looking for.'

Otto sat up on one elbow and sent a thin stream of tobacco smoke into the atmosphere through narrowed lips. 'What the hell's that supposed to mean?'

'Two of your SS cronies were here tonight. They said Geli Rosenbaum had been picked up hiding in one of our old foresters' huts and that you'd identified her for them down at headquarters.' Horst's voice was clipped and bitter, very bitter.

Otto stared up at him from the quilt. How the hell did the little brat know that? He stuck his nose into too many things that didn't concern him these days. 'So?' Otto drew heavily on his cigarette then blew a perfect pair of smoke rings. He watched as they floated lazily up towards the ornate ceiling to dissolve into the charged atmosphere, then he turned his gaze back to his younger brother. 'Who the hell did you expect me to say she was – the Virgin Mary?'

'Please don't joke,' Horst said, through gritted teeth. 'That was a despicable thing you did. She's Jewish. You know what will happen to her.'

'She'll be resettled, that's all.'

'Resettled!' Horst attempted a hollow laugh that did not come off, and his voice broke as he almost shouted, 'This so-called resettlement is a sham! You must know they're sending them to their deaths out East. They're killing them, Otto, for God's sake! These so-called enemies of the Reich – these men, women and children that were our friends – they're murdering them in the name of the German people – our name! Or doesn't your beloved SS handbook go into that?'

Otto sat up straight on the bed and his eyes hardened. 'Who told you that rubbish? Who the hell have you been talking to?' There was no way his kid brother could have just made up a thing like that.

But Horst was in no mood for revealing anything. 'I want you to stop them,' he said, surprising himself at his own vehemence. 'I want you to see that they let Geli go.'

'*Verdammt noch mal!* Do you know what you're asking? Do you want me arrested as an enemy of the state? For that's what it would amount to, conspiring to let a real enemy escape.'

'Be reasonable, Otto, for God's sake! Geli is no enemy . . . For pity's sake, she was my friend. She was once *your* friend!'

His brother looked at him, a cold, hard stare, in which the blue of his eyes looked quite grey in the light of the bedside lamp at his elbow. As cold and grey as *Karstenstahl*. 'Go to bed, *Kleinster*,' he said grimly. 'Go to bed and grow up.'

His blond head jerked in the direction of the window. 'If you look out there you will see there are still lights burning at the Berghof. The Führer has been talking to the Englishman Chamberlain all day. The British say they want to avert war, but we are already at war. We are at war with all enemies of the Third Reich, whether they be within our own country or across its borders. We are building a new world in Germany – a new Reich that the Führer himself swears will last for a thousand years.'

His eyes took on a softer, dreamier look as he continued, 'Think of it, Horst . . . The Thousand-Year Reich – and we are privileged to be part of making that dream come true. True soldiers of the Fatherland, ready to lay down our very lives if need be . . . You are ready to lay down your life, too, aren't you?'

Horst stared at the figure on the bed and no longer recognized him as the brother he had once known. The body and soul of what had once been Otto von Karsten was no longer the human being he had known and loved as a child growing up; it was one of Hitler's fighting machines lying there on that quilt. His own brother was as much a part of the growing war machine as any gun or tank. To his embarrassment he could feel the hot sting of tears in his eyes as he turned on his heel and left the room.

Once back in his own room, he threw himself down on his bed and lay staring up at the ceiling. He felt a deep sadness within him that was almost unbearable; it was weighing down his very soul. He felt alien here, in this household that, more than almost any other in Germany, was committed to this war they all knew was coming. And committed for good reason – had not their entire wealth come from the tools of war? From being one of the wealthiest families in the land at the beginning of the Franco-Prussian War of 1871, at the end of the 1914–18 war Germany's *Jahrbuch der Millionare* had stated that Otto von Karsten, with three hundred million marks to his credit, was the richest man in the country. Blood money, his great-grandson thought bitterly. And one thing was certain, he himself would be no part of that war machine when it rolled into action next time round.

'Dear God, let me have the courage to refuse,' he prayed softly. 'Don't let me simply close my eyes like so many in the Fatherland today.'

Chapter Eighteen

'The Rosenbaum affair', as it became known in the von Karsten family, proved to be the most traumatic time ever endured by its youngest member. That there would be trouble if Geli's hiding place was ever discovered Horst had never had any doubt, but nothing had prepared him for the anger that awaited him once his elder brother became involved. It took less than a day after the discovery of their old doctor's daughter in the foresters' hut for a bag of dangerously damning evidence to land on the Himmelhof's dining-room table.

'Just look at this!' Otto Junior commanded, as he opened the leather satchel and decanted its contents on to the highly polished surface, then stood back to gaze at the resulting pile with a look of both disgust and rage. He had not even paused to divest himself of the black leather coat of his uniform, but had marched straight into the house, calling out loudly for them all to gather round. And it was only when the whole family had responded to his call and had assembled in the dining room that he opened the satchel that he carried beneath his right arm.

The action was executed with such a flourish that it sent the contents of the bag skidding across the smooth tabletop and brought a gasp from his mother as the delicate Venetian glass centrepiece shook, but thankfully did not fall.

The whole family was gathered round, all five of them, including Elsa who, having just arrived from Berlin a few hours earlier, did not quite understand what all the fuss was about. The young woman stood leaning against the door, stifling a yawn, in her blue quilted dressing gown, her fair hair tousled from the nap she had been aroused from so rudely by her elder brother. Devoid of make-up after a bath, she looked childishly pretty but petulant at being summoned so abruptly from her bed. It was typical of Otto to throw his weight about like this, she thought, scowling through a wayward lock of hair; he had become even more unbearable since getting into uniform. But what could be so important that it warranted all their undivided attention like this? 'What on earth are you doing with those things?' she asked.

But the young man in the SS uniform did not even hear the question. He was far too taken up with his own thoughts as he tossed the empty bag aside and pointed to its contents, now piled high before their eyes. He turned and glared at his younger brother. 'The evidence!' he declared in a triumphant voice. 'Do you realize there is enough here to have you locked up and the key thrown away for good?'

Horst gazed at the pile of books, as they lay in an untidy heap in front of them. There were seven in all, most of them expensive leather-bound volumes, their titles tooled in gold leaf. His father's pride and joy. He recognized all the names, and did not have to look inside any of the covers to see what all the fuss was about. Each and every one bore the telltale sticker '*Ex Libris: Otto von Karsten*'. Each and every one from his father's own library. Most had belonged to his grandfather, and his great-grandfather before that. And each and every one had been found in the hiding place of Geli Rosenbaum.

Their father, who was standing only a few feet away, was almost beside himself with rage. A phonecall from his elder son from the SS headquarters in Berchtesgaden just before his arrival had already alerted him to the situation, and it had taken their mother all her tact, and in the end her sheer physical strength, to avert what could have resulted in a very nasty scene before Otto's arrival. He had been intent on having it out with his younger son there and then.

For several seconds there was absolute silence as they all gazed at the pile. Then: 'You damned little fool!' Otto von Karsten could control himself no longer. He lunged at Horst, who managed to duck out of the way of the flailing arm as his mother grabbed hold of her husband by his other arm. It was the first time Otto had raised a hand in anger to any of his children, but there had never been a situation anything like this.

Despite his wife's earlier entreaties to remain calm, that raising his voice or hand would accomplish nothing, the sight of those books — *his* beloved books — now proved too much. How dare he! How dare he! The damned little fool! Didn't he realize what this could mean? Was he really so stupid? His colouring, already alarmingly florid these days, grew an even deeper pink as he fixed his furious gaze on his younger son.

'Otto, please! Don't distress yourself!' his wife pleaded. 'The boy has been a fool. We all know that. He must know it, too, but it will do no good for you to get yourself worked up over it. You know what the doctor said only last Easter!' The fact that it was old Doctor Rosenbaum who had warned his patient of the dangers of becoming over-stressed, after having already displayed the first symptoms of heart trouble, was an ironic twist to the situation that was completely missed by both husband and wife, as Gertrud von Karsten kept a tight, restraining hold on her husband's arm.

'What's all this about?' Elsa demanded impatiently, her blue eyes wide with concern at the aborted display of violence she had just witnessed. Had they all gone quite mad? What did they think they were doing falling out over a pile of old books? Had she come home to a madhouse?

She turned to her elder brother who was standing grim-faced on the other side of the table. 'What on earth's going on here, Otto?' She demanded. 'What are all these books doing here? They're not banned, are they?' Surely there couldn't be this much fuss over some old books that had somehow escaped the official burnings? She walked across and picked up a copy of Schiller's poems and turned it over in her hands, as if looking for some sign that might enlighten her.

'You'd better ask that little fool of a brother of yours,' Otto replied bitterly. Then addressing himself personally to Horst, he added with even more venom, 'How dare you! Just how dare you besmirch the family name like this! How dare you bring all of us down into the mire by your own stupid – no, criminal – actions! Don't you realize you were not only harbouring an enemy of the state on our own premises – you actually left the evidence of your criminal act! By leaving these you must have known you would be implicating our family if she was found.' He shook his head in incredulity at the sheer stupidity of it, his fair skin a blotchy pink and white with barely suppressed anger.

Horst stood ashen-faced at the end of the table, all eyes on him. He could almost feel the anger coming at him in waves. It matched in kind his own anger; the anger that burned deep within him at being an unwilling part of a society that could stoop to such depths as to do what was being done to a helpless, innocent young woman like Geli Rosenbaum. And worse, much worse, he was part of a family that not only upheld, but actively supported that society. The fact that none of them could even see that fact almost choked him.

'Well, what have you got to say for yourself, boy?' It took his father all his time to get the words out coherently; never had he felt such rage towards any of his children.

With his wife still clutching his arm, he stood alongside

364

his elder son and namesake, and the two Ottos glared in unison at the young man less than six feet across the table. And at that moment, Otto Senior wondered at the strange genetic happening that had created the young man that was Horst. There was neither physical nor mental resemblance between them. It was no longer enough to blame it on poor Gertrud's relatives. It was as if he was looking across the table at a complete stranger. He himself was tall and thick-set, like his elder son, and both had the same head of fine blond hair and pale grey-blue eyes. These physical characteristics had been borne by von Karsten males for the past four generations, as had the burning devotion to the Fatherland and the desire to uphold its laws that now seemed so entirely lacking in the object of all their wrath.

And as Horst looked back at them he too was aware as never before of the gulf between them. He had seen that same look in his father's eyes so many times during his growing up. He neither looked nor felt as he knew he was supposed to. True Aryans were like them: they were tall and strong, with blond hair and blue eyes and put loyalty to the Fatherland above all else on this earth. But he fell far short of that ideal: he was tall, it was true, but he was not strong, and eighteen years of being closeted away down here for the so-called good of his lungs was the price that he had had to pay for his physical shortcomings. And while they were fair, with fine straight hair, pale eyes and regular Aryan features, his own hair was an indifferent light brown and prone to curl girlishly around his ears when he waited too long between haircuts. And the eyes that gazed back at them all were too dark a blue to be fashionable, his features altogether too aquiline, and his tall body far too thin to feature on any of the coloured posters extolling Nazi youth that were to be seen all over the place these days. In short, he was a disappointment to his family, both physically and mentally. He had always been a disappointment. He knew it and they knew it. And never more so than at this moment.

Ever the peacemaker, his mother broke the oppressive silence that had descended. And her voice was clipped and very formal, as it always was when she was trying to control her temper, and be fair into the bargain. 'Yes, Horst, I think you at least owe us an explanation. It was bad enough that you knew of that young woman's presence on our property, but actually to furnish her with books from our own home . . . in essence to implicate your own father in that criminal act!' Gertrud von Karsten shook her head. 'That really defies belief.'

'Is anyone going to tell me what's going on here?' Elsa's voice rose plaintively as she continued, 'Have I come home to a madhouse, or haven't I?' She turned to her younger brother. 'What on earth have you been doing that's so terrible, Horst? Have you killed the Führer – or broken Mother's best Meissen vase?' Both would rank as capital offences, she had no doubt. 'Tell me, for heaven's sake!'

Horst looked his sister straight in the eyes. Poor silly Elsa, whose mind was never filled with more than the latest fashion or popular song. She really didn't give a damn either about the Führer or this so-called New World they were all supposed to be building. All Elsa wanted to do was to find a young man as rich as her father and as good-looking as one of those American film stars she loved to read about. But she was his sister and she deserved the truth. 'I have been living by a code of honour given to me by my great-grandfather,' Horst said quietly, but with real pride in his voice. '*Der Alte* would have been proud of me. I have not betrayed my friend.'

And with that he turned and walked from the room. He could sense their shock in the silence that greeted his words and could feel their eyes on his back as he walked, head high, to the door and closed it behind him.

366

He half expected one of them to run after him or call him back, but no one did, and there was a cold satisfaction in his heart as, step by step, he slowly climbed the stairs to his room with his head still held deliberately high.

He closed his bedroom door behind him and slumped down at the desk by the window, to find to his disgust that he was shaking all over. He had never felt more alone. He gazed out through the glass over the countryside that he loved so much. But he was no longer part of it. He was a stranger here. A stranger in his own land.

In front of him was a journal in which he wrote down anything that happened to appeal to him. It gave him succour in times of stress. With trembling fingers, he opened it at the page marked by the thin red ribbon and gazed down at the words by the English writer E. M. Forster that he had copied from a British newspaper some months before: *'If I had to choose between betraying my friend or my country, I pray to God I would have the courage to betray my country.'* Never had words on a page seemed more appropriate.

What became of Geli Rosenbaum he never succeeded in finding out, although through Anna Marie and her sister he made several attempts. Because of what had happened, he was not able to ask any direct questions of anyone himself, and even the Zimmermann sisters found it difficult to probe too far. People who asked the wrong questions did not do so for long these days.

For several days afterwards both Anna Marie and Heidi had expected to be pulled in by the SS for harbouring an escapee, but it never happened, and in a way that made it even worse. It meant that Geli had not cracked under interrogation and given away her helpers. That knowledge made all three of them feel very humble and also very small and impotent.

'We should have known,' Anna Marie said in despair to Horst on his first visit to the Zimmermann home the

Sunday after the arrest. 'We should have guessed they would be searching the area because of the British Prime Minister's visit. It's our fault. It's our fault she was caught. She trusted us. She relied on us, and we let her down.'

Horst knew those words would continue to echo in his mind long after the affair had been forgotten by the rest of their families. Geli Rosenbaum's silence after her arrest had been an object lesson in loyalty to them all. He knew exactly what Anna Marie must be going through and he did his best to comfort his friend. 'That's nonsense, Anni,' he said, putting an arm around her shoulders. 'It's no good tormenting ourselves. We did all we could.' But he knew that if he could not convince himself of that, how could he ever hope to convince anyone else? It was something they would both have to learn to live with, that was all.

There was so much they were having to learn to live with just now. So much had happened this past year: the *Anschluss* in March had united Austria with Germany, and now the British Prime Minister, Neville Chamberlain, on his visit to the Berghof, had all but handed the Sudetanland to Hitler on a plate. Germany was developing a ferocious appetite for gobbling up its neighbours. Where would it all end, Horst wondered? What would be next? Would the Nazis decide they wanted East Prussia back and march into Poland to 'liberate' it for the Reich?

In many ways it would be a relief to leave the Obersalzberg, for after the Hitler–Chamberlain meeting this area had become a hotbed of political speculation as to what lands the Führer would lay claims to next. And while this sort of thing provided his father and brother with the excuse for endless hours of discussion, it both bored and repelled Horst. This strident, militaristic nationalism was anathema to his basically gentle, contemplative nature, and he longed for a life where the conversation at the dinner table did not always revolve around high politics. Being a von Karsten was a heavy cross to bear at times and one which he knew he would gladly lay down if given the chance.

But that was wishful thinking, and he knew it. One could not just disavow one's birthright. And at times like this his eyes would inadvertently be drawn to the shiny white scar on the palm of his left hand. 'The brand of Karsten Steel' they had called it, in order to pacify him as a child. But it had not just been his physical body that had been burned in the fire that had forged Karsten Steel for four generations; he knew now that it had also scarred his soul. The knowledge that it was the money from his father's furnaces that had helped this government to power, and was still supporting it, was a fact of life that was becoming more and more difficult to live with.

The nights were drawing in now, and as the leaves of the forests turned to red and from yellow to a deeper gold, Horst knew that his days at the Himmelhof were drawing to an end, and in so many ways he was not sorry. The old place now held too many sad memories for him to want to remain here much longer. Anna Marie was already out there in the world earning her living, as were all the other young people of his age whom he had got to know over the years. He was no longer a child. He had to start thinking about entering the adult world, and that meant he had to start thinking seriously about studying for his *Abitur*, the examinations essential for entry into university.

There had been a tacit family acceptance that he would let his parents know when he felt fully capable of returning to the regimentation of school life for the one concentrated year his tutors here had estimated would be needed to give him any chance of passing his examinations. There was no doubt, that time had now come, and if he did not bring up the subject, he knew that his mother or father would be sure to do so before long. He waited a few days to let the heat of the Rosenbaum affair cool down, then he spoke to his mother about the possibility of returning to Berlin with her to enrol in school. And Gertrud von Karsten lost no time in relaying the news to her husband just before his return to Essen.

Otto von Karsten had not found it in himself to have a meaningful conversation with his younger son since that confrontation over the books, but it was no secret that he too felt it high time Horst set about finishing off his education. And, as far as the head of Karsten Steel was concerned, that meant only one place, Berlin.

'Get the boy certificated as A1 in health and see about getting him a place at the Kaiser Wilhelm, then. And you'd better be quick about it,' he told his wife. 'Any delay and it'll be too late and we'll have him wasting his time down here for another year. And heaven only knows what other kind of mischief that might result in!' He no longer trusted his younger son as far as he could throw him. And in his own present state of health, that wasn't very far at all these days.

His wife did not require a second telling. She was on the telephone immediately to the Blutenberg Klinik in Munich and an appointment was made for a week's time, when Horst would be seen by Professor Doktor Klaus Brinkmann, one of the country's leading lung specialists.

Horst travelled to Munich with his mother for the appointment in good spirits. He loved the Bavarian capital, with its historic Old Town Hall and beautiful churches. Whenever he went there as a child, they would always dine at the very best restaurants and he would be allowed to buy a bag of his favourite chocolate marzipan animals from a special sweet shop on Maximilianstrasse. But he was no longer a child, and on the day of the appointment there was to be no dining before his examination – on doctor's orders.

'Do you want me to come in with you, *Liebling*?' his mother asked, when his name was called at eleven o'clock precisely.

Horst shook his head. 'I'm a big boy now, remember,' he said with a smile. 'I can even tie my own shoelaces.'

Gertrud von Karsten gave a rueful smile and sat back down on the waiting-room couch. 'Mothers are entitled to forget occasionally.'

Horst shot her an encouraging smile as he left to follow the white-uniformed nurse down the corridor. His mother was even more nervous than he was.

His shoes echoed on the highly polished floor and the corridor seemed to go on for ever. Then he was shown into an examination room that appeared to be the last word in the latest technology. Everything was white: white ceiling, white-tiled walls and a white-tiled floor. There seemed to be an abundance of chrome fittings, spotlights and gadgets that he could not begin to imagine the use of, but it was to what was on the gleaming white wall immediately in front of him that his attention was drawn.

On the wall directly behind the examination couch was a set of three posters designed to illustrate the physical superiority of the Aryan race over the Jews. Blue-eyed, blond, even-featured young men were shown alongside what purported to be typical examples of the Jewish male. The result was what would have been a quite laughable caricature were it not quite obviously being taken so seriously. But Horst had little time to dwell on the posters or anything else as Professor Brinkmann appeared almost immediately from an adjoining room.

He was a tall grey-haired man in his fifties, who exuded an aura of quiet confidence and put his patient at ease straight away by asking Horst about his hopes and plans for the future. The examination itself was exceptionally thorough and took the best part of an hour, and at the end of it Gertrud von Karsten was called in.

Professor Brinkmann gave both mother and son a reassuring smile. 'As far as I can tell, there is no reason why you should not return to your studies tomorrow, young man. Your lungs seem to have improved considerably from what your notes say, regarding your previous examination. You feel well in yourself?'

'Oh yes, perfectly well!'

The Professor smiled as Horst pulled on his shirt. 'Perhaps a little more beef on that frame would not go amiss, but apart from that, you'll do. I wish you luck with your *Abitur* when the time comes! Have you made up your mind which school you'll be attending?'

'The Kaiser Wilhelm I in Berlin,' Gertrud von Karsten answered proudly for her son. 'It offers one of the best classical educations in the country and is within walking distance of our apartment on the Unter den Linden. The Director will be delighted to hear he is actually coming.' She had spoken to Herr Kempten herself less than a week ago and the old man had been only too pleased to assure her that a place would most certainly be found for the son of Otto von Karsten.

'Good. I'm sure you'll do your family proud, my boy.' The specialist held out his hand to Horst, who shook it gratefully.

'I hope what the Professor said turns out to be right, Horst dear,' Gertrud von Karsten murmured, as they walked together back down the corridor. 'I hope you will do us proud.'

On their return to the Himmelhof, preparations began immediately for the journey to Berlin. After all the time he had spent in their Bavarian home – almost his entire childhood and adolescence – Horst was surprised to find that as the day scheduled for their departure grew nearer, a great reluctance to say goodbye to the old place descended upon him.

'You are just being silly,' his mother told him. 'You will love it in Berlin. And haven't you complained for long enough about not being able to join us there?'

Horst knew that to be true. Just as he knew it to be true

that in leaving the Obersalzberg he was leaving his youth behind for ever. Berlin would mean hard work. Obtaining the grades in his *Abitur* necessary for his admittance to university would not be easy. But worse than that, worse than the knowledge of the work that lay ahead, was knowing that in leaving Bavaria for Berlin, he was entering the lions' den. He was leaving behind this lovely land of mountains and fresh air to enter the heart of darkness itself, for that was now what he always thought of when he thought of their nation's capital. Thousands of black-shirted soldiers goose-stepping their way down the Unter den Linden and filling the air with their Nazi songs.

But he kept his private thoughts to himself as he made his preparations for the long journey north with his mother, scheduled for just under a week's time. His father was now back in Essen, and with his brother and sister also gone, Horst found he had just enough time left to say goodbye to his favourite friends and members of the household staff before he was due to set off.

His last goodbye to Anna Marie he found particularly painful. They had gone through so much together, especially this autumn. He decided to say goodbye at her work, hoping it would be easier with other people around.

'Do well in Berlin, Horstchen,' she said to him, as she clasped his hand for the last time. 'Do well and get to university. Become a good and learned man. God knows, our country needs such men.'

And there were tears in both their eyes as he forced a smile to his lips. 'It needs good women too, Anni,' he said softly. 'People like you and Heidi.'

Anna Marie nodded, her heart almost too full to speak. 'We are not the ones who are wrong, Horstchen,' she said. 'And if we do not live long enough to see the truth told, then history will tell it for us. It will tell it for people like my father, and Geli and her family, and for the thousands of others . . .'

Despite his resolve to keep it as unemotional as possible, he clasped her to him as her voice tailed off. And they stood there clinging to each other at the kitchen door of the small café where she worked, until an impatient voice from the direction of the sink called, 'Anna Marie, there are customers waiting!'

He was to think of that moment often on the journey up to Berlin, as he sat in the back seat of the family Mercedes with his mother and watched the countryside flash past. He knew he was leaving behind a real friend, someone who shared his values in life, and they were few and far between these days. Would he find such a friend at the school his parents had enrolled him into, he wondered? Just one would do. Someone to reassure him he was not alone, that he was not a freak in believing there were still such things as goodness and humanity in the world, and that they still mattered.

To his relief, at the Kaiser Wilhelm I Gymnasium for Boys where he enrolled on 17 October, things did not turn out half as badly as he expected. Horst found he was to a great extent closeted away from the world of personal involvement in high politics that had disturbed him so much at home. At this particular school the emphasis was very much more on the past than on the present, with Greek and Latin prose to be read in far greater quantities than modern German, and few of the masters appeared to take much notice of what was happening in the daily newspapers. With this complete change of emphasis, the relief was enormous, and he felt as if a huge burden had been lifted from his shoulders.

Although he had not expected to like it there, he soon found that the whole ethos of the place appealed to him. With its lofty, echoing corridors, grand carved-oak staircases, and rooms with wide windowsills on which sat the marble busts of all the great figures of Western civilization from the Greeks down through Martin Luther and

Goethe to the present day, it was like a little oasis in the cultural and spiritual desert that now existed outside.

The only teacher who appeared indisputably Nazi was the sports master, Dr Knebel, who looked like the model for the many posters depicting Aryan health and fitness that he had plastered up all round the sports hall. But, as Horst was not particularly sports-minded, he succeeded in exchanging most of his games periods for extra language lessons, so Dr Knebel's political predilections did not really affect him, and this one enthusiastic Party member was more than made up for by the many others who patently were not.

It came as something of a surprise to him to find that not all his classmates were ardent members of the Hitler Youth, and that there were actually some like himself who were secretly appalled by the sight and sound of their country proudly marching down the path to war once more. By the end of the first semester, seven of them had got into the habit of meeting regularly in the back room of a local *Kneipe* owned by Manny Schnelldorfer, an old ex-Communist, who had escaped incarceration only by proclaiming a complete change of heart and displaying coloured posters of Adolf Hitler on the walls of his *Bier Keller*. 'But old dogs like me don't really change,' he told Horst and his other young pacifist friends. 'We only learn some new tricks to keep the bloodhounds off our backs!'

'Bloodhounds in black shirts, with long black leather coats!' Konrad Bauer, a doctor's son from Potsdam grinned, and someone else jumped to his feet, barking loudly and giving the *Hitlergruss* of the right arm raised in salute.

Yes, they had fun in Manny's back room all right, before returning to their respective homes to pore over their school textbooks far into the night. It was there that Horst learned to drink beer with the best of them, and they lustily sang songs a world away from those sung by the likes of Horst's brother Otto and *his* friends.

'In Mannys Kneipe bei Wein und Pfeife
Da sassen wir beisammen
Ein guter Tropfen von Malz und Hopfen
der Teufel fuhrt uns an.

'Hei, wo die Burschen singen
Und die Klampfen klingen
Und die Mädel fallen ein.
Was kann das Leben Hitlers uns geben
Wir wollen frei von Hitler sein!'

'In Manny's bar with wine and pipe
We all sit together,
A goodly drop of malt and hop,
And the devil calls the tune.

'Hark, the hearty young pals sing!
Strum that banjo, pluck that string!
Let the lasses all join in!
What can Hitler do for us?
Let's be free of him!'

The rousing last bars of that their favourite song were still ringing in their ears, on the night of 9 November, as Horst said *Wiedersehen* to his friends outside the *Kneipe* and prepared to make his way home. Thankfully it wasn't far to his parents' apartment on the Unter den Linden and no matter how much beer he had drunk in the course of an evening, he usually managed the journey in under twenty minutes.

Tonight, however, he had had only three steins of beer and was far from drunk as he looked about him. 'What in heaven's name is going on tonight?' he found himself saying, as they were pushed aside on the pavement by a group of young Blackshirts, some obviously very drunk indeed, and all yelling obscenities, aimed mainly at the Jews.

'Didn't you hear?' Konrad said. 'There was something on the radio today about demonstrations planned for tonight against the Jews . . . I'd forgotten all about it until now.'

'*Juden 'raus! Juden 'raus! Juden-Scheisse! Juden-Scheisse!*'

A cropped-haired youth wielding a pot of white paint in one hand and a brush in the other was running along the pavement yelling, 'Bring out the Jewish pigs!' He paused in front of Horst and his friends. 'Know where any Jewish swine live or have businesses around here?' he demanded.

He was met by a wall of silence, but a passer-by – a well-dressed young woman in a fur coat, called over, 'Beck's the jeweller's is owned by a Jew.' She pointed to a well-lit shop window some distance away. 'It's down there.'

The young man with the paint pot shouted his thanks and set off in the direction indicated.

'Why did you tell him that?' Horst demanded as the young woman drew nearer. Surely she could see that lot were up to no good tonight?

The woman shrugged. 'It's only the Jews they are after. Why should it bother you?' She looked at him quizzically as a small crowd began to gather. 'You're not a Jew-lover, are you?'

Horst bristled and was searching for a suitable retort when he was pulled aside by Konrad. 'Come on, *mein Freund*! It's time we were going home!'

As their small group pushed their way through the gathering crowd in the direction of the Unter den Linden, Horst protested, 'I should have said something. I shouldn't have let her get away with that!'

'Then you would have been protesting at half the population of Berlin,' Konrad informed him. 'Just look at that lot!'

They were approaching the young man with the paint

pot again and, to the applause and rousing cheers of a small crowd, he was daubing white swastikas all over the windows, door and walls of Beck's the jeweller's.

Then, to their horror, one of the crowd pushed a booted foot through the glass. After that there was mayhem as passers-by jostled with one another to get at the goods on display.

'Let's get out of here!' Konrad Bauer shouted, and Horst and the others needed little telling. Things were happening around here tonight of which they wanted no part.

By the time Horst got back to his parents' apartment he felt quite sick inside. All Jewish property within sight had had those same swastikas daubed on it, in dripping white paint. And almost all had their windows kicked in, and he saw at least one synagogue ablaze. There seemed to be fires all over the city, for as far as the eye could see there were red glows lighting up the night sky.

It was after ten o'clock by the time he found himself standing at the drawing-room window looking down on the milling crowds on the pavement below. Most of the cinemas and theatres were out by now and the home-going crowds were becoming caught up in what was beginning to look more and more like a Nazi rally, as gangs of Blackshirts marched down the centre of the road waving their red, white and black banners and yelling their patriotic songs. Scores more sped past in open-topped military vehicles, gesticulating and waving their flags as they hurled anti-Jewish insults into the night.

Their apartment was on the fifth floor and it gave superb views across the city in the direction of the Brandenburg Gate, which seemed to have become one of the focal points for the night's activities. From his vantage point Horst could no longer actually hear any of the shouts or singing, but he had no doubt what the sentiments were. This was the nearest thing to a pogrom he had ever witnessed and the whole spectacle filled him with both revulsion and a deep shame.

His father was still in Essen at the moment, and his mother and sister at their house on the Wannsee, so apart from the staff he was alone. The last thing he was expecting as he went into the kitchen to make himself a cup of coffee was to hear the front door open and his brother's voice shout, 'Anyone at home?'

Horst hurried through to the hall to find Otto and two fellow SS officers standing there.

'Ha! Little brother!' Otto removed his black leather coat and indicated for his colleagues to do the same. He then bundled all three garments on to Horst. 'Hang these up, there's a good lad, and if that's coffee I smell in there, put out three extra cups, will you?'

As Horst stood open-mouthed by the kitchen door, weighed down by the heavy black leather garments in his arms, Otto and his friends made for the drawing room, laughing and joking as they passed him by without a second glance.

Instead of hanging up the coats, Horst dumped them on the kitchen table, then wondered, should he or shouldn't he act as maid and make them their coffees? Otto's high-handed manner was a never-ending source of irritation to him. He saw more of his elder brother than he liked now that he was living in Berlin and on almost every occasion there was friction between them. Otto just could not seem to accept that his younger brother had a mind of his own, and that that mind had no wish to dedicate itself to the Nazi cause.

The coffee pot was bubbling and there was certainly enough for four cups in the pot. Perhaps on this one occasion . . .

He carried them through to the drawing room on a tray and bowed ceremoniously as he deposited it on a side table next to the chair in which his brother was slouched, his long legs outstretched.

'*Vielen Dank!*' Otto drawled. 'By God, we need this – and will require something a good deal stronger before the night's out!'

'Heaven knows what they'll do with them all if it goes on like this!' one of his companions added, with a shake of the head. 'The jails will never hold them all.'

'They'll have to get the transports going before the night's out,' the third officer put in. 'They say the trains are already leaving from the Putlitzstrasse goods yard with their precious cargoes.'

'What precious cargoes?' Horst asked from the vicinity of the door.

'Why the Jews, of course,' the young man replied. 'We've been arresting them by the score down there.' He nodded in the direction of the window. 'I'm surprised you haven't been out there joining in the fun!'

Seeing the expression on Horst's face, Otto cut in quickly. 'My little brother is something of an innocent in such matters. He even claims he would rather go to university than join our ranks when he finishes school next year!'

'And which university might that be?' It was the first young man who spoke, who asked the question. 'Will you go to dear old Heidelberg and gain your duelling scars for the Fatherland?'

'I have put my name down for the Wilhelm Humboldt.'

'Aha!' the third officer smiled. 'Berlin's pride – and hotbed of subversive elements ever since that bloody evil Jew Karl Marx!'

'Not all Jews are evil,' Horst said, quietly trying to remain calm.

'Don't be a bore, Horst,' Otto said in a world-weary voice. 'They're all after one thing. Self-aggrandizement at other people's expense! Look after Number One and to hell with the rest – that's the motto of every member of that race I've ever met.' He lit a cigarette and waved it in

Horst's direction as if to dismiss him from their learned company.

'That's just not true,' Horst replied in a cold but quiet voice.

All three visitors laughed in unison. 'Name one who isn't!' Otto demanded. 'Name one Jew you can think of who wasn't out for himself!'

A silence fell as Horst looked at all three in turn, then said quietly, 'Jesus Christ. Will that do for one?'

He saw very little of Otto after that. Whether his elder brother was deliberately staying away from the apartment or was merely busy, Horst could not tell. He suspected the latter, for as the year wore on the undeclared war against the Jewish population of the city gathered momentum and Horst began to find it increasingly difficult to ignore what was going on around him. One thing was for certain: he could no longer talk to his own family about it, but found a welcome outlet in the evenings spent with his student friends over a glass of beer. They were to be his salvation.

The life of German students through the ages had revolved as much around the *Burschenschaften* – its student societies – as around the lessons, and it was a great comfort to know in your own small group there were kindred spirits who thought as you did – that you were not alone in hanging on to what you believed to be the only good and true values in life: to respect and value your fellow men and women, whatever their colour, creed or political beliefs.

But several evenings a week spent putting the world to rights over a glass of beer did not mean that the young men who attended those regular *Kneipe* gatherings worked any the less diligently when it came to studying for their final examinations, and Horst was no exception. Never had he worked so hard and for so long, and by the time that winter had passed into spring, then spring into early summer and the fateful weeks of the examination came round, Horst felt as if he was simply too full of knowledge ever to be able to regurgitate it in any way coherent enough for the examining board.

When the news finally came one hot, balmy day in July that he had passed with distinction in English, Latin and Greek, and had been accepted for a place at his chosen seat of learning, the prestigious Wilhelm Humboldt University, he could barely believe his good fortune. And it seemed to come as a similar shock to his parents.

'Well, I must admit, *Junge*, I began to doubt you had it in you.' His father beamed as he shook his son's hand on hearing the news. 'Not as dumb as you'd have us believe, eh?'

'No, Father, perhaps not.' He had long since dropped the familiar Papa.

And Otto von Karsten's smile had become even broader as he slapped him heartily on the back. Perhaps his youngest son might even make an acceptable member of the human race, after all.

'You are now ready to take your place in the adult world, and you could not have chosen better than our Wilhelm Humbolt University, here in Berlin. Some of our greatest men have taken their places in that seat of learning, my boy; men that have changed the world, for good or ill.'

And Horst had known that by 'for ill' his father meant Karl Marx – the man whom Trotsky had once referred to as 'the greatest Jew since Jesus Christ'. The great economist and philosopher had been a student at that same university a hundred years before, and he had been both a Communist and Jew – the very epitome of all he knew that his father most detested.

But could it really be to Germany's or the Wilhelm Humboldt's advantage that men of that calibre would no longer be granted a place, but were instead locked up by society as 'subhuman'?

'I will do my best to live up to the honour, Father,' Horst

promised. And he could not wait for October 1939 to come so that he too could walk through that same door that had welcomed some of the finest minds in modern German history, whatever their religion.

It was decided that he would read English and Theology. English because it was his best subject – having been brought up during the first ten years of his life by a Scottish nanny from Aberdeen had made him almost as much at home in her language as his own. Nellie Morrison never could get her tongue around the German vocabulary, so with his parents away so much, and by far the greater part of the year spent closeted away at the Himmelhof with Miss Nellie, his nanny's native speech became as familiar to him as his own.

'Yes, English I can understand you wanting to concentrate on, *Liebling*,' his mother commented, when he had informed her of his choice of subjects. 'But why Theology, for goodness sake?'

Why indeed? It was something Horst was still wondering about himself. Perhaps it was simply some sort of romantic, personal rearguard action he was carrying out, because he believed there was a definite move in Germany today to do away with Christianity and replace it with this thing they called the Old Religion. From what he could make out, it was little more than devil worship wrapped up in the national flag.

'You don't really want to be a priest, Horst, do you?' his friends had asked him in amazement when they had heard his choice of subjects, and he had shaken his head. No, he didn't really want to be a priest, he just wanted to know more about what he was supposed to be rejecting in order to be a 'good German'.

Although they normally spent a good part of September at the Himmelhof, the dramatic turn in political events, with what seemed like the great powers issuing ultimatums to each other every other day, meant that Horst was in Berlin, along with his mother and sister Elsa, on Friday, 1 September 1939, as the international crisis deepened. Everyone wanted to be where it was all happening, and that place was Berlin. Only Otto von Karsten, Senior, was not in the country's capital city; he was busy seeing to affairs in his factories on the Ruhr, where business had not boomed so much in over two decades.

Sunday 3 September dawned clear and balmy, with the promise of even more sunshine to come. The weather was the last thing on anyone's mind, however, as the talk of war with England intensified by the hour. Ever since Hitler's speech at the Opera House on the Friday morning, Berliners had been convinced that the die was cast. And by the Sunday morning things had reached such a fever pitch that Gertrud von Karsten even forsook the family home by the Wannsee to spend the day in their palatial apartment so she would be at the very heart of things if the unthinkable happened.

In no mood for country pursuits, Horst and his sister Elsa decided to join her, and the three of them had just sat down to lunch at midday when loudspeakers all over the city blared out the fateful news they had all been waiting for, yet dreading to hear.

They heard it first themselves from a passing government car which relayed the message to the inhabitants of their apartment block just as the maid left the room after serving the meal. Great Britain had declared itself at war with Germany.

Gertrud von Karsten laid down her knife and fork with a clatter and looked at her two youngest children. Her face had gone quite white. Despite all the advance speculation, it came as a dreadful shock to think it had actually happened. Her mouth had gone quite dry and she licked her lips before saying softly, 'May God protect the Fatherland and us, my children, for I doubt if things in this land or this family will ever be quite the same again.'

Horst asked to be excused and rose from the table, his appetite completely gone. He made straight for his room and lay down on his bed. He picked up his diary from the bedside table and opened it to record the fateful news, and his eyes fell on a few lines by the English poet laureate that he had written down the day before:

> As Priam to Achilles for his son,
> So you, into the night, divinely led,
> To ask that young men's bodies, not yet dead,
> Be given for the battle not begun.

War had been declared, and now that battle of which the poet wrote was about to begin for young men both here and across the English Channel. But another battle was already raging in his heart. Could he – should he – fight for his country under the Nazi swastika? Up to this moment the question had been purely hypothetical and he could be as positive as he cared to be with his friends at the *Gymnasium*, for he did not have to stand by his brave words. Now it was quite a different matter.

For generations von Karstens had been the first to take up the sword of the Fatherland. And more than that, they had been the ones to forge the sword that their own young men would carry into battle. His own grandfather, *Der Alte*'s only son, had carried that sword and died with it in his hand on the battlefield of the Somme during the Great War. And now, a generation later, their country was at war with England once again. That sword had fallen to his own hand to be picked up and held aloft, and he could just hear his brother's taunt, 'Aren't you man enough, then? Aren't you man enough to fight for your country?'

He closed his eyes then opened them again to stare at the ceiling. The question really was, was he man enough not to? That indeed would demand far greater courage.

Chapter Nineteen

It took Horst very little time to realize that soon there would be no choice in the matter; either he enlisted in a section of the armed forces of his own choosing, or the government would decide for him and he could end up at the Front in hand-to-hand combat with an enemy he neither chose nor recognized as such. But could he square this with his conscience? It was a dilemma that absorbed his attention to the exclusion of all else as he found himself saying premature goodbyes to scores of young men with whom he had hoped to be entering university in October.

As soon as war was declared, almost all males of eligible age that he knew volunteered for active service and, despite all their brave songs and promises to each other, all six of his comrades from Manny's *Kneipe* were among the first to go.

'It's not Hitler we'll be fighting for, Horst old pal,' Konrad Bauer told him, his good-natured face serious for once, as they sat together over a beer, in front of the ancient tiled stove that warmed the tavern. 'No, it's not for any political system. It's for the Fatherland. It's all very well not liking Hitler and his lot, but you can't turn your back on your country when the time comes that it needs you. I could never go home again and face my father or grandfather again if I didn't enlist.' And Konrad's voice had lowered as he said with some emotion, 'My father went right through the Great War for me, after all, and his father fought against the French at Sedan.'

And whoever he turned to, the decision was the same: it was all very well to espouse pacifist beliefs, and extol the merits of international brotherhood, but how did you explain to your mother and father that your brothers and cousins were signing up, but you were not?

'You can't just say you don't believe in this war, or even wars in general,' Paul Kramer told him, over a stein of beer the day after war was declared. 'It's like saying you don't believe in your country. It's heresy, Horst. Just plain heresy. And maybe you have the guts for it, but I certainly don't!'

Horst listened to Konrad and to Paul, as he listened to all his other friends, and felt both confused and sometimes rather ashamed inside. Was there something wrong with him that he didn't respond to the current political situation as they did? Was it something lacking in his character that the warrior in him did not immediately rally to the flag like all good Germans? But who were the 'good Germans' these days? Were they only those lucky enough to be designated as 'good' by the Nazi Government? He had thought old Dr Rosenbaum was a 'good' man; you had to be 'good', hadn't you, to devote your life to healing the sick? And Anna Marie's father, Herr Zimmermann, had been a fine man – a good God-fearing family man, whose only crime had been to be a supporter of the Socialist Party. And over the past few months there had been dozens of others he had known, or heard about, who had been arrested, or had just 'disappeared' overnight. Despite what anyone else tried to tell him, he would never believe that the majority of those people had been anything but 'good Germans'. No one could ever convince him that they were simply *Untermenschen* to be got rid of like vermin from the body of society.

No, despite his friends' decisions to enlist, he knew he might be the one who was out of step, but he was not the one who was wrong. There was something deeply amiss with society these days. The old Christian values on which it had been founded were being subverted by a dangerous political clique who espoused other, more sinister, beliefs. Germany – his beloved Fatherland – was entering the darkest age in its history and something must be done to stop it, to halt this mad march to Hell.

But still that one vital question continued to haunt him. Knowing what had happened to the thousands of others who had raised their voices in protest, was he man enough to stand up for his beliefs? Did he have the guts to go against them all?

He took the dilemma to Manny, his old friend in the *Kneipe* down the alley off Friedrichstrasse where he had spent so many happy hours during the past year with his friends.

The old Berliner shoved up the ancient black sailor's cap he always wore and scratched the crinkly grey thatch beneath. 'I am not an educated man, young Horst,' he said in that hoarse smoker's voice of his. 'What book-learning that has filtered into this old head came more from being forced to attend church twice every Sunday as a child than to paying attention at school. But a certain person's thoughts on this very subject have remained with me throughout my life. A very wise man once said that war is the greatest plague that can afflict humanity; it destroys religion, it destroys states, it destroys families. Any scourge, he said, is preferable to it . . .' He squinted through the smoke of the cigarette that dangled permanently from his bottom lip and paused to allow the words to sink into the consciousness of the young man on the other side of the bar, then he said quietly, 'The man who said that was perhaps the greatest German who ever lived. Greater than Barbarossa, greater than Frederick the Great, greater even than Bismarck. It was none other than Martin Luther himself. And I remembered those words when the Great War broke out in 1914.'

Horst straightened up on the bar stool and set down his empty stein on the counter as he leant forward to ask, 'What did you do then? How did you get out of it – get out of taking up arms?'

Manny gave a wheezy laugh as he drew his young friend another stein of beer. 'I enlisted in the Merchant Navy, that's what I did.'

'But I can't stand the sea,' Horst groaned in disappointment.

'Neither could I,' his old friend said. 'In fact, I got seasick having a bath! But you just have to find a way round your problems.'

Horst looked at him bleakly. 'What do you suggest I do?'

'Volunteer for something else,' his friend said practically, as he pushed the foaming stein across the counter. 'There are lots of options open for someone like yourself with a decent brain. Use it, lad! Put your thinking cap on! You don't have to take up arms if you don't want to kill; you can be of service to your country some other way, like I was. Then you can still look your friends and your family in the face without having compromised your principles. Bertolt Brecht did it too in the Great War, and thousands of others. It wasn't just me.'

Horst raised his eyebrows. 'Brecht?' he said, repeating the name of Germany's banned playwright. 'He managed it too?'

'Sure he did. He enlisted as an ambulanceman. You don't have to take up arms, you know. Like I said, there are lots of ways round it.'

His old friend was right. There must be lots of other options open to him. It was up to him now to discover what they were. 'Manny, you're a genius.'

'No, I'm not. If I were that I wouldn't be spending my old age behind the bar in this place. I'd be retired to a nice house on the banks of the Wannsee. It needn't be too big, not like that stately pile your old man's got out there. Something a little less showy would do champion.'

He gave a rueful grin that showed his missing front tooth as he mopped up the spillage on the counter. 'A house on the Wannsee! Now that's a fine thing for a decrepit old Marxist like myself to admit to hankering after, isn't it? But they say every man has his price,' he sighed. 'And that'd be mine. A house by the lake and a nice deckchair to snooze away my old age in . . . *Ein kleiner Himmel*, Horst my young pal. My own little heaven on earth.'

And so, as the hundreds of keen, bright young men like himself, ready to enter the hallowed portals of the Wilhelm Humboldt for the autumn semester, set about postponing their education for an indefinite period, Horst began to give much more thought to Manny's advice. But just how did he go about finding out about these other options that were available? He couldn't bring up the subject at home, for it was already a sore point that he had not applied to join his brother Otto in the SS. To start enquiring of his father about the availability of non-combative jobs would bring a reaction from Otto von Karsten, Senior, that his younger son could well imagine.

But, as the autumn winds grew chill, and sent the leaves from the lime trees on the Unter den Linden scurrying along the pavement beneath the fashionable shoes of the hurrying shoppers, and the black jackboots of the men in uniform who seemed to infest the city, the answer to his question came sooner than he expected. And it came in the totally unexpected guise of a tall, good-looking aristocrat whom he had known at a distance all his life, but with whom he had never really had a proper talk until one evening in early September. It was at a gathering at his parents' apartment that they met once again. The word party was never used these days, for it was considered not quite the done thing to hold such frivolous events when one's country was at war.

Graf Helmuth von Moltke was an old friend of the von Karsten family; in fact the von Moltkes and the von Karstens went back a very long way. But the von Moltkes went back a great deal further than not only the von Karstens, but further even than Germany's old royal family, the Hohenzollerns themselves. Neither Horst's relatives nor the old Kaiser's had anything like the pedigree of the proud military family who had played such an important part in the history of their country since the thirteenth century.

Unlike the von Karstens, whom many in the German aristocracy might look down upon as simply *Geld-Adel* – owing their exalted place in high society more to wealth than breeding – the von Moltkes were undoubtedly *Land-Adel* – a vastly superior breed, whose titles and estates went back to almost the beginning of the Second Millennium.

But, despite the difference in the length of their pedigrees, there were enough similarities between the von Moltkes and the von Karstens to have kept them circulating within the same social orbit for several generations. Also Gertrud, Horst's mother, was more than a little taken by the charming, fair-haired aristocrat, who was not only extremely good-looking but was also better travelled and more cultured than just about any of her other well-connected acquaintances. He was certainly a great deal more sophisticated and intelligent than most of the Nazi hierarchy who frequented her regular salons, and even her husband found much to interest him in the conversation of the Graf. Apart from admiring von Molke's political acumen, Otto enjoyed comparing notes on the running of their country estates – something he could not do with the vast majority of the Nazi Party hierarchy, who might have had the money to buy an estate, but did not have the faintest idea of how to run it.

The von Moltke estate of Kreisau stood in the beautiful

land of mountains and gently undulating green meadows that straddled the border of what had once been old Prussian Silesia and Austrian Bohemia and was not unlike the countryside that surrounded the von Karsten estate in Bavaria. Horst had once paid a visit there with his family as a three-year-old child, over the Christmas period of 1920, but could not remember the occasion, although he had been told he had sung '*Stille Nacht, Heilige Nacht*' quite beautifully, and had had Helmuth's mother Dorothy in tears at his childish piping voice and winsome ways. It was still his favourite of all Christmas hymns, but he doubted if his mother would admit to him having very many winsome ways these days.

Although of noble German lineage on his father's side, Helmuth's mother's family were Scottish and, as well as practising as a lawyer in Berlin, the Graf had also studied at Oxford, passing the examinations necessary for him to practise in England. This personal experience of the two societies seemed to have endowed him with an enlightened cosmopolitan outlook on life that greatly appealed to Horst.

One other more important factor that emerged in the course of a long, quite intimate conversation in his mother's drawing room, was that here, in the person of this highly intelligent aristocrat, Horst began to see that he had Manny's advice personified. A committed Christian, Helmuth von Moltke had been strongly opposed to the war and had sought to find himself a niche that would prevent him being called upon to bear arms and kill those whom he admitted to Horst he could in no way regard as his enemy. This he had succeeded in doing by obtaining an appointment as a War Administrative Counsellor to the Foreign Countries Division of the *Abwehr* in the Supreme Command of the German Armed Forces.

'It is the ideal position,' he told his young companion, as they sat in a quiet corner of Gertrud von Karsten's elegant drawing room, and he accepted another glass of *Sekt* from the butler's tray. 'It gives me official justification for keeping in touch with the outside world, and with Britain in particular.'

Horst shifted excitedly in his seat. His interest was aroused even more. 'What exactly do you do – if that's not too awkward a question?' He knew the *Abwehr* was a highly secret organization, involved with the procurement of intelligence and counter-intelligence, and for sabotage and subversion of the enemy. But he knew this much only by eavesdropping on conversations between his father and brother and one or two of the highest-ranking house guests they so frequently played host to, either here in Berlin or back in Bavaria.

Helmuth toyed with the glass in his hands, his long, handsome face pensive. Then he sipped thoughtfully before admitting, 'None of my work is too original, I'm afraid. A good deal of it consists of evaluating the secret intelligence material that has been gathered by others. And I read a lot – the English and American newspapers mainly, and whatever other intelligence comes in in that language.' He gave a wry smile. 'Sometimes I get quite snowed under by the amount of stuff that lands on my desk. What I really need is someone equally fluent in the language of "our enemy" to help me out!'

Horst sat up on his seat, his heart racing. 'I could do it.' He had not meant to blurt it out so quickly, but could not contain himself.

His companion looked puzzled. 'You speak fluent English?'

Horst nodded vigorously. 'Almost as good as my German. My nursemaid was Scottish and I was left in her company for . . .' he gave a sheepish smile, 'well, for most of my childhood, really. And she couldn't speak German.'

'Well, I never!' The Graf placed his wine glass on a side table next to him then sat back in his chair, crossing one long leg elegantly over the other, as he pressed his fingertips together in an attitude of prayer and regarded his young companion thoughtfully. He had felt from the beginning there was a special affinity between himself and von Karsten's younger son, and now he was sure of it.

'You can test me if you like!' Horst leaned forward, his hands clutching the arms of his chair in his eagerness to impress. He just knew this was what he wanted to do. Something had told him immediately the Graf began to speak about his work that this was the answer to his prayers. If he had to do something for the war effort, and there was no doubt he would be called up in the very near future, then this was it. And what was more, he would be working alongside a man with whom he felt complete empathy. 'I really don't mind – written or spoken, it's all the same to me.'

Helmuth von Moltke smiled. 'Test you? I really don't think that will be necessary.' Then his brows furrowed above the clear, wide-set eyes. 'What do you think your father will think of this?'

Horst sank back in his chair. 'Oh, my father . . . To tell the truth, I think my father will be hugely relieved I've found something I feel I can do – and do well.' He made a rueful attempt at a smile. 'I think he's beginning to despair of me and is quite terrified I'll end up in prison as a conscientious objector!'

Helmuth von Moltke did not return the smile, but nodded understandingly. He could believe that. It must be no easy task being the son of their country's biggest arms manufacturer at a time like this. He felt sympathy for this pale-faced young man with the intense dark-blue eyes and quiet manner sitting across from him.

His own eyes moved to the side of the room to where Horst's elder brother was having a boisterous conversation with a high-ranking Nazi. He never could stomach Otto, whom he felt to be all too typical of the bombastic young SS officers he so often encountered in his job. There was no escaping them: young men on the way up, who would stop at nothing to get where they wanted to go. And he knew that young Otto von Karsten was more determined than most, for as the heir to the Karsten Steel empire, he made no secret of the fact that he wanted to make as great an impression on his country's history as had the legendary *Der Alte*, and this war was an ideal vehicle in which to achieve that ambition. But young Horst here was something else entirely. He was a young man with a conscience; a rare bird indeed in Germany these days.

'You will see what you can do for me, won't you?' Horst pressed, sensing his companion's attention wandering.

'Leave it to me, my boy,' the Graf replied. 'I'll get back to you on this before the week is out.'

And he was true to his word. Horst was still in bed the following Saturday morning when the message came via the maid that he was wanted on the telephone. 'The gentleman says it's important and he must speak to you personally.'

'Did he give a name?'

'Graf something . . . von Moltke, I think.'

From a half-asleep stupor, Horst was wide awake.

'Herr Horst – your dressing gown!' Gretel, the maid, looked quite shocked as he made for the bedroom door dressed only in his pyjamas.

'*Scheisse!*' He knew he shouldn't swear in front of a member of the opposite sex, but excitement got the better of him as he doubled back to grab his dressing gown from the chair by the bed, then raced along the landing, to tear down the main staircase and snatch the phone from the butler's hand. It had to be him. It just had to be. 'Hello? Horst von Karsten here.'

It was him. But it was a bad line and Helmuth von Moltke's voice was faint and sounded as if it was coming from the other end of the country, instead of the same city. Horst had to strain to hear.

'Von Moltke here ... I have had a word with my superior and he is quite interested.' A crackling chuckle came over the line. Quite interested was putting it mildly. 'In fact, to tell the truth, I think he would regard it as something of a coup to have a von Karsten on the payroll. They are very choosy about who they accept here, you know. The security vetting is the tightest you can imagine. But as I told him, if you can't trust the son of the man who is supplying the country with the weapons to fight this war, then whom can you trust?'

Horst gave a wan smile into the phone. He had always determined that the family name would never be allowed to influence his getting a job. 'A von Karsten has never let the Fatherland down yet,' he said mechanically.

'That is just what they want to hear. Can you get over here for nine o'clock?'

Horst turned to glance at the longcase clock against the wall at the foot of the stairs. It had just gone eight. 'That will be no problem.'

'Good. You know where my office is on the Bendler Strasse. When you get to reception ask for me by name. I have left instructions for you to be sent straight up ... *Wiedersehen.*'

'*Wiedersehen.*'

Horst could barely contain his excitement as he hung the phone back on its hook. Heinz, the butler, was standing nearby and he shot him a nervous smile. 'I think I may have a bit of news for you all when I get back later on this morning, Heinz.'

The elderly man raised a bushy eyebrow. 'Really, Herr Horst? I trust it will be something your parents will approve of?'

Horst smiled. The butler had been the unwilling witness to far too many family quarrels of late to have any rose-tinted ideas about the youngest member of the family's schemes. 'I am about to investigate the possibility of serving my country,' he said, with a deliberate air of righteousness. 'There can be no objection to that, don't you agree?'

'Indeed, Herr Horst. Indeed I do!'

He chose his suit with care, choosing a dark slate-grey that had been bespoke-tailored by Berlin's leading gentlemen's outfitter, and matching grey leather shoes. He also wore a grey soft felt hat above his dogtooth tweed overcoat, feeling that would lend a certain air of gravitas to his appearance. And, as he surveyed himself in the full-length mirror of his dressing table, he was quite pleased with what he saw. He offered a silent prayer of thanks that his skin had cleared up of late. The acne that had plagued his teenage years had all but gone, except for the occasional spot now and again around his chin, and that was a blessing indeed, particularly when going for a job in what was undoubtedly a real man's world.

Although he could easily have walked it from their apartment, he took a taxi to the address that Helmuth had given him. The Graf's office was situated in the Supreme Command of the Armed Forces – the OKW building – which had one entrance on the Tirpitz Ufer and another on the Bendler Strasse, just south of the Tiergarten, in Central Berlin.

'Keep the change,' he told the delighted taxi driver, before sprinting up the steps and in through the Bendler Strasse entrance.

He was stopped immediately by two uniformed soldiers who first searched him, then asked for his identification and reason for being there. His feeling of importance and excitement faded somewhat as he allowed himself to be frisked and then waited for his *Personalausweis* to be returned.

'You may continue,' one of the soldiers said, handing

back his card, then standing smartly to attention. *'Heil Hitler!'*

'Heil Hitler!' He still felt foolish every time he was called upon to give that salute.

The grim-faced, bespectacled woman behind the desk in the vestibule picked up an internal phone, after checking his identification once again, then confirmed he was indeed expected. 'You will be escorted there,' she said, indicating a young SS man standing nearby.

'Danke.'

It was strange how even quite innocent people could be made to feel guilty just by the presence of such a person, Horst thought as he walked a couple of paces behind the black-uniformed figure up two flights of stairs and half-way along a corridor.

'Heil Hitler!'

'Heil Hitler!' Horst gave the Nazi salute once more in return as the escort took his leave.

He stood looking at the closed door, his heart racing. Then he knocked three times.

'Herein!'

He found himself in a large, high-ceilinged office that seemed to have its walls covered in maps with pins stuck in them, and coloured lines drawn all over them. An oil painting of the Führer hung over the black marble mantelpiece at the opposite end of the room to where two men waited. Helmuth von Moltke was standing behind the large mahogany desk at which was seated a dark, swarthy-looking man, who rose to greet him. He was not nearly so tall standing as he looked sitting.

'Heil Hitler!'

'Heil Hitler!'

Once the essential greetings were over, Helmuth said, 'Admiral, I'd like to introduce you to my young friend Herr Horst von Karsten.'

'Horst, I have the honour to introduce you to Rear-Admiral Wilhelm Canaris.'

'It is a great honour and pleasure to meet you, Admiral,' Horst said, shaking hands with the man he had never met, but had so often heard referred to as 'the little Greek'. He was sure the ex-sailor had little or no Greek blood, but he certainly looked Mediterranean in appearance.

He had had no prior knowledge that the Admiral was the man in charge of the *Abwehr*, and was rather surprised to find an ex-naval officer at the Head of Military Intelligence. Any doubts he might have harboured, however, as to the man's fitness for the post immediately evaporated as, over the next half-hour, he was given a thorough grounding in what his job would entail should he be given the post. 'It is hard work and long hours, young man, make no mistake. But your reward will be the triumph of the Fatherland over its enemies. The richest prize of all.'

Horst caught the Graf's eye and the older man's expression was totally noncommittal.

He was then escorted on a rudimentary tour of the building, before being taken into a special office where he was subjected to an hour-long grilling from a panel of three men in plain grey suits. He had to be very careful indeed as to what replies he made. At no point must he say or indicate anything that might make them suspect him of anything other than total loyalty to the Führer and his government.

'We won't bother putting you through the English-language tests, Herr von Karsten,' he was told. 'We already have the results of your *Abitur* on file.'

Horst looked surprised. They certainly lost no time in getting information in this place. He had no doubt that in the short time that had passed since his initial conversation in his mother's drawing room with the Graf all sorts of checks had been run on him. Even a von Karsten would not be immune as far as the *Abwehr* was concerned. Whatever information they felt they required they had obviously got hold of, and got hold of fast. And perhaps that should be an object lesson to him. You would have to be up to it just to survive five minutes in here.

He was then offered a cup of coffee and asked to wait in an anteroom where he passed the time reading some old copies of the English *Times* newspaper. He was halfway through the Anglo-Saxon version of the invasion of Poland when the door opened, and through it came the familiar figure of Helmuth von Moltke.

The Graf was smiling and held out his hand to be shaken. 'Congratulations, my young friend,' he said. 'And welcome to the *Abwehr*.'

Horst rose unsteadily to his feet, the newspaper falling to the floor beside him. 'You mean they have accepted me?'

The Graf nodded. 'They have indeed.' Had his young friend but known, the decision had been made even before his visit today. Admiral Canaris had been only too delighted at the prospect of having a von Karsten on the staff. There was not a government department that did not benefit from having a member of the Establishment on its payroll.

Horst shook his head. It seemed much too good to be true. He had made it. He was now a member – albeit a very junior one – of Germany's most secret and highest military intelligence organization. 'Thank you, Herr Graf,' he replied, a trifle shakily. 'I only hope I am worthy of such a position.'

Helmuth von Moltke's clear eyes were grave. 'I only hope it is worthy of you, my young friend,' he answered quietly.

And there was something about the tone of the Graf's voice that brought a distinct feeling of unease to Horst as he reached out to shake his new colleague's hand. And that unease grew with the tiny package the Graf handed him before he left. 'Inside there you will find a small glass phial,' he said quietly. 'We all carry one – all of us with knowledge that could be of use to those they call "the enemy". I do not have to spell out to you what it is for. Let us just say you will be expected to use it should the need arise.'

That tiny package now lay at the bottom of his pocket and its presence on his person heightened that sense of unease he had begun to feel before he left the *Abwehr* building.

He decided not go straight home, but instead took a taxi out to the Tiergarten, Berlin's popular animal park. An hour or so in the fresh air, he thought, would give him the chance to do some proper thinking about his future before he actually broke the news to his family.

The Tiergarten had been one of his favourite spots as a child, but, to his surprise, on his arrival half an hour later, as he looked at the animals behind their moats and bars, the place had a curiously depressing effect upon him. As he strolled the well-tended walkways, he felt a sense of empathy towards them, as if he too knew what it was like to live without real freedom; to spend one's life in an alien environment. For that was what Germany was to him now. He did not belong here in this society that accepted willingly the imprisonment of its fellow men and women, because of their religion, race or political beliefs.

He had mixed feelings even about his acceptance into the *Abwehr*. In his heart he knew it was the coward's way out, and no one of his age liked to think of themself as a coward. Youth was the time of idealism, of following one's dream, wherever it might lead. But his dream had died the day they captured Geli Rosenbaum. That, more than anything, had brought home to him the real depths to which his country had sunk.

He sat down on a bench in front of the monkey house

and watched a young couple throwing peanuts to the animals. The young man had on the black uniform of an SS officer. It could have been Otto standing there. He felt nothing but contempt for his elder brother now. It was funny, really, how their father was so proud of his eldest son. 'Otto is a real man, a true von Karsten,' Otto Senior had declared after Otto Junior's last visit. 'A man with a backbone forged of finest steel; a man with fire in his blood.'

Horst gave a bitter smile at the memory. How many times had he heard those words or something similar? He glanced down at the palm of his left hand. The pale shiny skin of the old wound glinted in the autumn sunshine. That was all Karsten Steel had done for him. The fires that had made the family rich, and had helped Adolf Hitler to power, had scarred both his body and his soul. He was not proud to be a member of that family any longer. He was not even proud to be a German.

A young mother and her small son were looking at the monkeys now. The infant had a red balloon on a long string and, as Horst watched, the little boy let go of the string and a wail of anguish filled the air as the balloon sailed straight up into the heavens, to take off over the treetops, until, very soon, it was out of sight.

That sight of that red balloon sailing into the atmosphere remained with Horst as he made his way slowly back to the main gates half an hour or so later, to head for home. There had been something intensely liberating about the whole spectacle, and how he had wished he could sail with it, away up there beyond all the misery that was a country at war. But he couldn't. He was as much a prisoner here as these animals he was leaving behind. Unless he had the guts to do something about it, that was. But did he? Did he?

It was a question that was to haunt him for the next four years.

402

'He came unlooked for, undesired,
A sunrise in the northern sky:
More than the brightest dawn admired,
To shine and then for ever fly.'

Coleridge

Book Three

THE OFFCOMER

Chapter Twenty

Lot's Farm,
UTHERDALE,
Spring 1944

The old limestone farmhouse stood where it had stood for generations, solid and unpretentious, and as much a part of the Utherdale landscape as the crag itself. In its early years it had played host to the remnants of Bonnie Prince Charlie's army as, tired and defeated, the Highlanders had plodded wearily northwards towards the border and home. And now, almost two centuries later, the young woman who regarded it as home listened with renewed interest to the old folk of the area who had known the place as a thriving farm before the Great War and recounted as much of the history of the old house as they could remember.

Miss Wright, the postmistress's grandmother, had been born there when its water had to be fetched by pail from the beck that ran along the foot of the neighbouring field, and though that had now been superseded by a cold tap and stone sink in the kitchen, the old place still left a lot to be desired in terms of modern conveniences. There was no electricity and the hot water had to be heated in a small boiler that enclosed the fire of the shiny black range that the Colonel had had specially fitted for the newly-weds in the oak-beamed kitchen. But in the heady weeks of first moving in, the young couple had paid little regard to the dampness, peeling plaster and other imperfections that came of age. Simply to be together under their own roof, despite its leaky slates and wormed timbers, was enough.

Nevertheless, Bethany and Jack had done their best in

the early months of their marriage to make the old house as habitable and attractive as time and finances would allow. With paint pots stacked by the back door, and heavy tomes of wallpaper patterns and swatches of curtain material to choose from, they had set about the task with all the optimism and vigour of youth. For Bethany in particular it had been a whole new experience, being able to decorate their new home in exactly the way that pleased them and no one else. Catalogues were pored over and colour schemes chosen with infinite care, so that by the end of their first year, the old place was barely recognizable.

The fact that they had been able to make a start in their own home here at Lot's Farm and had not automatically moved in with the family at Wolf Hall was something for which she knew she would be eternally grateful. Jack had known she was not keen on the idea of beginning married life under the same roof as the rest of his family and, with the Wolf Hall estate finances under severe strain, he had managed to persuade his father that if he could make a go of Lot's Farm, and save it from total dereliction, they would all benefit.

The decision to allow him to resurrect the old place and turn it into a working unit once more was agreed upon by the Colonel only on the understanding that Jack also helped him oversee the management of Wolf Hall itself, and to this he readily agreed. It made for an exceptionally busy start to married life, but the arrangement kept both his wife and his father happy. What more could he ask, he had to keep reminding himself, when eventually he succeeded in flopping into bed at night?

The change they wrought on the old farm in the first few months of their occupation was regarded by many as little short of a miracle. And it was not only inside the house that the difference showed. Outside, the knee-high grass and banks of nettles and brambles that had disfigured the entrance had been cut back, and soon the withered spires of rosebay willowherb that had grown tall between the old York stone flags of the path leading up to the door were nowhere to be seen. Even the tangle of briar roses that bordered the path had been carefully pruned to encourage the flowers that now provided a scented guard of honour throughout the summer months for inhabitants and visitors alike.

On the outside of the house, the greying wood that had not seen paint in living memory was now protected by two layers of best black gloss bought from Webster's, the ironmonger's in Butterslack. 'We might as well do as much as possible now,' Jack Greville told his young wife. 'You just never know. We might not get the chance to attend to such things before long.' Neither of them had realized then just how true those words would turn out to be. Less than two and a half years later, both he and Fred, the painter who had assisted him in his transformation of the old place, were in uniform and hundreds of miles away.

Throughout the first two years of their marriage the threat of war with Germany was a cloud everyone in the dale hoped would remain very much beyond the horizon. But as the summer of 1939 drew to a close, those hopes began to dwindle along with the light. The evenings were drawing in, and the red and gold of the falling leaves that swirled on the breath of the Helm Wind through the narrow streets of Utherby had not yet turned to brown when, down in London, the nation's capital, on 3 September 1939, to cries of 'Speak for England!', Prime Minister Neville Chamberlain rose to his feet in the House of Commons to tell the world: 'This country is now at war with Germany. We are ready.'

Bethany and Jack had been working in the fields when that declaration was made. But news travelled fast and that evening they had attended a packed church together to hear Kenneth Barden tell his parishioners to 'gird their loins for the coming fight'.

It was with heavy hearts they had walked back to Lot's Farm through the balmy evening air. It had been one of the loveliest September days in living memory, with not a breath of wind and a golden autumn sun shining from a clear blue sky. There was an air of unreality about it all. How could the world be going to war on a day like this? It didn't make sense, somehow. Bethany had clasped her husband's hand that bit tighter and they had spoken little on the way home. Too many thoughts crowded both their minds to give them voice.

They listened together to the wireless that evening to hear King George VI tell his subjects, 'We can only do the right as we see the right, and reverently commit our cause to God.'

Jack Greville had looked at his young wife. He knew that he too could only do the right as he saw the right. And to him that did not mean closeting himself away here at home while others did the fighting to defend their country. For several weeks now, other young men throughout the dale had been rushing to enlist. To wait for call-up was in many eyes to be branded a coward. 'I could remain here, you know,' Jack told Bethany. 'I don't have to go. As a farmer they would probably grant me an exemption.'

But Bethany had known they were only words. Within a few weeks of war being declared and seeing most of his friends rush to exchange their civilian clothes for military uniforms, there had been no real argument about it. Her husband was young, healthy and keen to go; there was no way she could have stopped him, nor would she have wanted to.

'You'll still have Joe and Sam to see to the really hard stuff around the place when I'm gone,' Jack had told her, and she had nodded reassuringly. 'Don't you worry about me,' she had said. 'I'll manage fine.'

It was exactly what Jack wanted to hear. That he felt a certain amount of guilt at leaving her there was no doubt, but she had both her family and his own on the doorstep, he told himself. And, with his lame leg, there was no question of Amos ever having to enlist. Knowing that his younger brother would be here to look after his wife made all the difference. 'And don't forget, you'll have Amos to turn to when I'm gone,' Jack reminded Bethany, with a reassuring smile. 'I'll let him know I'm relying on him to keep an eye on you.'

Bethany had gone quite cold at those words. That they were meant to comfort her, she had no doubt, but they had exactly the opposite effect. If only he knew. If only he knew how she shuddered at even the thought of his younger brother coming anywhere near the place once he had gone. But he would never know – not if she could help it. He had made it very clear to her early on in their relationship just how much his brother meant to him and she could not be the one to break his heart.

'I'm sure Amos will have quite enough to do running Wolf Hall, without bothering about me,' she had said lightly. And Jack had reluctantly agreed. If the truth be known, he was not at all happy at leaving the Wolf Hall estate almost entirely in Amos's hands, but he had comforted himself with the hope that his brother would grow enough in the job to be every bit as much a help to the old man as he himself had undoubtedly been.

But all that was over four years ago now, and no one could have guessed that the war would still be dragging on into the middle of the decade.

Neither could Jack have guessed just how quickly his father's health would deteriorate once he had gone. It was as if the leaving of his eldest son for war had dealt a mental and physical blow to Philip Greville from which he would not recover, and the passing years only made matters worse. Of late, the Colonel's heart trouble had increased to the extent that Amos had now practically taken over the complete running of the place, and, with his well-known predilection for 'a drop of the hard stuff', as he liked to put it, both The Hall itself and the estate were slipping into a state of decay that Bethany found quite depressing, whenever she spared the time to think about it. Her whole life, since Jack's departure, now revolved around making a go of Lot's Farm, and that, she kept telling herself, was quite enough to be going on with, without worrying about Amos's job for him.

As for the help that Jack had left her with: Joe Winstanley and Sam Brookhouse. She had to smile, otherwise there were times when she could certainly cry. One was even keener on the bottle than Amos, and the other was all of sixty-three. Not the best or most reliable pair of workers to help her run the farm, but they were the only ones available, so it was no use wishing for the impossible. Almost all the best young men had volunteered even before war had been declared and, of those that didn't, nearly all had gone by the time Jack himself had been due to leave.

Bethany had watched her young husband don his uniform with a heavy heart on the morning of his departure. It was raining outside – not the gentle drizzle that so often came with the dawn over Uther Crag, but a harsh, biting rain that caused the drain in the yard to overflow and muddy rivulets to wend their way across the cobbles and out into the road. That same road down which they would soon be setting off for the station and the eight o'clock train.

She had stood by their bedroom window, gazing out as he dressed. The moors beyond Lot's Farm had disappeared in a grey bleakness that echoed the feelings in her heart. 'I don't want you to go,' she said in a tired voice. Then more vehemently, 'I don't want you to leave!' She turned to face him and he paused in adjusting his tie in the small cheval mirror on the dressing chest. Their eyes met in the glass and he turned.

He came over and placed his hands on her shoulders. She had never said those words to him before and they tore at his insides as he looked down into her troubled eyes. 'I thought you understood,' he said quietly.

Bethany shook her head as her eyes filled and she clung to him, pressing her cheek against the roughness of his lapel. She had thought she understood. She had been oh-so-understanding about it – until now. Until the time had actually come for him to leave. 'Blast Adolf Hitler!' she said bitterly. 'Blast him to hell! And blast all those who have done this to ordinary people like us!'

He prised her gently from him and reached inside his trouser pocket for a clean handkerchief. 'Here,' he said gently. 'Dab your eyes and blow your nose and promise me that lower lip will never tremble again.' He gave a rueful grin as he watched her obey his order. 'How could I ever survive out there knowing my Squirt was falling to pieces back here at home?'

Bethany forced a smile to her lips as she blinked back her tears and pushed the handkerchief back into his pocket. He was right, of course. She had to be strong, for his sake. 'I'm sorry, Jack,' she whispered. 'It's just that it all seemed like a dream that would never actually happen – until now.'

'I know.'

He reached out and kissed her for the last time; a long, heart-rending kiss that expressed all the pain and un-certainty that was in both their hearts. Who knew when they would ever kiss this way again? Who knew *if* they would ever kiss this way again?

They said very little after that. In having everything to say in such a short time as they had left, they said almost nothing. And as she watched him drink his last cup of tea at the kitchen table, Bethany thought of all the things she had meant to tell him. How very much he meant to her. But he knew that already, didn't he? Didn't he? All sorts of silly little things crowded into her head. Things about the farm or the animals that she had meant to mention to him. But now it was too late to bother him with trifles like that. Now it was too late for everything.

The station platform had been already busy when they arrived, with more than a sprinkling of khaki and air-force blue among the figures who jostled with bags, boxes of vegetables, and the odd sheep and goat. They had both made it clear to their respective families that they would prefer to say their last goodbye alone, and both were thankful for the relative privacy as they stood together waiting for the final whistle to blow.

'Look after yourself, Squirt,' Jack said softly, reaching down from the open window of the carriage door to touch her cheek.

Bethany clutched his hand to her wet face and kissed it. 'And you take care, Lieutenant,' she answered, attempting a resilient grin that didn't quite come off. 'I'll keep the home fires burning, don't you worry!'

And then he was gone — all that was left of him was a khaki-clad arm waving into the distance. She had watched the train until it disappeared round the edge of the crag on its way to Butterslack — a grey blur in a haze of mist and white smoke.

Several people spoke to her as she made her way hurriedly from the station, but by the time she reached home she had no recollection who they had been or what they had said, as she slumped down at the kitchen table and reached out gently to pick up the cup with the remnants of his last drop of tea. She would not wash the cup, she resolved. She would sit it up there on the dresser and pretend he had only just popped out for an hour or so — jumped into the car to go down to the village for some errand, perhaps . . . But no, that was silly. That was just the kind of thing she knew Jack would not want her to get up to. She had to be strong – for his sake as well as her own.

She had got up from the table and walked to the window. It was still raining outside. She turned and looked about her, at the familiar room where they had spent so much of their short time together. All of a sudden Lot's Farm seemed a cold and lonely place, with more work attached to it than she could ever cope with, with or without Joe and Sam to help.

Situated on the outer reaches of the Wolf Hall estate, on the edge of the old drove road between Utherby and Butterslack, the old farmstead and its neighbouring barn and outbuildings were known to few who had not grown up in this neighbourhood. Only a handful even knew of its existence, for no one ever passed this way now. There was no need to; the new road, built at the end of the old Queen Victoria's reign, by-passed it by a good half-mile.

But even without Jack, there were times when Bethany did not mind the solitude – a word she much preferred to the 'isolation' used by her mother – for it lent a timelessness to the place. Almost nothing had changed in those three hundred years since it had been built; the modern world with all its upheavals and strife had not impinged, and now that she was used to it, sometimes even this terrible war seemed like a tragedy that was taking place on some other planet.

It was not a grand house like The Hall, but with its homely stone-flagged kitchen, front parlour, two upstairs bedrooms and two tiny rooms in the attic, there had been room enough for the two of them and any family that might have come along. And it was private. More than anything in the first years of her marriage, Bethany had valued that. She had had her own front door, with her own key. They had been determined not to be beholden in any way to the remainder of the Grevilles still at The Hall.

415

Whatever income they succeeded in generating from the hundred acres that came with Lot's was theirs and theirs alone, although Bethany suspected that any surplus would find its way eventually into the coffers of Wolf Hall. After all, as Jack had kept reminding her before he left, he would be Master there in the not too distant future.

Although sometimes it seemed only yesterday she had seen him off to war on that rainy winter's morning, over four years had now passed. Five years of back-breaking toil as one season slipped slowly into another, and life in the high reaches of Yorkshire's North Riding got harder, not easier, and the war – that damned bloody war that had robbed the dale of its finest young men – dragged on and on.

Spring came late to Utherdale in the year of 1944 and the hard ground responded slowly to the season of rebirth. But come it did at the beginning of May, and on the tangle of old-fashioned rose bushes that bordered the path to the door of Lot's Farm, the crinkled new leaves were appearing, ready to burst forth any day now, and in the nearby pear tree, the golden buds were bursting into leaf, as its resident chaffinches began to sing and display their courting finery.

In the hawthorn hedges too, that bordered the lane between the farm and Lot's Barn, the hedge sparrows were twittering their greetings to the tiny blossoms the size of pinheads that promised the drifts of white flowers in a few weeks' time. And in the grassy verges of the old road, pale-yellow primroses clustered, and celandine and blue periwinkle, where only a few short weeks before clouds of snowdrops had seen the last of the hard frosts that kept the ploughed fields ribbed with iron and the hill farmers looking anxiously to their pregnant ewes.

Even now, on the upper slopes of the hills, it was still a bleak cold landscape in which to welcome the new life that was waiting to be born. Although lambs had been scampering about the fields of the lower reaches of the dale for months now, up here on the rougher land of the fells that composed most of Lot's Farm's hundred acres, lambing was still in progress, and the young woman dressed in a thick Arran jersey, dungarees and a pair of black, muddied wellington boots was looking more anxious than most.

'Hold still, old lady, it's coming . . . it's coming!' Bethany Greville gripped the bleating, writhing ewe with her left hand, while her right slid over the slimy head of the unborn lamb. 'Once more and we've got it!' Taking a deep breath, she grabbed hold once again and, with a deft twist of her wrist, she got the small creature under the chin and pulled.

With a rush of bloodied fluid, the torso slithered to the grass to land with a faint plop behind the mother. The ewe gave a plaintive bleat, then immediately tried to scramble to its feet to attend to its latest offspring.

'God, that was a hard one!' Bethany said to no one but Glen, the border collie, by her side, as she watched the new mother stagger to her feet to lick life into the bedraggled lamb on the grass beside her.

She bent down and wiped the afterbirth from its eyes and forced open its mouth to make sure its passageways were clear before picking it up by its hind legs to rub her right hand over its heart. The creature gave a twitch then let out a loud pathetic bleat. The sound brought an immediate response in kind from its mother and a smile to the face of the young woman who had acted as midwife. She had wrestled with this particular ewe since early morning and had all but given up the unborn lamb for dead. A surge of emotion rose within her at that first cry. 'You'll be OK, little 'un,' she said, lying it back down beside its mother. 'If you can survive that, you can survive anything.'

As she straightened up, she pressed a hand into the

small of her back and groaned out loud. God, she was tired! She had been at it since daybreak. She glanced at her watch. Almost six hours ago. Almost a whole day's work packed into one morning. How she dreaded this part of the year with Jack gone. She had never expected the war to drag on for so long that she would find herself into this, her fifth lambing season, without him. And it had not got any easier. It was hard enough with a capable man around the place, but one woman alone, with only occasional help . . . Well, that was another story entirely.

Yes, it was now over four years since Jack had enlisted. Four lonely years when she had often begun to wonder if she still had such a thing as a husband, and if this damned war would ever end. He was now a Captain in the Military Police, at present somewhere in North Africa or Southern Italy, she thought. But letters were infrequent, and heavily censored. The fact that sometimes she almost forgot what it had been like to have a husband around the place was understandable, for he had been gone so long. But then this bloody war had been going on for an eternity, or so it seemed. Nobody had ever imagined when the Prime Minister, Neville Chamberlain, had broadcast to the nation that they were at war with Germany, back in the autumn of 1939, that nearly five years later they would still be in the thick of it. No one she knew had thought it would be like this – that it would be 1914 all over again. Even Jack himself had joked with her when she shed a tear at the first sight of him in uniform. 'Don't worry, Squirt,' he had said. 'It won't be anything like the last one. It can't be. With all these new-fangled aircraft and tanks and things they have nowadays, it can't possibly take half as long as the Great War. It'll be over and done with in no time, you'll see.'

Well, 'no time' was turning out to be a very long time indeed. And now even her two young brothers, Tom and Teddy, had reached the age of call-up and were over there in Italy with the Eighth Army. If it went on much longer even Sam, the baby of the family, would be man enough to don the khaki. And that she knew was her mother Betty's greatest fear. In the past few years she had seen all her children leave the nest, both girls to marry, and her two eldest boys to go to war. All she had left was Sammy. Sammy and her husband, Kenneth. For the widowed Betty Baine had married her chief comforter, the Reverend Kenneth Barden, less than two years after her daughter Bethany's marriage to Jack Greville. That such a match might well be on the cards had come as no surprise to Bethany, who had been more aware than anyone of the support Kenneth Barden had given her mother since the death of her father. It seemed hardly a day passed without the minister calling in for his customary cup of tea, and the middle-aged cleric had found not only words of comfort to give, but had come to realize he had much in common with the grieving widow, who was herself a 'daughter of the cloth'. They were kindred spirits in their staunch faith in the Good Lord, and Bethany, in particular, hoped that the relationship she had watched deepen in the early months of her mother's widowhood would prove just the emotional crutch the sensitive Betty Baine so badly needed and would continue to need in the years to come.

The quiet wedding in the local church had delighted almost everyone. Who could make a better wife for the middle-aged preacher than his predecessor, Harrison Hetherington's only daughter? Only a few had carped, for Utherby was no exception in having its fair share of those who got no pleasure from the happiness of others. But, on the whole, Betty Baine was better thought of than most, and there were few who could think of much to hold against Kenneth Barden. Well-meaning was the description most commonly given to the tall, rather gawky man, with the gaunt, lined face that belied a hearty appetite for his food, and a deep appreciation for all the comforts of home now offered by his new wife.

'I just thank God he's over forty-one,' her mother confessed to Bethany after hostilities were declared. 'I couldn't bear it if Ken had to go too.'

And so, apart from those deemed too old to bear arms for King and Country, such as Kenneth Barden, they had left the dale; one by one, the young and not so young men who had wanted nothing more than to go about their daily business each day and return home to their waiting families at night, had exchanged their civilian dress for the uniforms of His Majesty's fighting men, and their women-folk had watched them go, for the second time in living memory for many.

That it had been raining the day that Bethany had seen Jack off at the local station had seemed fitting somehow, and her heart still missed a beat when she thought of how he had looked that morning. He had been so handsome in his uniform, for those years in Australia, and then that precious, but heartbreakingly short time working the farm here had turned him into a fine figure of a man. 'As fine a figure as his father was at his age,' an old lady from the village had told her on his first walk in Utherby in uniform. Those words were painful to remember, for the Colonel was now a pitiful shell of the man he had once been and Bethany shuddered to think what Jack's reaction would be if he could see his father now. By the spring of 1944, two more heart attacks and an increasing case of senile dementia had turned Philip Greville into a bent figure in a bathchair – someone now totally unrecognizable as the proud military man who had come through the trenches of the Great War with more medals than most.

Yes, these past few years had not been kind to her family or to anyone else's, come to that. But Bethany had tried not to let it get her down, for so many women were in her position these days. And many, such as her old friend

Nancy over in Butterslack, had been left with young children to bring up on their own. She and Jack had not been blessed with offspring, so her mother said she had much to be thankful for in that regard. 'It would have been much worse if that had been the case,' Betty Barden had told her daughter. 'You would have had real cause to complain with a couple of hungry infants to cater for.'

But Bethany knew she *did* mind, nevertheless. And she minded terribly that it had been Jack that had gone and not Amos. Amos, with his lame leg, the result of that fall so long ago from the barn loft, was still lording it up at Wolf Hall, where his father was now almost totally confined to his room.

And that left only Ned . . . And poor Ned was still . . . well, just Ned. And Bethany's heart went out to her husband's younger brother whenever she thought of him left up there with only Amos and their invalid father for company.

'You'll be needing a cuppa, lass. I brought you one.'

Wiping the ewe's afterbirth from her hands on the piece of sacking she had tied around her waist as an apron, Bethany spun round to see the figure of Old Carnforth coming towards her across the field, a small Thermos flask in his hand.

'Thanks, Warton, you're a good lad.' She had never even discovered the old man's name until after Jack had gone off to war, and she had never failed to call him by it ever since. His surname, he informed her, was that of a good old Lancashire railway town, and his Christian name was from its neighbouring village of Warton, where his forebears had come from – a perfect combination, his mother had thought. But just about any name would have done by then. 'You're not too choosy by the time you've given birth to nine, I reckon, Bethany lass!'

'How are you this fine morning, anyway, you old rascal?' she asked, as she unscrewed the lid of the flask.

Old Carnforth scratched two days' growth of grey beard and sighed. 'Ah'm nobbut middlin', lass. But I mustn't grumble. We've all got our fair share of problems these days.'

'Aye, that's certainly true.'

He looked on as she poured the hot tea from the Thermos into the cup-lid and took her first sip. 'Aaah, that tastes good!' She squinted through the mid-morning sunshine at the old man. 'I heard tell you were invited to attend that piano recital they held in the village hall on Saturday night.'

The old man looked away in some embarrassment. 'Oh aye.'

'Oh aye, indeed,' Bethany continued with a smile. 'A little bird tells me it was Mrs Borthwick, the old tailor's widow, who did the asking. Did you enjoy it?'

'Nay, lass,' the old man replied in all honesty. 'To tell the truth, I felt like a fish out o' t'watter sitting there – and when she saw me turn up in me best suit she looked at me as if I were one an' all!'

Bethany suppressed a smile. Warton Carnforth in his ancient three-piece suit, with his wing-collar framing his scrawny neck, was a sight to behold. She knew, because it had come out of mothballs specially for her wedding to Jack. 'I think it would be nice if you returned the compliment, all the same,' she said. 'Invite her to the pictures at Butterslack, say. I heard tell *The Thirty-Nine Steps* is coming.'

'Thou thinks too much, lass. Me and Mrs Borthwick are chalk and cheese. She's a fine God-fearing woman, I'll give her that, but she has one thing agin her.'

'Oh, and what might that be?' Bethany looked at him in some amusement as she sipped the hot tea.

'She talks a lot but says nowt,' the old man said with some feeling. 'And I never could abide a natterin' woman – especially an old 'un.' Then his expression softened as he looked at his young companion. 'But nobody could accuse you of being one o' them, lass, have no fear.'

Bethany laughed. 'That's probably because I'm always too darned tired these days to spend extra energy on gossip.'

'You'll be packing it in for the morning now.' It was more of a statement than a question and the old man looked at her in some concern. One of these fine days she was going just to flake out way up here on the fells, and what would happen then? He knew that her brother-in-law, Amos, had more than enough on his plate these days, with The Hall and the quarry to supervise. And with old Sam Brookhouse off with a bad attack of his sciatica for the past week, and Joe Winstanley more often drunk than sober, it was not a happy prospect. 'I reckon thou needs help, mysel', lass. A body can only carry on for so long like this, thou knows.'

'Are you suggesting we apply for another of those Land Girls?' Bethany asked, with some scepticism. The last one they had had, just before Christmas, had gone off with a young Scotsman she had met at a local dance and had never been seen since. And the one before that had become pregnant, although disclaiming all knowledge of a boyfriend. 'The Immaculate Conception', as she became known throughout the village, stayed on until her eighth month and then went home to her mother in Bridlington. Bethany had received a postcard from her some time after the baby's birth. It had been a girl and she had named her Concepta. They had all had a laugh about that in the local pub. 'Being a girl, it couldn't have been the Second Coming, then,' Hector Wilks had commented, as Bethany went in for her weekly supplies. 'So that Concepta was the next best thing to calling the little blighter Jesus.'

'Land Girls,' Bethany mused. 'I don't know so much . . .' While she was sure the Women's Land Army was an august and much-needed national asset, and that there were thousands of young women who were very good, they would always be associated in her mind with Sheila and Meg, and the type of silliness that was typified by the government's Dig for Victory campaign. There wasn't a serious farmer she knew who couldn't see those silly grins on the faces of Potato Pete and Dr Carrot, the cartoon characters, far enough.

Dig! Dig! Dig! And your muscles will grow big,
Keep on pushing in the spade!
Never mind the worms
Just ignore the squirms
And when your back aches, laugh with glee
And keep on diggin'
Till we give our foes a wiggin'
Dig! Dig! Dig! to Victory!

Was Old Carnforth seriously suggesting another of the same? 'Do you really think we'd be better off with another Land Girl?' she asked.

'Mercy, no, lass. I was thinking on one of yon lads from t'POW camp. There have been quite a few let out to farms in t'area and some are right well thought of an' all.'

'You mean Heaton's Crag?' Bethany asked, mentioning the old disused army camp about seven miles the other side of Butterslack that had been given over to housing prisoners of war. 'You think we should apply for someone from there?'

Warton Carnforth puffed a shag of his precious tobacco into life in his old briar pipe and nodded. 'I don't see why not. Others in less need have. You can be too proud, thou knows, lass. We get no medals in heaven for working ourselves to death.'

Bethany smiled and drained the last of the tea from the flask lid. She screwed it back into place and returned it with a smile. 'Thanks, Warton. I appreciated that. And I

424

appreciate what you have just said. I'll think about it, I promise.'

And she did think about it over the next few days and by the end of the week she had just about had enough of soldiering on alone.

Her younger sister, Libby, who was married to a local lad, Will Denyer, now in uniform with the rest, came over from her home in Butterslack to suggest they go to the pictures together that Saturday night. 'It's Leslie Howard in *The First of the Few*,' she said. 'You like him, Beth . . . Remember him as Ashley in *Gone with the Wind*?' She sighed like the star-struck adolescent she still was as she continued knowingly, 'Of course this is not quite as romantic as that. It's the story of that chap who invented the Spitfire. One of the lasses who works in the shop with me saw it earlier on in the week and said he were right good. She really enjoyed it.'

Bethany looked up from the stove, where she had milk for the motherless lambs heating. 'Oh, I don't know, Lib, I'm awful tired these days.' She thought of all the effort involved: getting herself washed and dressed to go and sit in a darkened cinema for a couple of hours didn't really appeal.

'Too tired to see Leslie Howard?' Libby looked at her sister, askance. 'I tell you this for nowt, our Beth – if you're tired of Leslie Howard, you're tired of life!'

Bethany gave a weary smile as she poured the milk into three babies' bottles sitting ready by the side of the kitchen range, in front of which she had three newly-born lambs, wrapped in an ancient blanket, warming in an old orange box. Tired of life? She gave a resigned shrug. 'You could just be right there, our Libby. Maybe that's just what I am.'

They had grown quite close of late, although they had little in common except blood and husbands at the Front. In some ways Libby, although still in her teens, was much more wordly than her elder sister. She knew all the latest

425

popular songs and, having been given her Grandmother Hetherington's old Singer sewing machine from her mother as a wedding present, she never ceased to amaze Bethany by managing to run up quite an array of dresses, and a very fashionable spring jacket, on just a private's pay. Even the official 'Make Do and Mend' campaign run by the government could learn a thing or two from her young sister, Bethany decided.

It was funny, really, how they had never been close until now. But perhaps the gap in their ages had been too great as children. And Bethany had been acutely aware when she married Jack that her own family felt rather overawed by the sudden relationship to the Grevilles that had been thrust upon them. They would never just pop into the farm unannounced, but always waited for an invitation. It had upset her at first, but she understood. They did not want to 'impose', her mother said, but Bethany had been left with the feeling that in many ways she now knew Jack's family, the Grevilles, better than her own. She seemed to have been part of them for so long. But while familiarity might not breed actual contempt, it certainly did not encourage closeness in that particular household. What contempt she did feel was reserved purely for Amos, for she knew she would neither forgive nor forget what had happened to her as a young girl at his hands. For Jack's sake she had tried to put it behind her, but just being in his younger brother's presence was still, after all these years, almost unbearable.

Although she made her obligatory visits to Wolf Hall for the sake of her father-in-law, these were becoming much less frequent of late. Philip Greville had few lucid periods these days and she was finding it increasingly distressing to see his mind and body deteriorate so rapidly before her eyes.

Since Jack's departure, her world seemed to have shrunk to the life in and around Lot's Farm, which was something she never could have imagined as a young child when she wandered the fells and surrounding area and looked down on this old place from the top of her beloved crag and wondered if it would ever again be inhabited.

And so, after Libby had left to gaze at Leslie Howard in the picture house alone, Bethany sat there that evening and stared into the red glow of the fire, in the large, square kitchen. It was a room that brought comfort, with its shiny black range, bordered on either side by gleaming horse brasses inherited from Tabby on the old lady's death the previous year. On the well-scrubbed shelves of the old-fashioned Welsh dresser against the far wall was displayed the fine set of Doulton dinnerware given them as a wedding present by Jack's uncle in Australia. It had arrived in a box sent all the way by rail from Harrods in London and she could barely remember ever having been so thrilled. A dinner set from Harrods was a far cry from the plain blue and white crockery sold by Webster's, the ironmonger's in Butterslack where most folks around here bought their tableware. But of all the things in the room which brought her pleasure, place of honour went to her beloved boomerang: her first ever present from Jack. It had pride of place on the very top shelf and was lovingly polished every week.

She yawned as her eyes rested on it and she sat back in her chair and absent-mindedly stroked Glen, the sheepdog, who sat by her side. He was not allowed in the house when Jack was at home, but life was different now in so many ways.

By her side on a little side table lay a letter addressed to Captain John Greville, and she felt relieved that she had written her bit to Jack for that evening. But even that had taken more effort than she had the energy for. She wrote almost every night, even if it was just a paragraph or two, and posted two letters a week. She hadn't a clue how many got through and she hadn't heard from him herself for several weeks now. She was trying not to worry, for letters got held up for all sorts of reasons, and she just kept on trying to sound cheerful in her own to him. That was important, for whatever she was going through, there was no doubt he was enduring far worse. Far, far worse. She knew he liked to be kept up to date on what was happening on the farm and with the family, but she was choosy in what she wrote. There were some things best left unsaid in a situation like this, some people best left undiscussed. And his brother Amos was one of them.

Since Jack enlisted her situation here at the farm had become difficult to cope with from many angles. Not only was the work too much, with Joe and Sam being so unreliable, but as 'acting head of the family', as he liked to call himself, Amos was posing an ever-increasing threat to her physical well-being. While Jack was still at home, she found she could cope with her detested brother-in-law, mainly because he was seeing a young woman from a farm near Sedbergh on a fairly regular basis, and this must have helped burn off much of his surplus sexual energy, but just lately that romance seemed to have cooled and his attentions were turning to her once more.

She never could quite make out exactly what it was that Amos felt for her. In her more charitable moments she even believed he might actually be in love with her, but then her next experience of his crude remarks or gauche attempts at embraces changed her mind. How could he be in love with her and act like that? But one thing was for sure: whatever it was he felt for her, it was no flash in the pan, for she had endured around a decade of his attentions. And her blood still curdled at the thought of that very first time she had witnessed him going through that strange ceremony in front of his bedroom fire and what had followed.

Although no mention was made these days of the

British Union of Fascists, and all the Grevilles had renounced any connection with the organization as soon as it became obvious that to retain their ties was to risk imprisonment, Bethany had no doubt where Amos's loyalties still lay. She was equally certain that, whatever black magic or voodoo, or other nonsense, he had practised all those years ago, he was practising still. She had no direct evidence of this, for the shenanigans at the barn had stopped long since, but it was just an inner feeling she had always had. There was something evil about Amos Greville, something lurking behind those dark eyes and that sidelong glance that brought her skin out in gooseflesh just to be alone in his company.

The swarthily handsome looks of the young man he had been in his late teens and early twenties had coarsened through the years, and there was something distinctly unsavoury now about his almost gypsy-like unkempt appearance and the aura of brooding sensuality that surrounded him. Her old schoolfriend, Nancy, had once told her that Amos reminded her of Heathcliff in *Wuthering Heights* and Bethany had been quite horrified at the comparison and wondered what Emily Brontë would have made of her handsome hero being compared to a molester and drunk. Yes, and maybe even a murderer, for if others seemed to have forgotten that he had once been questioned about poor Sarah-Jane Youdell's murder, she certainly had not. There was a malign presence surrounding Amos Greville; a malign presence that could not be ignored.

Bethany often wondered if she was the only one to feel this way about him. Certainly none of the rest of his family had ever indicated any hint that they shared her unease. Except perhaps Ned. Poor daft Ned. A warmth welled in Bethany's heart whenever she thought of the Colonel's youngest son, for age had not improved his lot; it had made it harder. 'Ned, Ned, daft in the head! Daft as a brush and better off dead!' Kids could be cruel all right, and those cries still taunted his every walk through the village. And he understood, she had no doubt about that, and that's what made it all the harder to bear.

She would watch him sometimes shambling about the streets, his hair now long and unkempt, his clothing undone, and that vacant stare and smile of his bestowed on all and sundry. He was still the friendliest of souls, but people would look away and cross the road rather than get entangled in his pathetic attempts at conversation.

But while it might be understandable for outsiders to be cruel, she found it difficult to forgive the deliberately high-handed way that Amos treated him. With his father a chronic invalid, and his other brother away at the war, Ned looked to Amos both for companionship and leadership, and got neither. Instead, he got pushed aside and was made to feel a stranger in his own home. 'Bugger off and play with the sheep, will you? They're more on your level!' Amos would bellow as Ned hovered in the background, embarrassingly grateful for any bit of individual attention that might be thrown his way.

It was painful to witness, and Bethany tried to make up for the treatment he got at Wolf Hall by keeping open house for him at Lot's Farm, but Ned had stopped calling so frequently of late, and she couldn't help laying the blame for that at Amos's door.

'He hasn't said anything about you coming here so much, has he, Neddy?' she had asked one Sunday just before Christmas when he called round with some holly he had cut for her from the tree by the front door of The Hall. She had seen so little of him of late that she had begun to get quite worried. But poor Ned had only given her that silly grin of his and shaken his head. He wouldn't tell anyway; he was as scared of Amos as she was, although her own nervousness around Jack's younger brother was something she would never admit to a living soul. Especially Amos Greville himself.

Chapter Twenty-One

'Is it true?' Amos Greville demanded of his sister-in-law as, flushed in the face and panting from the exertion of the ride, he dismounted from Zephyr, his favourite gelding, and threw the reins over the handle of an upturned cart.

Bethany stood at the open door of the shippon, a pail of water from the tap in the yard in each hand. Amos in a paddy was the last thing she could do with at present. Totally ignoring his shouted question, she turned and headed inside.

He followed her, his lame leg making a scuffing sound on the cobbles as he determined not to let her off without answering. 'Have you applied for help on the farm from those bloody Nazis up at Heaton's Crag?' Old Carnforth's casual remark as he had been saddling his horse this morning had brought him over here at the gallop and he was determined to get to the bottom of it.

Bethany looked up from her task of emptying the fresh water into the trough and gave a noncommittal smile. So they were 'bloody Nazis' now, were they? Time was when Hitler and his friends were all things wise and wonderful to the British black-shirted young men of not so long ago. It was amazing what the threat of jail could do to one's beliefs.

'Bloody well answer me, woman! Have you asked for enemy help or haven't you?'

'Happen.'

Amos stood by the side of the shippon door and glowered in at her as she went about her work. Little puffs of dust rose in the shaft of sunlight from beneath his foot as he kicked at the floor, and he reminded her for all the world of an irate horse pawing the ground in frustration. 'Pa won't like it, you know – having Nazis around this place. And what's more, Jack would be bloody furious. Good God, woman, he's out there fighting the swine, while back here his own wife is entertaining the idea of having some of the bastards working on his own land! I ask you! Have a heart!'

'I have a heart,' Bethany replied patiently, hanging the empty pails back up on their hook, then wiping her hands on an old towel that hung beside them. 'And I also have two arms, two legs and a body that's just about fagged out working this bloomin' place!' She adjusted the belt that kept her dungarees from flapping too loosely around her slim figure and pulled down her sleeves as she closed the door to the stall, then added impatiently, 'Anyhow, they're not all Nazis. From what I hear the vast majority are ordinary conscripts . . . Hitler's equivalent of the poor bloody cannon fodder of the last war.'

'It makes no difference, they're German, aren't they? The bloody enemy. That's all that counts.' He moved back slightly to allow her to pass, then followed her into the yard, his voice rising in agitation. 'You can't tell me it's right to treat them like normal people. They're our enemy, for God's sake! If we were over there on the Continent or in North Africa, or wherever, we'd be shooting the bastards. Those blighters that are over here – that have been lucky enough to get caught and not killed – their mates are still out there shooting our chaps. Decent, God-fearing blokes like Jack – your own husband, for God's sake! Doesn't that mean anything to you?'

Bethany paused in her stride halfway across the cobbles to turn and face him, hands on hips. Her patience was rapidly running out. What right had he to come here and interrogate her like this, or to raise objections to whoever she had working for her? Wolf Hall was his concern, not Lot's Farm. He was not the one who had all the work to do about the place whenever Joe decided to disappear, or old Sam had one of his bouts of lumbago. 'Quite frankly, no, Amos. It doesn't mean anything to me. I don't really give a damn if they're Germans, Martians, or any other species you care to mention, as long as they've got two arms and two legs and a back that doesn't mind being broken like mine is with this endless work there is around here.'

He continued to glower at her, his dark brows meeting in the middle, beneath a forehead that had two deep furrows across the sallow skin. 'You always were a wilful little bitch,' he said bitterly. 'Wilful and stubborn at the same time. God knows why our Jack ever chose you to hitch his waggon to! Could have had the pick of the dale, he could. Why he settled for you I've no idea!'

Anger flared in Bethany's eyes. 'Yes you do. You know exactly why Jack chose me. Because he was attracted to me, that's why, just like you are, Amos Greville. Only in Jack's case he didn't have to take what he wanted by force – it was always freely given. And that's something you can't stand, isn't it? You never did like playing second fiddle to your big brother, even as a kid.'

She gave a pitying laugh as she pulled the scarf from her hair and ran her hand through the thick auburn mane. This morning had been warm for May and her brother-in-law's interference and jibes had not exactly helped in cooling her down. Perspiration shone on her brow as she passed the back of her hand across it and gave him a scoffing smile. 'I can just imagine the two of you as lads at a sweet-shop counter. You would be the one who grabbed without bothering to pay, while Jack wouldn't even have to pay. Folk took to him, that's why. They liked him and so would be happy to give freely of what they had. And oh, how that must have rankled with you! It would've rankled then and it still rankles now, every time you look at me.'

His eyes had never left her face and they narrowed, as did his lips, as he spat out the word, 'Bitch!' and grabbed her right wrist. The anger that had been welling within him ever since hearing the news about the POWs from Old Carnforth now boiled over. Her whole attitude was provocative, but then it always had been. Both mentally and physically, she was doing what she had always done – provoking him into a response. What she said was calculated to bring retaliation. It went too near the bone – far too near the bone. He had his pride, after all. He couldn't let her get away with that. She had meant to rile him and had succeeded. 'You damned little bitch!' He made a grab for her and caught her by the arm, twisting the limb back behind her until she was forced to let out a yell of pain.

'Let me go! Stop it – you're hurting me!'

But Amos would not let go. She had asked for it, after all. And he was enjoying seeing her suffer, witnessing the pain in her eyes as he led her round the centre of the yard in a grotesque dance, her arm doubled back behind her back. She had sought to inflict pain on him with her tongue – well, two could play at that game.

'Le'me *go*!'

He was forcing her to high step, no easy task in a pair of muddy wellington boots, and she almost lost one and had to struggle to keep it on as she let out another yell of pain at the limb twisted so grotesquely behind her. The pain was excruciating now, and she could feel the heat of tears springing to her eyes but was determined not to cry in front of him.

They were approaching the shippon, the door to which was still wide open, and his gaze fell on the pile of hay just inside on the flagged floor. Lovely soft, inviting hay. His pulse quickened at the sight of it. He pushed her towards it, his fingers digging into the soft flesh of her wrist.

'Let me go, Amos!' she panted. 'You're hurting me! You're breaking my wrist!'

But the entreaties were ignored as, with one deft flick of his own wrist, he sent her spinning through the entrance of the shippon. A sharp prod of his riding crop then sent her staggering backwards to fall heavily and painfully on to the hay.

'You bastard!' She landed on her already tender wrist and for a moment lay there, glaring up at him as she fought to keep back the tears. 'You think you're so big, don't you? So big and powerful standing there. But you don't have to be big and powerful to attack a woman – it's small and weak you need to be inside to do that!'

'Shut up!' he commanded. 'Just shut your face and don't say another word! You've said more than enough already.' The sight of her lying there on the hay at his feet brought a powerful surge of the emotions already burning inside him. Anger fermented with revenge and the constant slow-burning lust that lay within him for this woman who could infuriate him as no other, and his breathing quickened and became more laboured as he stood there looking down at her. This need, this yearning, it was always there torturing him, nagging at him; night and day it lay just beneath the surface, ready to burst into flame at any provocation. And, by God, she was giving him provocation now. He began to move slowly towards her.

The sight of him bearing down on her was too much for Bethany. She attempted to scramble up, but her rubber boots slithered on a wet patch of hay, where she had spilt some of the water a few minutes before. Sensing his chance, he immediately grabbed a pitchfork from the rack at the side of the door and moved forwards towards her, holding it in front of him, until she could smell the manure still clinging to its prongs. She froze in horror as what was potentially the most lethal weapon on the farm came within a fraction of an inch of her face then moved slowly down until it reached her neck. She gasped in shock as she felt the cold metal touch her skin and fear widened her eyes as she gazed up at him. 'Don't be a fool, Amos,' she gasped, almost too terrified to move a muscle to speak. 'Put that thing down.'

But he had no intention of putting it down. He had her at his mercy now and they both knew it. Slowly a smile spread across his features, and she could see he was enjoying this. The bastard was really enjoying it. The smile – that familiar, twisted, mirthless smile – fanned the cold, impotent rage boiling within her.

Then the smile faded and his expression became more intense. The only sound was his breathing, heavy and hoarse. The blood that had been quickening within him was urging him on. It throbbed in his loins and brought a sweat out on his skin beneath his riding habit. A bead of perspiration glinted on his upper lip. She was at his mercy, all right. He knew it and she knew it. And they were quite alone. There was not a soul to hear within a mile. Even that old blighter Carnforth wouldn't be back to blunder in on them for ages yet. He had gone to the village for the week's provisions, and that other old codger, Brookhouse, was out on the fell. He had passed him on his way here.

'I've got you now, Bethany Baine,' he said through gritted teeth.

She stared up at him, transfixed. It was the moment that she had dreaded – that she had been waiting for ever since Jack had been called up. It had taken four years to arrive, but arrive it had, and panic froze her mind and body. She could neither move nor think.

'You're at my mercy now.' His voice was low and taunting, and his dark eyes seemed to glow with a strange sort of madness as he made a slight stabbing movement with the pitchfork in his hands.

Her mouth was dry as she pleaded hoarsely, 'Please, Amos . . . Put that thing down. Be sensible.'

The smile flickered back for an instant. 'Sensible?' he

mimicked. 'Sensible? What makes you think I won't be sensible?' She knew why just as well as he did. But he could taunt her every bit as well as she had tried to humiliate him. 'Is it not "sensible" to fancy some of those illicit sweets you were on about so eloquently a minute or so ago?' he asked softly. 'Is that not "sensible"? After all, it was you who put the idea into my mind, wasn't it? I'd have been quite happy just to head on home to The Hall. But no, you had to go and say things – give me ideas. It really wasn't very "sensible" of you, now was it, Bethany?' He was taunting her all right, teasing her, playing with her fear and enjoying every minute of it.

She stiffened and succeeded in moving back a fraction on the damp hay, her eyes still locked with his. She would call his bluff. They were both fully grown adults. She was his brother's wife, for heaven's sake. She had to make him see sense.

But the pitchfork was moving closer until a prong was poised on each side of her neck. She could feel its presence half encircling her throat like some hideous collar on top of the small St Christopher medallion she always wore. 'I know what you want, Amos,' she whispered, trying to summon up much more bravado than she felt. 'But you can't force me. You can't make me do it.'

'Can't I?' he hissed back softly. 'Do you really believe that?' Their eyes were still locked in a trial of strength. 'You really think I can't make you?' He moved an inch or two closer and she could see the perspiration now beading his upper lip. 'Just watch me,' he said softly. 'Just you watch me.'

Panic engulfed her. That look in his eyes – that devil-take-the-hindmost look that said he would have what he wanted at all costs –brought it all back. It was playing in her mind in glorious Technicolor like some Hollywood movie she might have gone to the pictures in Butterslack to see the second time round. They were no longer in the

437

shippon out here on Lot's Farm; they were back in his bedroom at The Hall. The whole room flashed before her, even those disgusting foxes' tails. If he moved an inch closer she knew she would be able to smell the whisky on his breath once more. It was bound to be there, for he was still as fond of the bottle as he had ever been.

Then, from somewhere out in the yard, there was a clattering sound, like a pail being knocked over on the stone cobbles. It was probably only Glen or one of the farm cats, but hope surged in her heart. It was worth a try. It might just be Old Carnforth, or Sam Brookhouse. The latter had reported back for work this morning and should be around somewhere. Despite the proximity of the prongs to her throat, she opened her mouth and let out one long prolonged scream that echoed around the empty shippon.

'Shut up, bitch!' The fork was thrust forward, so that the metal curve between the prongs was now hard up against her neck, the cold steel pressing into the skin of her throat, forcing her to gag, then collapse backwards until she was flat against the floor. The implement was then pulled back and tossed aside. It clattered to the ground about six feet away as he almost fell on top of her, his great bulk hitting her ribcage and stomach, almost completely winding her.

'No-o-o-ooo . . . !' It took her only seconds to find enough breath to make a fight of it. Her nails clawed at his face and hair, drawing blood on his right cheek as he fought to regain control of the situation. But this time there was no way she would give in as weakly as before. She was a grown woman now and was determined to make a real fight of it, even if she did come off worst in the end. She would never submit without a struggle. And soon she was struggling so much and making so much noise as they wrestled on the floor that neither of them was aware of the two pairs of eyes watching them in some confusion, then mounting concern from the open doorway.

After little more than a few seconds, one of the visitors decided this had gone on long enough. What they were witnessing could in no way be a lovers' roll in the hay. That woman was fighting for her honour, if not her life. The two strangers looked at one another and both silently concurred. It was high time someone intervened.

The younger man moved forward and bent down, then a decisive hand reached for Amos's collar. He was dragged up by the scruff of the neck in one mighty jerk to find himself looking straight into a pair of strange dark-blue eyes that burned indignantly into his own. 'I may be mistaken, but I think the lady was saying no,' the stranger said as he let go of the collar, to send Amos staggering backwards.

'Who the hell are you?' Amos's lame leg had almost given way beneath him, and he had to steady himself against the door jamb of the shippon as he looked in consternation at the two strangers. His already ruddy colour heightened even more as he adjusted his riding jacket and stared in mounting anger and hostility at the tall figure beside him and at the slightly smaller, older one in the doorway. That accent didn't come from anywhere round here, that was for sure. And those clothes they were wearing looked like some sort of uniform.

'My name is Horst von Karsten,' the taller one said. 'And this is my comrade Dieter Hoffmann.'

Amos's mouth dropped open as he straightened his dishevelled attire and stared at the two men dressed in the drab grey of Heaton Crag camp. 'Bloody Germans!' He might have known! He turned angrily to Bethany, who was still on the floor, but who had by now scrambled to her knees. She too was looking in some amazement at the two newcomers. 'You didn't tell me the bastards were already here!'

Bethany got up slowly, her eyes never leaving her rescuer's face as she brushed the strands of hay from her clothing and passed a hand over her hair, picking out the dried grass. 'I had no idea they had arrived,' she said in all honesty, and immense relief. 'But it looks like it wasn't a minute too soon.'

The whole situation was too embarrassing for words, and although she was incredibly grateful to her rescuers, she felt an irrational sense of guilt, as if she had somehow been a part of it – a willing party to the awful scene they had just witnessed.

Making a deliberate attempt to act as if nothing untoward had been going on and what they had just seen take place there on the floor might well have been an everyday occurrence, she held out a welcoming hand to each one of the new arrivals in turn and said in as light a voice as possible, 'I'm very glad to make your acquaintance, gentlemen . . . My name is Mrs Bethany Greville and this . . .' She turned in her brother-in-law's direction. 'This is Mr Amos Greville.'

The taller, younger one, who had pulled Amos off her, shook hands solemnly and gave a perfectly executed bow, with a Prussian click of the heels. 'I am pleased to make your acquaintance, Mrs Greville.' He was nice-looking as opposed to handsome, and more French than German in appearance, she decided. With his rather lean, intense face and finely-boned features, he seemed more poet than soldier or farm labourer, and was not at all what she had expected. He spoke perfect English with almost no trace of an accent and, as she shook his hand, she noted his felt soft to the touch, as if he had never known what it was to do a day's real work in his life.

With a rather strained smile, she passed on to the older man behind him who, with his grey, balding head and rather squat peasant build, was another kettle of fish entirely. But his eyes were kind and his smile was just as genuine as he took her hand warmly in both of his and she felt the calluses that spoke of a lifetime's hard toil long before this war had even begun. '*Hallo, gnädige Frau,*' Dieter Hoffmann said, in his heavily accented German. '*Tut mir leid, ich kann kein richtiges Englisch.*'

'My friend apologizes for not speaking any English,' Horst von Karsten said. 'But he is a good man and keen to learn.'

He turned to Amos, who was standing stoney-faced by the shippon door, and held out his hand. 'I am also pleased to know you, Mr Greville.'

Amos deliberately ignored the extended hand. 'That's the last bloody thing you'll be,' he said, casting a still furious glance back at Bethany. 'For if I have anything to do with it, you'll be off Greville land before you can say Adolf bloody Hitler!'

Anger flared in Bethany's eyes, but she bit back a retort. The two newcomers had seen quite enough of Greville family altercations. Then all three of them watched as Amos turned on his heel and strode as resolutely across the yard as his crippled leg would allow, in the direction of his tethered horse.

Horst turned to Bethany. 'Your husband seems very angry,' he said.

Bethany's brows rose a good half-inch, then she laughed out loud for the first time that day. 'Good God in Heaven, that's not my husband! If it were I think I'd shoot myself!'

The young man standing next to her looked surprised, then faintly amused. 'Oh no, Mrs Greville. I think there is enough shooting in the world already!'

Bethany smiled. 'You're right there,' she said with feeling. 'You're absolutely right.'

As they walked out of the shippon she saw a khaki-uniformed guard standing enjoying a cigarette on the other side of the yard, and he smiled and came towards them. 'Sorry to spring this on you a bit sooner than you expected, Mrs Greville,' he said. 'The truth is, these two were assigned to go to farms in the Ingleton direction with four others, but the lorry left without them. The Sarge thought since they were all signed out to leave they might as well go somewhere, so as you were next on the list, you've got your help a week earlier than expected. Do you mind?'

'Do I mind?' Bethany looked from one to the other. 'I'll say I don't.' Then, casting her mind back to several minutes previously, she added with conviction, 'In fact, you could say they arrived not one moment too soon!'

But now that she was landed with them, the problem was what to do with them? She had not really given it much thought as yet, and pondered over the question throughout the next half-hour while the four of them sat together in the kitchen drinking tea and enjoying the eggless cake she took out of the tin to cut specially for the occasion.

She thought it was odd the way the guard sort of talked over them, as if they were both deaf mutes and incapable of either understanding or answering for themselves. She realized this was almost the case with the smaller and older of the two who could understand no English, but it was certainly not the case with the younger, the one who called himself Horst von something.

'Of course most farms have a loft or the like above a barn,' the guard was continuing in his distinctive West Midlands accent. 'I noticed you have a fine old 'un a half mile or so down the road there that would do fine, by the looks of it. That type of thing is usually enough for the likes of them. These lads are quite used to that sort of thing, you know. A lot of them are peasants back home, you see Mrs Greville, and wouldn't expect much else.'

Out of the corner of her eye, Bethany caught the ghost of a smile that flitted across the lips of the younger prisoner. That one at least was no peasant, she decided. And anyway, who had ever heard of a peasant with a 'von' in front of his name? 'Oh, I wouldn't worry about their sleeping accommodation, if I were you, Corporal,' she told the man who had brought them. 'This is a big enough old place to put us all up in some degree of comfort, without having to resort to the barn.' She could have added that she could tell a fine tale about the loft of that barn he mentioned, but she kept her peace. No one would believe her, anyway.

The guard took his leave after another cup of tea and another generous helping of cake, and Bethany was just on the point of wondering exactly what to do next with the two men who were now part of her workforce, when there was a knock at the door and Sam Brookhouse entered.

The elderly man looked quite taken aback at the sight of the two Germans sitting there at the kitchen table, and he began to back away. The last time he had had any direct contact with the likes of them had been in the trenches in 1918. He had been told this morning on his return to work that his employer had applied for POW help, but he had not expected to find them here already, and it made the reason for his visit all the more embarrassing. He removed his bonnet and scratched his balding crown as he shifted uneasily from one booted foot to the other.

'Is anything the matter, Sam?' Bethany asked, surprised to see him back at the farmhouse at this time of day.

'Well, you could say that,' the elderly worker replied.

'It's not your back playing up again, is it?' she asked in some concern. 'You don't think you've come back too soon?'

'Nay, it's not me back,' Sam assured her. 'It's young Joe I thought I'd better see you about.'

Bethany's brows rose as she got up from the table to fetch another cup for the new arrival. 'And what about Joe?' she asked, in some irritation, as she set about pouring another cup of tea. She had just about had her fill

443

of Joe Winstanley, who was to be found more often drinking out of hours in the back room of the Pig and Whistle in Utherby than helping here on the farm. 'According to the last I heard, he'd gone down with some mysterious ailment, not a million miles removed from a hangover, I'll be bound.' She would have got rid of him years ago if she hadn't felt sorry for his wife and child. 'You haven't spoken to him recently, have you?'

The farmhand shook his head. 'Nay, not him personally. But I've had a word wi' his missus. Ran into her this morning, I did.'

'And?' Bethany handed over the cup of tea and looked quizzically at the elderly man.

Sam looked distinctly uncomfortable as he shot another glance at the two Germans sitting quietly at the kitchen table. 'It's to do wi' them,' he said at last. 'Joe reckons it's not right.'

'What's *not right*?'

Sam took a deep breath. 'Expecting him as a young man to work alongside them, that's what. Not seeing as his two brothers are over there fighting the beggars.'

Bethany's mouth opened, then closed again as she sat back down on her chair. She took a mouthful of tea to calm herself. There was no good her exploding, that was for sure. According to quite a few around here, he would have a valid point. 'And just what does he intend to do about it?' she asked, in a strained voice.

The farmhand finished his tea with a slurp and replaced his cup on the table, carefully avoiding the eyes of all three as he said quietly, 'His missus reckons he'll not be back . . . Not here at Lot's Farm, anyroads, seeing as how things are now. And if he can't get tekken on any place else, he'll enlist.'

'Enlist!' Bethany hooted. 'I'll be surprised if they get him sober long enough to sign on the dotted line!' Then her smile faded, as she added quietly, 'In other words, you're here to tell me Joe won't be back?'

The elderly man scratched his head once more before replacing his cap and making a move towards the door. 'Aye, it amounts to that,' he said in a tired voice. Then, casting a wary eye towards the two newcomers sitting next to her, he added, 'And I'll better warn you, Mrs Greville, there's plenty more who thinks as he does around here. Fraternizing wi' t'enemy some call it.' Then seeing the concerned look on her face, he added quickly, 'Not that I'd go as far as that mesel', mind. But I can't say as I'm happy about it. And you have to be honest, don't you?'

Bethany gave a weary sigh. 'Aye, you have to be honest, Sam.'

An embarrassed silence followed the elderly man's departure. She knew that the older of her two new workers had not understood a word, although he could sense the atmosphere around what was being said. But the younger . . . She threw a glance at Horst, who was looking at her with some concern in his eyes from the other side of the table.

'It is understandable,' he said quietly. 'I just hope our arrival does not cause too much trouble for you, Mrs Greville.'

Bethany gave a strained smile. 'I've never been one to shy away from trouble,' she said, with a quiet determination. 'And I don't mean to start now.'

She rose from the table and affected as bright as smile as she could manage. 'I think it's time we thought about your quarters, don't you?'

But what to do with them? Her mind had been working on the problem ever since their arrival and she had come up with the only decision possible, as far as she was concerned. There were two bedrooms on the floor above. One was hers and Jack's; the other was done out as a guest room for the visitors they had never had. But somehow it didn't seem quite fitting to put them into the room next to her own. No, the two small attic rooms on the floor above that would have to suffice. They weren't up to much, but at least they would have one each and they were wind- and weatherproof, which was more than could be said for that old barn the guard had suggested.

'Well, if you follow me, gentlemen,' she said, 'I'll introduce you to your new home for the time being.' She gave an embarrassed smile. 'They're not exactly Buckingham Palace, I'm afraid, but being at the top of the house, the view's excellent.'

They followed her in silent procession up the steep stairs to the two tiny rooms in the eaves of the house, their feet causing the ancient wood of the treads to creak loudly with each step.

The landing at the top was wide enough only for one person, so she threw open both doors for them to see inside, then beckoned them to follow her into the room on the right.

The taller, younger one brought up the rear, and had to duck his head to pass beneath the lintel of the door which stood no more than five and a half feet high.

The air was musty and caused the older, smaller man to sneeze. Bethany rushed to open the skylight. There had obviously been no fresh air in here for decades. The window stuck and she stood aside gladly as the taller one succeeded in prising it open for her.

The rooms must been used for a family at one time, for each was equipped with a single wooden slatted bed, still with its straw mattress, squeezed against one wall; a small table stood beside it, and a bentwood chair completed the furnishings of each. They looked so old that perhaps they had been made for the original Lot who had given the farm its name, Bethany mused to herself. At any rate, the sparseness was even worse than she remembered, for she had seldom ventured up into the attics, and she gave an embarrassed shrug as she looked about her. 'As you'll see, they're not up to much,' she said. 'But I've no doubt the conditions here may be somewhat better than what a lot of men are enduring right now. My husband included.'

The comment brought a thoughtful silence and, as they stood there on the bare boards looking about them, a shaft of spring sunlight broke through the dusty pane of the open skylight above. It pierced the dim light of the room to fall on a rough wooden crucifix hanging on the wall behind the bed. It seemed a curiously touching thing to happen, and Bethany wondered if they felt it too, for it was not the most usual situation in the world for a young woman to be standing in her own home apologizing to the enemy for the drabness of their accommodation.

Horst saw her looking at the sunbeam on the wall and smiled down at her. '*Post nubila Phoebus*, Mrs Greville,' he said.

It sounded like Latin to her ears, but she couldn't be sure. 'I'm afraid I don't speak any foreign languages,' she admitted with a rueful smile. 'Very few English people do.'

'It means: "After cloudy weather comes the sun",' he informed her. 'That seems so true for us today in so many ways.'

Chapter Twenty-Two

Horst paused to wipe a bead of sweat from his brow and let his gaze fall on the slim form of the young woman working about a hundred yards away, where the hayfield bordered the old drove road past Lot's Barn. He had worked here on her farm for over three months now, but he still knew very little about her. Despite his excellent English she had not encouraged familiarity, either towards himself or Dieter, so the latter's progress in the language had progressed very little and for his own part he had been loath to risk a rebuff by appearing to expect more in comradeship than she was prepared to give. It wasn't that she was unfriendly, more that she seemed afraid, somehow; it was as if she were frightened that any degree of real friendship could be misinterpreted, and there were plenty of those around all too ready to do just that.

He knew that their arrival here at Lot's Farm had created a good degree of antagonism within the Greville household at Wolf Hall. Her brother-in-law, Amos, to whom he had had such an unfortunate introduction, had made no secret of his hostility at having Germans working on the land. Horst had seen him on several occasions around the place since then; with his familiar grey riding jacket and pronounced limp it was impossible to mistake him. He also knew that whenever Amos Greville paid a visit to Lot's Farm, there would be tension in the air and his employer would have a distinctly depressed look on her face for the rest of the day. There was something uncomfortable in the relationship between the young woman in whose employ he now was and the man who was her brother-in-law. Horst could not yet put his finger on what it was between them that had caused this situation, but the longer he lived here the more obvious it became.

He had also heard raised voices downstairs in the kitchen on one or two occasions late in the evening, as he had lain in bed in his attic room. On one particular occasion there had been a distinct clattering and the sound of things being banged into, as though a scuffle was taking place. He had been sorely tempted to go down to investigate, but as no shouts for assistance could be heard, he had resisted for fear his intrusion might be resented.

He had gone to his attic window on that particular night and had witnessed Amos Greville staggering towards his waiting horse. The man obviously had a drink problem and seemed to choose those nights when he had had a few too many to come round to visit his sister-in-law. Perhaps he needed Dutch courage for whatever he had to say or do. At any rate, Horst decided, the young man who now ran Wolf Hall was a pathetic figure and more to be pitied than reviled, despite his posturing and blustering and foul mouth.

It was obvious his crippled leg had prevented his call-up and perhaps this accounted for his bitterness and his particular animosity towards himself and Dieter. Their presence here must be a constant reminder to him of his failure to be out there doing his bit for his country, particularly with his own brother away doing his, and almost every other young man in the dale into the bargain. Yes, perhaps it was no wonder that Amos Greville drank.

He also seemed to spend most of his time in the saddle, which was just as well, otherwise he would surely have ended up dead in a ditch or injured, or done the same to someone else long before now had he been driving a car.

'You must excuse my brother-in-law,' Bethany had once been forced to comment diplomatically when he had even had trouble staying aloft his horse. 'He is having problems with his balance today. If that poor animal didn't know its own way home, heaven knows where the two of them would end up.'

Over the next few weeks, Amos Greville having trouble with his balance, as his sister-in-law so tactfully put it, became a familiar sight around the place, and when he was not in the vicinity of Lot's Farm itself, the sight of the caretaker owner of Wolf Hall and his pack of baying hounds tearing across the countryside became a familiar sight to the two Germans as they worked in the surrounding fields. The hunting season as such meant nothing to Amos, who would set off across the fields whenever the fancy took him, fox or no fox, and on two separate occasions he actually made a point of diverting the chase into the field in which Horst and Dieter were working. On the last occasion, less than two weeks previously, he had ground his mount to a full stop at Horst's side and looked down at him with such a look of contempt and pure hatred on his face that it had quite taken the young German's breath away.

'Can I be of assistance?' Horst had asked, quite taken aback, but feeling it important to be polite nevertheless.

'Aye, you can fall on that bloody scythe of yours and do us all a favour!' had been the reply. Then, after aiming a mouthful of spit at Horst's feet, Amos Greville had taken a piece of card from the inside pocket of his riding jacket and thrown it to the ground. It had landed a few feet from where Horst was standing.

Horst had looked down at it, uncertain quite how to react, as the Englishman glared down at him from only a few feet away. Then, with a cry of 'Halloo!' to his hounds, he had taken off back over the fields in the direction of Wolf Hall.

Horst stooped down to pick up the card and a cold feeling came to the pit of his stomach as his eyes took in the black edge to it and the drawing of a swastika at the top. At first glance he thought it might be English propaganda – a text vilifying the Nazi Party and Germans in general, but it was nothing so simple, and despite his excellent English he had never come across anything like it. It was only after the second reading when he got back to the farm that night that he realized it could only be one thing: it was nothing to do with the war really; it was a piece of literary black magic aimed personally at him. The thought both perplexed and horrified him and a shudder ran through him as he reread the lines in his room that night:

> Behold, saith Satan, I am a circle on whose hands stand the Twelve Kingdoms. Six are the seats of Living Breath, the rest are as sharp sickles, or the Horns of Death. Therein the creatures of Earth are and are not, except in mine own hands shall ye know which shall sleep and which shall rise. As it was, so it shall be that the Mighty Throne growled and there were twelve thunders that flew into the East. And the eagle spake and cried aloud: I am the deathless one who rides the whirlwinds. Ye will be driven from the House of Death, for I have prepared a place for you. Your time is nigh to join me in the Kingdom of Hell.

The more often he read it, the more the words both sickened and upset him. He had not expected to be welcomed with open arms on his arrival here, but this was more than simple anti-German prejudice. There was hate here, real hate, and an undercurrent of something he had never expected to find in this small, isolated community. This was England, after all – one of the most civilized countries on earth. But then he had thought the same about his own land until he had learnt better.

He had torn the card up that same night and burned the pieces to ashes in the small grate in his room, but the memory of it and the words he had read lingered, leaving a distinct sense of unease within him. It was not a happy thought knowing that someone could hate you enough to do such a thing; someone who didn't even really know you; someone who had never even had a proper conversation with you.

There was so much hate, so much misunderstanding in this world already, that encountering it at such a personal level was an upsetting and disturbing experience, particularly for someone who had never felt the least animosity towards the English and had done his best throughout the past few years to bring an end to hostilities between their two countries. And most upsetting of all, he knew that Amos Greville was not alone in his hostility. While his might be aimed personally, there were many others among the villagers who also bitterly resented the presence of Germans in their midst.

Within days of their arrival at the farm they had been the butt of quite a bit of stone-throwing by children and name-calling by both adults and children alike. In a close-knit society like this all 'offcomers', as the locals termed strangers, were regarded with the utmost suspicion, if not outright hostility, so what hope had they as Germans of ever fitting in? And the hostility was not only aimed at them, for the old man they called Carnforth had told him that his employer, Mrs Greville, was being shunned by a good many of those whom she had once called friends in the village because of their presence around the place. 'Spat on the ground she walked on, some of 'em did,' the old man told him. 'And called her some right names int' bargain!'

Horst listened with growing unease. That thought upset him greatly. The idea that a young woman could be being victimized for agreeing to their presence on the farm seemed so grossly unfair. After all, in their own way they were aiding the British war effort with all the work they were doing here. He had even tried to broach the subject with her on one occasion, but Bethany Greville had politely but firmly brushed him aside. 'Evil minds think evil thoughts, Herr von Karsten,' she had told him, with a weary smile. But he had noticed she had been even more unapproachable after that, keeping herself to herself both at work during the day and in the evening when it would have been the most natural thing in the world to discuss how things were going on the farm.

In fact, it was embarrassing really, for in her desire for privacy and to keep an invisible barrier between them, she had given over her front parlour to himself and Dieter for eating and relaxation, retaining only the large farm kitchen as her own private world. She would serve their meals in the parlour, with two places neatly set out on the oak dining table by the window, then she would retire to take her own food quite alone at the kitchen table. Horst was certain they must be the only prisoners of war in the whole of the country who got to use the best room in the house, while the owner was relegated to the kitchen.

There was no doubt, however, that she was personally grateful for their presence, despite the wagging tongues it had caused in the dale. Since their arrival Lot's Farm had never looked better. Within weeks all the stone walls had been repaired; the door to the shippon had been rehung on its hinges so it opened and closed with ease, and umpteen other little jobs around the place had been attended to, apart from the normal daily routine of a working farm.

To Horst's delight, he had even learned an amazing amount about sheep from old Sam Brookhouse since he had been here. At first the elderly man had been suspicious of both himself and Dieter, but gradually, after a real effort on Horst's part to win his confidence, the atmosphere had thawed and the old farmhand found a willing listener to everything he had to pass on about the animals he had spent a lifetime tending. 'For an offcomer – aye and a foreigner at that – you're a quick learner, I'll say that for you!' Sam had declared after less than a week of working together. Horst had beamed with pride. Old hands like Sam were as sparing with their praise as they were with their cash, so the elderly man's approval had meant a lot, and the marvellous thing was he was actually enjoying learning the new skills and knowledge required to run a hill farm such as this. It was a way of life he would never have come into contact with back in Germany. Von Karstens simply did not mix with struggling hill farmers, let alone dirty their own hands with such work. He wondered what his father and brother would make of it all if they knew. But as the days passed, Germany and his family receded more and more into the past and his new life began to absorb all his waking hours. He found he picked things up quickly and actually enjoyed the process of learning from the old hands around him such as Sam and old Warton Carnforth. He now prided himself in being able to pass on to Dieter the virtues of a flock of fine-boned, blue-faced, long-wooled Wensleydales as opposed to the larger, more stocky, white-faced Cheviot, or any of a half-dozen other breeds favoured by farmers in the area.

His arrival in the middle of the lambing season on the farm had been a revelation, for never in his life at Himmelhof had he experienced anything quite like it. To help bring new life into the world was both an intensely satisfying and very humbling experience, and he knew that as long as he lived he would remember these weeks, and how he had once sat up all night, at the end of a long hard day, and helped Mrs Greville bring two ewes through very protracted and painful labours, to welcome two healthy lambs at the end of it all.

There had been a peculiar closeness during those hours in the lamplight and cloistered warmth of the shippon that had made him feel that perhaps come morning the ice might have thawed a little between him and his employer. But no. Come daylight and the cold reality of another day, he found that the invisible wall remained, and no matter how much he would have liked to scale it, he knew there would be nothing for him on the other side. Bethany Greville had made it very clear she was a respectable married woman, whose husband was overseas fighting just such people as themselves, and while she was grateful for their help, it ended there. Theirs could only ever be a working relationship, nothing more.

Not that Horst would have dreamt of presuming anything other than friendship, he told himself. That was what he desired more than anything and he felt that she needed it, too. For his own part he still had Dieter, of course, but Dieter had been a small-time farmer from the cold flat lands of Schleswig, in the north of Germany around the Danish border, and Dieter's civilian life and interests were as far removed from Horst's own as could be imagined. He felt sorry for the older man with the kind eyes who spent so much of his time worrying about how his wife and family were coping back home on their small farm. Effi Hoffmann was in almost the same position as their employer Bethany Greville had been before their arrival. And she had four children all of school age to fend for into the bargain. And what was more, according to her husband, Effi had spent some time in a sanitorium for TB as a young woman and Dieter's eyes would mist as he told his young friend how he could feel in his bones that she would not be able to cope much longer on her own.

'When you have been as close as we were, you know these things – you can feel each other's pain, even though you are apart,' he would tell his young friend. 'I know what she's going through right now. And I know the work involved. She's just not up to it, Horst. God help me, she's not up to it.'

At such moments Horst would wish with all his heart he could think of something to lighten Dieter's load of worries about home, but they were all powerless. On both sides there was so much suffering, and that same rage he had felt all those years ago over poor Geli Rosenbaum still burned within him for the people who had brought this about. They were not the ones who were suffering – who were bearing the brunt of this awful war.

He was grateful to Dieter in many ways, for while Sam had instructed him in the specifics of hill farming, the older German had taught him much about the general work on a farm, so that in a very short time Horst did not feel quite such a fool when their employer was around. In fact, he decided, it was just as well that Bethany Greville did not speak German, for it saved him from many an embarrassing moment; half the time she thought he and Dieter were merely chatting in their native language as they tackled a job, he was actually taking instructions from his older and wiser friend.

Despite his lack of a proper education, Dieter was also sharp. '*Alles zu seiner Zeit*, Horst,' he had told him one day after observing him watching Bethany going about her business. Everything in its proper time . . .

Horst had given a rueful smile. Maybe Dieter was right. Maybe there would come a time when she too would feel the need of a friend, just as he did, during these long, lonely years that they were all enduring. And perhaps that was the greatest agony of war – the loneliness, the separation from loved ones, the deep, crying need for companionship, for a real friend.

As the days went by and he watched Bethany go about her tasks alone and sit so often by herself in the kitchen at night, he wondered if she too felt within herself that need for true companionship.

Although she was often around, he could not believe her sister Libby Denyer fulfilled that purpose. Despite the wedding ring on her finger, to his eyes his employer's younger sister was little more than an overdeveloped child. With her bright-red lipstick, powdered face and rouged cheeks, and her hair done up in the style they called Betty Grable, she looked just like a little French doll once owned by his sister Elsa. It was hard to believe she and Bethany were even related, he found the contrast between them so great. And in a way he felt sorry for Libby, for no amount of powder and paint could ever turn those plain features into the fresh-faced beauty that her elder sister seemed to take so much for granted. Yes, she must find it hard living up to an older sibling who seemed to have everything. He knew that only too well, for hadn't he grown up in his brother Otto's shadow? Otto who was everything their father had ever wanted in a son. But he had never envied Otto the way Libby seemed to envy her sister, and if he was right, and there really was jealousy there, he was sure Bethany was not aware of it.

Old Carnforth had told him that Libby had a husband called Will fighting overseas. 'But what the eye don't see, the heart don't grieve over,' the old man had added, with a knowing wink, and Horst had puzzled over those words at first, until they very soon became clear through the behaviour of the young woman herself.

There was no doubt about it, she had been visiting her sister over here much more often since their arrival, for Warton Carnforth had said as much, and whenever she did so she had never failed to seek Horst out to pass the time of day. At first he had been flattered, for any extended hand of friendship in their situation was something to be grasped gratefully. But he was quickly becoming aware that perhaps there was more than friendship on the young woman's mind. Of late she had been lingering much longer, as if waiting for him to say something – that special word or phrase that would be the key she was waiting for; the key that would open the door on a new

457

exciting relationship to brighten the dull little life she was leading between work in the local chemist's shop in Butterslack and her cramped, two-roomed flat a few doors along, above Webster's the ironmonger. She even took great pains to describe the place to him and tell him of how lonely life was there.

'This war has done awful things to us young folk, don't you think?' she asked in that confidential tone she adopted so often when there were just the two of them around. 'Folk like you and me, we're not meant to spend our lives alone like this. It's not right. It's not natural.'

He was not a fool, and the message she was trying to convey was becoming quite unmistakable. He asked Dieter how he should handle it, for he did not want to risk offence to either Libby or her sister, Bethany, if the latter found out. The older man had given a knowing smile and told him he did not see the problem.

'When you are dying of thirst in the desert,' he had told him in his clipped North German dialect, 'and someone offers you a glass of water, you do not refuse it in case it gives offence to someone else should you accept. No, my young friend, you drink your fill!' Then he had chuckled and given a rueful sigh, 'I only wish someone would offer me that glass of water, for I have been dying of thirst for three long years now!' Then he had shaken his head. 'Well, perhaps not. I have been faithful to my Effi for over thirty years, so maybe it is a bit late in the day to think of straying.'

Horst had smiled, but pondered on his friend's words. Maybe as a young single man he was being ridiculous in having such scruples. He was sure Dieter must think so. But the point was he had no real desire to begin any sort of sexual relationship with Libby Denyer. Perhaps it was because four long years of war had cooled his ardour for that side of things, or maybe he quite simply did not find her attractive enough; whatever the reason, it was a

458

difficult situation he knew was not just going to go away of its own accord. And his forebodings were to prove more than justified much sooner than he expected.

Chapter Twenty-Three

It was one evening when Horst was finishing tidying up in one of the outhouses before turning in for the night that Libby Denyer came out of the front door of the farm, on her way home to Butterslack, quite obviously resolved to give him the push she was positive was needed to get things going between them. Whether she had heard him rattling around in the outhouse, or whether she had enquired of Bethany as to his whereabouts, he did not know, but he got the fright of his life to find her standing there in the gloom when he turned from his task of cleaning the scythes for the next morning's work in the fields.

'Mrs Denyer . . .' he said, looking up with a start at the figure in the doorway. 'What . . . ?'

But he got no further, as she laid a finger to her lips. 'Libby,' she corrected softly, sidling further into the gloom of the shed and looking at him in a way that left little doubt as to her thoughts. 'I've told you before I don't care for this Mrs Denyer stuff. Makes me feel old before my time, it does.'

Horst straightened up, as the trim figure in the fashionable swagger jacket, pencil skirt and high wedge-heeled shoes leant back against the wall and eyed him up and down.

To many men she would have been quite a prize, but he prided himself in being able to see beneath the surface trappings. And, anyway, he had never been one for collecting sexual trophies. After those first fumbled attempts with Anna Marie in the foresters' hut in the woods at Himmelhof, there had been only two other real sexual experiences in his life: one disastrous encounter that was best forgotten with a prostitute named Lotte in Berlin, and one with a young, very pretty friend of his sister Elsa's with whom he had kidded himself at the time he might even have been in love.

'I worry about you, Horstchen,' Elsa had said, back in 1939, shortly after he had joined the *Abwehr*. 'At your age a young man should have a regular girlfriend. It's unhealthy otherwise.' So she had produced Karen: Karen Margarete Braun-Muller, known to her friends as Kari, who had been two classes below her at school. And Kari had been fun. They had attended all the right parties together and he had spent the odd weekend, when he was not working, at her apartment on Leipziger Strasse in Berlin. And it was in bed there one day that Kari revealed that far from him being her first or even second lover, she had dispensed her favours to half her friends' brothers over the past two or three years. The thought that a whole list of young men had also enjoyed on a regular basis – and might still be enjoying – what he himself was enjoying had been the greatest passion killer imaginable. He could never feel quite the same about their affair after that. It wasn't that he was old-fashioned in that way; it was simply that love had to mean more than that. Even sex had to. Or maybe he was just one of those strange people who found it hard to separate the two. And he was still having the same problem four years on as he stood in the outhouse of Lot's Farm and regarded the young woman in front of him with growing unease.

He continued rubbing the rust from the scythe in his hands and did his best to avoid her eyes. Politeness should be the order of the day, he decided. He must attempt to keep his distance – keep it as formal as possible. 'Can I help you in any way?'

461

'My, aren't we formal! . . . Can you help me in any way?' she mimicked. 'Well now, that depends . . .' Libby Denyer had a funny little smile on her lips as she continued to look him up and down quite unashamedly. Perhaps he was just shy, she decided. Some men were like that, and who knew what kind of straitlaced upbringing he might have had? Germany was a funny place, by all accounts. But Bethany had said he didn't act like a German — not like any they read about anyhow, who bayoneted babies and did all sorts of awful things to the Jews and other people they didn't like. 'Quite a gentleman,' Bethany had said. 'Keeps himself to himself and is not at all forward.'

Her gaze took in the lithe body bent over the implement and the sinews beneath the tanned flesh of his arm as he rubbed at the tarnished metal. Maybe all that he needed was a bit of coaxing. A bit of encouragement. Her heart began to beat faster beneath the thin material of her blouse. She had intended to make a move tonight — had even tidied up her flat specially. 'It's a bit cold in here,' she said, underlining her words with a theatrical shiver. 'Do you mind if I close the door?'

It was a warm — stiflingly warm — night, with barely a breath of wind, and what was more she was wearing a jacket. 'No, not at all,' Horst answered a trifle hesitantly, putting down the scythe and unconsciously running a hand through his hair. He was sweating now and could feel the perspiration trickling down the small of his back.

He watched in growing apprehension as Libby turned and closed the door. It creaked on its hinges and immediately threw the outhouse into an even deeper gloom. 'That's better.' She moved closer and leant against the wall beside him and he could smell her perfume; she was wearing lily of the valley. He recognized it; it was his mother's favourite scent. 'I came to talk to Bethany,' she said quietly, in that faintly petulant voice of hers, 'but she says she's too tired to natter. She's always too tired these days. You won't turn me away, will you?'

'Of course not,' Horst answered, with more certainty than he felt. 'In what way can I be of help?'

'I'm lonely,' Libby said. 'You know that. You must do. I'm lonely and have been for over a year now . . . That's how long it's been since Will got leave.' Her voice fell even more until it was barely above a whisper. 'Do you know what that can do to a person?' she asked, edging a few inches closer along the wall. 'Can you imagine what that feels like, spending night after night alone in a small flat with only the four walls to talk to . . . Only your pillow to hug?'

'It must be terrible.'

'It is terrible,' she insisted, her childlike voice more querulous now as she thought of all those lonely evenings she had endured since she last saw her husband. 'And I have had to put up with it for all these years . . . But there comes a breaking point, you know, Horst. You see your life – your youth – slipping away from you, and there comes a time when you just can't take it any longer . . .'

'And that time has come?' His heart was beating much too fast as he anticipated an answer he could well do without.

'You noticed! I knew you would. I knew from the start that you knew – that you realized what I have been going through.' She laid a hand on his arm, her slim fingers stroking the soft down of brown hairs. 'Horst . . . Horst von Karsten . . . It's a fine name – a strong name. It's silly and childish of Amos to make a fool of it and call you the Horse, for you're not a bit like a horse. You're young and lean – and sensitive to the needs of a woman like me.'

She was talking straight out of one of those American movies he used to see in Berlin before they were banned. It was pure *Woman's Own*, or whatever they called that magazine that her sister Bethany often left lying around the house and he would pick up and read for want of anything better.

Libby's fingers gripped his forearm, pulling him towards her. If she had to force the pace, she decided, then so be it. She wasn't proud. She was far too fed-up at the moment for that. Fed-up with seeing the best years of her life sailing past without an end to her predicament in sight anywhere on the horizon. 'Would you prefer we stay here, or go to my place?' she whispered urgently. 'We could go there . . . It's a risk, I know. But we would be more comfortable there and what is life if we aren't prepared to take a risk now and then?'

Horst looked down at her in the half-light as her face turned up to his. Her lips were parted, inviting him to kiss her.

'We are young, Horst,' she breathed, warming to her role now as temptress. 'Young and vital.' Her hand reached up to touch his face. He took hold of it, kissing her fingers by way of compensation as he backed off.

'I cannot come with you, Mrs Denyer,' he said. 'I am not allowed to leave the farm without permission.'

Libby drew back slightly, her upper lip curling in derision. What sort of reaction was that? 'Not allowed to leave the farm without permission! What are you, a man or a mouse?'

Horst said nothing as he let go of her hand. It fell limply to her side, then she deliberately wiped his kiss from the back of it as she took another step back.

'I'm sorry,' Horst said. 'But that is how it is. I cannot leave here. It is not allowed.'

'Not allowed!' Libby repeated scathingly. 'Not allowed! You're not a man at all! You're a mouse, that's what you are, Horst von-bloody-whatever-your-high-falutin' name is! You're a bloody mouse!'

Then she gave a laugh, a high-pitched forced sound that was more of a cackle as she added bitterly, 'Or maybe

Amos is right . . . You're not a mouse at all! It's a horse, that's what you are! A great big clumsy horse that doesn't deserve anything better than the bloomin' stable to live in. Which is where he says the likes of you should be – not living there in the farmhouse like Lord Muck!'

Horst made no reply, but let her have her say. He had embarrassed her and she had to vent her spleen. He felt sorry for her and the position he had put her in. It was not a pretty sight witnessing a woman scorned and suddenly he felt very weary inside that he had had to be the one to do it. Life was difficult enough just now without this type of thing to contend with. But his silence infuriated her even more.

'You know what they're saying in the village, don't you? They're saying that you're having it off with our Beth. And I wouldn't put it past you or her!'

This was too much. The English was colloquial but he got the gist of it all right. Anger surged through him, for Bethany's sake, not his own. They could say what they liked about him, and probably would. But not about her. He rose to his employer's defence immediately. 'No! That is not true!'

'Oh, isn't it now? I reckon you're a bit quick in jumping in there and denying it, if you ask me.' Libby moved towards the door, pushing imaginary hairs back behind her ear. Her face was flushed beneath the powder. 'I'd watch it if I were you, Horst von bloody Karsten. Folk round here can't stand the likes of you. And it wouldn't take much for them to let you know that in no uncertain terms. We're at war with you and your kind, you know. My husband is out there risking his own life to kill the likes of you! . . . Just watch it, that's all I say. Just you bloody watch it!'

Then she was gone.

Horst breathed a sigh of relief and leant against the rough stone wall for support. How long he stood there he was not quite sure. But there was no doubt that what had just taken place and what had been said had disturbed him. Until then he had chosen to believe that there were only the isolated few, such as Amos Greville and one or two others, and the silly kids who threw stones, who resented their presence at the farm. But what he had just heard confirmed what he had feared: it went much deeper than that. If what she said were true, then almost the whole community resented it. They were not welcome here in Utherdale. It was not a comfortable feeling.

But that was last night and this morning was another day, and a fine day at that, not a day to be mooning over what had been said in the heat of the moment by a disappointed young woman. Out here in the fields it was almost possible to forget the troubles they were all going through, whether here or over in his homeland where the bombs were falling, or in other lands where the battles were raging. Here all was as it had been for hundreds of years. In the cloudless sky above him, little flocks of peewits flew and larks soared, and along the lane he could see one of the first loads of hay being brought in from one of nearby Wolf Hall's fields. The old cart, weighed down by its bulky load, creaked and swayed its way along the bumpy surface, dropping wisps of hay on to the honey-suckle that weaved its sweet-scented way through the hawthorn hedges tht bordered the road.

It seemed incredible to think that had things worked out differently he might not be here to experience this. If his plane had not come down up there on the lower slopes of the Howgills, and that old farmer had not seen it descend spewing its black smoke from the engine, he would be lying up there still on that Cumberland hillside, just one more nameless casualty of this hellish war.

It had never entered his head his mission could fail – too much rested on it. Too many hopes – too many people's lives – depended on it. But things had been going badly for the *Widerstand* – the German resistance to Hitler of which he was a part – and especially for those of his colleagues within the *Abwehr* itself. His boss and friend Graf Helmuth von Moltke had been arrested in a Gestapo swoop in January. He had been rounded up along with several other of his *Abwehr* colleagues and those in a resistance ring centred around Hanna Solf, the widow of the former Ambassador to Japan. The arrests had created panic among those remaining undetected and had made them all the more determined that something would have to be done, and done quickly, to bring this war to an end.

Anything was worth a try, no matter how foolhardy it might seem at the outset, to get rid of that madman Hitler who was leading the whole German nation on a crazy dance to its own death. Although it was still treason even to whisper such a thing, and no one could be sure of trusting even their best friend with their opinions, as one of Helmuth von Moltke's closest colleagues and confidants before his arrest, Horst had grown increasingly aware that there were many others who thought as they did, and that somehow, someday soon, Hitler must be stopped, before it was too late to save their country from certain destruction.

He had even suspected that their boss, Admiral Canaris, the head of the *Abwehr*, was also anti-Hitler, but he had had no personal confirmation of this. It would not have surprised him, though. Many people, particularly those in high places and of the old Junker stock, bitterly resented Adolf Hitler and his henchmen, and what was happening to their country. Most of all, they resented the replacement of good Christian values with what they regarded as the totally immoral values of the Devil. From that perverted crooked crucifix – the swastika – that they had chosen as a symbol of their New Order, through their laws that flouted all human decency and natural justice, the

Nazi Party ideology was corrupt and it was time to make a stand against it before it was too late.

The decision to send himself and Willi Feldman, the pilot, on this mission was taken at the end of 1943, just before von Moltke's arrest, and only after much agonizing on the part of the innermost group of what had become known among those of the *Widerstand* as the Kreisau Circle. This small group, mainly from similar privileged backgrounds to himself and the Graf, met at irregular intervals on the von Moltke country estate at Kreisau to discuss ways of saving the Fatherland from further ruin.

The idea for his own mission had been inspired by Hitler's deputy, Rudolf Hess's ill-fated flight to Britain in May 1941 and Horst could remember the moment the proposition was put to him as if it were yesterday. They had been sitting in the conservatory at Kreisau, overlooking the sweep of green velvet lawns, and drinking a rummer of the Graf's finest vintage cognac. Helmut von Moltke had raised his glass and examined the contents, swirling the spirit thoughtfully around the crystal goblet as he said quietly to the young man opposite him, 'You too must head for Scotland, my boy. But unlike poor Hess, you will be making for nowhere near the Duke of Hamilton's estate. No, you will be headed instead for a large country estate in the Scottish borders. Balnadrochit it's called – halfway between Melrose and Kelso. Old friends of my own Scottish mother's family live there. They will act as go-betweens between yourself and British Military Intelligence. This mission will be of the utmost importance. It will act as a prelude to the plan now being devised by others of our friends here to put an end to our country's misery.'

Horst had guessed immediately what that meant. It could mean only one thing. And only that one thing could save Germany now. They were planning to assassinate the Führer.

The older man had looked at his young friend and colleague with some concern in his eyes as he took another sip of his drink. 'Will you do it, Horst? Are you ready for such a task?'

Horst had had no hesitation. '*Jawohl*, I am not only ready – I will be proud to carry out such a mission.' The thought that it might end as ignominiously as Hess's had never entered his head.

But even Horst, although party to it, was not privy to the full implications of the task he was about to carry out. All he knew for certain was that the assassination attempt was provisionally scheduled for sometime in midsummer. Exactly where and when this was to be carried out and who was to be the one brave enough to do it, he had no idea. All he was certain of was that the top-secret plans he was to present to the British Government regarding the cessation of hostilities once this had been accomplished were accompanying him on the plane, and his greatest regret and worry ever since was not knowing what had become of them after the plane crashed. It was something that had haunted him ever since.

Of the actual plane crash itself he could remember very little. From what he could gather, most of the aircraft had been burnt out and he could only surmise that the documents had also perished, otherwise he would surely have been interrogated far more than he had been afterwards. As it was, after a fortnight's intensive questioning by British Military Intelligence, he been left with the distinct feeling he was being dismissed as little more than a headstrong, idealistic young man who had been more intent on saving his own skin than in saving his country. That hurt more than anything, but you could not argue with the British, and – as they were quick to point out – he was in no position to argue with anyone at that point. He was, in fact, very lucky to be alive.

On the first night of their arrival at Lot's Farm, Dieter

had asked, 'How much do you actually remember about your crash, *Junge*?'

But Horst could only shake his head. 'Almost nothing,' he had told his friend. 'I do remember vaguely having my face licked by a black and white collie and hearing an old man shouting, but I must have been drifting in and out of consciousness, for the memories are all disjointed. They did tell me afterwards, though, that it was an old farmer and his dog that found me.'

Of the first few days that followed the discovery of the crashed plane he could remember very little either. Perhaps the local doctor who first attended the scene had given him something for the pain, and that had dulled his senses. And pain there had certainly been. Even now, all these months afterwards, he could still feel a nagging ache in his chest and abdomen from time to time, after exerting himself too much.

'You know what I regret most?' he had told Dieter. 'Apart from the failure of the mission itself, what I regret most is not being in a fit enough state at the time to thank that old man for saving my life. There's no doubt that if he hadn't spotted our plane falling from the sky, I wouldn't be here now.'

'And so one of the first things you will do when the war is over is to go back up to Cumberland and say thank you to the old fellow and give his dog a bone!'

Horst had beamed across at his friend. 'Why not?' He could think of nothing that would give him more pleasure. But saying thank you to the old farmer was only one item on his mental list of things to do once this awful war was over. 'I just hope we all live long enough to see that day,' he told his friend. Poor Willi, his pilot, had not been so lucky. From what Horst had been told afterwards, his friend had not even survived the crash.

Horst had spent the next few weeks in a special military hospital until his broken bones and other internal injuries were deemed well enough healed for him to be discharged. Several broken ribs, various lacerations to the body, and a damaged spleen had been the main problems but, luckily, despite his slim physique, he had been in good physical health before the crash and had made a rapid recovery.

Heaton's Crag had been the most obvious choice of where to send him, as the prisoner-of-war camp lay less than twenty miles from where his plane had come down, and it turned out to be far better than he expected. The regime was a fairly easy-going one and boredom had been the main complaint from its inmates.

For the first few weeks there, Horst had found himself suffering from an irrational sense of guilt for having survived the crash in which his friend had perished. But gradually this faded, leaving his sadness at the death of his pilot as yet one more unhappy memory of this awful period in his young life.

He had been at Heaton Crag for just over a month when the chance came to work on the farm and he had jumped at it. They wanted young men who had energy to spare and, once his injuries were healed, he had that in plenty. The thought of a springtime and summer spent in the clean fresh air of a farm was too good an opportunity to pass up. It was at this time of year, when the evenings were long and the earth was green, and the sun was molten gold in the clear blue of the heavens, that he missed Himmelhof most of all. There was a special magic to the countryside in high summer that he had longed to experience once again. He had missed that during all those years in Berlin, and how strange of fate to grant him his wish to savour those delights once more, not in his own homeland of Germany, but here in England.

So here he was. But life as an English farm labourer was not turning out exactly as he had expected. And there was no doubt about it, the worst aspect of it was the loneliness, for apart from Sam, who seemed to disappear for days on end when his lumbago was bothering him, almost the only person he could have any type of real conversation with was Dieter. He gave a wry smile as his shoulders bent into another sweep of the scythe – the only person apart from the likes of Libby, that was.

'Herr von Karsten!'

He looked up to see his employer on her way over to him, Glen the sheepdog at her heels.

Bethany's face was red with the sun and shiny with perspiration as she strode across the stubble of the newly-cut part of the field. She stopped a few yards from him and said, 'I'd like you to ask your friend if he'd mind beginning the field beyond the barn. We're nearly finished here and I'd like that begun before we break at twelve.' She glanced at her watch. 'It's just gone ten. It'll give him two good hours at it.'

'Of course.' Horst strode over to where Dieter was turning over some hay that had been cut the previous day and relayed the message. The instruction was met by a weary nod. 'If those are my orders . . .' the North German sighed. It would have been so much easier just to remain here and finish up than begin scything again in a new field in this heat.

'He'll be glad to go,' Horst lied diplomatically on his return, and they stood for a moment watching the middle-aged man wearily pick up his scythe and water bottle and head for the gate that led to the lane.

'Would you care for a cup of tea, Herr von Karsten?'

The question took Horst totally by surprise. How could she produce a cup of tea out here in the field? And anyway, they never stopped for cups of tea outwith the normal breaks. 'That – that would be very nice, thank you,' he said formally, but with a smile that left no doubt of his appreciation.

'Good. Well, I'll go and put the kettle on. Perhaps you'd care to join me in ten minutes or so.'

Horst watched in some wonderment as she set off back across the field in the direction of the farmhouse, her slim body blurred in the hazy sunshine, and the sheepdog trotting at her heels. He scratched his head and then stretched his back before setting back to work. A cup of tea indeed.

He was at the kitchen door in precisely ten minutes; just in time to see her pour the boiling water from the kettle into the brown earthenware teapot. 'Come in. You're just in time,' she said with a rather shy smile.

He took off his cap and had to bend his head to get through the door, to stand uncertainly in the middle of the stone-flagged floor. The room had a comfortable, homely feel to it, but he felt alien in here, as if he had somehow intruded into her own hallowed sanctum. His eyes took in the tall dresser with its colourful display of crockery, and the polished horse brasses on their leather straps, hanging on either side of the fireplace. Above on the mantelpiece itself stood a large photograph of a young man in military uniform. Her husband, most probably. He could not recognize what regiment or corps he belonged to, but he had a pleasant enough smile. In fact, he looked a nice person. A really nice person. He was happy for her sake, and his heart went out to her once more. It was not an easy situation she had been left in, and it must have been really hard trying to cope here on her own. The last thing she needed was any hostility from her husband's family and friends over his own and Dieter's presence here.

'Do please sit down.' Bethany indicated a chair on the other side of the table from her own. There was a plate with digestive biscuits and two mugs into which she proceeded to pour the tea. 'You're supposed to leave it to brew,' she said with a smile. 'But I like mine weak. I don't take anything in it, you see.' She could have added that they were all taught to do without milk or sugar in their tea as children. It saved precious pennies back then in the

473

Hungry Thirties, as they were now so rightly calling them. 'Please, make a long arm, as we say in Yorkshire,' she said, indicating the plate of biscuits. 'Do help yourself.'

She looked even prettier when she smiled, he decided, and it was not a common occurrence. At least not when they were around. There was a fragility to her beauty, despite the sunburnt skin and lack of make-up. Her attire did nothing to enhance her appearance. She seemed to live in that old set of dungarees. In fact, in the three months he had been here he had never seen her in a dress and he smiled to himself as he imagined her dressed up as her sister Libby had been last night.

As if reading his thoughts, she said suddenly, 'You're probably wondering why I asked you in . . . Well, it's about Libby.'

Horst let his mug of tea down with a clatter on the tabletop as he looked at her in surprise. 'Your sister, Mrs Denyer?'

'Yes,' Bethany said in a resigned voice. 'My sister, Mrs Denyer.' She paused, gazing down into the hot brown liquid in her mug. 'I'd better not beat about the bush, Herr von Karsten. The truth is, I suspect she may have formed some sort of crush on you.'

'Crush?' His English was good, but wasn't 'crush' what you did when you pressed something very hard?

Bethany gave an apologetic smile. 'I mean she appears to have become rather too fond of you for her own good – or yours come to that . . .' She paused, remembering the times she had caught Libby furtively nosing around in the attic bedroom the young German occupied, when he was safely out in the fields for the day. That was something that really shocked her, for it was something she would never dream of doing herself. She had tackled her sister about it, to get the immediate rejoinder, 'What harm does it do? I'm not pinching anything. You're always picking on me, our Beth. Lay off, will you?'

Bethany had immediately felt guilty. Was she really always picking on her? She certainly didn't mean to and, if the truth were known, she felt sorry for Libby with Will away. Her sister was young still and couldn't come to terms with the situation as she herself had done. 'I need to have a man around,' Libby would complain constantly. Then one day last week she had been more explicit. 'I can't stand it on my own,' she had said. And she had looked at Bethany with a strange expression as she added quietly, 'Don't you need a man around, our Beth?'

Bethany had laughed and exclaimed, 'I'll say I do, with all this work about the place!'

But Libby had frowned and shaken her head. 'No, I don't mean it like that. I mean, don't you miss . . .' She had begun to colour beneath her make-up. 'Well, you know what I mean . . .'

Bethany had stared at her and found herself flushing in return. 'Heaven help us – no!' To hanker after another man while Jack was away had never entered her head. Life was complicated enough just now without that.

'But you must get lonely.'

'Oh, aye, I get lonely, all right.'

'And it never enters your head that you've got a good-looking fella living here right under your own roof?'

Bethany had been quite taken aback. 'You mean Herr von Karsten?'

'Well, I certainly don't mean t'other!'

'Well, no . . .' The thought of making any kind of a pass at her German help appalled her. And heaven only knew what the young man in question would make of it. He looked and acted the perfect gentleman at all times. She looked quizzically at her younger sister. 'You're not taking a fancy to him, are you?'

Libby had shrugged and said a noncommittal, 'Happen.'

Bethany knew her sister of old. If Libby wanted something she would get it, by hook or by crook, and the concern she had felt about the whole situation then, she felt still as she looked at the young man, who now sat rather awkwardly at her kitchen table sipping his tea.

'I can see you are worried,' Horst said quietly. 'But you need not be.'

Bethany gave a weak smile. 'I wish I could be so certain! I – I'm rather afraid my sister may choose to make her feelings known to you in the near future and I want you to realize the consequences that could result if you responded in kind.'

Horst was silent for a moment, then gave a wry smile. 'You mean if I respond in the way she wishes I either get stoned to death by the villagers, or I get sent back to the camp?'

Bethany smiled. 'Something like that.' Her fingers toyed with the handle of her mug. She felt annoyed and exasperated with Libby for putting this genuine, quiet-mannered young man in an awkward situation like this, and she felt partly to blame for allowing it to get this far. She should have been firmer with Libby from the outset. But she always had been far too soft where any of her younger siblings were concerned. Perhaps it had been something to do with the fact that she had married out of the poverty which to a great extent they still had to endure.

'Are you married, by any chance?' she found herself asking Horst. It was none of her business, but somehow she wanted to know.

'No, I'm not married . . . But you are.' Their eyes met.

'Yes . . . I am.'

'Is that your husband?' Horst indicated with his head towards the photograph on the mantelpiece.

'Yes,' she answered fondly. 'That's Jack.'

'You must miss him.'

She nodded, a look of pain flickering across her features for a moment, then she said brightly, 'But I can't complain. This war is no picnic for anyone.' She gave a wistful smile. 'You'd think we'd have learnt our lesson in 1918, wouldn't you?'

> 'Goodbye, Nellie,
> I'm going across the main.
> Farewell, Nellie,
> This parting gives me pain.
> I shall always love you
> As true as the stars above,
> I'm going to do my duty,
> For the girl I love.'

He sang it softly to the tune of 'I Wore a Tulip' and she burst out laughing at the end of it.

'Who on earth taught you that?'

'My nanny. She was a wonderful old Scotswoman who, I think, lost her love in the trenches. Her name was Nellie. Nellie Morrison. I suppose that's why the song appealed to her.'

Bethany looked across at him, her interest obvious. 'Well, who would have guessed? You're quite a surprise, Herr von Karsten.'

'Could I ask you to call me Horst?'

'Oh, I . . .'

'Please . . . It will be the first time since I left Germany a woman has used my first name.' He deliberately did not mention Libby.

She smiled. 'I might just manage that. But only when we're alone, mind. And you may call me Bethany . . . But only when we're alone.'

'Bethany . . . It's an unusual name. A very pretty name.'

Her eyes lit up. 'My father chose it. It's a form of Elizabeth – my mother's name – and means "born in the house of poverty". It seemed appropriate at the time, I suppose.'

477

'You don't come from a family with money?' Somehow he had imagined that, to have a husband heir to a large house like Wolf Hall, she must have done.

'Oh no. My family were very poor indeed.' She spoke with pride and this touched him somehow.

'Poverty is no crime . . .' he began, but she interrupted him.

'Please don't quote the Bible to me,' she said with more than a touch of impatience. 'All that stuff about the rich man not getting into Heaven may be true, but I can tell you, Herr von Karsten, the poor man will already have served his time in Hell before he even gets there.'

Her words hung between them. She had spoken with such passion that it had taken him aback and she could see he was uncomfortable. 'I'm sorry . . . Tell me about *your* family,' she said.

His discomfort increased. 'My — my family are in . . .' He was about to say armaments, but changed it to steel. Then she surprised him once more.

'Like Krupp.'

He nodded. She was not stupid.

Then her expression changed as realization dawned. 'Von Karsten . . . of course! Karsten Steel! My God!'

'Please!' he protested. 'We cannot choose our parents.'

'But your family . . . It's one of the most powerful in Germany, isn't it?' She had read articles before the war about their factories on the Ruhr and how the head of Karsten Steel had taken on the trade unions and won.

'One of the most powerful?' Horst looked surprised. He had never thought of it quite like that. 'Perhaps. But even the very rich are poor in influence when we have a government like Adolf Hitler's.'

She looked at him quizzically. 'You are not a supporter of the Führer, then?' It was all too easy to claim that in his position. But somehow there was something about the way he said it that made her almost believe him.

478

'I have never supported the Nazi Party. They are not only destroying my country physically, they are destroying it spiritually. That I can never forgive.'

Bethany sat up in her chair. Despite her reservations, there was something about this young man that made her want to know him better. It was the first time she had felt that since her first night out with Jack. She felt she could talk to him and somehow he would understand. He seemed as many light-years away from her brother-in-law, Amos Greville, in character as it was possible to get. 'It – it must be hard for you,' she said. 'Being a prisoner.'

He sipped his tea. 'Yes, it is hard.'

'What is it you miss most, being in captivity, if that's not a silly question?'

'It is not a silly question,' he said slowly, as he pondered on his reply. 'And this may sound – may I say "silly" to you – working on a farm here, out in the fields all day as I do. But you really want to know what I miss most? It is being able to just go for a walk – a long walk. Back home in Bavaria, we have mountains that reach straight up to heaven . . . I can see them from my room, just as here I can see that small hill this side of the village.'

His eyes took on a faraway look as he continued, 'I look out of my window at that hill last thing at night in the moonlight, and first thing in the morning as the new day dawns, and I wish, oh how I wish, with all my heart, I could take a walk up there and . . .' He paused, searching for the right words. 'Well, just breathe free, I suppose, is the best way of putting it.'

There was a silence, then she said softly, 'That small hill as you call it is Uther Crag, and it means a great deal to me too.'

As long as she lived Uther Crag would mean both heaven and hell. Her own father was killed by it, but it was also the place where she had first run free and felt the cool Northern air whip the colour to her cheeks and send the blood coursing through her veins as she realized this was *her* land. She was as much a part of this cold Northern landscape as the very limestone out of which it was hewn, the stone that her father had given his life to; the stone that had taken his life in the end.

Tears misted her eyes as she looked at the young man across the table from her. 'You shall walk up Uther Crag,' she said softly. There were too many deprivations already in this world right now to deny him that small favour.

Chapter Twenty-Four

When Horst got back to the field, he felt as if he could at last see light out through the invisible prison bars that surrounded him. For the very first time since his arrival here, he and the woman he had known until today as Mrs Greville had reached across and touched one another. Not physically; it had been a meeting of minds, and that meant much more. And much, much more than what her sister Libby had to offer. A cynic might say he had simply been suffering from female starvation and was getting excited over nothing, and while that might be partly true, there was much more to it than that. He had sensed a kindred spirit hidden beneath that formal, rather distant exterior of Bethany Greville, and the fact that she had, for the very first time, been prepared to let down her guard – to treat him like a normal human being – was quite something indeed. He had to tell Dieter.

He knew his friend was working in the next field and he set off at a run to find him. The summer sun was warm on his face and running through the sweet-smelling hay brought back those long, hot summer days at Himmelhof when he would play silly games with Anna Marie in the fields – chasing each other round the haystacks and through the long, uncut meadow grass until their faces glowed red and the perspiration ran in rivulets down their backs. And then they would make for the bend in the river that skirted their land. There was a small waterfall there that was pure bliss to stand beneath and let the water cascade over your bare skin. It was just such a day when he had seen a young woman naked for the first time, and Anna Marie, with her pink and white, well-rounded flesh had been a sight to behold. Even all these years later, it was still one of his favourite memories.

A rabbit scampered out of the hedgerow in front of him and he found himself whistling that funny little song that was all the rage on the BBC at the moment, 'Run, rabbit, run, rabbit, run, run, run . . .' and then grinning all over his face. All of a sudden, because of one cup of tea and a short conversation, life was good again. How silly, how gloriously silly life could be, even at a time like this.

He spotted Dieter at the far side of the field, standing by the gate to the lane. He seemed to be resting his head on his arms. Horst called from about twenty yards away but got no response. He couldn't be asleep in that position, he thought, slowing his pace as he approached his friend. Maybe the heat had got to him. Dieter had been slowing up of late, showing his age. Although not yet fifty, two years of war and two of captivity had taken their toll and hot days especially got him down. Sometimes he would be quite worn out by evening. But this was still only morning; the day had barely begun.

'Dieter, old man!' Still no response. Horst shook his friend by the shoulder and slowly the older man turned his face towards him. Running in two furrows down his cheeks, through the dust and grime of the morning, were the twin tracks of tears, and the friendly open expression that was usually there had given way to one of such bleakness and despair that Horst stepped back, quite shocked at the transformation. 'Dieter . . .'

Embarrassed at this show of his own weakness, his friend turned his face away once more and Horst could see he was holding a piece of paper in his right fist; it was crumpled into a ball.

'What is it? What's wrong?'

Dieter Hoffmann shook his head, unable to speak, as he sniffed and wiped his nose with the back of his hand.

Horst gripped him by the shoulder. 'Tell me, Dieter. I'm your friend, remember.'

With his face still averted, Dieter handed the crumpled ball to Horst, who opened it out. The heavily wrinkled buff-coloured paper was difficult to read at first, but as he smoothed it with his fingers the message became unmistakable. It was an official form advising his friend of his wife's death.

Horst read, then reread the neat black typescript so there could be no mistake. Two lines of it there were; two clinical, matter-of-fact lines that could shatter a life in the few seconds it took to read them.

'My friend, I am sorry, so very sorry . . .' He gripped his friend by the shoulders with both hands and shook his head in despair. They had not invented words for a time like this. He wanted to hug him, to let him know properly how much he felt for him, but natural reserve held him back, and platitudes would be too easy, too trite.

Dieter turned away, staring bleakly out across the green fields and hills of this foreign land. 'She was forty-one, Horst. Only forty-one. Her life was not half over. It was this war, this damned war that did it. I knew something like this would happen. When they made me put on that damned uniform, I knew it would never be the same again for us . . . But somehow I thought it would be me. I was sure it would be me.' His throat tightened once more as he choked back the tears. It *should* have been him. Guilt and grief in equal measure overwhelmed him and, unable to contain himself any longer, he sobbed his misery into his hands.

Horst stood with his arm around his friend's shoulders until Dieter had composed himself enough to talk. And that was what he needed most of all. There was so much to tell, so much to share. To bring her back to life, if only in words, was to cling on for a few precious moments to that which had gone.

It was as if he needed his young friend to know all there was to know about the woman that had once been Effi Hoffmann, his first love, the mother of his children. And as they stood there by the old wooden gate, he talked too of their life on the small farm that had been their home, on the wide flat lands of Schleswig, Germany's most northern land, where the horizon was endless and they said when you looked out of your window in the morning you could see who was coming to supper. Her body would be lying there now in the parlour of their little wooden house, by the shores of the Baltic. They would be gathered around the coffin – Dieter Junior, Hans, Paul, Margit and the baby of the family, little Hilde, with her freckled face and long brown braids.

Who would they turn to now? Both sets of grand-parents had gone to meet their Maker long since. 'Who will take care of them, Horst?' he cried. And Horst had no answer. Who would look after his friend's children? Who was there left who could be both father and mother to them while their father remained here a prisoner in a foreign land, a land whose language he did not speak, whose people he did not love?

'What am I doing here, Horst?' Dieter Hoffmann asked bleakly. 'What perverse God has sent me here to tend the land of another woman, a woman whose language I cannot even understand and whose husband may be at this moment in my own land killing my own people – threatening the lives of my children? Are we taking part in some crazy game?'

Then he shook his head as a great bitterness welled within him and he answered his own question. 'Yes, it is a game all right. It is a game of life and death. But it is not the guilty who die. It is not the ones who started this crazy war who pay for it with their lives . . . Oh no, they sleep safe and well in their beds at night. It is the innocent who die. It is people like my Effi . . . God rest her soul . . . And I cannot even be there to lay her to rest. I am bound here in a prison without bars, in this land I do not love, amid a people who are not my own.'

There was such a desolation in his voice as he continued to stare out over the green fields of Utherdale that Horst knew no platitudes of his could ever relieve his agony. It would do no good saying how time was the great healer. Time was now the enemy. Time was what separated him from his home and children. And as long as this war lasted he would remain a prisoner here doing time for a crime he did not commit. For Horst knew it was not simple, good men such as his friend Dieter who were the criminals; the criminals were those who had started this war that was sending countless millions to their deaths.

'All I want is to go home, Horst . . . Just to go home . . .'

'I know, my friend . . . I know . . .' And as he stood there, Horst was reminded of a poem taught to him once at school. It was called '*Heimweh*' – homesickness – and he spoke the words softly to his friend in their native tongue, as he stood with his arm around the older man's shoulders:

> '*Ich kann die Sprache*
> *Dieses kühlen Landes nicht,*
> *Und seinen Schritt nicht gehn.*
>
> '*Auch die Wolken, die vorbeiziehen,*
> *Weiss ich nicht zu deuten . . .*'

> 'I know not the language of this cool land,
> And its ways are not mine.
>
> 'Even the passing clouds
> I know not the meaning of . . .'

Dieter was silent for several seconds as the words sank in, and the few lines brought a glimmer of hope to the eyes now seamed red with tears. He nodded his head slowly. Those words – they could have been written by him . . . He was not alone. Someone had known. Someone had understood. In this crazy, brutal world, someone had been been there before him. Someone had gone through what he was now going through and had survived. Never had a poet's words been more gratefully received, and by a man who had never taken the trouble to read a poem for pleasure in his entire life. '*Danke, Mein Freund*,' he said softly. '*Danke sehr . . .*'

The knowledge of Effi Hoffmann's death cast a cloud over the rest of the day and totally changed Horst's mood of elation to one of deep and impotent grief for what he knew his friend was going through. He suggested to Dieter that he go back to the farm to rest, telling him he would explain to Mrs Greville what had happened. But his offer had been refused with a weary shake of the head.

'What would I do in my room?' Dieter had said wearily. 'How would I rest? By sitting and thinking of my wife and my poor children – by suffocating in my own misery in that little room? . . . No, Horst, my young friend, Effi is with me out here in the fields far more than she is with me back there surrounded by four walls.'

But Dieter did go to his room directly after supper. Grief was an exhausting emotion and he had not been able to eat much of the fresh vegetable salad that Bethany had prepared.

He had spoken only once during the meal – a few words murmured to himself in a quiet whisper of desperation that matched the bleakness in his eyes and heart as he sipped his tea and gazed with unseeing eyes out through the parlour window. 'My children . . . Dear God, help my poor children . . .'

He excused himself after finishing his cup of tea, leaving

Horst sitting alone in the room. The younger man watched him go, and silently cursed the people who had brought this about: the inhuman monsters who believed that wars benefited anyone.

An old newspaper was lying on the arm of a chair and to take his mind off his friend's agony, Horst leant over and picked it up. Its headlines screamed at him: 'HITLER'S SS IN FRENCH VILLAGE OUTRAGE'. He gripped the pages until his knuckles showed white through the tanned skin. They were writing about the Führer Division in which his brother Otto was a Captain. And as he read on a sickness welled within him that was physical as well as mental:

Reports from our sources in France indicate that SS troops of the Führer Division have totally obliterated the village of Oradour-sur-Glane, sixteen miles from Limoges. Only seven out of more than seven hundred inhabitants are known to have survived.

It is reliably reported that at 1.30 in the afternoon, the SS ordered the entire population to assemble on the village green at gunpoint. The entire male population were then taken in groups of twenty into a nearby barn and shot at point-blank range. The women and children were herded into the local church, along with a large box of explosives which was placed on the altar. The entire village was drenched with petrol and set alight. Within seconds sheets of flame engulfed every building and, inside the church in which the women and children were held at gunpoint, the box of explosives ignited, turning the place into an inferno. According to eye-witness reports, women and small children, their clothing ablaze, were gunned down as they tried frantically to scramble out of the windows.

All that remains of the village, its church, and its people are charred ruins. Even the church bells melted in the intense heat. Eye-witnesses who entered the village some time after the atrocity reported the charred remains of some of the children were still visible, standing upright in the Confessional.

The SS Company Commander in charge stated afterwards that the action was a direct reprisal for the killing of one Nazi officer in the vicinity. But when pressed he then admitted they had set fire to the wrong village in mistake.

Horst was unable to read any further. They had not given the name of the Company Commander or of any of his brother officers, but they did not have to. He was almost certain one of them must have been Otto. Mass murder, that was what it had been. His own brother, whom he grew up with, and had loved, had once even admired, was a mass murderer who made war on innocent men, women and children.

Sick at heart, he turned the paper face down on the arm of the chair, then got up slowly to stare out of the window. His stomach churned and he thought he would surely bring up his tea. He could feel the hot sting of tears in his eyes as he stood alone in the quiet of the early evening. It was a peaceful pastoral scene out there, grotesquely at odds with what he had just read, with what was going on elsewhere in Europe. He felt almost ashamed of being alive, of standing here with food in his belly and a safe roof over his head. People were dying by their millions just now all over Europe. Innocent people, dying in their untold masses because of the megalomania of one man, a man who had once called him '*Junge*' and ruffled his hair as a child, a man whom his father and mother had been proud to call a friend. And he wondered what *Der Alte* would have made of it all, of the whole bloody mess that was now the Fatherland that he had devoted his whole life to, and had loved with a passion never felt for a mere human being, no, not even for his own wife.

'Herr von Karsten . . .' The woman's voice came from the doorway. Then a more tentative, 'Horst . . .'

He turned to see Bethany Greville standing there, and his eyes that had misted with thoughts of war, blinked in surprise. She was wearing a blue and white spotted summer dress and white low-heeled sandals, her hair tied back at the nape of her neck with a white cotton scarf.

She smiled, then glanced down as a faint pink blush rose

to her cheeks. 'You probably don't recognize me in a frock. But I thought I'd show you I do possess one nevertheless.'

'Please – sit down!' Horst said hastily, indicating the sofa a few feet away and feeling rather foolish to be offering her a seat in her own home.

'Oh no, I won't, if you don't mind,' Bethany said, then she hesitated. 'I was wondering – seeing as Mr Hoffmann would rather be alone this evening – I wondered if you'd fancy that walk up the crag we spoke of earlier.'

'Well, yes . . . Yes, indeed. I would like that very much.'

'Good, then we can go whenever you're ready.'

Horst did not need a second telling. This was just what he needed. He would surely have gone mad left alone here with the agony of poor Dieter and half the world on his mind. 'If you'll excuse me for a moment.'

He left her standing by the window as he dashed upstairs to smarten up. As he pulled a comb through his hair he could not help but wonder at the knowledge that he was not only about to enjoy his first real walk in almost a year, but that he was to be accompanied by a young woman, and a very attractive one at that.

He had barely recognized her at first, so great was the change in her appearance. Those terrible dungarees that she wore and that scarf she had permanently tied around her hair had given her an almost sexless quality and had given little indication of the pretty, slim young woman that lay beneath. But he musn't get too carried away, he told himself. This was no ordinary evening stroll; she was still his employer, and a married woman into the bargain. He must be careful not to overstep the mark and read into it anything more than what was simply a very thoughtful gesture on her part.

And so they walked together through the fields of Lot's Farm towards Uther Crag, and from a distance they were simply two young people out for an evening stroll.

Bethany deliberately did not take him by the usual path up past the quarry for fear of running into any local people who might have fancied a walk themselves in the cool of the evening. Instead, they took the long way round, past the small wood that skirted the west of the crag and bordered her own land. That way they would avoid even the village children who stuck to the quarry side for their games.

Although her companion had never complained, she knew that children as much as their parents could be cruel in their comments when those they perceived as 'the enemy' were around. She had seen them on several occasions, standing by the field in which either Horst or Dieter was working, and swinging on the barred gate while they called names to the two men as they toiled.

Some of them had even got hold of Amos's sarcastic pun on Horst's name and she had heard them yelling in that sing-song way of theirs: 'There goes the Horse! Gee-up! Gee-up!'

She had even caught one or two of the older boys throwing stones at them and had had some choice words to say on that particular occasion. But her intervention, when out of sight of Horst and Dieter, had only served to add to their fun. They had then turned their attention on her: 'Mrs Greville's a dirty devil!' and 'It's raining, it's pouring, and Beth'ny Greville's snoring. Went to bed wi' a Jerry instead and couldn't get up in the morning!' Her face still flamed to think of it.

No, the long way round was definitely preferable. 'It's longer, but safer,' she told her companion. 'We'll have the path to ourselves. And it's a fine night – the extra few hundred yards or so won't do us any harm.'

Horst murmured his agreement. It was a lovely night all right, and the air all around them was alive with the sights, smells and sounds of high summer. Although geographically quite different, in many ways it reminded him so much of Bavaria; there was something about the clearness of the air up here that made his longing for the Himmelhof almost unbearable, and a deep yearning gnawed within him for a time and place now long gone from this present life.

But somehow even that memory was now tainted. It was tainted by reports such as that one in the newspaper, lying back there in the front parlour. Nothing could ever be the same again back home after the likes of that. Not at the Himmelhof, not anywhere in Germany. For how would they look each other in the eyes again when this war was all over? It was a question he found impossible to answer.

As they passed the copse of trees that skirted the foot of the crag, the sound of birdsong above their heads brought Horst to a full stop in his tracks. And placing his hand on Bethany's arm, he said, 'Listen, do you know what that is?'

She listened, cocking her head to one side. 'It's a woodpigeon, isn't it?'

He nodded and the bird did a repeat performance, as if especially for their benefit. Horst began to hum in tune, then broke off with a smile. 'Did you recognize it? It's Beethoven.'

'Beethoven?'

He nodded and grinned. 'The first five notes of the woodpigeon's song are the first five notes of the after-storm melody from Beethoven's Pastoral Symphony. It's quite obvious when it's pointed out.' It was something *Der Alte* had once told him years ago.

She looked at him in wonder as the familiar sound once more filled the soft evening air. 'Beethoven was a wise man,' she said. 'You cannot do better than copy nature.'

There were wild fruit bushes along the path and they picked an assortment of berries to eat on their way. It was the first time Horst had picked wild berries since that day he had filled his pockets with fruit for Geli Rosenbaum, only to find he had eaten most of them by the time he arrived at the hut. He had spoken to no one in the intervening years about what had happened that summer, but so vivid did the memory now become in his mind that he found himself telling the young woman by his side. And Bethany made a sympathetic audience to what he had to say. At first she felt rather awkward and embarrassed, but within minutes she was totally absorbed in listening to him tell her of a life and lifestyle so far removed from her own. The thought that this gentle, personable young man she was sharing her home with had once had Adolf Hitler himself as a neighbour was quite incredible.

He gave a rueful smile at her comment on that fact. 'Someone had to live next to him,' he said matter-of-factly. 'And, anyway, we were there first.'

'I suppose so,' Bethany agreed. 'But, your family certainly moved in elevated circles, nevertheless.'

'Elevated? You mean because Himmelhof was built halfway up the mountainside?' Horst teased.

'You know very well I don't!'

Then Horst's smile faded. 'Elevated in some ways, perhaps. But lower than vermin in others.' Then suddenly his voice took on a bitter tone as thoughts of that newspaper article came back to haunt him, and all the other loathsome things he had had to learn of and accept that had been carried out in the name of his homeland.

And as they walked on he began to unburden his heart, to tell her of how ashamed he felt of his fellow countrymen who had let this happen to them. 'We never question – we never imagine as children that our own flesh and blood could be capable of such inhuman acts as are taking place all over Europe as we speak. On the contrary, as children we learn that our own families and friends are part of a nation that is the most just, the most civilized in the world. And we thank God that we have been lucky enough to have been born into such a society.'

He was silent for a moment and their pace slowed. He would dearly have loved to have had the courage to have told her about that newspaper report – to tell her of his sorrow and shame knowing his own brother had almost certainly been part of that atrocity that had just taken place in France. He felt tainted by the knowledge – as if he himself were somehow guilty by association. But his courage failed him as they walked together up the winding path of Uther Crag. Some things were just too painful even to think about.

He talked instead about his home in Bavaria and of his longing for a Germany that he knew had now gone for ever, for no matter what happened after the war, things could never be the same again. Bethany listened in silence and she knew that what she was hearing was coming straight from the heart. And his words both deeply moved and deeply troubled her, for no more could she think of this man as her enemy. His sensitivity and concern for what he knew to be happening were totally genuine and it seemed a cruel twist of fate that had made him her prisoner. Yes, in effect, that was exactly what he was. 'It's a strange world we live in,' she said as they climbed the last few yards to the top of the crag. 'A strange and beautiful world, contaminated only by the people who inhabit it.'

They stood side by side on the summit and it was like looking down on their own private world as the whole of Utherdale stretched out before them. Horst knew that the tears he had fought so hard against earlier in the evening were not far from the surface of his eyes as he gazed on the land that was and never could be his land. But he already knew how much it meant to the young woman by his side.

'I love this place,' Bethany said softly. 'I was born here and I will die here. It is as much a part of me as my flesh and bone.'

Horst said nothing, but felt it all. He knew exactly what she meant, for his beloved Obersalzberg had meant the same to him. Hitler had taken his people to war for *Lebensraum* – living space – as they called it, but there was space enough for all in this world. Millions did not have to die to give one people more land. God gave the land to all His people, whether they be here, in Germany, or in any country on earth. Land was land the world over. Only men made boundaries – frontiers that others could not cross. And sent young men, husbands and fathers, with guns and tanks to kill for those lines their leaders had drawn on a map.

His eyes searched the far horizon. 'I want you to believe me. I want you to know I hate this war,' he said passionately. 'I hate it with every breath in my body.' He hated it for what it had done to Effi Hoffmann, for what it had done to Geli Rosenbaum and her family, for those poor villagers in Oradour-sur-Glane, and for all the unknown millions that had already died, and were still to die before this madness was at an end.

Bethany half-turned and met his eyes. 'I believe you,' she said softly. 'I believe you, for I hate it too.'

At that moment Horst felt something pass between them – a sense of understanding that was almost tangible. He wanted to say more, but no words would come. They stood for a moment or so longer, looking down across the valley below them, then of one accord, they turned and began the slow, steep descent back to the farmhouse.

'Tell me about your husband,' Horst found himself saying, after they had walked in silence for a minute or so. But no sooner were the words out than he immediately regretted them. He was being too presumptuous – far too presumptuous. He glanced across at her in some embarrassment, but she was smiling.

'Oh, you'd like Jack. He's not at all like his brothers – either of them.'

494

'You mean he has another brother apart from Amos?'

'Oh, yes . . .' And Bethany's face softened along with her voice. 'There is another brother. Haven't you met poor Ned yet?' Why did she always prefix Ned's name with the adjective 'poor'? She felt immediately guilty and said quickly, 'Neddy's not half as daft as they make him out to be – not by a long chalk. He'll surprise us all one of these fine days.' 'A gradely, gormless bugger' was how she had heard him described often enough in the village, but Ned was more than that, much more than that.

'Ned . . . ?' Horst said. She couldn't mean that young man he had taken for the village idiot, who was always hanging around the place, hovering at a distance, as if scared to come too close? 'You mean that . . .' he searched for the correct English word as 'idiot' sounded too cruel. 'That simple young man with the smiling face is your husband's brother?' The one thing he had noticed about him was that he always had that fixed smile on his face.

Bethany sighed. 'Yes, that's our Ned . . . Jack, Amos and Ned. Each as different as chalk from cheese, but I reckon I got the best bargain by far in Jack.'

Horst looked down at her. There was something about the way her face lit up when she said the name Jack that made him envy this stranger – this young man he had never met and, had things turned out differently, might well have been friends with. How grotesque that fate should have decreed that young Captain – her husband – to be his enemy. 'What is he like? Does he look like me?' Whatever made him ask that? One day, he decided, he would learn to keep check of his tongue and not to embarrass himself like this.

'Look like you?' The question made Bethany smile as she cast a quizzical eye over her companion. 'Well, no, not really, although there are certain similarities. He's tall, but not quite as tall as you are, and he's heavier built . . . Yes, distinctly heavier built.' All those years in the Outback had turned an already well-muscled frame into quite a powerful build. 'And his hair is darker than yours and perhaps a bit curlier, and his eyes are brown, not blue.'

She continued to study his profile as they clambered down the path together. He had a finely-boned look to his features that did not quite fit with her vision of the square-headed, square-jawed, blond gods that the Nazis used on their posters. 'You don't look like a typical German,' she said. 'More French really.'

Horst smiled. 'I take that as a compliment. The French are a fine race and have produced some of the best thinkers the world has ever known.' And suddenly he was telling her of all his heroes – of Rousseau, of Voltaire and of all the other great humanist writers he had known and loved from his schooldays. And to his amazement, she actually listened – not just out of politeness. And she asked questions – questions that he could answer and expand upon, as they walked back, side by side, down the steep, meandering path of the crag.

'You're quite a revelation, Horst von Karsten, do you know that?' Bethany said, as he took hold of her hand to help her over a quite nasty rocky outcrop. 'You're not exactly the usual run-of-the-mill farmhand, are you?'

He smiled, and kept hold of her hand. It seemed right somehow. 'I am many things to many people right now, it seems. To my family . . .' he gave a half-hearted laugh, 'to my family, I suspect I am something of a disappointment. Getting caught – being a prisoner of war – it is not exactly a glorious way to do one's service to the Fatherland, is it?' He could just imagine the pride with which his father would have told his friends: *'Mein Sohn hatte die Ehre, fur den Führer und Vaterland zu sterben!'* ' "My son had the honour to die for the Führer and Fatherland" – now that's something my father could have boasted about over his cognac and cigars in his *Herrenklub*. But to have a son

496

stupid enough to get taken prisoner . . .' He shook his head. 'That is ignominy indeed!'

'You don't like your father, do you?'

Horst looked surprised. 'Is it so obvious?' He felt almost ashamed.

Bethany gave his hand a comforting squeeze. 'None of us can choose our parents,' she said quietly. 'I can imagine it's no easy matter being the son of the head of Karsten Steel.'

Horst gave a wry smile and concurred, then added with feeling, 'You know something I decided a long time ago? It does no good at all anguishing over who our parents or grandparents have been. How much more important to concentrate on the kind of human beings our children and grandchildren will be.'

She glanced up at him as his words sank in. 'You know, Horst, you're quite a philosopher!'

He shook his head and laughed. 'Not really. I have probably just had more time on my own to think recently, that's all. It's not everyone who gets the chance to be a prisoner, after all!'

She stopped in her tracks and, keeping hold of his hand, she turned to face him. 'You may be a prisoner in the eyes of the British Government,' she said softly. 'But you are simply a friend to me.'

Their eyes met and held. 'Thank you, Bethany,' he said, using her name for the first time. 'I appreciate that.'

His fingers tightened on hers as they continued the last few hundred yards of their journey, and they were still holding hands, although in a comfortable silence now, as they turned the corner into the yard behind the house.

'Oh my God!' Bethany let go abruptly, as through the gathering dusk her eyes looked straight into those of Amos Greville.

Her brother-in-law was waiting astride his horse outside the farmhouse door. He had obviously ridden over in the hope of finding her in and had been about to leave. The look on his face at what he had just seen said it all, and she thought for one awful moment he was about to jump from his horse and attack them both.

His mouth twisted into a word she could not hear, but could certainly guess at, as the horse's hooves sent up a cloud of dust and he galloped past them, his riding crop thrashing the gelding's buttock with more venom than was ever necessary.

They watched as he bent low over the horse, his right hand still working the riding crop, as the hooves clattered over the cobbles of the yard, then he turned and headed for the road that would take him back to Wolf Hall. When he was finally out of sight, Horst turned to Bethany. 'I'm sorry,' he said. 'I may have got you into trouble. I don't think your brother-in-law liked what he saw.'

Bethany shrugged and attempted a nonchalant smile. 'To hold a friend's hand is not a crime. And anyway, Amos Greville is not my keeper. He cannot choose my friends for me – or my enemies.'

He looked down at her in the dying light of a day they would both long remember. Despite her resolve and what she had just told him back there, life was not quite as simple as that. 'To your government and your people, I am still your enemy.'

She shook her head. 'No, you are not my enemy, Horst von Karsten. I have told you – you are my friend. My very special friend.' And as she spoke, something inside her told her, a real friend was what she needed most of all right now.

Chapter Twenty-Five

Dieter disappeared from the farm during the night. It was Horst who discovered his friend had gone, after knocking at the adjoining attic-room door to find out why he was not coming down to breakfast. After several knocks and no reply he had tried the handle and it had opened at once. The bed was neatly made and everything in order. Only the occupant was missing.

Horst had stood and looked around him at the sparsely furnished little room beneath the eaves that had been as much a prison as if it had had bars at the tiny window that overlooked the glowering presence of Uther Crag less than a mile away. What agony had his friend endured in here last night? How many tears had been shed for his dead wife and his five motherless children, as he sat alone in this confined space that was now home? And men did shed tears at a time like this. There was no shame in it.

Horst closed the door, and a deep melancholy pervaded his soul as the latch clicked into place and he made his way slowly down the narrow staircase. It was as if he knew he would not see his friend again, either in this house, or in the fields outside where they had toiled for so many long hours together in the past. Today and tomorrow, and for all the days to come in this foreign place where fate had decreed they must spend their days, there would be no Dieter to share his sorrows and occasional joys.

'I know what has driven him to it,' Horst told Bethany over his cup of morning tea, some fifteen minutes later. For the first time he was breakfasting with her in the kitchen. It did not seem strange. On the contrary, it seemed only sensible as they pondered over the situation they now found themselves in. 'It does not surprise me at all. He needs to get back to Germany. He was worried to death about his children, with Effi dead.' His voice was bleak and a deep sense of emptiness once more filled his heart as he thought of his friend.

'But he doesn't speak any English,' Bethany reminded him as she lifted the heavy brown earthenware teapot from its stand and topped up both their cups. 'Not even understanding the language, he'll not get any distance without being discovered. He'll get picked up immediately.'

Horst sipped the hot tea and frowned. She was right, of course. He doubted if Dieter would even make it out of the dale. But that did not matter. Even that was better than doing nothing. That feeling of helplessness he knew his friend must have endured since getting the news must have been worse than anything. 'He had to try. He could not have forgiven himself if he had not at least tried.'

Horst took another sip of tea, then sat silently looking out of the window, lost in thoughts of his friend. Bethany watched him with a growing sense of being torn in two. She found she could no longer think of these two men who had shared her life and work on the farm as enemies. They were human beings with feelings, with hopes and fears for loved ones back home, as any soldier had anywhere. What that poor man, Dieter, must be going through just now she could barely imagine. 'I'll have to report it,' she found herself saying, and hating the position she was placed in. It made her feel like a prison warden, which in essence she was. 'I could be in real trouble if I don't.' She studied a tealeaf swimming round in her cup then looked up and their eyes met across the table. 'But I won't let on to the authorities for a couple of days.' That should at least give him a head start.

Horst reached across and clasped her hand. They both forced smiles to their lips that belied the sorrow in their eyes. No more was said.

Bethany worried at first that Dieter's disappearance might mean she would not be allowed to keep Horst – that she would be deemed an unfit employer for letting one of her workers escape. But the official who arrived from the Heaton Crag POW camp three days later, to get her to sign the statement informing them of the escape, soon put her mind at rest. 'Don't you worry, lass, they'll not leave you without any help. But it might mean you're not top of the list for another worker just yet.'

'Oh, I don't mind that,' Bethany replied, unable to disguise her relief, as she bent over the kitchen table and scribbled her name on the line indicated. 'The one I've still got is fine. And after all, I had to manage without their help for long enough.'

The man patted her on the shoulder as he pocketed the official form with her signature at the bottom. 'How some of you ladies manage with your menfolk gone, I'll never know! By the way, did they tell you they got the beggar?'

Her eyebrows had shot up and she drew in her breath sharply. 'You mean Mr Hoffmann? They caught Dieter?'

'Aye – that's him – the one who did a runner.' He seemed surprised she hadn't heard. 'Didn't you know, then? Caught him t'other side of Sedbergh last night, they did. Reckoned he was making for the coast.'

Bethany's heart sank. Poor man. Only to get as far as Sedbergh. 'What will happen to him?' She knew Horst would be anxious to know.

The soldier put his pen back in his breast pocket and gave a shrug. 'Oh, jankers for a while, I reckon . . . That's back behind bars proper,' he explained. 'Then it'll be the recipe as before, except they'll not let him out on farm labouring again. Not now they know he's not to be trusted.'

Bethany said nothing as she showed her visitor to the door. Already she was imagining that poor German back sitting behind bars worrying himself sick about his children. She held out her hand as the man from Heaton Crag took his leave. 'Thank you for coming, Sergeant. You've put my mind at rest.'

'Thank *you*, Mrs Greville.' He touched his cap, then added, 'And a good afternoon to you . . . Oh, and just for the record, you've no complaints about the one you're left with?'

'No complaints.'

She made a special supper for Horst that night. She knew he would be disappointed that his friend had not got further than Sedbergh before being picked up, but in some ways it was also a relief that Dieter had been caught. The thought of him living rough, with no real hope of escaping the country at the end of it all was not a happy prospect.

The kitchen was fragrant with the smell of newly-baked bread and Lancashire hotpot when Horst emerged from his wash and brush up after the day's work ended. He listened in silence as Bethany recounted to him the news of his friend as she passed the plate of steaming food across the table to him.

'It has not been a good day,' he said quietly. He ate in silence for some time, his thoughts on Dieter, but Bethany had an uncomfortable feeling there was something else troubling him.

'You look worried, Horst,' she said, passing him the bread plate. 'Is it just Dieter, or is there something else on your mind?'

Horst remained silent for a moment or two, as if unsure whether to unburden himself or not, then decided that there was no point in hiding the truth. 'Take a look on that hook at the back door,' he said, tearing a piece of bread with his fingers and dipping it into his gravy.

Puzzled, Bethany rose and opened the back door to be

confronted with a very ancient but particularly vicious gin-trap, the type once used locally to trap rabbits, foxes and other vermin. 'Good God, where did that come from?'

'From just inside the gate of the field I've been working in,' he said, his face grim. 'It was a miracle I didn't step right on it.' He could have added how it was cunningly disguised beneath a sheaf of hay, but he refrained. The shocked look on her face told him she was already thinking exactly what he had thought at the time.

'Amos! It must be. My God, has he taken leave of his senses?' She had no doubt whatsoever her brother-in-law was at the back of it. 'That thing could have had your leg off at the ankle – or it could have got Glen!' The thought of either him or her beloved dog being the victim of that thing horrified her, and her face was white with shock as she closed the door on the offending item and looked across at Horst. 'They're lethal, those things are.'

'I know,' he said. 'We used to have similar ones on our estate in Bavaria.' He gave a mirthless smile as he dabbed his bread in the gravy once more. 'I think your brother-in-law is trying to tell me something, don't you?'

'He hates you,' Bethany said quietly. 'He hates you because your being here means he can't just come and go as he likes. He knows if he tried to start anything . . . anything like you saw that day of your arrival, you'd never stand for it. You didn't then and you certainly wouldn't now. And he hates you even more now it has become common knowledge that Dieter has gone.' She shivered although the evening was warm. 'I'm frightened, Horst. I'm really frightened for your sake.'

Horst put down his knife and fork and looked at her, then he got up from the table and came across to where she was standing. He put his hands on her shoulders and looked down at her. There was the glisten of tears in her eyes as she looked up at him. He drew her closer, till her cheek was resting on his shoulder and he stroked her hair.

It smelt sweet and clean in his nostrils and felt like the smoothest silk beneath his work-callused hand. Just holding her, touching her, seemed to renew his strength, his hope for the world. In her slight body, she seemed to personify all that was still good in the world, all that was good and strong, yet gentle and just. She trembled in his arms and he clasped her closer. 'You must not worry,' he said softly. 'I am here. No one is going to harm you – or me.'

Then his eyes looked up and straight into those of the young man in the Captain's uniform in the photograph on the mantelpiece. Her husband. Jack Greville's dark gaze made him look away. No matter how much he might wish it otherwise, she was not only another man's wife, but fate had decreed that he was that man's enemy. He had read stories of women in other countries, like France, who had consorted with the enemy and had had terrible things done to them – and often by those who had been their friends and neighbours. He held her closer, as if to give her strength – to give them both strength. It felt so right to be holding her in his arms. He buried his face in her hair, then slowly, gently, he prised her body away from his as his conscience got the better of him. 'Look,' he said, attempting a smile he did not feel. 'Our food is getting cold. And after all your hard work in making it, I think we'd better finish our meal, don't you?' For just a fleeting second he thought he saw a flicker of disappointment in her eyes.

They sat together in the kitchen that night, Bethany knitting and Horst mending and sharpening knives and threshing implements as they listened to the radio. They talked little, but each drew comfort from the nearness of the other. There was a report from London, where the German V-1 bombs they were nicknaming 'Doodle Bugs' were terrorizing the population. Thousands of mothers and children were being evacuated to the rural areas, and farmers and other country dwellers all over Britain were being asked to open their homes to them. 'You might be asked to take some people in,' Horst said, after listening to an outside broadcast with some evacuees from London's King's Cross Station. 'Would you mind?'

Bethany looked up from her knitting and met his eyes. Would she mind? A few short months ago she would have been delighted at the prospect of company, but not now. Definitely not now. A curious feeling had been growing within her for this young man on the other side of the fireplace from her. No matter how much she tried to deny it to herself, it was there and she knew he could sense it too. Perhaps he even felt it too. She could feel her cheeks colour and dropped her eyes to the knitting in her lap. She was silent for a moment. Should she lie? 'Yes, I would mind,' she answered softly. 'Wouldn't you?'

Her words hung in the air between them and she could feel gooseflesh cover her skin as he laid down the knife he was holding and got up slowly from his stool. She could feel her fingers stiffen on the knitting needles in her hands as he came towards her.

Now he was standing over her, looking down at her, but she dared not look up. She dared not meet his eyes.

'Stand up,' he said softly, holding out his hand. His heart was racing. For the past two hours he had been wrestling with his feelings. He knew it was wrong. Dear God, it was wrong. It was a sin in the eyes of the Church and the world. But then, out of all the great sins being committed in the world right now, was theirs such a very great one? Was feeling this way about another human being really so terrible? 'Stand up,' he repeated, his voice huskily low.

Her knitting dropped to her feet as she obeyed.

She was trembling as he took her face in his hands and lifted it up so their eyes met. She was aware of thinking how blue, how deep, dark-blue his were, before their lips met.

His kiss was soft and very gentle, as if she were some

505

fragile china figure that might at any moment shatter into a thousand pieces; then as her body began to thaw in his arms, his lips became harder, his kiss became stronger, more urgent, and then she was kissing him back, making little moaning sounds in her throat as his lips moved over her face and down the pale arch of her neck. Her hands moved up behind his head, her fingers moving through the short brown hair, then caressing the faint stubble of his cheeks as tears began to well in her eyes. She didn't know why she was crying. Was it out of happiness? Or despair? Or even guilt?

'*Endlich . . . Endlich . . .*' His lips were moving over her face as he murmured words of love in German that she could only guess at. 'Bethany, *meine Liebe . . . Endlich . . .*'

She buried her face in his shoulder as he carried her through to the bedroom and laid her on the soft quilt of the bed. Then he lay down beside her and held her in his arms. He did not ask why she was crying. He understood. He was crying too, inside. He merely lay there, with her head in the curve of his shoulder, his long fingers stroking her wet cheek as he murmured words of consolation in his own tongue. '*Fur tausend bittere Stunden sich mit einer einzigen trosten, welche schon ist . . .*' For a thousand bitter hours, take comfort in one that is sweet . . . And his heart wept silent tears for those countless thousands of bitter hours; and for those countless thousands, millions perhaps, who had died in this futile war, and who were out there dying now as they lay here together and savoured the sweetness of this moment.

They were still lying there as the sky beyond the net curtain grew dark. He did not attempt to make love to her. It would have been quite wrong somehow. What they needed most right now was each other. But not in that way. Not yet . . .

Dawn came early, filling the small bedroom with a hazy yellow light. Bethany awoke first, and for a moment she thought it was Jack's head there on the pillow next to her own. But the tousled lock that fell across the closed eyes was not so dark a brown, and the mouth on which the ghost of a smile played was not so full. He was still fast asleep, but at least it must be a good dream, she thought as she lay there unwilling to move and break the spell.

There was a peace about this time of day, when the first rays of the morning sun lit the wall against which rested the head of the old oak bed. It was a moment she used to savour when Jack had been at home, for she was always the first one to wake up, and she would lie here and think how lucky she was to have a man like him beside her.

But this morning there was another man's head on the pillow. Another man with whom she had known a closeness, a kinship, that she had never shared with another human being. His gentleness, his understanding, was something she had never known before, not even with Jack. No, not even with Jack.

She moved her head slightly on the pillow and rested her eyes on his face. It was a gentle face, a kind face, that mirrored the sensitivity within. There was the bluish shadow of morning stubble on his cheeks and his skin glistened with the faint sheen of perspiration. It had been a warm, humid night and he was still fully clothed; they both were, and a great feeling of tenderness overwhelmed her for this young man who had come to mean so much. She thought of Amos and the brute force with which he had tried to make her his and contrasted it with the tenderness she had known in this man's arms. He could have made love to her last night. If he had insisted, she doubted if she would have had the will to refuse. And it would not have felt wrong, for how could love if freely given and gladly accepted ever be wrong? But he had not done so. He had known, as she did, that what they were feeling – the love that was growing between them – was still too new, too fragile a thing to risk by making rash decisions.

Quietly she slipped from the bed and went to the mirror of her dressing table to tidy her hair. In the glass she could see him still lying there, his breathing steady and even, like a child's. She smiled tenderly at his sleeping figure as she pulled the brush through her tangled locks.

When she had finished, she got up from the dressing stool and looked down at him, and as she stood there at the side of the bed, his eyes opened. He blinked in the light, then returned her smile.

He held out his hand and she took it, sitting down on the edge of the bed beside him. There was a tenderness in his eyes that brought tears to her own and she had to look away. Her gaze dropped to the long, tanned fingers encircling her own and, gently, she stroked the palm of his hand with her thumb. Then her brow furrowed as she noticed the white, shiny skin where once a lifeline had been. She touched the old wound with her fingertips and glanced up to meet his eyes once more.

'The brand of Karsten Steel,' he said softly. 'Their fires burn all who bear this name, one way or another.'

'Will you go back?' she asked. 'When the war is over, will you return to Berlin and your family?' She hardly dared breathe as she waited for his answer. It was a long time in coming, and was prefixed by a question of his own.

Somehow he knew he could not lie to her – not now. Not ever. 'Would you want me to?' he asked softly, his fingers tightening on hers.

She tensed and the tears that had been hovering behind the surface of her eyes, glistened in the light from the window as she gave a helpless shrug of her shoulders. 'I – I should say, yes. It is right for you to return – to go back to Germany . . .'

'But . . . ?'

'But I can't.' A pinkness coloured the skin of her neck as a blush crept up to flush her cheeks as she looked across at him. 'God help me, I can't.'

She extricated her hand from his and rose quickly to look out the window as it all became too much. 'I'm a married woman,' she said in a tired voice. 'And I'm married to a good man – a fine man . . .'

He rose to stand behind her, his hands resting on her shoulders as they both gazed out across the fells, now bathed in the full glow of the early-morning sun. 'You don't have to remind me,' he said softly. 'But that does not alter anything, does it?'

She shook her head. How could it? How could you stop yourself from falling in love? 'I've never really been in love before,' she found herself saying, and she knew it to be the truth. What she had felt for Jack had been nothing like this. There was a bond between herself and this young German that made her next question almost irrelevant, but she had to ask it all the same, 'Have you?'

'No, I have never been in love before.' His fingers tightened on her shoulders and gently he turned her towards him.

'Tell me what to do, Horst,' she implored him. 'Tell me what is to become of us.'

He drew her towards him, and he stroked her hair as her head rested on his shoulder. What answer could he give? What could he say to relieve her of the question that was plaguing his own heart? 'Only God has the answer to that question, *mein Schatz*,' he said softly.

'Maybe it's the war,' she heard herself saying. 'Maybe it makes people imagine things that would not be there had they met under normal circumstances.' She was trying to rationalize it, for both their sakes.

Horst shook his head as he prised her away from him and looked down into her eyes. 'Do you really believe that? Do you really believe if we had met six years ago we would not have felt the same?'

She gazed at his face; every line, every feature was now so familiar. It was as if she had known him all her life. And

509

she knew without a shadow of a doubt, she wanted him near her for the rest of it. She wanted him just as much as she knew he wanted her. She wanted him, never to let him go again. Never, never . . .

Her hand reached up touch his cheek, then it froze in mid-air. 'What was that?'

'What was what?'

She stiffened. 'That noise. Did you hear it? I'm sure there was a knock at the door.'

Horst was about to deny hearing any noise when it occurred again. Three faint taps of the brass knocker on the front door downstairs. They looked at one another. 'Who on earth can that be at this time?' Bethany glanced at her watch. It was just after seven. 'You'd better stay here,' she said, making for the door. 'I'll yell if I need you.' She had little doubt who it would be.

Horst grabbed hold of her arm. 'No, you don't!' he commanded. 'You may be my boss on the farm, but I am taking charge for once. You are staying here. *I'll* shout if *I* need *you*.'

She was about to protest but he was already on his way, making for the bedroom door. She could hear his stockinged feet padding on the staircase as the knocker rattled once more. If it really was her brother-in-law he would have him to face first and the thought sent her heart racing. Amos Greville drunk or sober was someone to be reckoned with.

Horst braced himself for the worst, but when he threw the door open his brow creased in confusion. It was not Amos Greville standing there, but a clergyman. A grey-haired man in late middle age stood on the step, obviously as surprised as he was to see someone he had not been expecting to encounter.

But the stranger composed himself immediately, glancing behind Horst's shoulder into the small hall beyond. He had been expecting Bethany herself to answer his knock and the sight of the young German momentarily disconcerted him, although he did his best not to show it. 'I've come to speak to Mrs Greville,' the Reverend Kenneth Barden said stiffly. 'Who might you be?' He was only too well aware who Horst was, but he wanted it confirmed before he went any further.

Horst held out his right hand. 'My name is Horst von Karsten,' he answered politely. 'I am employed here on the farm by Mrs Greville.'

Then, much to his surprise, the clergyman ignored his extended hand and all but pushed his way past him to enter the house.

'Bethany!' Kenneth Barden's voice, a tone higher than usual, called impatiently upstairs, as he stood at the foot and pointedly ignored the figure of Horst still standing by the door.

Bethany appeared at the top of the stairs and stared down in some surprise. 'Ken! I didn't expect you!'

Her mother's husband made no reply but his expression left his thoughts in no doubt.

'Is anything wrong?' Bethany asked anxiously as she came hurrying down the stairs to join them.

'That depends.'

The enigmatic reply, delivered through thin lips, seemed to echo in the quiet of the morning air as all three walked into the kitchen.

'I'll put the kettle on,' Bethany said, indicating for the others to take a seat. 'Then you can tell me what brings you here at this ungodly time of day – if you'll excuse the expression!'

Kenneth Barden did not return her smile as he said solemnly, 'I'm sorry to appear on your doorstep so early in the morning but I wanted to catch you before you went out to the fields.' He could have added that he had just endured a sleepless night with a wife distraught at what she perceived to be a situation with her elder daughter

511

that was getting out of hand and, in order to keep the peace, he had promised to pay Lot's Farm a visit the first thing after breakfast.

'It must be important.'

'It is.'

Bethany placed the kettle on the fire and took a deep breath as she sat down at the table across from him. 'OK. Let's be having it.'

Her stepfather looked deliberately at Horst. 'What I have to say is something of a private matter.'

Bethany stiffened in her chair. 'I'm sure Mr von Karsten here can be trusted,' she said, glancing across at Horst.

'I would prefer it if he went while we spoke.'

Horst rose to go, but Bethany held up a restraining hand. 'No, Horst, stay where you are!' She turned back to her stepfather. 'I told you, Ken, anything you have to say to me you can say in front of Horst. I have no secrets – nothing to be ashamed of.'

'That's not what they're saying in the village.'

Bethany's heckles rose immediately. 'And just what might that mean? Just what exactly *are* they saying in the village?'

Kenneth Barden looked distinctly uncomfortable; this wasn't how he had envisaged the conversation going at all. And to have to sit here explaining himself with the German present. He took a deep breath. 'This is a delicate matter for me, Bethany. Not easy at all.' He glanced across at Horst once more, who was now leaning forward in his seat, anxious to hear exactly what this was all about. 'You see, it concerns this gentleman here.'

'You mean Mr von Karsten, my employee?'

Kenneth Barden nodded. 'Aye, if that's all he is.'

'Ah-ha!' It was just the innuendo she was waiting for. Bethany rose from her seat, to stand hands on hips looking across at her stepfather. 'So that's it, is it? Dirty tongues have been wagging. Who was it this time, Ken? Was it my dear brother-in-law again, or are they all at it by now?'

'Amos is only one party who's upset,' Kenneth Barden said defensively. 'There's more than him concerned with how things are up here. Especially now that the other chap – that older fella – has gone and there's only the two of you left in the house. It's not right. Not right at all. I tell you, Bethany, there's a lot of ill feeling down there in the village over this situation. They thought a lot of Jack, you know. And what with him off doing his duty . . . Well, they don't take kindly to this. They don't take kindly to it at all.'

Bethany's colour rose with her voice. 'Don't take kindly to what, may I ask?'

It was Kenneth Barden's turn to rise from his seat now, as he nervously got up and took a step back towards the door. He swallowed, his Adam's apple protruding above his dog-collar as he cleared his throat. There was no good in beating about the bush. He might as well come out with it. After all, he had promised her mother he would put it to her straight, and Betty would want to know what had been said, word for word, when he got back to the vicarage. 'Cohabiting, I believe is the word most often used.'

Bethany hooted. 'Co-hab-it-ing!' she mimicked. 'So that's what's being said, is it? That, I very much doubt! They wouldn't waste breath on fancy words like that in Utherdale. Isn't "bedded-up" the expression they're using, Ken? Or "having it off"? Or . . .'

'Bethany, please!' Kenneth Barden's face had gone quite red. He hated this sort of thing, but because of his profession he always seemed to be the one called upon to do it. The conscience of the Parish was what he was supposed to be, his wife had once informed him – and even when the conscience that needed pricking was within his own family, it was a duty he could not shirk.

513

'I'm only reporting what gets back to me, Bethany love, and I wouldn't have come except it's upsetting your mother. She's been getting more agitated by the day. Hardly a wink's sleep either of us got last night . . . You're all right, up here at the farm. You're not down there in the village, having to take it all. There's never a day goes by but she gets something said to her, either in the shops or stopped in the street, and it can't go on. The whole thing's getting out of hand. There's even talk of a deputation getting up in the village to come up here and . . .'

'And what, Ken? Run Horst out of town? Or me? Or both of us?' Bethany gave a bitter laugh. 'There's going to be a showdown, is there – just like in those Hollywood pictures? Well, let them try, that's all I can say – just let them try!'

Horst, who had been listening with a look of growing concern on his face, now got up, so all three were standing in the middle of the kitchen floor. 'Perhaps I have no right to speak,' he said. 'But from what I can understand this is something directly to do with me – with my friendship with Mrs Greville here. What exactly are they saying in the village? Can you tell me, please?'

Kenneth Barden looked him straight in the face and said very slowly and deliberately, 'To put it quite brutally, Mr von Karsten, they are saying that you and my stepdaughter here are – are . . .' He paused, unwilling to say the actual word. 'Well, you can't deny you are living here under the same roof. That you have your feet under the table, as the saying goes.' He glanced down meaningfully at Horst's stockinged feet. 'There seems to be no question of you living in the barn or elsewhere.'

'Yes,' Horst confirmed. 'That is true. We are living in the same house. My bedroom is in the attic and Mrs Greville's in on the first floor. Are you saying that is not so?'

'No, I'm not denying that,' Kenneth Barden said impatiently. 'It's easy enough to claim you have separate bedrooms. But you have legs and folks round here have imaginations – vivid ones at times.' He looked imploringly at Bethany. 'I'm not saying there's anything improper been going on between the pair of you. It's not for me to sit in judgement – only the Lord God Almighty can do that. All I'm saying is, there's talk. Lots of it. And a great deal of ill feeling into the bargain. In short, it's a situation that can't go on.'

Bethany bristled. 'And if it does?'

'If it does, I'll not be responsible for what might happen.' He was backing towards the door as he spoke. 'But you can't say I didn't warn you, Bethany love. You can never say that.'

Placing his hat back on his head, and with a cursory nod in Horst's direction, he turned and left the house.

The outside door rattled on its hinges, leaving Bethany and Horst looking at one another in the silence of the kitchen. For a second or two neither spoke, and the only sound was the longcase clock ticking beyond the open kitchen door, in the hall beyond. Then Horst held out his arms and Bethany rushed into them.

'It's you and me against them,' she whispered into the rough cotton of his shirt. Then she shivered and closed her eyes.

Horst held her tightly to him as, from the mantelpiece beyond, a pair of eyes stared down at him from beneath the peaked cap of a British Army officer. Those damned eyes seemed to see everything. They were always there, accusing him, reminding him she was another man's wife. *His* wife. His enemy's wife. And he shouldn't care, but he did. God help him, he did.

Chapter Twenty-Six

Kenneth Barden's visit cast a cloud that both Bethany and Horst found hard to disperse, so at Horst's prompting, Bethany decided to pay her mother a visit at the vicarage two days later. Leaving it for two days was just about right, she decided; it showed she had nothing to feel guilty about – there was nothing going on at Lot's Farm to cause her to rush back to the bosom of her family to confess.

But when the time actually came to get on her bicycle and head for the vicarage, things seemed slightly different. More than anything, she hated talking about her private life, whether she had reason to feel guilty or not. As she pedalled the two miles along the rutted lane that led to the village, the clouds that were gathering dark and threatening in a cigar-shaped roll along the top of the crag seemed ominously at one with her feelings.

This was headache weather, overcast and oppressive. The whole dale knew that the Helm Wind was out there somewhere in the far north-east waiting to pounce and lay waste to the fields of crops not yet gathered. And, if Ken Barden and her mother were right, there were people in this dale waiting for more than the Helm Wind; they were eagerly awaiting their chance to pounce and lay waste to her life. But she would not – she could not – allow it to happen. At all costs she had to stand up for herself. For far too long individuals in these small communities had been at the mercy of the evil-thinkers, and Bethany knew there were far more of them than the so-called evil-doers upon whom they had seated themselves in judgement.

The only trouble was, too few people were willing to speak out against this type of malicious gossip which could sweep the dale as swiftly and wreak as much devastion among its people as that great north-easterly wind did to the land itself.

From her earliest years as a child, when she would climb up there among the clouds that wreathed the top of her beloved crag, she would look down on the valley below and ponder on the people who lived there: her people. In so many ways they were as one with the landscape that bore them: hard and unforgiving on the one hand and yet, for a few precious moments, soft and yielding on the other. And as she cycled between the leafy hedgerows that bordered the lane on the last hundred yards of her journey, she could feel that summer softness in the landscape around her, and that never failed to lift her spirits; just being out here in the fresh air seemed to lighten the load on her mind and ease the headache that had been pounding since breakfast. 'Fresh air is the best medicine,' her mother used to say, and it certainly was – for the mind as well as the body.

The dale was at its best at this time of year and so often during high summer Bethany would look longingly on the lusher pasture land and meadows at the valley bottom and wish that Lot's Farm was as fortunately endowed. But in her heart she knew she would not change her craggy fell country for all the sweet green meadows in the county. And, as she pedalled slowly past the church, her eyes fixed once more on the upper slopes of Uther Crag – her crag – and she was a child again, her bare feet running carefree across its limestone outcrops and dangling in its mossy pools, where childish hands would snatch beneath the limpid water to capture some poor unfortunate newt, or other small creature, which would be carried back in triumph in an empty jam jar to be proudly displayed in the school playground the following day. Two newts were

517

worth one frog, and two frogs fetched a whole selection of birds' eggs, and so it went on. Golden days they were at this time of year. Nature's breathing space, her mother used to call it – that time between flowering and fruit-picking, when the world was green and the harvest plenty, with the grain standing tall and yellow in the fields of the lower slopes. Mother Nature was holding her breath, pausing to survey her handiwork before giving forth her bounty. Even the birds seemed hushed in their song during this magic moment before the land turned golden and the harvest was gathered safely home.

How different things had seemed then as a child. And who could have foreseen the apocalypse that awaited them all just around the corner? The 1930s had been a cruel decade for many, but looking back it seemed the essence of peace and tranquillity compared to the trauma the whole world was going through at present. The war to end all wars, her father had called the Great War of 1914, and a strange, haunted look would come into Cheevers Baine's eyes as he cast his mind back to those days of blood and hell in the trenches of Flanders. 'I thank the Lord my own lads will never have to go through what we went through,' he would say, shaking his head. 'Thank God, we learned a lesson never to be forgotten after that.' What would he have said if he had lived to see both Tom and Ted now at the Front, Bethany wondered? At least death had spared him that. And it had spared him the anguish she knew her mother was now going through on her account. For this war did not only cause pain for those in the field of battle – it was causing all sorts of problems for their loved ones left at home, too.

But in a strange sort of way, this morning Bethany felt almost detached from the situation in her life that she had heard was causing so much trouble for her family down in the village. Exactly how much of it was exaggeration on Ken's part she could not be sure. Certainly her mother's

518

'nerves' had always been a problem and even the most everyday worries would tend to get blown up out of all proportion and, as she cycled the last few yards, Bethany comforted herself with the thought that maybe this was one such occasion. Not that she would put it past some of the folk in this village to be having a field-day over her suspected relationship with a German. She could just imagine the delight with which her private life would be discussed in the queue at the post office, or behind the counter in Hector Wilks's grocer's shop. Hilda Capstick and the like would be having the time of their lives.

But it was all speculation, for none of them knew the truth, and she hardly knew it herself, for none of the books she had ever read had dealt with a situation quite like this. That people did not keep from falling in love just because they had a wedding ring on their finger was a fact of life, and some of the best stories ever written had had just such a theme. But in most of those stories the situation was quite clear; the husband was a wicked or indifferent type who did not deserve the heroine's love anyway. What red-blooded young woman did not feel for poor Anna Karenina when she fell in love with the dashing Vronsky? But what happened when the husband did not deserve to lose his wife to a rival? And what happened, Bethany wondered, when part of you still loved your husband, but another part was gradually falling helplessly in love with his enemy – with an enemy of the people?

'An enemy of the people', Bethany spoke the phrase aloud, as her cycle wheels bumped along the road. She had heard that very expression used in the post office less than a week ago. The farm on the other side of Butterslack that Nancy Turver's father had gone to work on in the early 1930s had just applied for 'an enemy of the people' as extra help with the harvest, the woman had said. Bethany had known the expression was aimed at her ears, as the details of the farmer's application were relayed across the post-office counter by an old neighbour of theirs from The Row. And although she was not even glanced at during the exchange, Bethany, as well as the three other customers waiting, were well aware the comment was made specially for her benefit.

Well, let them talk and think their dirty thoughts – she could no more contemplate sending Horst back to that POW camp than fly in the air. And, quite apart from their growing feelings for each other, how on earth would she manage if she did get rid of him? With old Sam now more of a hindrance than a help, and Joe Winstanley gone, did they want her to work herself to death? No, it was unthinkable, and she would make that clear to her mother. There came a time when one did not bow down to gossip. She had done nothing to be ashamed of, and whatever she felt for Horst was nobody's business but her own, and she was determined it would stay that way.

It had taken her just over twenty minutes to reach the vicarage, and as usual she parked her cycle against the back wall before entering the flagged courtyard, carefully closing the gate behind her. Sam, her youngest brother, was on his knees at the back door mending his own bike. She tousled his hair as she passed. 'Afternoon, Horror.'

The young lad squinted up at his sister. 'Hello, our Beth. Can I borrow your pump? Mine's knackered.'

'Help yourself.' She smiled fondly as he rose to a gawky height of almost six feet and dashed off with a grin of thanks. They really shouldn't have him still in short trousers at that height, she thought; it wasn't fair. He was growing up fast; soon he'd be Brylcreeming his hair and taking an interest in the opposite sex. And in a few years he'd be old enough to fight in this ghastly war, if it lasted long enough. It was a depressing thought that she did her best to banish as soon as it entered her head.

Mrs Simpson, the family cat, mewed loudly and

brushed against her legs as she pushed open the back door and entered the large family kitchen. Betty Barden was baking at the table in the middle of the room, listening to a play on the Home Service, when her daughter walked in. She wiped a flour-caked hand across her brow as she looked up in surprise at her visitor. 'Well, I never! Look what the wind's blown in!'

'Hello, Mam.'

Her mother reached for a cloth to wipe her hands and although she made an attempt at a smile, there was a set look to her mouth that Bethany knew only too well, as she reached for the Off switch of the radio and said pointedly, 'You've taken your time in showing your face and no mistake.'

Bethany shrugged but gave no apology; the welcome was no more than she expected. 'I've been hard at it. You know this is one of the busiest times of the year for us.' It was a lame excuse, and not even true, and her answer did not fool her mother.

'For *us*?' Betty Barden looked at her daughter sharply as she reached for the kettle.

Bethany averted her eyes and gazed out of the window to where young Sam was still fiddling with his bike in the back yard. She sighed. She might have known her mother would lose no time in coming to the point. 'I haven't come here to fight, Mam,' she said wearily, turning back to the older woman. 'I came because I gather from what Ken said that you've been concerned about some gossip you've heard in the village, and I want you to know that's all it is – gossip.'

'You can't deny the pair of you are living there together, though – and alone at that!'

'That's hardly our fault. The other chap ran off and they won't replace him – not yet at any rate. What do you want me to do, for God's sake – give him up and manage the damned place on my own? For that's just about what it would amount to.'

'There's no need for that kind of language, thank you very much!' Betty Barden set two cups on the wooden tabletop with a clatter. 'What decision you come to is up to you in the end, our Beth, but we felt it important you learn what folks are saying round here, that's all. You keep yourself far too cut off up there and that's half the trouble, if you ask me. If you came down here into the village and mixed a bit more – showed your face more, you might say – I reckon there wouldn't be half the tittle-tattle there is now.'

Bethany looked up to the ceiling and folded her arms. 'So it's stuck up I am now, is it? Just because I don't make a habit of attending their blessed beetle-drives!'

'There's a lot more to village life than beetle-drives, Bethany, and you know it. There's such a thing as a community spirit. We have to keep going at a time like this. In fact, it has never been more important than it is now, with so many of the menfolk posted missing or worse . . . By the way, have you heard from your Jack recently?' She looked at her daughter quizzically as she spooned the tealeaves into the brown earthenware teapot.

Bethany felt a stab of guilt; she had barely given Jack a second thought for days now. 'I – I wrote to his unit last week,' she answered truthfully. 'It's several weeks now since I had a letter. But I haven't been too worried – he always said to regard no news as good news, as they'd inform me immediately if anything happened to him.'

'Hmm.'

Bethany picked up a copy of *Woman* from the window-seat and it fell open at the 'Dear Evelyn Home' page. Almost every letter seemed to be from or about unfaithful wives. It was obviously quite a problem throughout the country, but the knowledge that that was how she was now being regarded around here was not a happy thought. She closed the magazine and tossed it back down on the seat with a grimace. 'We haven't *done* anything, you know, Mam. You do believe that, don't you? I haven't "committed adultery" with him or indulged in any of the other Seven Deadly Sins you all seemed so concerned about.' She looked her mother straight in the face, her tone defiant.

Betty Barden coloured and went to the stove where the kettle was now singing. Bethany watched in silence as her mother poured the boiling water into the waiting teapot. 'You do believe me, don't you?' she repeated, louder this time.

Her mother sat the kettle on the side of the stove and sighed. 'If you tell me you have nothing to be ashamed of, then I have to believe you. Your father and I brought you up to tell the truth.'

It was a noncommittal answer, but Bethany knew it was the best she was going to get. 'What would you have me do?' she pleaded in exasperation. 'Tell me what you suggest I do that would improve things – that will stop them from gossiping?' She was asking for the impossible, she knew that.

But her mother's face brightened. 'There's a bit of a do here in the church hall tonight, in aid of the war effort. You could show your face at that for a start.'

Bethany groaned inwardly. She knew exactly what that entailed. Miss Bunter, the infant mistress, at the piano and Scottish reels interspersed with old-fashioned waltzes until the menfolk who were still around – and that meant mainly the old and the infirm – were too drunk to put one foot past the other. The fact that drink was banned on church premises didn't stop them from filling up at the local pubs before the dance began. 'You really think that would make a difference?'

Her mother nodded emphatically as she passed across a cup of tea. 'I'm certain of it. Folks can only gossip about you behind your back, Bethany. When you're always there in their midst it takes the wind out of their sails and they have to find someone else to pull to pieces.'

Bethany managed a weak smile as her eyes fell on the embroidered sampler hanging on the wall opposite. 'Home Sweet Home,' she read aloud. 'There's no place quite like it, is there, Mam? If they don't throw you to the wolves, they make damned sure they devour you themselves!' It was at times like this when the Greville family motto seemed quite sickeningly appropriate.

Betty Barden made no reply. There was too much truth in what her daughter was saying to deny it.

They went on to discuss the latest war reports on the BBC, for being tuned to the Home Service from morning till night had become a part of life. These days, however, there was good reason for tuning in as frequently as possible. The Allies seemed to be going from strength to strength in Normandy, with the Germans on the run in many places. How much of it was true they had no real way of knowing, but morale among the general public had never been higher. Then her mother showed her Tom and Teddy's latest letters. Although both less than two pages in length, they seemed cheerful enough and Bethany said as much as she passed them back across the table.

'Have you seen much of Libby recently?' she asked as her mother pushed the letters back into a drawer. 'She's normally round at least twice a week, but I haven't seen her for quite a few days now.'

Betty Barden's lips pursed as she lifted her cup to her mouth and took a sip of the tea. Her younger daughter had indeed been around recently and had been very voluble indeed in her condemnation of her elder sister's new farm workers, particularly the one who was now the cause of all the gossip. 'Tried it on with me the first time we met, the younger one did,' she told her mother in feigned indignation. 'Shouldn't be allowed out of POW camp, if you ask me. They're not safe around respectable young women.' It had been fuel indeed for the older woman's fire and confirmed all her worst suspicions. 'Libby's quite well,' Betty Barden told her elder daughter, choosing her words carefully, 'and I'm sure she'll have plenty to say to you next time you meet.'

Bethany regarded her mother quizzically across the kitchen table, but made no comment. She sensed more could be said on that particular score, but that somehow it would not be in her best interests to pursue the matter.

She did not linger for long after finishing her cup of tea, but did succeed in leaving the semblance of a smile on her mother's face as she took her leave. 'If it really means that much to you, I'll come tonight,' she promised, as she pecked the older woman's cheek. 'But I'll not make a habit of it, mind!'

'Thanks, love. You'll not regret it.'

Bethany told Horst of her decision over tea that evening.

'Do you really think that is wise?' he asked her, visibly concerned as he looked up from his plate of lamb stew. 'Your brother-in-law might be there.'

Bethany gave a strained smile in reply. 'I can handle Amos,' she said with more bravado than she felt. 'He can't get up to much with half the village around!'

Horst was unusually silent for the remainder of the meal and Bethany knew that he was worried. The idea of him accompanying her even as far as the church hall was unthinkable and it had left him feeling both impotent and frustrated. The situation in which he was living here divested him of almost every shred of dignity, and pride meant a great deal to him, she knew that. If he was no longer a man in his own eyes, how could he be one in hers?

He had to struggle to contain himself as they said goodbye at the door at a little after eight. His eyes had lit up as she came down the stairs. She had donned a new peppermint-green striped cotton dress and with her thick auburn hair loose and glossy down on her shoulders he thought she had never looked more beautiful, or more vulnerable. It was strange how capable she looked in her dungarees working around the farm, but dressed like this . . . '*Schon . . . Wunderschon . . .*' he murmured as he lifted her hand to his lips.

She smiled back, blushing momentarily at the admiration in his eyes. 'I look like a stick of Blackpool rock in this get-up, if the truth be known,' she laughed. 'But seeing as you've never had the delight of coming across such a thing you wouldn't know.' She tiptoed up and placed a peck on his brow. 'I won't be gone long, never fear. I'll be back before dark.'

Glen was tied up in his kennel just outside the front of the house and she stopped to fondle the animal before setting off down the path towards the village. 'At least you never think ill of me, do you, old boy?' she whispered. 'You could show them down there in the vicarage a thing or two when it comes to loyalty!'

When she had told her mother this morning that they had done nothing they need be ashamed of, she had not lied. That she and Horst loved each other there was now no doubt, but automatically to brand her an adultress was somehow to defile what there was between them. If love itself was a crime, then yes, she was guilty – they both were – but as for anything else, then the good people of this dale could gossip till they were blue in the face; they could not make her feel guilty for a sin she had not committed. It made this public appearance she was being called upon to put in tonight all the more of a charade. But then so much of life was a charade, she thought wearily. People spent half their lives saying and doing things they didn't really believe in just to keep other people happy. Bethany was well aware that her mother's 'nerves' had been the excuse for her having to make all sorts of compromises over the years and even now as a fully-grown woman herself she could not decide whether this was for the best or not. Often it was surely more honourable to be true to yourself.

She could hear the noise of the music and laughter before she turned the final corner, some fifty yards away, and it was no surprise to find that the hall was already full and the dancing in full swing as she entered the open double doors.

The sight of the tattered bunting strung from bare light bulb to bare light bulb and the smell of too many bodies in too confined a space brought it all back – all those embarrassing Saturday nights she had been allowed off as a young girl to attend the local dances to celebrate harvest home, or some such occasion. Nothing had changed; even the coloured portraits of the old King George and Queen Mary were long out of date. Had no one told them there had been an Abdication since then, and a new King and Queen had been on the throne for almost a decade?

The hall itself was just the same: originally distempered a pale beige, the walls had now darkened to a dirty khaki through years of tobacco smoke, and even tonight a faint fug already hung in the air, from the pipes of the old men who were seated on the side benches, their booted feet tapping in time to the music. The stage, where the music was coming from, was at the far end of the hall, with two of the local quarrymen providing the fiddle and accordion accompaniments, and Miss Bunter, the school infant mistress, on the piano. The wooden benches, on which the old and infirm were already seated, ran down both sides of the room, and at the top were four tables for the use of the church committee and their wives. Blatant discrimination and snobbery some folk called it – not at all in keeping with the Methodist tradition – but tonight Bethany viewed them with some relief. With her step-father the Chairman of the committee, it meant she could at least sit down and ignore most of the proceedings if she chose to do so.

In front of the benches the younger folk congregated, some to gather in small gossipy cliques, and others to snatch a furtive drink from the ubiquitous hip-flasks carried by the local youths, and some just to stand and stare. A quick glance told her she knew almost all of the faces present, but the only one she was genuinely pleased to see was Ned. Dressed in his best Sunday suit with his collar and tie askew, he was leaning against a pillar, halfway down the left-hand side of the hall. Her heart went out to him. She had not the slightest doubt that he would dearly love to ask a pretty girl to dance but would never dare to. He had already had too many rebuffs in his young life to go looking for more. Just how much sadness there was hidden behind those dark eyes she could only guess, but she had known him for too long to doubt that he had feelings just like the rest of them. He could get hurt just as easily, and knew joy and despair as keenly as anyone present.

A St Bernard's Waltz was just finishing as she set off to walk the length of the hall to where her mother was sitting with her stepfather at one of the privileged tables. The cessation of the music seemed to coincide with her long walk through the dispersing dancers and she was aware of a distinct buzz that went round the hall as her high heels began to tap their way across the polished wooden floor.

At first she thought it was only her imagination, but then she realized it was more than that. Within seconds the excited buzz had turned into an ominous silence as people froze where they were and all eyes turned to her. She had never experienced a feeling like it; the hostility seemed to come at her in waves, and although she deliberately avoided all eyes, she was aware of the antagonism and downright hatred in the stares she was receiving from these, her own people. She had heard of the small hairs at the back of one's neck standing on end but had never experienced it until this moment.

Then just as she was about a third of the way to her destination the hiss began. It started by the outside door and grew louder with every step, until it seemed to be taken up by everyone in the hall. The sound seemed to vibrate through her very being and she was sure her legs were about to give way under her as she struggled to keep her head high and her pace even. Then from the corner of her eye she saw the familiar figure of Neddy shambling across the floor towards her. And part of the hissing turned to ribald laughter as Jack Greville's youngest brother took hold of her hand and placed it inside his arm. He was going to escort her to her table. Neddy of the inane grin and shambling gait was going to shepherd her through the hissing mob.

'Fancy a bit of what the Kraut's gettin' for supper, do you, Ned lad?' someone shouted from behind.

'Has your Jack sent you, then Ned? She needs more than a chaperone, that one!'

Each comment was met with jeering laughter by the young men present as their partners ostentatiously held in the full skirts of their dresses in case she should accidentally contaminate them in the passing.

Bethany was only too acutely aware of the incongruous sight they must make as she slowed her pace to allow for Ned's lame leg and shuffling gait. The booted foot that he trailed made a squeaking sound as it scraped along the talcum-powdered floor and the more he tried to keep in step with her, the more he seemed to fail. His head, which normally swung unbidden from side to side, she was aware of his making a giant effort to keep under control. And the laboured sound of his breathing was in direct response to the effort he knew he was making to appear as normal as possible for her sake.

As she walked the last few yards on his arm, she felt her

heart would burst with love and pride for this young man who had been destined to spend his life as the laughing-stock of these people, yet who had been the first and only one to sense her discomfort and come to offer his support. Yes, they could jeer at her and make a fool of him, but the lot of them had less humanity in their whole bodies than he had in the little finger of the hand that now clasped her own so tightly.

'Thank you for that, Neddy,' she whispered in a tight voice as they reached the table by the stage reserved for the Minister and his guests. She leant over and kissed her brother-in-law on the cheek. Beads of sweat were stand-ing out on his brow and upper lip and he giggled as his grin grew wider and the colour flared in his already florid face. He backed away from her, his dark eyes gleaming until, overcome with embarrassment, he turned and fled into the body of the hall.

She stood and watched him go, doing her best to ignore the dying hisses and comments that were still flying around her. At least she had one true friend in this place.

Also doing his best to ignore the sounds that were now thankfully lessening in volume, Kenneth Barden stood up quite deliberately to welcome her, then after kissing her on the cheek and pulling out a chair, he turned to the band who had witnessed the whole scene and were also gazing down from the stage at the new arrival. He made an impatient gesture with his hand for them to begin the next dance, and reluctantly they obeyed.

As the strains of 'If You were the Only Girl in the World' filled the hall, her mother turned to Bethany and spoke for the first time. 'You certainly could have timed that better. Or did you mean to arrive late and make such an entrance?'

Bethany's hands were shaking as she sat down and smoothed the full skirt of her dress over her knees. Her whole body began to tremble as her mother's comment found its mark and she bit back a retort as she mentally relived that grotesque walk with Ned. Why had he been the only one to feel for her in that awful situation? Her mother must know how embarrassing that had been, but instead of showing sympathy and solidarity like Ned had done, the villagers' reaction had merely added fuel to the flames already burning in her mother's mind. They had all turned against her – all except Ned. He had seen what was happening and had tried to shield her, but her mother was merely thinking of the embarrassment she had caused. It was all turning into a grotesque pantomime with herself cast as the role of the baddie at whom they must all hiss and call names. What would happen next? Were they already lining up the rotten eggs and tomatoes? But it was no joke; this was far worse than she had ever imagined. She stared ahead of her, avoiding all eyes, particularly those of her mother. 'They must really hate me,' she said in a choked voice. 'I had no idea.'

'We did try to warn you, lass,' Ken Barden said.

Bethany shook her head. It seemed as if all the feelings of vengeance engendered by this war, all the hatred, were being directed at her personally, and for once she felt her confidence begin to ebb. All that resolve that had hardened in her heart on the way here was crumbling by the minute.

'It'll not stop, you know. Not till you get rid of that German.'

Somehow even to hear Horst being referred to as 'that German' made her feel sick inside. She could feel tears of rage and frustration rise within her and she blinked them back as her stepfather shot a warning glance at her mother then held out his hand. 'Let's dance, lass,' Ken Barden said, sensing she was on the verge of tears. 'They'll all be too drunk before long to know who's here and who's not, anyroads!'

She danced three more dances with her stepfather over the next hour, and sat the others out as she sipped her tea

531

and attempted to make painful small-talk with her mother. Although several of the male parishioners asked Betty Barden to dance, it was pointedly obvious they chose to ignore her daughter. Bethany could not remember time ever passing so slowly. When the clock above the stage eventually reached ten, she checked it with her watch and said with ill-disguised relief, 'I think it's time I was getting back, I've got . . .'

But she never finished the sentence, for a tap on her shoulder made her turn in her seat, to find herself looking straight into the eyes of her brother-in-law. But this time it was not Ned.

Her heart sank. 'Amos!'

'Nice to see you, Amos!' Ken Barden half-rose from his seat to shake hands with the Colonel's second son, then his wife did likewise. 'Good of you to come, Amos,' Betty Barden added, with genuine feeling.

'I'll always turn up in aid of a good cause,' Amos Greville replied with a pious smile. His normally swarthy face was tanned an even deeper bronze with a summer spent mainly in the saddle, and his teeth seemed quite dazzlingly white as they aimed a smile in Bethany's direction. Then he held out his right hand and she had no choice but take it.

'I see you're dressed to kill tonight,' she said, with an ironic glance at his well-worn riding habit. It was not the usual attire for a village dance, but it was fast becoming the only outfit he was ever seen in these days. He made no reply to the remark, but the smile remained fixed on his face, and Bethany was aware of her mother and Ken Barden smiling in relief at this show of family support as Jack's younger brother led her past the other tables and on to the dance floor. But her own heart was sinking.

'Going hunting tonight?' she asked ironically, as he took her in his arms and swung her into the middle of the other dancers.

'You could say that.' His answer was as cryptic as his expression as he gazed down at her.

Those eyes – how she hated those eyes. And that familiar smell of Scotch on his breath. His palm was sweaty over hers. It was all so familiar, so sickeningly familiar. The very nearness of him had an almost paralytic effect on her and he chided her on her stiffness as they waltzed their way round the floor.

His dancing was not a patch on Jack's and for once, apart from the comment on her inability to relax, he made no attempt at conversation as they wove their way through the other dancers. Bethany knew she should at least try to make it look as if she was enjoying herself and that they were on the best of terms, if only to put on a show of family solidarity in the face of all the antagonism in the place, but somehow small-talk would not come. There was too much hatred in her heart for this man who bore her husband's surname, but for whom she felt no brotherly love, only a deep and abiding contempt.

It was only when the dance was nearing its end that the silence was broken. 'You won't take a telling, will you?' Amos said suddenly, and with a vehemence that took her aback. His fingers tightened on her right hand. 'You always have to be the one who calls the tune. But didn't anyone ever tell you, Bethany Baine, that whoever calls the tune in this life also pays the piper?'

She stared up at him as the last strains of 'I'll be Seeing You' filled the air, and he swung her round for the last time. 'I – I don't know what you mean,' she said, breathless now from the exertion of the dance.

'Don't you?' They were standing at the side of the dance floor as he looked down at her. 'Then I'll put it another way. There's an old Yorkshire saying that goes, "You don't get owt for nowt". You've heard of that, have you? In plain English, everything in this world has to be paid for . . . Like I said, whoever calls the tune pays the piper. And folks in this dale reckon that in certain quarters it's time the piper was paid. I'm just warning you, that's all.'

She extracted her hand from his as if from some filthy glove. 'You can't threaten me any more, Amos,' she said, looking back at him in defiance. 'This is a free country and I've done nothing wrong — nothing to be ashamed of!'

She spat the words back at him far too loudly and they were heard by far more people than she intended as she turned on her heel to head back for her table. The dancers surrounding her seemed to part like the Red Sea to let her through and once more she could feel their stares burning into her as she made her way back to where her mother and stepfather were sitting.

'I think it's time I was getting back,' she said, unwilling to sit down and prolong this miserable evening another minute. 'I've a hard day ahead tomorrow.'

Ken Barden made to get up. 'Would you like me to see you part of the way?'

Bethany shook her head. 'No, thanks all the same, Ken. It's not quite dark yet and, apart from the wind that's getting up, it's a fine night.'

She could feel their eyes on her as she made her way towards the door but, happily, this time a Scottish reel was being set about with gusto and she was met with only the occasional crude remark as she walked quickly towards the exit.

'B-b-bet'ny!'

She turned to see Ned shambling towards her. But for once there was no familiar smile on his face. 'What is it, Neddy?' She looked in concern at the beads of sweat on his upper lip and the saliva that oozed from the sides of his mouth. That always happened when he was agitated about something. 'Is something wrong?'

Neddy grabbed her arm and shook his head. 'N-no go, B-bet'ny,' he blurted out, shaking his head furiously. 'N-no go!'

'But I must go, Neddy dear,' she said patiently. 'I have to get up in the morning, remember. I'm a working woman.'

But he was still shaking his head. 'N-no, no . . . No g-go.'

She began to walk on in the direction of the door, but he held fast to her arm. She shrugged herself free. 'Please, Neddy dear. I must go . . . Let go of me!' A crowd was beginning to gather now and the insults and coarse remarks were beginning to fly once more. She pulled at his fingers to free herself. 'Let go of me, damn you, Neddy, *let go*!'

Tears of frustration sparkled in the young man's eyes. He could not remember her ever shouting at him before. He shrank back. He had angered her; he had incurred her rage and that he could not bear. Chastened, he let go of her arm and backed away towards the hall, leaving her to rush off in the direction of the outside door.

It was almost dark when she reached the fresh air, but thankfully the wind seemed to have dropped. An uneasy calm seemed to permeate the air all around her. She found herself panting for breath, but it was not from the stifling atmosphere; that final encounter with Ned had upset her almost as much as what had gone on before. She hadn't meant to hurt him. All she wanted to do was to get as far away from this place as quickly as possible. She would make a point of seeking him out tomorrow, she resolved. She knew Amos had forbidden him to come around Lot's Farm any more, but it was high time she paid the old Colonel at The Hall another visit. The old man seldom even recognized her these days, but it was a habit she knew she must not break, for Neddy and Jack's sake if nothing else. Yes, she would seek Ned out tomorrow when she visited Wolf Hall and apologize. He would understand. He knew as well as anyone what she had endured at the hands of this village tonight.

The moon was full above Uther Crag and its silver light lit the landscape as far as the village green and the start of the path she was to take back to the farm, past the old barn. Although, to her relief, the wind that had been threatening all day had not yet developed into the feared Helm Wind, a stiffish breeze was now blowing and she clasped her arms around herself for warmth as she set off in the direction of home.

Once out of the vicinity of the village the path became more twisting and much rougher and a mixture of tiredness and the half-light found her stumbling several times on the uneven ground as she neared Lot's Barn. Thankfully, the moon was quite full, so she did not need the small torch she carried in her jacket pocket. Passing Lot's Barn, however, always made her shudder, even in broad daylight. She had never liked the place, and although seldom a day passed but she caught sight of it or had actually to pass it on her way to the village, it never failed to remind her of that awful night all those years ago when she had witnessed what her stepfather, Ken Barden, would certainly regard as the work of the devil.

Because of her intense dislike of the place, she had got into the habit of averting her eyes as she passed its ancient bulk, and tonight was no exception. Her gaze was fixed firmly on the distant lights of Butterslack several miles down the dale when a noise like a breaking branch from somewhere behind her made her jerk round.

'Dear God in heaven!'

From the vicinity of the old barn several hooded figures loomed out of the darkness at her. They were those same awful white hoods she had seen in this place all those years ago.

'Let's get her, lads! Let's get the Jerry whore!'

She stood frozen to the spot in horror for a second as at least five or six figures began to run towards her. Then, summoning all her energy, she let out a shriek and began to run in the direction of the farm.

'Get her! Don't let her get away!'

Voices raged behind her, cursing her flight and egging each other on as booted feet sped over the rough ground much faster than her own high heels could run.

Panic had almost paralysed her at the sight of them, but now she fled in front of them in a state of sheer terror. They must not catch her! Dear God, don't let them catch me, she prayed, as each breath became more painful and her legs began to turn to lead.

It was like some awful nightmare where she was running with all her might but was making no progress, for she could feel them gaining on her with every step. She had got less than a hundred yards when they were upon her. A hooded figure of about her own height made a lunge and brought her to the ground in a flying rugby tackle. She landed heavily on the stony ground but so great was her terror she barely felt the pain as rough hands pulled her into the long grass at the side of the path.

'Jerry whore! Traitorous bitch!'

The insults were spat in her face from all directions as hands grabbed at her and attempted to pin her struggling figure to the ground. At first she succeeded in screaming, but within seconds a thick, callused palm was wedged over her mouth so firmly she felt she was going to suffocate. Then before her terrified gaze one of them produced a knife. Its blade glinted in the moonlight and the sight of it sent her rigid with shock.

The man who was standing over her held it up before her terrified gaze so there could be no mistake. 'Maybe you've heard what they do to Jerry whores like you in civilized places like France, have you, *Mrs* Greville?'

She made a muffled groan beneath the suffocating hand and attempted to shake her head, but she was pinned too securely by at least three of the hooded figures for any freedom of movement.

The man with the knife knelt astride her, holding the weapon only inches from her face as the others crowded round. It was a steel hunting knife with a black ebony handle, similar to the ones they used to slice off foxes' tails. Similar to Amos Greville's. But this was not her brother-in-law wielding it tonight. 'Aye, they've got it down to a fine art by now — what they do to them as consorts wi' the Hun. First we mek 'em a little less attractive to the enemy, that's what we do! Like this . . . !'

With a grab of his left hand he bent over her and yanked forward a thick lock of her hair which he hacked off at the roots with a skilled flourish of the weapon in his right hand. There was no doubt about it, this was a hand that had done the same to many a poor fox's brush and, as he brandished the glossy reddish lock in front of her terrified eyes, her mind flew back to that gruesome glass display case in Amos Greville's bedroom. That this was one of his hunting henchmen she had no doubt, just as she had no doubt Amos Greville was here in person gloating among these hooded devils as they heaped humiliation on humiliation upon her with every stroke of the blade.

The tugging of her hair and scything of each handful in turn was as painful as it was humiliating and tears blinded her eyes and ran down in hot, bitter streams over the hand that was still pressed suffocatingly over her mouth as lock by lock she was shorn of her hair until there was nothing left except a patchy bloodied stubble.

She could feel the wind chill around her bare scalp when, at last, her chief tormentor decided that that part of her ordeal was complete. But there was more to come.

'Happen, that was the bit you didn't enjoy,' the man said with a mirthless laugh. 'But we're fair men, Mrs Greville. We're fair men. We won't let you go without making it up to you!'

His voice was familiar, but she could not put a specific name to it. Was it Billy Sedgwick, or one of her other ex-classmates? It certainly sounded like him. But whoever it was, his ominous promise was met by a chorus of ribald laughter that sent a chill through her rigid body.

'Aye,' another put in. It was the one whose palm was suffocating her who was speaking. 'We have a real treat in store for you now!'

The man with the knife got up from his knees, where he had been astride her midriff, and to her horror he began to undo his belt. 'He's quite right there,' he said. 'We all know how much store you set by entertaining the enemy, Mrs Greville – why the whole of Utherdale knows that – so we reckon as good, loyal Utherdale lads you'll be only too delighted to do the same for us!'

'Call it doing your bit for your country,' one of them put in from somewhere behind her right shoulder. 'You seem to enjoy doing it for the enemy, so think how much more you'll enjoy doing it for your own kind!'

'This is wartime, Mrs Greville! Lie back and think of England for a change – not bloody Germany!'

'Aaaaaaaaaah!'

In his excitement to get his own trousers undone, the one who had been holding her mouth let go for a second, only to clap his hand back over it as she screamed for all she was worth.

'Get a bloody sock stuffed in there!' the one who seemed to be the leader commanded, and almost immediately she was well and truly gagged.

What happened next was a nightmare from which she began to believe she would never awaken, as one after the other all six of them took it in turn to subject her to indignities she had never even dreamt of, before finally raping her in prolonged and brutal succession. The ordeal, which seemed eternal, lasted over half an hour and left her lying semi-conscious and bleeding in the long grass by the side of the road.

Exactly how long she lay there she could not tell, for her

head spun and her whole body, now defiled and bloodied, ached more than she thought she could bear.

Then, out of the darkness and pain, she was aware of a figure kneeling above her in the grass, and something splashed on her face. She struggled to open her eyes to find the face of Ned gazing down at her. Silent tears were streaming from his eyes and he made no attempt to wipe them away as he took her head gently in his arms.

'Neddy . . . I'm so sorry . . .' What she was apologizing for she did not know as he rocked her in his arms.

They were both crying as they clung together, two dishevelled figures by the side of the ditch. And as Bethany sobbed her hurt and humiliation into the fine worsted cloth of his jacket, Neddy made funny little cooing noises of comfort through his tears. He was rocking her in his arms like a baby as he did so. He – Daft Ned – the one they had made such a fool of for all of his young life. He was comforting her as a mother would a distraught child. Then suddenly he extricated himself from her grasp and staggered to his feet.

'Don't leave me, Neddy . . . Please don't leave me . . . !' Bethany gasped and held out a hand in desperation as she pleaded not to be left alone. He couldn't desert her. Not like this. Not now.

'Do-n' wo-o-rr-y . . .' Neddy backed off from her, placing his hands together in front of him as if in prayer. He was telling her not to worry, but where was he going?

She watched in growing despair and apprehension as he disappeared into the darkness, leaving her to face the coming night alone.

Chapter Twenty-Seven

The longcase clock in the hall of Lot's Farm struck eleven and Horst closed the volume of John Masefield's *Collected Poems* and stared into the gloomy darkness of the kitchen, beyond the small paraffin lamp at his elbow. This had been a long evening; in many ways the longest since his arrival here, and he was surprised to find how much he missed her. Being all alone in the house like this – her house – had seemed strange, yet so much of her remained. Little touches like the vase of fresh flowers in the middle of the table spoke so clearly of the type of person she was. Beauty mattered to her, but it was not the beauty to be found in artificial things such as her sister Libby set such store by; it was the beauty of nature that Bethany loved, and in this strange, hard land she would seek it out and find it, and make it as much a part of her daily life as breathing. She was at her happiest when out in the fields, with the sun on her face, the wind in her hair, and her beloved Uther Crag keeping watch in the background. Yes, that's always how he would think of her – the memory he would cherish – no matter what happened in the future.

He glanced down at the book in his lap. He had chosen the volume at random from the bookcase in the parlour and had been skimming through it to pass the time till she got back. There had been one poem in it entitled 'I Went into the Fields' that had touched his soul and seemed to have been written especially for him. It had been a quite incredible experience reading the poet's words. All that he had been feeling, all the agony he had been going through as he fought against his growing love for her was in there. He was not alone; someone else had gone through it too.

It was funny how we all imagined our feelings to be unique, he thought. No one has ever loved, has ever suffered like we have. And yet throughout the ages the whole of mankind — not just the poets — have laughed and cried over the same emotions that he knew both he and Bethany were going through right now. Almost every word written in that poem could have been written by himself — right down to that last strangely enigmatic ending. *'And the waters ebbed, the moon hid in a cloud . . .'*

Yes, somehow, he knew exactly what the poet meant. Now he too knew what it was like to be living through the high-water mark of an affair of the heart — that exquisite period when two spirits meet and touch. To the fortunate few it can happen once in a lifetime, but never twice. And all too often, like the bloom on the rarest blossom, it is too fragile, too beautiful a thing to last. Like the soap bubbles he would blow as a child in the gardens at Himmelhof, it would float from his grasp and sail away, to disappear before his very eyes, leaving only a beautiful memory of what had once been, but was now no more.

But he was being needlessly morbid, he told himself. He was simply depressed because Bethany had gone alone to the dance in the village hall tonight. Not all love affairs ended like that. Some went on to even greater happiness; the happiness to be found through a lifetime of shared companionship and love. Oh, that he might be so lucky . . .

He laid the book open at the page, face down on the small table by the sofa in the kitchen, then got up and walked through to the front parlour to look out the window. From here he could watch for her coming up the path.

She had promised to be home before dark — by ten, if he remembered rightly. And it was long past that now. A

542

distinct feeling of unease was beginning to creep into his thoughts. It was stupid to worry, for she was a grown woman who had lived in these parts all her life; it was not as if she could get lost on the way home or anything like that. But these were not ordinary times and there was no denying he had felt distinctly uncomfortable about her going to that dance alone tonight. There was hatred in this place, for herself as well as for him, and it had been manifesting itself much more than he had let her know of late. Even before that gin-trap incident there had been other quite sickening episodes over the past few days: rabbits with their throats cut and left hanging by the neck from the branches of trees near to where he was working alone. He had even had his jacket tossed into the beck the other day when he returned to the field from a midday snack in the farmhouse. He had hung it over a hawthorn bush to dry so she would not notice its wetness when he went home at night. He had tried to think no more about it himself, but such happenings gave him a funny feeling. Someone – or some people – were obviously watching him and were doing their best to make things as uncomfortable as possible – to warn him off, even. But he would not be warned off. What he had found here with her had been the only good thing in five years of darkness, for that was what this war had been.

He walked to the front door and opened it, breathing in the clean night air. Then he paused and listened. What on earth was that? There was a strange whining sound coming from the end of the house. He turned in its direction. 'Glen!' The sheepdog was straining at the rope that tethered it to the wall of its kennel and was making a persistent bleating sound that he had never heard from it before.

Horst walked over and attempted to quieten the animal. '*Was ist los?* What's wrong, old man? Aren't you well?' He had never known the dog to act like this before. 'Want to go places, is that it?' The collie made a habit of never fouling the area around the house and maybe it had eaten something it shouldn't have today. It might be stomach trouble. 'Just a minute, I'll untie you and we'll see if that helps.'

Horst bent to undo the stout rope with which Bethany kept her pet tethered, but instead of making for the back yard as he anticipated, the animal set off like the wind down the path in the direction of the village, barking loudly as it went.

Alarmed that it might run off and not return, Horst found himself running after it, calling its name, and as the barking grew fainter in the distance, to his surprise out of the dark loomed a figure, heading towards him. His heart lurched, then hope faded almost immediately; it was not Bethany.

At first, by the way it was staggering, he thought it was a drunk from the village hall who had simply lost his way. Then there was a moment's apprehension as he feared it could be Amos Greville on his way here to make trouble, after too many in the local pub. Then, as the figure grew closer, he realized it was not Amos at all but the hurrying, shambling figure of his younger brother, the one they called Daft Ned. He seemed to be heading straight towards him, gesticulating with his arms in a strange, agitated fashion.

As he came within a few yards, Ned's agitation became even more obvious as his face contorted and he gabbled out something that Horst could not even begin to comprehend.

'What is it?' Horst asked, by now quite perturbed. He had had almost no contact with the young man before and there was something both pathetic and almost repellent in the facial and bodily contortions he was witnessing. Was he drunk or simply trying to tell him something? It was impossible to tell. 'Is something wrong?'

Ned now had him by the arm and was pulling him down the road away from the farm. 'B-b-b . . .' His distress had made his inarticulateness almost complete. Even in the moonlight, it was obvious he had been crying and his tear-streaked face gazed into Horst's and saliva frothed at the sides of his mouth as he tried yet again to be understood, 'B-b-b-b-e-e . . .'

Fear gripped Horst. 'It's not Bethany, is it?' he asked, his voice rising. 'There's nothing happened to her?'

Relief flooded Ned's face as he nodded his head vigorously and pulled even harder at Horst's sleeve.

'*Ach, nein!*' He should have guessed! Horst did not need a second telling as he jerked his arm free from Ned's sweaty grasp and set off at a run down the road towards the village, leaving his companion to shamble after him as best he could.

He knew it! He just knew it! Something in his bones had told him she shouldn't have gone down there alone tonight. But it was always so easy to be wise after the event.

He could feel his heart thumping with every step he took and perspiration dampened his skin as he headed on into the night. What on earth had happened? Had she had an accident? Had someone said or done something to hurt her? All manner of thoughts crowded in on him as he strained his eyes against the darkness and ran on in the direction of the village.

It took only a few minutes to have his worst fears confirmed. It was the dog he noticed first, standing by the side of the road. Then his eyes focused with mounting horror on the crumpled figure at its feet. It could be no one else but Bethany, for Glen, her faithful collie, was already standing over her, his wet nose nuzzling her blood-streaked cheek. The animal began to bark loudly once more at the sight of Horst and started to wag its tail. It was as if it had known back there at the farm that something was wrong, and now it recognized that help was at hand.

'Bethany ... *Um Gottes Willen!*' Had she had an accident? Had she been knocked down by a car? He almost threw himself to his knees on the ground beside her and gazed down in consternation at the sight before him.

'Horst?' Her voice was no more than a whisper as relief flooded through her at his arrival. Then she averted her face from his, as shame and humiliation merged with the pain that wracked her body. She could feel her face bloated and bloodstained and winced in an agony that was both mental and physical as the fingers of the man whom she loved so much tenderly touched the bloodied stubble of her head.

'Oh, my love ... my love ...' Tears misted Horst's eyes as he gazed down at her and gently stroked the mutilated scalp; her hair, her lovely auburn hair — all gone. Thick strands of it still clung to the torn bodice of her dress and a long, severed lock was tangled in a clump of nettles by her head. Never, never had he imagined anything like this could ever happen. They could threaten him — yes, he could understand that; but threats were one thing — this quite another. How could they do this to a young woman like her? How could any human beings do this to another? She was one of them. She was born and brought up in this place. How could they do it to one of their own? Horst shook his head in disbelief as tears of anger, frustration and pity spilled down his cheeks. It was a sick world they were living in, all right.

There was a grunting, shuffling sound behind him. He half-turned to find that Ned had caught up. Horst moved over slightly as Jack Greville's youngest brother sank down on to the grassy verge beside them. His eyelids were red and swollen and his face was streaked with tears. His nose was running and he wiped it noisily on the sleeve of his jacket as a shuddering sob ran through him. Seeing Bethany once more, he threw up his hands in the air in a gesture of helplessness. He began to make little whimpering noises in his throat as he covered his face with his hands and began to rock backwards and forwards on his knees.

Bethany's dress, once so crisply laundered, was now covered in filth, its bodice ripped, the skirt bunched around her thighs, and her stockings torn. Her high-heeled shoes were nowhere to be seen. The sound of Ned's grief at the sight of her made her clutch tighter at Horst's hand and avert her head. 'Don't look at me,' she pleaded. 'Please don't look . . .'

But Horst could do no other than look at her and, in doing so, curse the fate that had brought this upon her. 'I'm sorry . . . I'm so very sorry, my darling . . .' In some terrible way he felt responsible for this outrage that had occurred here tonight. Had they never met, had he never been sent to work at Lot's Farm . . . Had the war itself never happened . . . Just how far back did you have to go to find the cause, to discover the real culprit on whom to pin the blame?

Bethany began to cry once more, her face still averted from his, and the sound of her anguish brought even louder sobs from Ned, still rocking backwards and forwards by her side.

'Come on, we're going home,' Horst said huskily, as he bent to lift her from the scrubby grass of the verge. He had to get her out of here as quickly as possible. Whoever was responsible for this crime couldn't be far away.

She was heavier than he thought, and she moaned slightly in his arms as, staggering momentarily under her weight, he got to his feet and, after making sure she was comfortable, he set off down the road in the direction of the farm.

Ned, in turn, scrambled to his feet and started after them. They made an odd little group, with Glen bounding on ahead, and Ned bringing up the rear, tears still blinding his eyes. He had tried to warn her, tried to tell her what he had overheard in the dance hall, but he had failed. And his failure had resulted in this. The horror of it still contorted his face as he struggled to keep up with the striding figure of Horst, as the German made his way back to the farmhouse, with Bethany sprawled in his arms.

Ned could see Bethany's head occasionally loll back from her rescuer's shoulder as he panted along behind them and it was as if a physical pain ran through him at the sight of it. He could have saved her; he should have saved her. If he had gone straight to the police he might have done. But no matter how much he might fear – even hate – Amos at times, he could not get him into that kind of trouble. Not again.

Scenes and sounds from long ago on Uther Crag now danced in a crazy jumble in Ned's head, just as those dancers had pranced around the Great Fire of Beltane. 'Ned! Ned! Daft in the head!' But not so daft that he had no feelings – that he couldn't fancy a pretty lass like yon Sarah-Jane. He had watched his brother and Sarah-Jane doing 'it' in the bushes that night, just as he had watched her doing it with others before him. All he knew about what men and women did together when they were grown up, he had learnt by watching in the woods on nights like that. He began to sweat even more at the memory as he struggled to keep up with the shadowy figure striding into the darkness in front of him.

What had been wrong with him having his turn? Why did Sarah-Jane have to start screaming like that with him, and calling him all those names? He knew what to do; he had seen it happen often enough. He had not meant to hurt her. He only wanted to shut her up – to keep her quiet so he could do it right. When she had gone limp there on the ground beneath him, he had thought she had fallen asleep with the drink like Amos so often did. It had come as a real shock to learn she had never woken up.

And then they took Amos away and started asking a lot of questions . . . But all that was a long time ago now . . .

He wished he had never left Wolf Hall to come to this dance tonight – had never seen what they had done to Bethany. He loved Bethany, more than he loved anybody, yet he could do nothing to save her. He had felt sick at the sight that had met his eyes after they had all gone and he had found her lying there by the side of the road. And, as he struggled on behind her now, he thanked God that the German had understood when he had run all the way to the farm to tell him. He could never have carried her back himself. Daft Ned, he was all right. Daft, bloody useless Ned . . . And tears sprang once more to his eyes to blind his vision as he stumbled on in Horst's wake.

The long walk back was not easy in the darkness, for the moon had disappeared behind a bank of cloud and the road was rough and full of unexpected pot-holes. Several times Horst had to struggle to keep his feet. In her exhausted state, Bethany's body felt like a lead weight in his arms by the time they had gone only a few hundred yards. The relief when the familiar bulk of the old farmhouse loomed out of the night was enormous. Soon he could lay his precious burden down and they could attempt to come to terms with what had just happened. He would make it up to her. Somehow he would make it up to her . . . 'We're almost there, my love,' Horst whispered, into the bloodied stubble of her scalp, as her head rested exhausted against his shoulder. 'We're almost home.'

He could feel both his legs and his arms almost giving out as he staggered the last few yards up the path to the door, which was thankfully ajar. He kicked it even wider open with his foot, before carefully manoeuvring her through the narrow opening. He could see the light on in the kitchen beyond the small hallway and headed for it, almost weeping with relief.

At first his eyes found it difficult to focus as they emerged from the darkened hallway into the comfort and familiarity of the lamplit kitchen. Then he gave a gasp of shock that sent him staggering backwards, almost dropping her in the process.

The figure of a tallish, dark-haired man in military uniform was standing staring at them from in front of the fireplace. His left arm and shoulder were heavily bandaged in a sling and there was a livid red scar running down his left cheek. The expression on his face was one of utter shock at the sight of Horst with Bethany in his arms. For a moment everyone froze, and time seemed suspended, then Glen bounded up to the uniformed figure, yelping and clawing at the soldier's legs in undisguised delight. But the man was not even aware of the animal. All he could see were the two figures before him.

'Dear God in heaven! What's this?' Jack Greville rushed forwards, unable to believe his eyes. He stared at the puffy, tear- and blood-streaked face of the young woman in the stranger's arms, and at her shorn head. The sight of the roughly sheared hair brought a sick feeling to the pit of his stomach. He had spent the past few weeks in France and had seen dozens of such sights as the Allies retook what had been Vichy territory. It meant only one thing for a young woman to receive such treatment at the hands of her own people. 'Dear God . . . Bethany!' He stared as if mesmerized by the sight as he shook his head in disbelief. 'Oh no, God, no . . . !'

At that point Ned came panting in through the open kitchen door, then gasped and shrank back immediately at the sight of his eldest brother. For a moment there was complete silence as all three males in the room exchanged awkward, almost fearful glances, then Jack attempted to gather himself sufficiently to demand of Horst, 'What the hell's going on? And who the hell are you?'

The sound of her husband's voice roused Bethany from her half-dazed state and, as she opened her eyes, Horst could feel her stiffen and then shrink back in his arms as she whispered the name, 'Jack!'

550

Almost too numbed mentally and physically to think straight, Horst walked over to the stuffed horsehair sofa and gently laid her down on the cushions, then sank down on the arm of the couch himself as he wiped a hand across his sweating brow. There was no mistaking the man who was now facing him across the kitchen floor; he had seen that face staring at him from the photo frame on the mantelpiece for as long as he had been here at Lot's Farm. Of all the times for them to meet . . .

A feeling of nausea swept over him. He wanted to be sick, whether from fatigue or shock, he was not quite sure. But one thing he was certain of: he must try to keep the situation as calm as possible. One wrong word or move and it could explode and, by the look of them all, that was the last thing that was needed.

Wearily and with not a little apprehension, he forced himself to his feet and walked over to offer his hand to the husband of the woman he loved.

Jack Greville looked suspiciously at the extended hand for a moment, then cautiously tendered his own in return.

'Mr Greville, my name is Horst von Karsten. I am pleased to meet you at last.' Horst knew that never had he told such a blatant untruth.

'You're German!' It was more of an incredulous statement than a question as the sound of that hated accent echoed in Jack's head, and he withdrew his hand from Horst's as if stung. Then his eyes moved to the prostrate figure of his wife lying on the sofa. The shock was still obvious on his face and in his voice as he demanded hoarsely, 'What the hell's going on here?'

He hardly dared utter the question, for he feared he already had the answer in all those desecrated examples of young womanhood he had witnessed in the liberated districts of France through which his unit had just travelled. And in comparison to some of the sights he had seen there, his wife had got off lightly. Tarring and feathering were the usual follow-ups to the shearing of the hair. Such treatment was meted out to young females for only one thing: consorting with the enemy. But never could he have dreamt he would ever meet that enemy face to face like this in his own home.

His first inclination was to attack – to knock the living daylights out of the bastard. But the idea was laughable. He was standing here a physical wreck, with one arm in pieces, part of his shoulder missing, and half his guts held together by surgical dressings and bandages beneath his uniform. An enemy shell had seen to it that he would do precious little attacking for a long time to come.

He cleared his throat and decided to play for time. 'Karsten, eh? No relation to the Ruhr bastard who was responsible for this?' he asked, with a bitter glance down at his wounded arm. Karsten, Krupp and Thyssen – Adolf Hitler would have got nowhere without them.

'No, no relation,' Horst said quickly, finding himself lying once more. Then he immediately regretted it, as *Der Alte*'s face flashed before him. He was denying his own family, just as Peter had denied Christ. What had this war reduced them all to?

But it was the reply Jack had expected. To have come home and found Otto von Karsten's son in his kitchen would have been almost as much of a shock as the sight of his wife with her hair shorn off. But he had to get to the bottom of this. Just how many bloody Jerries were there running around loose in Utherby? And was this one the one associated with what had happened to Bethany tonight? There was only one way of finding out: 'I'm not a fool, Herr whatever-your-bloody-name-is, and I know why they do things like this to young women in wartime, so just tell me one thing,' he said stiffly, addressing Horst. 'Just tell me if you're the one they suspect of carrying on with my wife while I've been gone.'

Horst opened his mouth, but no words would come. In the shadows of the room Ned shrank back nearer to the door. The silence that hung heavy in all their hearts was broken only by the soft sobbing of Bethany as she lay on the sofa, her head now buried in one of the cushions. It was all the answer that Jack Greville needed. And inwardly he cursed his mangled body that had once been young and strong. Not so long ago he could have made mincemeat of this Kraut bastard who stood here neither admitting nor denying his guilt. Frustration and rage rose within him, making his heart pound in his chest as he clenched his right fist and glared at the ashen-faced young man opposite him. 'Get the hell out of here, Jerry,' he said through gritted teeth. 'Just get the hell out of here if you value your life!'

Horst glanced at Bethany, who had raised her head. Their eyes met. In her gaze he read every emotion he was now going through mirrored in her eyes. The love that flowed between them in that look was almost tangible. Silently he implored her to give him a sign. Just one sign was all that was needed. Then, slowly, she began to nod her head. She was telling him to go. Telling him to get out of her life if he valued his own.

Jack Greville was looking from one to the other; there was real pain in his eyes, for at that moment he knew he was a stranger in his own home. It was a cold, sickening realization, without any words being spoken, and the pain it brought was almost physical. This was far from the homecoming he had expected. He had dreamt of this moment for so long, so very long. It was often all that had kept him going in the heat of battle. For four long years he had devoted his life to killing Germans, knowing at the end of it all he would return home to the woman he loved, the woman who loved him and would be waiting for him. And now that dream was shattered; instead, he had walked into a living nightmare. The enemy was in his midst – in his own home – had probably been sleeping in his very own bed, with his own wife! His fist clenched and unclenched as such emotions raged within him as he had never known before.

Horst could feel the temperature rising, and for a moment he stood motionless in the middle of the floor. This was the moment of truth. He knew one day it might come to this. But not yet, not so soon. Should he stay and fight for the woman he loved? If he was half the man he had thought himself to be, there would be no question of him walking out now.

'Go, Horst, please . . . Just go . . .'

From a few feet away Bethany's voice pleaded with him, imploring him to leave. He turned to face her. 'Is that what you want?' he asked softly. 'Is that what you really want?'

Tears streamed from her eyes as she gazed back at him, and silently she begged him to understand. This was not the ending any of the three of them had wanted, or deserved. This was the jagged, painful edge of the broken dreams that each had carried in their hearts throughout all this bloody war. The world – their world – could never be the same again for any one of them. She knew it, and they both knew it. And now she was being asked to choose between the man she now loved more than any other and the man she had married.

'Answer him, Bethany,' Jack said in a tight voice. 'Answer the bloody Kraut.'

She turned her head in her husband's direction. It was a gaunt, ravaged face that looked back into her own; a face that had gone to war a young man and had come back a generation older. He had seen mankind at its best and its worst over the past four years and he had few illusions left. She was looking into the face of a stranger, a stranger whose name she still bore, and whose ring she still wore, but for whom she now felt nothing but an impotent frustration that he should have returned at a time like this. It was too soon – far too soon.

Then her eyes moved to the young man standing between herself and the door. How cruel of fate to have brought them to this. How cruel to be asked to decide when there was only one decision possible. They were still at war. In the eyes of the world he was still her enemy. Where could they go together? The whole world was not big enough to hide them.

Slowly, painfully, she got up from the sofa and walked to where Horst was standing. 'For us the war is over, my darling,' she whispered in a voice so soft that only he could hear. Then from her neck she unfastened the small silver St Christopher medallion she always wore. She pressed it into the palm of his hand. 'God go with you, my love,' she said softly. 'Go now, and go quickly, for you take my heart with you.'

She turned from him and buried her face in her hands and he stood for a moment staring at the shorn and bloodied back of her head. Then, without a further glance at the man who stood glaring at him from the other side of the room, Horst turned and walked quickly towards the door.

Once outside, he stood in the middle of the path and gazed back at the farmhouse. He took a deep breath and shivered, for he had no jacket on and the wind that had been threatening all day was now chill around his bare arms. But he knew he could not go back into the house; he could not go back in there for a jacket, or for anything ever again. His legs were trembling, but not with cold, and suddenly that same feeling of sickness that had overwhelmed him inside, came over him again. He retched in the middle of the path, but nothing came up, although it made tears rush to his eyes. He wiped them impatiently with the back of his hand as he stared at the closed door of the farmhouse. Never had he felt so alone. He was not only a stranger in a foreign land, but he was an enemy alien who had no home and no friend to call his own. And worse, much worse, he had enemies here – real enemies, who this very night had shamed and mutilated the woman he loved.

He glanced anxiously around him in the darkness, and suddenly the whole night was his enemy. Where could he go? Where could he hide?

All he was sure about was that he must get away from this place – this dale – as quickly as possible. There was hatred here, real hatred such as he had never experienced before, and he now had an inkling of what it must have been like for poor Geli Rosenbaum who had found this happening in her own homeland. She had been de-humanized to the level of an animal to be hunted down by her own people, just as he knew would be the fate that now awaited him if he chose to remain in Utherdale.

He gave no thought to where his feet were carrying him as he began to walk quickly back down the road along which he had carried the half-conscious body of the woman he loved only a few short minutes before. He would head for Butterslack, then on southwards out of Utherdale. All he wanted was to get as far away from this place in as short a time as possible. Only then could he hope to make any kind of rational decision about his future, and decide whether to give himself up to the authorities or not.

It was only when he reached the vicinity of Lot's Barn that he realized he was not alone. A shout from the direction of the building froze him in his tracks.

'Is this him, lads? Is this the bloody Kraut?'

Not even pausing to consider his response, Horst leapt the nearest fence and set off running across the field as fast as his leaden legs would carry him. The wind was getting up and it began to rain, quite heavily, causing his feet to slip on the muddied ground. The events of the past hour had robbed him of most of his energy and it was a real struggle to put one foot past the other. He was aware he was heading in a roughly southerly direction and he hoped if he kept going long enough his pursuers would get bored and give up the chase. But, after five minutes or so, he realized he was not to be so lucky. In the distance behind him he could hear the sound of shouts and raised voices as others were rallied to the chase. If nothing else, his flight had answered their question. There could be no doubt in their minds now that with a bit of luck and enough moonlight to see by, they could have their quarry in their sights.

Exactly how many were after him he could not tell, but there were quite a few; he could hear their voices calling to one another, exhorting each other to keep going, and he knew they were those very same animals who had done that terrible thing to Bethany.

He felt both frustration and shame as on and on he ran across the wet fields. He should be standing his ground and making them face up to the foulness of their deeds. They should be confronted with their guilt and not run away from like this. With every step he took, he was handing them a victory; he was acting like some craven coward. But what was the alternative? He was only one man against many. And so he kept on running, for how long he did not know. All he knew was that he could not allow himself to rest until the sounds of their pursuit had disappeared into the night.

Thankfully, after about fifteen minutes the rain stopped and although the wind was still blowing, the going became easier. By the feel of the ground underfoot, it had not rained here at all and he took this as a sign; it gave him hope and the courage to carry on. Then after what he supposed to be another two miles or so, fatigue finally overcame him and he collapsed into a ditch at the side of the road. His heart was pounding fit to burst and the pain in his chest had become unbearable. For a long time he lay there panting and praying that the pain would subside and that it would not start raining again. Then slowly his eyes began to close. He did not mean to fall asleep, but sleep he did – sound and dreamless – until, just after daybreak, the sound of a hunting horn brought him back to consciousness with a jerk. Within seconds he was wide awake and sitting upright, his ear to the wind. For one fleeting moment he had forgotten the horrors of the night, but now it all came flooding back to him.

His clothes were damp with dew and he shivered violently and his teeth chattered as he stood up stiffly, then stretched himself and looked about him. His eyes travelled over the top of the hawthorn hedge beneath which he had spent the night, then narrowed as they moved in the direction of Lot's Farm and Wolf Hall just a few miles to the north.

'*Du lieber Gott!*' He had not expected this! One or two perhaps, but by the looks of it there was a whole hunt assembling back there, and there was no mistaking that mounted figure in the grey riding jacket in the middle of the group of other riders, about two fields away. It was none other than Amos Greville, and he appeared to be issuing orders for the chase to proceed.

Horst felt the panic grow within him. He had no doubt whom their prey was to be. It was to be no fox that was to be hounded over these fields here today. The quarry was to be human.

His first instinct was to hide as he looked about him in desperation. But where? Apart from the shallow ditch in which he had spent the night, there was nothing but open fields all around him. And so he began to run. And run. And run.

In less than two minutes he heard the sound of the hunting horn once more and the chase was on. He was crouching in a ditch by the side of the road when the mounted men first thundered past him, and he waited until they were at least three fields away before he had the courage to make a few hundred yards' dash into the next meadow. They would know he would still be in the area and were obviously determined not to give up until they had tracked him down. It was all good sport – marvellous sport. And he could tell from the way their eyes gleamed as they bent low over their saddles that no fox had ever inspired such determination to carry on until the prey had been run to ground.

The chase went on for hours. Would they never give up, Horst thought in desperation as, sick at heart and tired out, he hid in ditches and up trees as the mounted men scoured the neighbouring countryside, determined not to give in. Was there nowhere he would be safe from those pounding hooves? Bethany had told him once of some caves not too far south of here – great underground caverns beneath a limestone mountain even bigger than Uther Crag, called Ingleborough, the great flat top of which could be seen from the summit of her own beloved crag.

'Ingleborough's the most incredible crag in the whole of Yorkshire,' she had once told him. 'It's even bigger and grander than Uther. In fact, there's not a more mysterious place in the whole of England.'

And she had gone on to tell him of its great underground caverns, with names like Gaping Ghyll, Trow Ghyll, Yordas Cave and Hell Ghyll. 'Caves almost as big as Utherdale itself,' she had said. 'Full of lost souls, some say. Lost souls who are fated to wander their secret underground passageways searching for the light until the dawning of eternity . . .'

A lost soul searching for the light . . . If ever he felt like one of those, it was now. Perhaps he had been one all his life . . .

And her words repeated in his head as he set off south once more. Perhaps if he made for there he would be safe . . .

But as far as the man on the leading horse of the hunt

was concerned, his prey would never get as far as Ingleborough. He would not get out of Utherdale itself. It was to be a hunt to the death long before then, and Amos Greville's face betrayed the relish with which he now directed his men in pursuit of their quarry. Every so often they would come within hailing distance and Horst would break out in a cold sweat of fear as their horses' hooves pounded the hard ground, sending up a dust cloud only yards from his latest hiding place.

'Let's get him, lads! Don't let the bastard escape!' It was Amos Greville's voice he could hear above the others as they paused to muster themselves for another circuit of the outer reaches of the Wolf Hall estate.

They seemed convinced he was still in the area and, although over the next hour Horst would occasionally lose sight of them for as long as ten minutes, just when he began to imagine he was free of them, he would hear that dreaded horn again in the distance, then the pounding of hooves would send him running for cover once more.

The man in the saddle of the leading horse had the scent of victory in his nostrils and would not let go. All the hatred and rage that had built up in the heart of Colonel Philip Greville's second son now boiled over as he exhorted his horse to jump yet one more fence in search of the man who had taken what he was convinced was his by right. If any man had had a right to Bethany Baine with Jack gone, it was certainly not that Kraut bastard. He was the one who had wanted her first – the one who had gone through agonies, dreaming of her night after night throughout all those years, until Jack came back from Australia and laid claim to her himself.

And she would be his again, for God only knew when his elder brother would return from this war. Or *if* he would return. And in Amos Greville's most secret heart he prayed to his gods that his brother would never return, for then they would have come full circle. He would be the next Master of Wolf Hall, and it would be just himself and Bethany; Bethany and himself. And his heart would beat even faster at the thought as he lashed out at the chestnut flank of his gelding and raced on in pursuit of the only other man who now stood between himself and the woman he still desired more than any other. If he did not find him today, then he would find him tomorrow, or the next day. He would keep on and on in his search. No one knew this area better than he did. He knew every square mile of this ancient craggy land they called the North Riding of Yorkshire. There would be no hiding place for the enemy here.

And as Amos Greville rode on over the green country-side of Utherdale in pursuit of his prey, the man he was hunting ran on and on in quiet desperation, from ditch to ditch, tree to tree, more and more a hunted animal with every mile. The exhaustion showed on every line of his face and in every aching muscle of his body as he stumbled forwards, ever forwards. Where exactly he was heading for, Horst von Karsten now no longer knew nor cared. This war had robbed him of his country, his family, his freedom, and the woman he loved. What was left for him now?

At sunset, too exhausted to care any more whether or not they caught up with him, Horst flung himself down on the yellowing grass at the edge of a meadow about seven miles south of Butterslack, near the Ingleborough road, and closed his eyes. He had not heard that dreaded horn for almost an hour now, and the only sounds and smells that surrounded him were those of a high summer evening. There was peace here . . . Peace at last . . .

He was no longer an offcomer in this foreign land; he was a thousand miles away in his beloved Bavaria. And, as tears sprang unbidden to his eyes beneath his closed lids, he thought of the young woman who had come to mean so much. Yes, he had known happiness here over these past few precious weeks. In these warm summer days of this cold northern land, he had shared a love such as the poets wrote of, but few had ever known. There was joy in that — real joy. And he thought of her now, back there in that farmhouse kitchen with the man who was her husband, and the tears that trickled beneath his closed lids came from his very soul.

He rose at dawn, with a strange sense of exultation, and set off south for the last mile that would take him out of Utherdale, and out of the shadow of its crag and its people. In the distance behind him the Helm Wind was gathering; he could see its storm clouds darkening the silver of the morning sky above Uther Crag. And, as the land opened out into the fertile plain that lay between Utherdale and Ingleborough, he could feel its breath behind him, carrying him forward towards the great flat-topped mountain, with its strange underground caverns where lost souls were doomed to wander for ever in search of the light.

And suddenly he was running; his feet no longer leaden, he was running like a child again, along the pine-scented paths of his beloved Himmelhof. The Helm Wind was carrying him along and he was flying now . . . Flying onwards towards that mountaintop where they were all waiting for him . . . *Der Alte* and the others, they would all be there.

He was going home . . . Home at last . . .

Chapter Twenty-Eight

I went into the fields, but you were there
Waiting for me, so all the summer flowers
Were only glimpses of your starry powers;
Beautiful and inspired dust they were.

I went down by the waters, and a bird
Sang with your voice in all the unknown tones
Of all that self of you I have not heard,
So that my being felt you to the bones.

I went into the house, and shut the door
To be alone, but you were there with me;
All beauty in a little room may be,
Though the roof lean, and muddy be the floor.

Then in my bed I bound my tired eyes
To make a darkness for my weary brain;
But, like a presence you were there again,
Being and real, beautiful and wise,

So that I could not sleep, and cried aloud,
'You strange, grave thing,
What is it you would say?'
The redness of your dear lips dimmed to grey,
And the waters ebbed, the moon hid in a cloud.

'And the redness of your dear lips dimmed to grey, and
the waters ebbed, the moon hid in a cloud . . .' The last few
words of the poem echoed the emptiness in Bethany's
heart, and she closed the leather-bound volume with a

stricken look on her face, as Jack brought through a cup of tea and laid it on the small side table next to the sofa where she was still sitting. She had slumped down there after Horst's departure some fifteen minutes before, and she had not moved. Her red-rimmed eyes had stared vacantly ahead of her, until she had reached for the book at her elbow to try to take her mind off the unthinkable: Horst had gone. She had made the decision she had prayed she would never have to make, and she had settled for Jack. She had told the man she loved to go. And he had gone. The emptiness that was left was almost unbearable.

With only the ticking of the old clock in the hall to mark the passing of time, husband and wife had sat here, both nursing their own pain, their own private grief. Not a word had passed between them since Horst had left. Bethany had expected Jack to leave too, for even poor Ned had sidled out of the door within seconds of Horst's leaving, afraid of the scene that might follow.

But there had been no scene; her husband had merely slumped into that chair by the fireside and stared into the dying embers, without saying a word. Two people once so close, but with a gap between them that she was convinced was now completely unbridgeable. Then, to her surprise, a few minutes ago he had stood up and set about making a cup of tea. It had surprised her even more when he brought her through a cup and set it on the table at her elbow.

Bethany's eyes darted nervously in her husband's direction as Jack took his own cup and sat down heavily once more on the chair by the fire. She noticed his hand was trembling as he raised the cup to his lips. She reached out and took a sip of her own tea; and it was only then that the state of her hands registered. They were caked with mud and dried blood. God only knew what the rest of her must look like, she thought bitterly as she replaced her cup in its saucer and gazed down at her encrusted fingernails.

She could feel his eyes on her and she studiously avoided his gaze as, automatically, she passed a hand across the stubble of her scalp. Don't look at me, she wanted to scream. Please don't look at me like that! All she wanted to do was to crawl into a hot bath and scrub all the filth from both inside and outside her body.

But Jack Greville could not hear the thoughts that screamed in his wife's head. Nor could he see the filth. He was simply looking at the woman he loved. Yes, he still loved her, despite everything. A sigh ran through him and a feeling of overwhelming tiredness pervaded his being. What a homecoming! He had heard of this sort of thing of course; just recently one of his unit had gone back on leave after a year's absence at the Front to find his wife with a newborn baby. Yes, it happened all right; it happened all the bloody time in wartime. But always to other people. It never happened to you. Until now.

His lips twisted in a mirthless attempt at a smile as he recalled an incident that took place less than a month ago. 'It's all right for you – it never happens to your lot!' one of his corporals had told him, as he had tried to offer some words of comfort after the young man had received a particularly painful Dear John letter. 'Your wives and lasses don't have the temptations ours do.' How he had worked that one out, Jack could not imagine; but what would that same young Liverpudlian say now if he knew? Captain Greville had been cuckolded by an effing German! His own wife was not only no better than anyone else's – she was a bloody sight worse. She had chosen to sleep with the enemy!

He could have walked out on her there and then, he knew that; he could have just picked up his kitbag and marched straight back out that door. No one would have blamed him. In fact, no one would have blamed him if he had killed that bloody German. And he had been tempted. By God, he had been tempted. If it had not been for these

565

injuries, he might even have had a go. In fact, he *would* have had a go. But what would that have accomplished? He had not spent over four years fighting this war just to lose everything at the end of it. But more than that: he was tired. He was more tired than he had ever been in his entire life. It was as if all the tension, all the long nights without sleep, all the endless marching and driving, driving and marching, and all that chronic, numbing, indescribable weariness they called 'battle fatigue' had suddenly caught up with him when he had walked in through his own front door less than an hour ago. His shattered arm and the rest of his battle scars were as nothing compared to this feeling of being so dog-tired that even making the effort to breathe – to talk – to function as a normal human being was often too much.

That fatigue was now mirrored in his voice and in the bloodshot whites of the dark eyes that looked across at his wife. He could only imagine what she had gone through out there tonight, and it was not a pleasant thought. Had it been for any other reason than the one now torturing his mind, he would have committed murder on whoever was responsible for this outrage. But, in a twisted, sick way, what had been done had been done to avenge his own honour. The world had gone crazy all right. But then he had known that for these past four years.

Bethany moved uncomfortably beneath his gaze, and for the first time he realized how long he had been staring at her. Someone had to say something. One of them had to break this awful silence. It might as well be him. 'Just tell me one thing, Bethany,' he said quietly.

She looked up and for the first time since Horst's departure their eyes met.

'Just tell me if what they did to you out there tonight was justified – in their eyes. Just tell me the truth . . . Please, for Christ's sake, tell me the truth . . .' His voice cracked and there were tears now in his eyes. He had been determined not to cry. He had not cried once throughout the whole of this bloody war, but as he looked across at her, he was crying now; the tears were streaming down his gaunt cheeks like a baby's. He reached into the pocket of his tunic for a handkerchief and blew his nose into it. So much for the big brave soldier returning from war stuff, he thought bitterly as he shoved the linen square back into his pocket, then wiped his eyes with the back of his hand. Who was the weaker sex now? Certainly not his wife. She was sitting there like a bloody sphinx. Cropped hair or no cropped hair, he could not detect the faintest trace of repentance on her face. On the contrary, there was a look akin to indignation in the set of her features, as if a deep rage was burning within her. A tiny flicker of hope rose in his heart. Maybe – just maybe – despite everything, there was good reason for it. But, as his mind moved on to other questions, his wife's was riveted on one word.

JUSTIFIED . . . Was what they did out there tonight JUSTIFIED? Had she heard him right? Her husband's words rang like one of his brother's devilish incantations in Bethany's head. She wanted to scream at him: how could multiple rape ever be JUSTIFIED, for God's sake? How could any human being JUSTIFY the utterly repulsive acts that had been perpetrated on her body tonight by those animals?

She was aware of feeling frozen with horror once more as she stared straight in front of her and mentally relived those awful moments out there on the grassy verge by the old barn. She could not answer that question. She could never answer that question and remain in control of her speech or actions. So Jack would never know, just as he had never known so much of what had gone on around here in years gone by. Amos Greville and his like were her own personal devils she would have to exorcize in her own way, in her own time. Even if she had been capable, she could not inflict them upon him now. He was all in, mentally and physically. She had never seen him in a state like this. She had seen a man cry only once in her life before when, as a child, she had witnessed Tom Turver cry at the thought of losing his home and job. Men did not cry in these parts. Not real men, anyway, or so they said. But Tom Turver had been a real man. And so was Jack.

She looked across at him and barely recognized the person her husband had become. More than anything, she wanted to remove that pain from his eyes – those dark eyes that had once danced with the joys of youth, and were now looking at her across bloodied fields of pain.

But as he met her gaze, Jack Greville could read nothing in his wife's expression to bring him comfort. Bethany seemed devoid of all emotion, all feeling, as she sat there, her hands clasped tightly around that book in her lap. But he pressed on nevertheless. 'Answer me, Beth, please . . . Did you commit adultery?' he asked, hoarsely. 'Were you ever unfaithful to me with that German?' Maybe he was being a fool to himself posing such a question, but he had to know. It was important that he know. The whole of their future could depend upon it. But even as he sat there, tense and waiting, he had no idea what his reaction would be if she said, 'Yes.'

Bethany clasped the book tighter in her hands and took a deep breath as she looked her husband straight in the eyes. 'No, Jack,' she answered softly. 'I was never unfaithful . . .'

The sigh that was uttered by the young man by the fire echoed around the room, and the weight that had been lying heavy on Jack Greville's heart lifted as he slumped back in his chair. He would not – he could not – believe she was lying. She would not lie, not at a time like this; it was not in her nature. He continued looking at her for a long time without speaking as he repeated her words over and over in his head. Then he said softly, 'Thank you. Thank you for that.'

She gave a tight smile, wishing she could share his feeling of relief. But now it was enough that he was happy. She took a sip of the tea he had made, then after staring down into the brown brew for a moment, she lifted the cup in silent salute. 'Welcome home, Black Jack,' she said softly. 'Welcome home.'

For the very first time since arriving back in his own home, Jack Greville smiled. 'Thank you, Squirt,' he said, in a voice that was barely audible, as he lifted his own cup in response. He had waited so long to hear those words. More than four long years he had waited. They were not out of the wood yet, not by a long chalk. But they were on their way.

'We've come through a lot, you and me, Bethany girl, and it's not over yet. But we'll make it, don't you worry. We'll bloody well make it!' The last statement was said with a vehemence that made the cup in his hand rattle as he laid it in the saucer to light a cigarette.

They sat sipping their tea in silence, as the smoke from his cigarette curled lazily to the ceiling, and Captain Jack Greville laid his head against the back of the chair and watched it drift, then dissolve in the draught from the window, just as he had done so many, many times in years gone by. Glen was resting his head on his master's leg, and as Jack laid his hand on the animal's shaggy coat, for the first time since walking through that door tonight a feeling akin to peace touched his soul. 'Home . . . Home at last, Glen old boy . . .'

Bethany sat watching him – the man she would spend the rest of her life with, and she was happy for his sake. Happy that his worst fear had been unfounded. Happy too that the physical agonies that he had gone through were now over and his shattered body would have the time and peace to heal.

Then she thought of the man she loved, now somewhere out there in the darkness of the night beyond their

569

closed door. She got up and walked slowly and painfully to the window and looked out into the darkness. It was raining now, and he was out there somewhere in the cold and wet. She stared at the glass and watched as the raindrops trickled like tears down the pane.

She closed her eyes and she could see his face. And, as her eyes filled, the redness of his dear lips dimmed to grey. And the waters ebbed, the moon hid in a cloud . . .

Epilogue

The wind that blew chill and keen across the North
Yorkshire moors that grey, misty morning in early
autumn 1947, and whistled eerily around the clefts and
gullies of the mountain of Ingleborough, almost silenced
the shout of the young man before it left his lips. Along
with a companion, he had been scrabbling around the
entrance to Trow Ghyll ravine for almost an hour in the
hope of finding another way into Gaping Ghyll, the largest
of the network of great underground caves that honey-
combed the bowels of the mountain.

Now, with the removal of one particularly large rock
blocking a possible new entrance into the cave, he could
see inside. And what he thought he saw made his blood
run cold. He gasped aloud. Was he imagining things? This
was, after all, Ingleborough, the great rocky outcrop
around which so many legends had focused for over two
thousand years. He gesticulated impatiently to his companion working some feet away to lend a hand, and
together the two cavers worked frantically to remove
more boulders for a better view. After a period of intense
hard work, removing a whole stack of carefully wedged
stones, they stared in mounting horror at their gruesome
discovery.

Crouched in a sitting position, his arms still encircling
his bound legs, was the skeletal body of a young man. How
long he had been imprisoned there was impossible to say,
for the state of decay was already far advanced. Little
could be discerned as to his appearance, save that he was

tall, and the tufts of hair still attached to the skull were thick and light-brown in colour. Of the flesh that covered the bones of the skull, the little that remained was waxy and pulled so tight and thin that the features were now a travesty of human expression.

But gruesome as the discovery was, it was the circumstances of the death that horrified the finders more than anything. The body was trussed, the wrists pinioned, and still tightly clenched between the fleshless teeth in the final agony of death was a knotted scarf. Whoever he was, this wretched creature had not died by accident.

Despite months of investigations, the identity of the man was never established. The most the local CID had to go on in the way of clues were two small objects found beside the body: a tarnished silver St Christopher medallion and a tiny glass phial. It was around this latter piece of evidence that rumour grew in the surrounding area. With the Second World War barely two years over, popular opinion was convinced that the victim had been a German spy, complete with his phial of cyanide, and though his fate had been harsh, it was probably no more than he deserved.

The Coroner, basing his conclusions on facts rather than likelihoods, had no option but to record an open verdict. The case was closed and the remains were given a Christian burial. Only in the name that was given afterwards to the cave — Body Pot — is there today a grim memorial to the fact that this particular young man had ever lived and died.

> I know not the language of this cool land
> And its ways are not mine.
>
> Even the passing clouds
> I know not the meaning of . . .